I0761016

MARK OF MYTHICA

VERIHDIAN WARDENS - BOOK TWO

MARK OF MYTHICA

NIKKI ROBB

ISBN: Paperback: 9781964036007
ISBN: Hardback: 9781964036014

Cover and Interior Design by Rachel McEwan
Printed and Distributed by Kindle Direct Publishing

First Printing Edition

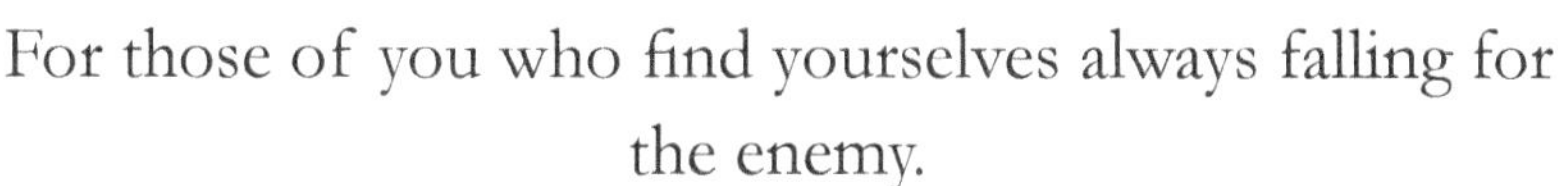

For those of you who find yourselves always falling for the enemy.

You're not alone…they're hotter.

Content Warnings

Mark of Mythica is a new adult fantasy novel that contains descriptions of drowning, nightmares, violence, choking, being restrained, description of torture, kidnapping, murder, death, and explicit sexual scenes. This novel also touches on feelings of intense guilt, including inter-familial guilt. Readers who may be sensitive to these elements, please take note.

Parliament
Golden Swamp
Guildhall
THE COURT OF SILENCE
Forsaken Quarters
Everwatch
Gate of Silence
THE COURT OF SHADOWS
Westville
Gate of Shadow
Verihdian Institute
Gate of Echoes
THE COURT OF ECHOES
Gate of Passion
Stormview
Sunken Province Prison
Dreamer's Gift
Pleasure Tower
Lustrada
THE COURT OF PASSION

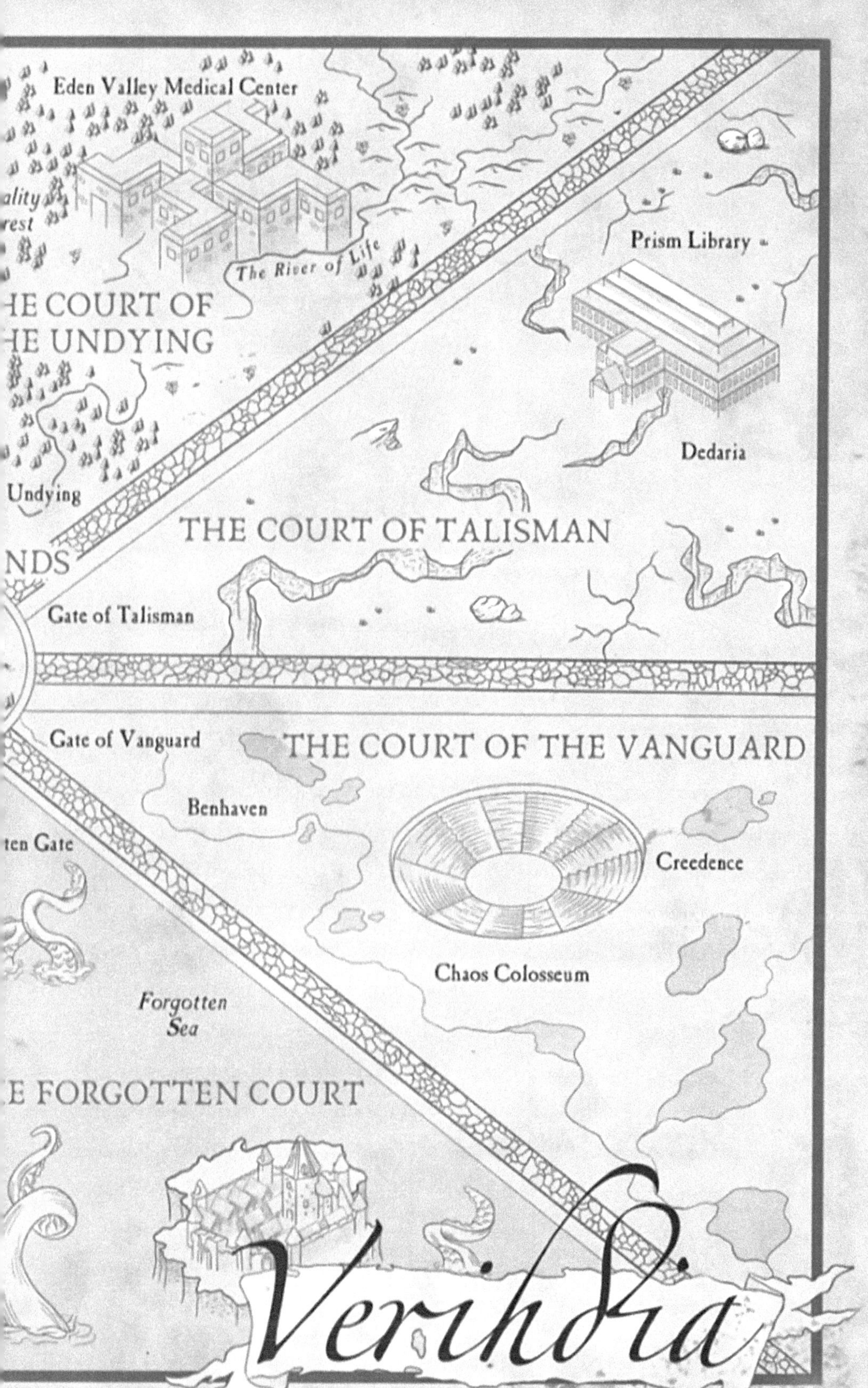
Eden Valley Medical Center
ality
rest
The River of Life
HE COURT OF
HE UNDYING
Undying
NDS
Prism Library
Dedaria
THE COURT OF TALISMAN
Gate of Talisman
Gate of Vanguard
THE COURT OF THE VANGUARD
Benhaven
ten Gate
Creedence
Chaos Colosseum
Forgotten
Sea
E FORGOTTEN COURT
Verihdia

Prologue

The decadent ballroom was filled with members of The Court of Shadows.

My Court.

Finally.

I had spent most of my adolescence and every second of my adulthood thus far planning for the day that I would be welcomed among the most cunning, dedicated, and influential individuals in Verihdia. I never wanted anything else, but I always wanted something more.

I shook hands with dozens of people congratulating and welcoming me, but none of them were who I needed to see me. None of them were the Warden. But one thing had become abundantly clear - he would never see me while *she* was in the way. Never in my life did I expect the biggest obstacle in my path to be the one person who had always supported me. What a laugh she must be having now.

I went to her room earlier, knowing he would find out we had been together. His showing up and actively witnessing my hands claim her body was only a happy accident. But that was when I thought he was just aiming for alone time to sell our Court to her. Then I found his letter. His stupid little admiration-filled letter.

'Little Storm,' he had called her. A nickname, a pet name. As if she was already some precious object to him.

That should be me.

I should be the most crucial person in this Court. I deserved to be. That mantra looped in my head as I pushed through the crowd of joyous dancing toward the throne.

"Chandler, you were not invited to approach the Warden," Lilith said as she stood and pursed her lips. Her hands landed on the table in front of her. I kept my eyes trained on the Warden. I didn't need him to know that I knew his Dean rather intimately, at least not until I could use that information to my advantage. Until that day came, I did not need Lilith Hargrove. It wasn't that she wasn't attractive to me, but the benefit that having a relationship with her gave me didn't matter anymore. Not since I received my Court Mark and was officially named a member of The Court of Shadows.

"My Warden, apologies." I tilted my head slightly. I intended to demonstrate respect to my Warden while conveying that we could operate on equal terms. He needed to understand the value I could bring to the table.

"You are making this a habit. Should I be concerned?" My Warden didn't look at me as he spoke. A slight twinge of anger rippled through me, but I reined it in. I had a plan - a good one.

"You need only worry if you do not wish to see such a proactive member of your Court," I spoke clearly. Confidently. I knew he heard me, although his body language said otherwise. He was ignoring me on purpose because he was jealous.

I had something he didn't.

Lexa Cromwell.

He felt my gaze on him and sputtered with a wave of his hand. "Do you need something, Mr. Wills?" I had to struggle to contain my reaction. He knew what he was doing just as clearly as I did. He was well aware of my identity. Soon, he would soon know more.

"Just to formally introduce myself and to offer my loyalty and service." The moment had arrived to reveal my cards, demonstrating to him my worthiness as I perceived it. The motivation for the forthcoming words was twofold: to assure my Warden that I could be a significant asset in obtaining what he desired most and to remind him of the unique qualities I possessed that he lacked. "As you've noticed twice now, I am quite close with Miss Cromwell." That caught his attention. His nearly glowing emerald eyes - the symbol of his stature in this Court - flicked toward me with heat behind them. A mental image of how I'd look with those eyes flashed in my mind. "My deep connection with her is one that I believe could work in our favor," I laced my words with a promise. A promise that I was willing to do everything within my power to secure Miss Cromwell's loyalty to this Court. To us.

Observing my Warden's shoulders rise and fall in a deep breath, I prepared for the anticipated acceptance. It was evident that he desired Lexa in this Court, a fact anyone with eyes could discern. I was poised to assist him in achieving this goal.

"Consider yourself introduced. Now, if you'll excuse me. I have a beautiful woman to dance with." His smirk was taunting as he watched Lexa move about the ballroom. My face fell with disbelief. Indeed, he hadn't heard me correctly because if he had, he would be shaking my hand and congratulating me on a brilliant plan. He should be thanking me for giving him an obvious advantage over his siblings, but instead, he began to move away.

"Of course, my Warden. Please do not hesitate to call on me. I intend to prove myself invaluable to you." He didn't respond, and the blood in my veins boiled until the world around me had a shadowed tint.

"Nice try," Lilith quipped, looking over at me. I turned to watch my Warden glide across the floor toward the source of all my ire.

"I don't understand. He wants her, and I can help him get her." My hands clenched into fists at my side. Lilith made a soft sound of acknowledgment. Lilith and I had developed a very peculiar type of relationship back at the Institute.

I visited her in her office a few years back to discuss my future in her Court. We didn't start anything physical until last year when she was confident I would receive a Court of Shadows result from the Final Trial. Even so, I had her promise me that even if I didn't receive that result, she would admit me when I pledged to this Court anyway. I enjoyed her company far less than Lexa's, but Lilith was far more valuable to me at the time.

Now, the tables have turned.

"Exactly," Lilith seethed, a dark fury lacing her words. "He *wants* her. He doesn't want you to have her. Or anyone else for that matter."

My head snapped in her direction. I knew he had developed some form of feeling for her. That much was evident from the letter I found next to the dress she wore tonight and their tense encounter in the hall when they thought I couldn't see them. But to covet her so entirely that he would turn down the chance I was offering was simply irresponsible. "I never got a chance to congratulate you on your Pledge," she said, switching the focus, but my mind refused to cooperate.

"Thank you," I retorted mindlessly, my eyes tracking my Warden across the ballroom as he approached Lexa.

"Come to my room tonight if you'd like to celebrate," she whispered. There was no rule keeping us from being together any longer, not like there was at the Institute, and perhaps that's another reason all the appeal had worn off.

"Not tonight, Lilith." And then I left her there. Moving across the ballroom floor as if I owned the place.

And one day, I knew I would.

*

"Another, Viktor," I grumbled, slamming a piece of gold onto the bar. I have visited this tavern every day since arriving in The Court of Shadows. Cheap and robust drinks, pleasant music, and its best quality of all, no Lexa Cromwell.

Being rejected by my Warden was one thing, but Lexa had never attempted to find me since our encounter. To apologize for what she did. To make it up to me. He is the Warden of The Court of Shadows, but she is nothing. Not yet. I did not deserve to be treated like that by an Uncourted Pledge.

"Coming right up," Viktor said, palming the gold coin and gripping my empty tankard. There was only one other patron here and he had been nursing the same drink since I arrived. I turned on my stool to look out the window that overlooked the town square. The sunlight was streaming in, and I was already on my third drink of the day.

I wasn't going to allow myself to wallow forever. Just until they leave. Once my Warden and Lexa begin their tour of Verihdia, this Court will be Wardenless for the longest it ever has. They will need someone to assist them. I will be that person. But until then, the drinks numbed the overwhelming envy that flooded my senses, and that was exactly what I needed.

I heard the splash first, then thrashing sounds in the water, a few screams, and some people running away. I was out of my stool and planted at the window in a heartbeat.

"Out of my way!" A voice boomed from the far side of the square. People listened. Of course, they did. It was their Warden speaking. "Everyone, clear the square. Now!" The patrons of various businesses quickly made their way down the alleyways and away from the commotion at the fountain. My Warden jumped into the water swiftly, grabbing the thrashing victim from the pool.

My blood ran cold.

Lexa.

Of course, it was her. Of course, he would make a scene for her. I rolled my eyes, watching as his hands made quick work of pumping her chest and his lips lowered onto hers. He looked worried, like a man in love. It made me sick. I couldn't bring myself to worry that she hadn't yet regained consciousness. Maybe this will be the end of her, and one of my problems will have solved itself. She coughed, water pouring from her mouth as my Warden cradled her and quickly left the square, drifting out of sight.

With an audible scoff of disappointment, I moved back to my stool at the bar, gripping my now full tankard and taking a long sip of the amber liquid. Warmth spread through my body as the alcohol attempted, unsuccessfully, to dull my jealous mind.

"What makes her so special?" The voice was weak, like he hadn't meant for anyone else to hear it, but as the man from the corner of the bar approached me, I knew he had intended to address me. He paused near the empty stool to my left, eyeing it and then me. I nodded, gesturing to the seat, and he climbed up, settling in beside me. "It's like he's not even our Warden anymore."

My eyes flashed over to Viktor to see if he had heard what this stranger said to me. He was far off on the other side of the tavern, cleaning glasses with a rag. I looked back to the man beside me; he wore a hood that blanketed his face in shadows, but I could see his strong chin and pale white skin.

It might have been the drinks or the anger that had been festering for days, but this stranger gave me precisely what I needed - an excuse. "It's pathetic." My speech wasn't slurred, but I had to focus more than usual to ensure the words came out of my mouth.

"Why is she more important than all of us?"

I nodded at the man's statement, raising my glass in agreement. "Exactly," I agreed. He took a sip of his drink, and I followed suit. "She doesn't deserve this attention. She's a nobody." Every bit of bottled-up anger and jealousy poured forth from my lips uncontrollably. Trying to restrain them was futile.

"If you had the chance to make sure she wasn't a problem anymore…would you?" The man whispered.

I stilled, inhaling a sharp breath. What was this man proposing? Was this a trap? Was My Warden testing me somehow? I looked around the room again for anyone else who may be listening.

"I'm sorry, that was inappropriate of me to say." The man shifted away slightly and indulged in another prolonged sip of his drink. I observed him. I should have left it at that, and two drinks earlier, I would have. However, against my better judgment, I leaned in closer to this unfamiliar face.

"You mean… kill her?" I whispered. He turned back to me, his head tilting slightly up, just enough so I could see his face. He was utterly ordinary-looking, with nothing identifiable about him, nothing special - the type of person who could do something entirely unnoticed.

He shrugged. "Killing someone isn't the only way to ensure they aren't an issue anymore." He spoke so calmly, so casually. I nearly said, 'May the Gods damn you,' but instead, I considered his words.

Did I want Lexa gone, truly gone? Like never to return, kind of gone?

Yes.

The realization surprised me, but it was true nonetheless. I nodded to the stranger slowly.

His lips lifted into a smile. "There's a door in the kitchens. It's used for deliveries of foods and goods for the Forsaken Quarters."

I nodded again, unable to speak. My mind was at war with itself.

"Leave it open tonight. And you can say goodbye to your little problem." The stranger reached into his pocket and placed a gold coin on the bar before leaving. And just like that, I was alone again. Only this time I had a choice to make.

Viktor refilled my drink once more, and with the help of liquid courage, I started formulating my plan.

I nearly tumbled off my horse as I rode back to the Forsaken Quarters, the drinks taking control of my senses and mind.

Each second, as I drew closer to the castle, the benefits began to outweigh the costs. If I couldn't use my connection with Lexa Cromwell to my advantage, she was only getting in my way. With her gone, the Warden would need someone to rely on. Perhaps he would need a shoulder to cry on, someone who also cared for his 'Little Storm.' Maybe he needed someone to take on duties that he would be too distraught to carry out alone. Perhaps, he would need a right-hand man.

By the time I arrived in the castle and made my way to the kitchens, I had decided. So when I propped the door open, allowing room for air - or anything else- to slip in, I felt nothing but relief.

ONE

There was a vicious irony to fleeing a place I felt unsafe, only to find that the place I retreated to was the more dangerous of the two. The figure's hand closed around my mouth, stifling the scream that erupted from my throat. With one mighty arm, this man held my body flush against him, painfully squeezing, sending memories of restricted airways soaring through my mind. His skin was calloused, and the smell of paint was thick on his fingers from the Forgotten Court Marks he plastered on the canvas of my room. I couldn't tell if this was the same man who attacked me in the carriage. I hadn't yet seen his face, but this hand felt familiar. How horrible was that? This hand that was attacking me, aiming to harm me, felt familiar, like an old memory that refused to dissipate.

I thrashed against him, but he managed to hold me still, stuck within the cage of his hostile arms. My throat, still tender from my encounter at the water fountain, throbbed in pain. I was tired of feeling weak. I was tired of being unable to protect myself. I was tired of being unable to breathe. Drawing on a lesson from one of the few times I met with Joanne, my trainer, my teeth clamped down on his hand, and with a curse, he instinctively pulled it away. Fighting for breath against his hold, I screamed. But not for help. No, I screamed in anger, in pain, in revenge. In warning. My blood burned with the resentment and the fury that had been building in my soul since the first moment my nightmares took control. His hand came back to my mouth, but his hold had loosened just enough that I was able to grip the emerald hilt of the dagger strapped to my thigh. It was clumsy but far more controlled than it would have been just days before. I had only taken two lessons thus far, which I deeply regretted now, but I managed to call on my little training.

With a grunt, I thrust the dagger backward toward my assailant, and the blade sliced through his clothing as he dodged. But I didn't stop. Unrelenting, unforgiving, unafraid. I swung my arm frantically, yet calculated. The figure behind me released the hold on my face to try and calm my wild swings, but he was too slow. My blade found purchase in his gut, and a loud, painful grunt spilled from him as his arms fell from me completely. I spun from his hold, facing him quickly. The bloody obsidian dagger in my hand was dripping crimson onto the wooden floor.

"Gods damn you," the figure hissed, his hands pushing against his wounded abdomen. I recognized his mask—the same dark one from the night at the carriage. Rage blinded me, and I thrust forward again. His blood-soaked hands caught mine before my dagger was able to meet his flesh again. Bringing his head forward, he slammed into my face. Air evaded me, and I felt my nose throb but not break. I couldn't give up, not now. No matter how much pain I was in. I didn't have the luxury. I kicked forward, and my knee made contact with his groin. He doubled over in pain, making himself vulnerable to me. His mistake. His head slumped down towards the floor as he folded. I gripped his head and brought my knee directly up into his face. The crack was sickening as his nose broke from the pressure. He let out a violent scream as he fell to his knees. The symphony of his pain was like music to my tortured ears.

Time slowed. This man was on his knees before me, blood pouring from his nostrils and his side. Before I knew it, I was down on my knees before him, the tip of my dagger pressed against the skin of his neck. I didn't have time to consider the similarity between this moment and the moment I had just shared with Lysander. The difference was that this time, with this man, I felt entirely willing and ready to plunge this dagger the rest of the way. There were no reservations in my heart. I ripped the mask from his face, revealing an unassuming young man with plain features. The dark cloud of Mythica surged within me, begging for a chance to rip his soul open and lay it out for all to see. I was willing to oblige.

What do you want with me?

My silent question was a shriek, a pained, desperate cry of a woman who refused to be the victim any longer. I felt the desperate tendrils of my Mythica seep into his mind, sinking its violent claws into the very depths of him. The figure's eyes narrowed, blood running down into his mouth, painting his teeth with a deep red film. He spoke unwillingly, through gritted teeth, as my Mythica dragged his devious desires from the darkest parts of his subconscious. The part of him that only I could see.

"We need you, Lexa. To save us," he spat.

I was blinded by too much fury to comprehend his words entirely. His throat was strained from trying to hold his truth in, to keep it from me as if he could ever hide from me. As if anyone could ever hide from me. My Mythica nearly screamed at the resistance, wrenching itself deeper into his head with vicious ease.

What are you so afraid of?

His pulse quickened, his throat bobbing as he swallowed the panic bubbling under the surface. He shook his head, fighting to keep his lips closed, to hold back the answers he wasn't willing to give. I may be easy to overcome physically and may still be weaker than I wished,… but my Mythica wasn't weak. No, my Mythica was the strongest it's ever been, a Titan among men, an inescapable force - and this man was practically begging me to show him the true reach of my power. I was more than willing to demonstrate.

"If you aren't …good enough," he began, straining against every word forcefully dragged from his lips. A devious smile crossed my lips at the sight of his struggle. A sickening pleasure erupted through me at the sight of his pain, a fact I'd leave myself to rectify later. "We are out of options."

I had a million questions, and things I wanted to know, but logic could not infiltrate my mind. When I looked at this man, I didn't see answers. I saw someone who tried to hurt me, use me. Twice now, this man has assaulted me. Twice now, this man has taken away my peace.

Never again.

He moved quickly, lunging to get his hands around me, but I was faster. My dagger pierced his throat, sliding through the flesh to the life within. His eyes went blank, and his fingers cupped the wound, attempting to keep the blood from spilling out onto the floor. The sound that filled the room was haunting. It was the whispers of Kamatyan coming to collect another victim, another soul. I watched from my knees as the man before me took his final, blood-filled breath.

The dark crimson pool spread across the floor, seeping from his lifeless form, flooding each crevice, filling each crack, mixing with the still-wet paint, and marring the Mark of The Forgotten Court with the essence of death. I watched it spread toward me until it surrounded me, too, painting my skin with the dark hue of his life—the life I had taken from him. My Mythica began to encircle me, surging as it celebrated its victory, satisfied that it had done its duty.

Reality crashed into me. My breathing was ragged. Verging on the edge of panic, I looked around the room for the first time. My eyes landed on the figure in the doorway. I suddenly felt the urge to run, but whether I wanted to run to him or in the opposite direction, I couldn't tell.

Lysander's eyes were filled with worry as he assessed me. "Gods, Lexa, are you okay?" He didn't move forward. Instead, he looked as if he was braced for an attack. His gaze bounced around the room, the space above my head. I knew what he was looking at. My Mythica felt wild, unrestrained, like a dam had burst, and it was finally released from its moral prison.

"He attacked me." It was quiet. Nearly silent. The swirling rush of Mythica continued its relentless storm in my chest.

"Are you ok?" he asked again. He braced himself against the door frame, watching the space as he prepared to cross the distance between us.

"He's dead." I was in shock, I decided. That is why I couldn't answer his question and why I couldn't feel the pain from the impact of the dead man's head against my face. I felt numb.

Lysander, gathering the courage he needed, sprinted inside and fell to his knees beside me, gripping my face in his hands and titling my face away from the body on the ground in front of me. His emerald eyes held a type of sorrow I didn't understand. How could he care for me like this after what he did? After what he authorized?

"They cannot remain without a Warden, and we cannot let the Warden remain."

I pulled my face from his grasp as the haunted memory of his words returned. I was instantly ashamed of how comforting it felt to have his murderous hands on me. My eyes trailed down to the pool of blood at my feet.

"Don't look at him, Lexa. Please. Look at me." Desperation laced every word.

I didn't want to look at Lysander, but I couldn't look at the death at my feet anymore. My vision blurred with my tears as I focused my attention back on the Warden of Shadows. He scanned my face, his fingers delicately brushing against the skin around my nose. There would be another bruise to add to my growing collection. I struggled not to pull from his reach again.

"Are you ok?" He asked again, deliberately emphasizing each word. His gaze held mine captive the way it had all those nights ago at the Courting Ball.

It felt like a different life.

"I don't know," I answered truthfully. My adrenaline began to fade, making way for the sharp pain in my face. I was barely aware of the tremble that had started racking my body.

"Come on, let's get you out of here. Can you walk?"

I nodded but made no move to stand. Lysander's arm snaked around my midsection, and I rose with him when he stood. Numb and drenched in the blood of a man I had just killed, I let him lead me from the room. I think he closed the door, but I couldn't be sure. Truthfully, a door could never be strong enough of a wall between me and the memory of those lifeless eyes that were now imprinted on my soul. Lysander ushered me quickly but tenderly up the stairs toward his quarters. I didn't have enough willpower to stop him.

The moment we entered his room, he directed me to the bathing chambers, bypassing the bed he and I had laid on together only a few minutes ago.

How could everything change so fast?

His supportive hand never left me as he quickly drew a bath, letting warm water fill the large pool. A pungent aroma flitted up to me, the scent of cinnamon mixing with the coppery smell of blood. I nearly vomited.

Lysander moved precisely, never removing his guiding hand from my skin, as my mind waged a war within. As desperately as I didn't want his hands to meet my skin, I wasn't sure I could survive this moment without the reassuring touch.

It's a strange and painful sensation to both desire and loathe the touch of the same person.

Blood was beginning to dry on my skin, cracking with each step, making each movement tense and wrong. Tears fell from my eyes involuntarily. One of Lysander's hands gripped my shoulder and the other held me up by my midsection, leading me to the top of the stairs of the bathing pool. He slowly released his hold and allowed me to climb into it alone. Lysander's draped tunic on my body, now stained and torn, pooled around my waist as I continued into the depths of the bath.

It was automatic, like I was in a trance. I found my way out to the center of his large pool of water and moved my hands aimlessly across the surface, creating delicate ripples at my side. I don't know how long I stood there, idly, waist-deep, staring out before me. But then I looked down.

The moment my gaze landed on the water around me, running red with blood, I felt something snap.

"I need to get out of here! I can't be in the water. I can't. Please!" My breathing came raggedly, and panic seized my heart. I felt the world tilt on its axis as I struggled to calm the cresting fear.

I didn't register the disturbance in the water until Lysander was in front of me, his hands wrapped around my waist and pulled me into his body. I clutched his shirt, damp from his frenzied dive into the water. I held onto him like the lifeline he was. Like I would succumb to the dread threatening to pull me under if he didn't stop me. There was a certain uncomfortable irony to the whole ordeal, being afraid to bathe because of my waking nightmares but needing to bathe because I killed a man. Killing a man because I ran from Lysander. Running from Lysander because he may have orchestrated the genocide of an entire Court. And now, the Court that he may have eliminated was causing my waking nightmares.

I was disgusted with him, deeply and thoroughly, but I needed something that only he could give me at that moment. I buried my face into the crook of his neck, clutching onto him. He held me tightly against his chiseled frame; the dark skin of his neck was stained with my tears and the single trail of blood from where my dagger pierced his skin. Each drop of salted, pained liquid from my eyes was another reminder that I wasn't safe here.

He didn't move. He didn't rush me or ask me any questions. Instead, he stood there, waist-deep in the blood-tainted water, holding me until I could breathe again.

Minutes passed before my sobs slowed, and my heart settled into a normal rhythm. Lysander made a brief move to grab the soap off the ledge, and I clung to him tighter at the threat of him leaving me behind to face the water alone.

"It's ok, little storm. I'm not going anywhere."

I relaxed into his embrace, which tightened in a silent promise around me.

"Is it alright if I help you?" He held the soap in one hand, a gentle and worried expression crossing his face.

I swallowed hard and considered it. My hate for him could wait a few minutes because the thought of being alone in the bathing chamber, surrounded by water that could decide to come back and finish the job at any moment, was enough to make the panic return. I caught the slightest reflection of my face on the surface of the gleaming water. How was this fragile girl looking back at me, the same one who just forced her Mythica to tear a man's subconscious to shreds? She was confident. She was angry. She was never going to be a victim again. And yet, here she was, terrified. I nodded.

So Lysander got to work, beginning with a delicate caress of my shoulders, rubbing slow circles into my skin with the lavender-scented soap. With one hand firmly around my waist, he washed all reminders of my sin from my pale arms. My tunic was sopping wet, but I was thankful he didn't aim to remove it. He spent a significant amount of time on my hands, scrubbing with a gentle force at the blood that had already stained. I watched him work. He didn't smirk or tease. He didn't make a joke or cause a fight. He simply guided water over my skin as if he could wash the demons away.

If only it were that easy.

"Put your legs around my waist," he ordered casually, his voice imbued with a type of care I was beginning to think was not as uncommon from this man as I once believed.

"What? I- No…" I shook my head and began to push against his chest. He rolled his eyes and held me in place.

"I need both my hands to wash your hair, little storm. Hold on to me so I can let go." His emerald eyes burned into mine. He was trying to prove to me how serious he was and tell me I could trust him.

And despite my better judgment and every bone in my body screaming at me, I did.

I slid my arms around his shoulders, folding them around his neck and hoisting myself until my legs wrapped around his waist. I was careful not to let my center, which was still completely bare, graze his clothed form. He tentatively removed his hands from my waist once he felt my limbs close around him. My fingers dug into the skin on his back instinctively to remind myself that he was still there and I wasn't alone.

His hands weren't gone for long, though they soon returned to my body, bringing a delicious-smelling soap to my scalp and lathering it slowly, spreading it down to the ends of my long hair. He was meticulous and focused, ensuring that every strand was thoroughly coated. His fingers at my scalp reminded me I was playing a dangerous game. His touch was so comforting, yet somewhere deep in my mind, I knew what those hands were capable of, what they'd done.

"We need to rinse now," he whispered, his breath hitting my cheek, alerting me to how close we had become.

My center was now flush against his body. I felt a blush creep onto my face.

"Lean back." He positioned one hand directly in the center of my back. His fingers splayed, and he urged me to follow his request. He must have seen the panic in my eyes because he spoke again, this time softer. "I've got you."

I nodded wearily but followed his instruction, leaning back, arching against his splayed hand as he lowered my head toward the water. My breathing quickened, and I felt the bruise on my neck strain against the movement. I watched the water's surface grow nearer and nearer with each inch.

"Close your eyes, little storm. Trust me."

Trust him?

I didn't think I was capable of trusting him. Not after seeing his guilt. After witnessing his darkest shame. But at this moment, he wasn't the Warden of Shadows. He was Lysander. I was quickly discovering the difference between the two. Logically, I knew there could not be one without the other, but there was a sort of beautiful duality to him, a duality that frightened and confused me but also allowed me at this moment to put it all aside, close my eyes, and let him take care of me.

I felt him lower my head towards the water's surface, stopping when the water reached my forehead, submerging my hair. His one firm hand remained strong against my back, a rigid barrier between me and the dangers lurking under the surface, while the other ran through my hair, washing away the soap and anything else that may have found its way there.

I felt weightless. Not just in the water but in his grasp. Like burdens that kept me tightly in their hold were loosening their clutches, letting me share the load with this man. Then he pulled me back up to face him. My wet hair hung heavily down my back as my eyes opened to find him watching me.

Without removing his gaze, he walked towards the ledge of the bathing pool. A hand came to either side of me, gripping my soft curves, and hoisted me out of the water, setting me on the edge as if I was as weightless as I had felt. I didn't have time to be embarrassed or worry about my lack of undergarments because he wasn't looking at my center. He was watching my face. His hands started at my feet, lathering each leg until he was nearly at my core but never quite breaching the distance. My eyes were glued on him as he made careful work of the dried blood and paint on my knees. His fingertips sent a calming wave directly through me with each tender pass as he brought a handful of water from the pool to spill over my skin.

Instinctively, I spread my legs. Not because I needed him at my core but because I wanted him closer. He moved to the wall, sliding between my thighs, my skin burning as his torso settled there. Still, his eyes never left mine.

He reached up to grip my waist, and this time, I wasn't afraid when he slid me into the water. I knew nothing could hurt me, not now. Not with him here.

I folded myself around him again, legs tightened around his waist, pulling my core against the fabric of his trousers and tossing my hands over his shoulders.

Lysander began walking for the stairs of the bathing pool, and I felt a tight panic seize me.

"I'm too heavy. Put me down. I can walk," I whimpered, my throat hoarse from the abuse it had suffered earlier and the screams that the attacker's suffocating hands had stifled.

He scoffed, not with malice, but with confidence, and I had no choice but to concede because he was walking up the stairs and into his chambers with ease. Holding me tight to his body as we trailed water across the wooden floor. My gaze stayed trapped in his, the way it so often was, as he walked me towards his bed. He hooked his hands under my thighs and motioned for me to set my feet on the ground.

It felt strange to release him from the hold of my legs. And the fact that it felt so was even stranger. My feet hit the ground, and he ensured I was steady before stepping back from my reach. I suddenly missed the warmth of his comfort.

He returned moments later with a new tunic for me. He placed it on the satin sheets and stepped back. "I need to take care of…" He trailed off. I nodded because I knew what he meant. He needed to take care of the body—the body of the man I killed.

The same man that was going to kill me.

His body tensed like he was fighting whether or not to leave and assess the threat to his Court or stay and protect me. But I didn't need his protection. No matter how nice it felt.

"Go. I'm ok," I reassured, not fully believing myself. Lysander's face contorted in a pained expression, telling me he believed my claim even less than I did, but then he went off to clean up my mess.

I slid out of the heavy, soaked tunic and into the fresh, dry one that Lysander had prepared for me and slipped beneath the covers on his bed. It smelled like us, if we had a smell. Fire and rain. Water and shadows. It was exhaustion that finally dragged me off to sleep, even among the images of the lifeless form bleeding out on the floor. Because if I had the choice, I would never close my eyes again.

Two

Leaving Lexa behind in my room after what she just endured was quite possibly the worst torture I had ever had the displeasure to experience, but there was a genuine, and currently dead, threat that I needed to deal with.

Once I closed the door to my chambers, I raced down the stairs to the floor below. My voice was tense and curt as I called out for one of the patrolling guards."Who was guarding this floor an hour ago?"

His eyes widened as my apparent rage seeped into my tone.

Despite the growing fury in my core, I had remained so calm in her presence. I wanted to rip this castle apart to discover how that man got into its walls. Into her quarters. I shuttered, remembering the surge of her Mythica. I had sunken to my knees after she ran from me, falling to the ground every bit the broken man she thought I was, but not for the reasons she suspected.

I felt a cold emptiness take hold of me as if a piece of my soul walked out of the room when she did - but just as I felt the nothingness threaten to consume me, her Mythica called out, vibrating the very ground beneath me, screaming for me the same way it did that night at the inn. As if it knew I was there and that I could help. I was sprinting down the steps and throwing open her door before I realized I'd even taken a step. That's when I saw her. She was kneeling over a lifeless body, the emerald-hilted dagger I gifted her in her hand, dripping dark crimson blood onto the floor. I couldn't focus on that. I couldn't focus on the painted symbol taunting me from every surface. I could only see her Mythica. It swirled around her head, filling every corner of the large room in a way I have never experienced. Not even in a room full of my siblings had I seen a Mythica so widespread as this. It thrashed in anger, in pain, in fury. For a moment, I was paralyzed. I couldn't bring my feet to move to her. Despite every rule and every precaution, her Mythica worked on me. It worked on a Warden. I knew she was powerful the moment I saw her, but not like this.

I wasn't afraid of her. Of course not. But I was more frightened of what the others would do when they learned of her capacity. At that moment, I promised that even if she chose to shun me, Pledge to a different Court, and forget all about me, I would do everything I could to ensure that none of my siblings learned what she could do. If this were the only thing she ever let me do for her again, I would do it well.

I had to brace myself against her Mythcia's wild borders before sprinting to her side, afraid it wouldn't let me near her in this state. However, the moment my feet bounded across the room, her magic parted for me, clearing a direct path toward her and ushering me safely to where she needed me most. When I gripped her face, her Mythica quieted to a dull roar, a sleeping fury. I didn't have time to analyze what it meant or why her Mythica seemed to want me near her; all I needed to do was get her out of that room.

"I was, sir," the guard answered timidly. I nearly growled.

"How is it then that you did not see an intruder enter Miss Cromwell's quarters?" I asked, my voice reaching a strained whisper. I knew better than anyone that voices carry in the atrium of my castle - having heard my fair share of secrets from this very spot - and I didn't need to cause any panic. "And how is it that there was a struggle that you didn't hear?" I fought against the impulse to grab the front of his leather armor and pull him in so he could feel the same fear I felt when I realized she was in trouble. When I realized how close I was to losing her.

"My Warden, I am the only guard on this floor. I walk the entire perimeter alone. I apologize for not being there."

He's right, of course. We have only ever placed one guard on each floor. It's ridiculous when you think about it. To get from this side of the atrium to the same floor on the other side would take several minutes. It all happened so fast. This guard probably hadn't even made it an entire lap around the floor in the time that Lexa was attacked, the man was killed, and I rushed her out. I let that thought soften me, as difficult as it was.

"I need Lilith and your Captain sent immediately to Miss Cromwell's quarters. Do you understand?"

He nodded fervently.

"But before you do that, I need two guards outside my chamber doors. A guard must always be present at that door, do you understand?"

The guard shook his head. "My Warden, forgive me, but we are not permitted on your floor."

I didn't have time for this. I was about to let go of the careful and waning grip I had on my anger. Never in my entire tenure as Warden had I felt as close to losing my calm, collected composure as I was right now. Lexa Cromwell had that effect on me. "Who gave the order for you to stay off my floor?"

He glanced around as if he could sense the trap within my question and was looking for an escape.

I felt my blood boiling again but took a deep breath to restrain myself.

"You did, my Warden." He was young, probably a relatively recent Pledge. His sandy blonde hair was tucked behind his ears, and he had a short blade at his waist. He looked strong despite cowering in my presence.

"Then I can be the one to change the rules then, can't I?"

He nodded, his throat bobbed as he swallowed.

"Go, now. I want guards at my door in three minutes and Lilith and the Captain to this room in ten. Do I make myself clear?" I wasn't intentionally trying to intimidate the poor kid, but I did need him to understand how important this task that I was giving him was.

He hurried across the floor, and I knew I should have rushed into Lexa's room instantly, assessed the damage, and figured out who the hell that man was. But I couldn't seem to step away from the base of the stairs. From here, I had the perfect line of sight to see the door to my quarters. I couldn't tear my eyes from it until I knew someone was there to watch it for me.

I didn't understand this constriction in my chest. Was it guilt that I wasn't fast enough to protect her? That she had to do it herself? Something she'll never forget. Was I angry at the person who infiltrated my home?

Yes, to all of the above, but it was more than that. I knew it was more than that. It had been more than that for days. My chest tightened at the thought of her in pain, in danger, not because it was my *job* to protect her, but because I *needed* to protect her. I needed to keep her safe. I needed her.

That thought scared me far more than the fact that her Mythica worked on me and that she stole my most profound guilt from me, viewing the tainted memory with her own eyes. She doesn't understand. And now, she quite possibly never would.

Three of my guards rushed past me, tossing wary glances in my direction as if they, too, thought this might be a trap, and bounded up the stairs to take positions in front of the door to my chamber. I released a breath I hadn't realized I had been holding.

She's safe.

With the question of her safety answered, I lowered my gaze to the closed door to Lexa's chambers. My eyes narrowed, and the restrained rage began to dictate every step toward the room. I slid inside quickly, opening the door only enough for me to slip in, hiding the contents of this room from any possible prying eyes. I steeled my nerves and turned to assess what Lexa had left behind.

To call it a horrific sight would be a severe understatement. Blood had continued spilling from the body long after Lexa and I retreated from the space. It flowed across the floor and covered an eerie amount of ground. I didn't have a weak constitution. I've seen plenty of death in my time, some at my own hand, but something about the way the crimson blood tinted the Mark of The Forgotten Court made my stomach turn.

I approached the figure, averting my eyes from the wicked-looking symbol. Lying within the blood, near this lifeless man, was the dagger. The dark obsidian blade glistened with the sticky remnant of a life stolen. I bent down, grasping it, carefully touching only the hilt. I tossed it onto the bed and folded the edge of the sheet over it, wiping the blood from the blade. The bright white paint soaking down into the mattress looked back at me. I gripped the edge of the sheet and ripped a corner off, large enough to use as a rag. I quickly moved around the room, marring the symbol of the Forgotten Court until it was nothing more than streaks, and the ominous image was unrecognizable, leaving only one untouched to show to my Dean.

Then, I made quick work of wiping the blood from the weapon. Once the dagger was clean enough, I ran my index finger over the single word etched into its blade. A tear fell from my eyes, but I quickly shook it away, and I slipped the dagger through a belt loop and turned back to the body just as the door to the chambers opened.

Lilith and the guard's Captain stopped at the scene before them. Their eyes widened in shock.

"Close the door behind you," I commanded flatly. They needed time to process, but we didn't need anyone poking their head in right now and seeing this before I was ready to explain.

If I'm ever ready to explain.

They shuffled in, shutting the door. Gregorio, the Captain, cleared his throat, composing himself. Lilith turned to face the wall, centering her gaze on anything except the body on the floor.

"My Warden, what happened here?" My Captain asked, his dark voice wavering with just a hint of insecurity. He was a talented guard, and he'd seen his fair share of *delicate* situations, but even I knew that the sight before him was one of nightmares.

"That is what I would like to know, Gregorio." I let the mask of Warden feed my cold tone. His eyes snapped up from the body to lock on me. "Would you like to explain how this man got into my castle and this room unseen?"

His throat bobbed as he swallowed hard. Fear coating his expression. "I assure you, I had guards on every entrance and every floor. As I always do."

I'm positive he's right. He's the best Captain I've ever had, and I've had quite a few throughout the centuries, but this was Lexa we were talking about. I needed my guards to be better than their best.

"I need you to find out how he got in."

He nodded, returning his gaze to the body.

"And I need a rotation of guards on my chamber doors until Miss Cromwell and I leave for The Court of Passion tomorrow."

Lilith's head snapped up, pulling her gaze from the blood to look at me. "She's staying in your quarters?"

I didn't miss the apparent jealousy oozing from her words.

"Did you expect me to ask her to remain in this room? Tell me, Lilith, do you think the blood makes for a good throw rug?"

She turned her gaze down, and Gregorio stifled a laugh with a cough.

"Gregorio, see that it's done," I demanded.

He bowed slightly at the waist, crossed his arm across his chest, and then slipped through the door, quickly closing it again.

Lilith didn't look at me.

"We are leaving tomorrow. And I expect you to keep my Court in one piece while we're gone," I remarked, although it felt strange discussing business with her while there was a dead body on the ground between us.

"You can trust me, my Warden," she assured me, but her eyes didn't meet mine. She was furious, no doubt. She had probably made plans to slither into my chambers tonight to try and sneak one last rendezvous in before I left for six months.

Even if Lexa weren't going to be sleeping in my room tonight, I wouldn't have indulged, not after knowing the sounds that Lexa makes when she climaxes. Nothing could ever sound sweeter. And I didn't want anyone else even to attempt to replicate it. I was completely and utterly addicted to the woman in my bed. I was addicted to the way she arched into me, the way the walls of her core tightened around my fingers, the way she pressed back into my hardened length. Ready just for her, especially for her. No, no one could ever compare.

I shook my head and focused on the angry blonde before me. "I know. That is why you are my Dean." I never told her that she was my Dean, not because of any merit on her part but because she was the only choice. She didn't need to know that. As long as she did the work and made my life easier, it was a solid enough arrangement in my eyes.

She smiled at that. Of course, she did. She was a member of The Court of Shadows. We need to feel like we aren't being treated as less than. "Do you know what this symbol means?" Lilith asked, glancing at the only mark I'd left untouched.

I focused all my energy on maintaining a calm expression.

"Not yet," I answered truthfully. I knew what this Mark used to be. But this bastardized version, this version that aimed to torment and harm… I had no idea what it was meant to symbolize. "If you see it again, tell me immediately. Use one of the messengers." It was a relatively common type of Mythica, the ability to send silent messages to other messengers. Each Court has a few members with that particular brand of Mythica so that the Wardens could communicate, should we need to. The messengers were also terrible gossips. "Discreetly, of course."

"Of course, my Warden." She looked down again at the body, disgust coloring her face.

"I need you to clean this up." She looked ready to argue, but I flashed her one of my looks that told her not to test me. "It is of the utmost importance that this stays quiet. Do you understand?"

She nodded solemnly.

"Go, gather what you need. You may enlist Gregorio's assistance."

She bowed her head and exited the room quickly, once again leaving me alone with my little storm's assailant. Now that Lilith had seen what she needed of the Mark, I quickly destroyed that one as well. Then I turned slowly to the body of the man that Lexa had killed.

"Who are you?" I asked under my breath, stepping forward to turn his head toward me. He looked young, mid-thirties or so. Too young to be dead. I shook the thought away and reached for the dagger at my hip. Using the tip, I sliced through the fabric of his shirt and tossed it to the side. I knew it was here somewhere. I just had to find it.

There, just above his pant line, climbing from his belly button to the center of his stomach, was the Mark of The Court of Shadows. It explained why he was here and why he was able to cross the veil. But it doesn't explain why this attacker would know about the Mark of The Forgotten Court. With one hand, I rolled him to his front, peeling away the rest of his blood-soaked shirt to reveal his back, tinted red from the pool of his own life that he lay in.

Gods save me.

Inked onto his shoulder blade was the very same Mark that marred the room. The silhouette of a raven, an autumn crocus hanging from its beak. The Mark of The Forgotten Court.

My breath stilled, and my heart seized. How could this be? This shouldn't be possible. This Mark has not been given out in nearly a century. There was no logical explanation for why this man should have this inked into his skin or why he bore the mark of my Court as well. Double Marked individuals were expressly forbidden, with the only exception being those branded with the Mark of Echoes so they could complete the one-way journey to the Sunken Province Prison. An eerie shudder wracked my body. Nobody could know of this.

I knew what I had to do, although it sent a disturbing sickness to my stomach. With shaking hands, I gripped the dagger and made quick, shallow cuts across the man's back, ruining the Mark until it was entirely unrecognizable, like the paint that now stained the room in indiscernible patterns. I fought against the bile that rose in my throat.

Once, I was sure nobody could piece together what he had inked into his skin. I stood, flipping the man to his back again. "Who are you?" I asked again under my breath before exiting the room and leaving the mysterious Double Marked man behind me.

THREE

It was morning. I could tell by the harsh light that kept me from opening my eyes fully. I don't know how long I slept. It could have been a few hours, could have been a day. After my encounter with the fountain, I must have slept for a few hours at least. It was dark outside when I woke up in this bed the first time, that much I know. It can't have been more than an hour after waking up before…

My body shook as the phantom memory of rough hands clamped down on my mouth. I jolted up in bed, my chest heaved, and my hands clutched my head, fingers digging into my still-damp hair.

I was still wet from the bathing chambers when Lysander washed my hair.

When Lysander washed all of me.

I let out a deep groan before falling back onto the bed and bringing a pillow to my face. How can someone make me feel passion beyond measure one moment only to frighten me the next?

How had I been so blind? Blinded by some pathetic seduction, too wrapped up in his euphoric sensualism that, I was unable to see the glaringly obvious.

Lysander Bladespell was a murderer. And so was I.

Tossing the pillow off my face as the unfortunate truth sunk into my bones, I swung my legs over the side of the mattress, and my feet landed on the wooden floor. Lysander scrubbed the blood clear, and thankfully, there was no longer a red tint to my pale skin, but I could still see it there. A part of me knew that I always would.

Sitting on the bedside table was a glass of water, the emerald-hilted dagger, and a note. I wasn't sure which of the three items I feared more. Water has proven that it was not the source of life that some claim it to be, at least not for me. That note was more than likely some half-baked apology from the man who ordered the execution of an entire Court and its Warden. And that dagger. That dagger is the weapon that I wielded when I took someone's life.

This bedside table was taunting me.

But I couldn't be afraid forever. Sooner or later, I was going to need a drink of water. I would have to talk to Lysander, and one day, I may need to defend myself again. This morning seemed as good a time as any to begin the long recovery journey.

Gripping the glass in my hand, I took large gulps of the cold liquid. Cold. Lysander was here recently. Did he sleep in here with me? I would have noticed that. His scent and his presence were so familiar to me now. Did he just step inside to place these things here before quickly rushing away? Did he stay long? Did he watch over me as I slept? If he did, how did I feel about that? I finished the glass and replaced it on the table, my hand hovered over the dagger.

If I picked it up, was that an admission that what I did was acceptable? That I killed a man, and it was okay. By holding this dagger, was I submitting to the title of murderer? Was I just as vile as Lysander?

I almost pulled away, left the beautiful weapon on the table, and stepped away from it and what it did because of me, but suddenly the feeling returned. That phantom touch across my face, the fear and panic that seized me when that man's arms encircled me, and I reached for the hilt. The moment my fingers grazed the cool jeweled hilt, the image of my assailant's lifeless eyes flashed in front of my eyes, and I pulled my hand back as if I had been shocked.

We were both killers—Lysander and me. But the comparison stopped there.

I was nothing like Lysander. I killed that man because he had attacked me. Lysander and the other Wardens killed The Forgotten Court because of their fragile egos.

My Mythica worked on him; I should be bracing myself for the possibility that he will notify the other Wardens of that little *development*, and together, they would execute me the way they did with the Warden of Forgotten. And undoubtedly with less pomp and circumstance because I was nothing special. Killing a Warden was a vast undertaking. Killing me would be nothing but a slight inconvenience.

I couldn't rectify that the man who spearheaded such a horrific act was the same man who held me together when I nearly fell to pieces in the bath last night. The same man who dove into the fountain to bring me back to the surface, whose fingers dragged the most intense moment of passion from my body. How could someone who does all that be a villain?

My fingers hovered over the word etched into the blade, not quite making contact.

'Vahlach'

I hadn't had a chance to ask Lysander what it meant. Maybe I should. If I ever wished to speak to him again, which wasn't proving to be high on my to-do list.

Leaving the dagger untouched on the table, I focused on the folded piece of parchment lying in wait. I must have sat there for several minutes, gathering the courage and weighing the benefits and the costs. Did I want to know what he said? Absolutely… not. Maybe. I wasn't sure.

That shining example of indecision was why, ten minutes later, I was still staring at the note.

Just read it, Lexa.

With a long, shaky breath, I reached for the note, gripping the smooth paper.

Unfolding it, I got a whiff of alcohol. I've smelled a similar thick, musky scent at the Verihdian Institute a few times. Oliver used to indulge on weekends or at events. He would smile, pull me in for a hug, and that comforting smell would wash over me. My heart constricted at the thought of Oliver, my mentor, my friend. I missed him desperately already. Perhaps I could be happy as an Uncourted, forget all this nonsense about choosing a Court, and choose none at all.

Shaking off the haunting longing that threatened to take hold of me, my eyes adjusted to the script on the page.

Miss Cromwell,

I've brought you some water, please drink it. You may not feel like it, but you are dehydrated - and if you're going to remain the surprising force you are, you need to keep up your strength.

I reread that sentence. Surprising? He certainly didn't sound like a man afraid of what I could do. Someone who'd sooner jump to murder than have someone show more Mythica aptitude than him. I shook away the doubt that crested because it wasn't a question. I saw that man with my very own eyes. I saw what he suggested. I saw what he did.

I've also brought you your dagger. Because it is… it's yours. And I have never been more thankful for a gift I've given before in my life. I know it may seem tainted now, stained. But hear me when I say this - you had no other option. And frankly, he's lucky that I didn't get to him first.

The image of Lysander coming to my rescue sent a strange sensation to my core. On one hand, it made me feel safe and protected. On the other hand, it reminded me that this Warden could kill someone without hesitation - and has. Even if not directly. It would have been so much easier to despise and write him off five days ago, but now, I've seen a different side of Lysander. A side that I liked - dare I say, respected. I tossed a melancholic glance at the dagger that sat idly on the table.

It is best to leave The Court of Shadows today and head towards The Court of Passion. It will take a few days for us to arrive at Pleasure Tower - I genuinely detest calling it that.

I chuckled softly, imagining his emerald eyes rolling in his head as his lips pursed. Then, a feeling of sadness washed over me. The thought of leaving The Court of Shadows and never returning left a sour taste in my mouth. How had so many of my opinions changed so quickly?

We will need to talk soon about what you saw in my mind - the guilt you were able to rip from me - and we will. I swear to you. Your things have already been packed, so you need not return to that room.

I released a sigh at his thoughtfulness. I never wanted to set foot in that room ever again. Of course, he would know that.

I'll be in my library when you are ready to leave.

With all the care in the world,

Lysander.

Tears sprang to my eyes. This man was confusing me beyond measure. I wasn't sure which way was up with him anymore. Was he the generous, flirtatious, kind man who his people loved? Or was he the bloodthirsty, egotistical, fragile Warden who brought nothing but death and destruction? I couldn't see how someone could be both.

I folded the note and placed it back on the nightstand. Sitting near the door, I caught a glimpse of my bags. Plus, a few extras. I reached for the foreign luggage and opened it to find a myriad of dresses, shirts, and pants. The styles and colors immediately told me these were native threads to The Court of Shadows.

Did he buy me clothes?

I couldn't stop the emotion that was building just inside my rib cage. I had lost one of my favorite dresses - luckily, the only casualty of my dip in the fountain. My fingers glided over the vivid reds, oranges, and greens crafted from exquisite fabric adorned with intricate swirling patterns and embroidery. These garments were beautiful displays of fine craftsmanship, evident love letters to the Court. Despite the kind and thoughtful gesture that swelled my heart, I couldn't bring myself to wear something purchased by a murderer. I closed the case and delved into my original bags for an outfit. While my hand hovered over comfortable pants suitable for a day of travel, a light grey shimmering fabric seized my attention. I had no compelling reason to dress up, appear presentable, or strive for attractiveness today—or so I told myself as I reached for the chiffon dress.

Slipping it over my head, it settled on my curves perfectly. It accentuated my soft hourglass figure and wide hips. Securing the high-neck collar that supported the top of the dress, I let out a sigh. It didn't completely conceal the bruise that decorated my throat, but it provided enough coverage to keep it from being the focal point. However, it did nothing to mask the darkened circles beneath my eyes, evidence of the forceful headbutt from my attacker the previous night. My black hair remained damp, hanging limply around my face. I gathered it into a loose braid cascading down the side of my head, delicately resting on my shoulder. Opting for sandals with long braided ropes, I crisscrossed the straps a few times, securing them up my calf just below the knee. Glancing into the wall mirror, I couldn't help but notice that, despite the bruise blooming along my nose, I still looked beautiful.

My hand was on the door handle when I felt the emptiness. The vacancy suddenly felt so prominent that I wasn't sure I'd ever be able to ignore it. My bare leg called out for the dagger on the bedside table. I wanted to leave it. To forget the man who gave it to me and the man whose life it took. I never wanted to see it again, but I needed it. It saved my life. Twice now. It made me feel safe. With a reluctant sigh, I crossed the space to the bedside table. Resting my foot on the edge of the bed, I fastened the leather holster, ignoring the memory of teeth pulling the strap taught against my eager skin, his fingers trailing up my thigh towards the center of my desire. I shook my head, letting the unwelcome intrusion dissipate. Then I reached for the dagger, hesitantly, cautiously. Expecting the dark memories to resurface the moment my fingers gripped it again, but instead, a wave of comfort blanketed me. Has it only been five days since he gave it to me? It seemed like this weapon had always been at my side, always made to fit against my skin, to protect me.

Feeling whole again for the first time since that man's death took a part of me, I left Lysander's room and headed toward his library.

Quietly, I acknowledged the presence of the two guards stationed just outside the chamber doors, appreciating Lysander's foresight in securing the room. Descending the stairs, I cast a lingering gaze around the atrium, a smile playing on my lips as I admired the foliage adorning the space and the warm light filtering through the stained glass ceiling. The air carried the rich fragrance of harvest—a blend of woods, spices, and crisp freshness. The Court of Shadows exuded a scent so full and vibrant, unlike anything I had experienced. At that moment, I was confident that I would miss it all. Every bit of it.

Even Chandler.

"Damn…" I halted on one of the landings, observing the few people in motion around me. I didn't know if Chandler was even still here at the Forsaken Quarters. The new Pledges were offered free lodging until they found a place of their own, and for all I know, he could have moved out by now. I should say goodbye. That would be the right thing to do. The years we spent together warranted that much.

Gregorio, the Captain - I think, was climbing the stairs in my direction, so I called out to him. When he saw me, he stopped in front of me. His eyes scanned my frame.

"Miss Cromwell, I'm pleased to see that you are well." His eyes held a secret behind them. He knew. Of course, he knew. Lysander had to inform his Captain of the guard that there was a breach in his security and a corpse bleeding out in one of the rooms.

I tried not to let my discomfort show.

"Thank you," I whispered. He bowed his head. "Do you know if Chandler Mills has moved out of the Forsaken Quarters yet?"

Gregorio's eyebrows furrowed, and his eyes flicked to the side as he tried to recall. "I don't believe he's found permanent lodging yet," he replied, unsure. I nodded twice, letting my gaze drift down to the ground.

"Would you mind showing me to his room?"

Gregorio looked over my shoulder briefly before his eyes trained back on me. "Of course. Right this way, Miss Cromwell." The Captain wore snug leather armor that highlighted his figure, with a dark tunic peeking out beneath the protective layer. His dark pants were neatly tucked into tall grey boots, and a long sword with a dark grey hilt rested at his side, accompanied by a dagger strapped to his opposite hip. His commanding presence mirrored that of Chandler and his manifested Mythica.

As we descended to the lower landing, I observed the back of his head, the echo of our footsteps resonating through the empty atrium. Gregorio's long strides presented a challenge for me to keep pace until we finally halted in front of a modest wooden door.

"Here we are," he turned back to me. His face was emotionless.

"Thank you, Gregorio." I smiled, and he bowed his head slightly. "If I don't see you before I leave, it has been a pleasure."

His face softened at that.

"I look forward to seeing you again when you make the right choice and Pledge to The Court of Shadows." And with what looked like the beginning of a smirk, he sauntered away.

My heart tightened. Last night, even if only briefly, I entertained the idea. I envisioned myself adorned in oranges and greens, savoring hot cider in the town square while vibrant trees swayed in the brisk autumn breeze. There was a fleeting moment when I believed I could find happiness here, with him.

Yet, like so many of the good things I've dared to dream, the vision unraveled. No, not unraveled— it crashed and burned.

What once held the promise of a bright and lively glimpse into a potential future now loomed clouded, obscured by a dark reminder of the harsh reality I've discovered about Lysander Bladespell, the Warden of Shadows. I still couldn't fathom the possibility that he might have committed such a horrific act.

But I saw it with my own eyes.

I shook away the thought and looked towards Chandler's door. I took a long, steadying breath and knocked softly.

My knuckles rapped against the wooden door, sending a dull thud echoing down the hall. I heard a groaning beyond the door and the shuffling of feet. When the door opened, I was met with the entirely unfamiliar image of a disheveled Chandler. Even after our frequent meetings in the bedroom, he never so much as had his shirt untucked or his hair uncombed. The man before me was a mere echo of the Chandler I thought I knew. His blonde hair was matted down and hung haphazardly onto his forehead. Dark and heavy circles framed his eyes. His chest was exposed, and his lower half was draped in light pants that sat low on his hips. He didn't look up at me as he slid the door open. Instead, he rubbed the back of his hand against his eyes as if begging them to awaken.

"I'm so sorry, Chandler. I didn't mean to interrupt," I whispered anxiously, turning to avert my eyes. It's not that I haven't seen him in far less clothing and far more inappropriate positions, but something about this moment felt vulnerable, and I didn't want him to feel ambushed.

"Lexa?!" He exclaimed boldly, his voice colored with shock and surprise. I lifted my head to look at him. His brown eyes were scanning me, up and down, as if he was looking for something or trying to decide if I was real. "What happened to you?"

I shrugged. Of course, he noticed the bruising. "I'm okay, I promise." It was a lie, but one that was easy to tell. After all, Chandler and I had been lying to each other for years.

His eyes continued their scan of my body.

"I just wanted to say goodbye. I'm leaving for The Court of Passion today."

His hands moved through his messy hair as he continued to look at me like he was shocked to find me there. "You're leaving?" He asked, the question coming out as more of an accusation. I nodded and took a step back. He followed me out into the hall. The two of us stood there, three feet apart, in various states of disarray.

I suddenly remembered that once I left, I would not have a single person to comfort me. Nobody would be around to help me feel safe. For a brief moment, I thought Lysander could be that person for me. But I was wrong. Unshed tears stung my eyes. "Yeah. It's time." It was a whisper—a confession. My eyes met Chandler's, and finally, the tears streamed down my cheek.

"Are you alright?" He asked again, but something about how he said the words told me he wasn't referring to the tears that fell but something that the eyes couldn't see.

"No," I answered truthfully.

"I heard about what happened at the fountain."

Panic seized my heart. My breathing became labored. Had Lysander gone around telling everyone what happened to me?

"I was in a tavern on town square when you … fell in?"

The tenseness in my muscles relaxed at the question in his voice. He didn't know the specifics of what happened, which means that Lysander didn't tell them. He hadn't betrayed me.

Again.

"I'm okay." That was all I could say. The distance between us seemed immense, as if the individuals we once were and the solace we once shared had become relics of the past. Logically, I acknowledged this reality but couldn't escape the sorrow weaving its way around my heart.

"Well," he started, his hand rubbing the back of his neck nonchalantly. "Safe travels." Casual. Detached. My heart ached for the relationship we used to have, as surface-level as it was.

"Thank you." I nodded. Silence fell between us. He sighed deeply before rushing forward to wrap me in his arms. I melted into his embrace, but this time, it carried a distinct and haunting sensation as my Mythica enveloped us. The wicked tendrils of my power circled him, but I didn't allow it to reach for him. But even as it danced in the air around him, I detected a strong emotion that stood out, one I could readily identify without even asking the silent question — guilt.

I ignored the dark storm within me that was begging to be released to question him on it. I would not ruin this final moment with Chandler just to see why his guilt felt so potent. When we pulled apart, I saw his eyes scan me again, this time with a hint of desire.

"So, there's no chance of you Pledging to The Court of Shadows?" Unlike Gregorio, he didn't seem to be tempting me or teasing me. He was simply confirming what he already knew.

I shook my head in answer.

"Then this is more than just a goodbye."

I nodded, afraid to speak in case my voice betrayed me.

"Well then, thank you, Lexa Cromwell," he said, extending his hand for a handshake. I laughed at the formality but lifted my hand to meet him anyway.

"Goodbye, Chandler Mills."

He smiled lightly, but that dark shadow of guilt still emanated from him.

"Don't get in too much trouble while your Warden is gone," I joked. I don't know why I was trying to prolong this exchange. I just wasn't quite ready to leave. Or maybe I wasn't prepared to face Lysadner.

Chandler's eyes darkened, and he tilted his head slightly. "Don't worry," he started, low. "The Court of Shadows will be in good hands."

I was aware of Chandler's connection with Lilith Hargrove, yet he had never praised her competence. In fact, he frequently spoke disdainfully of her Vacant status. I also remembered how he used to harbor a quiet desire to be appointed as the new Dean by Lysander during the Pledging ceremony—a secret I had extracted from the depths of his soul against his will. It surprised me to witness him now placing so much trust in her abilities.

"Take care of yourself, Lexa." Chandler did not lean forward to kiss me as I expected, but I was thankful for that. As much as I wanted to erase the thought of the last lips that touched mine, I also couldn't fathom kissing anyone else. *He's a murderer.* I reminded myself while squeezing Chandler's hand. With a final glance, I turned away, leaving Chandler and my last hope for comfort behind.

FOUR

The harsh sun bit my skin as I lay among the purple wildflowers. Oliver could do all he wanted to mimic the warmth of this Court from the safety of his classroom, but it paled compared to the power of this sun. My already tan skin, earned from several hours out on the front lawn of the Institute, had a slight red tint to it from the burn I garnered on my first day in my new Court.

My Court.

It felt incredibly surreal. After countless hours of hard work, dedicated training, sleepless nights immersed in studying The Court of the Vanguard, and numerous prayers sent to Banyad, I had finally arrived. This was my rightful place.

I was sprawled among the sea of purple flowers as the wind caressed my face, and the stems swayed, sending the delightfully fresh scent to my nose. Nothing had ever felt so right to me.

I found this hill on my second day here. I decided to take a run through the town and challenged myself by attempting an uphill sprint. Much to my happiness, I made it with minimal exertion, although when I stopped here to catch my breath, the view had stolen it from me. From this spot, I could see the city of Creedence bustling with activity. The faint sound of a blacksmith's hammer pounding could be heard across the distance. Then, just there, standing guard beside the city was the most beautiful sight I have ever and will ever see. The Chaos Coliseum. It was built into the earth, a large crevice of stone and honor carved into the ground. From here, I could see the empty seats begging their audience to return. It was the type of sight that made you thankful that you were alive. My entire body tensed at the sheer immensity and beauty of it. It looked different from up here than from within its stone arches.

My mind wandered back to the first night we arrived. Including me, there were eight new Pledges for The Court of the Vanguard. The moment we arrived, we were all escorted into the underbelly of the Coliseum, deep underground. I couldn't help but acknowledge that my feet were walking the same sandy corridors that the Verihdian Gladiators had, and with each step, I felt my destiny fall into place. I had never doubted that this Court was where I belonged, but if I had, any insecurity would have been thoroughly washed away the moment I took my first step into the arena. We exited the tunnels leading to the sand-covered arena floor to the thunderous sounds of cheers and warrior chants that echoed off the stone like the Gods themselves were amplifying their praise. The roars filled my ears and sent shivers of excitement down my spine. I had read about this Coliseum and the fights housed within its confines, but nothing could have prepared me for this. Nothing came close to the reality of it. The experience I had earned. One I had fought for.

So, I took my run and ended it here every morning since that night five moons ago. Each time I crested the hill, the sight would steal my breath like it had the very first day. I would never get used to this. I hoped I never did.

A few days ago, I found myself in a cozy cottage just outside of Creedence. Its roof still needed to be repaired, and the windows were all but busted, but it could be home. It would be home.

I spent most of my life growing up knowing that I wasn't anything special.

Knowing that because I was Vacant, I wouldn't just slot in someplace as perfectly as Riley had. The instructors at the Institute spent so long convincing us that having or not having Mythica was not the most crucial factor in Pledging, but we all knew it was. They didn't even believe their own polite lie. In a world that was designed for Mythica-wielders, I was Vacant. It wasn't easy, but I worked hard. I trained, and I knew I would have to mold myself into the perfect fit for one of the Courts. At first, the idea of being a Gladiator scared me, especially knowing I was no match against powerful Mythica. However, it all crystallized when I first heard that gladiators weren't permitted to use their Mythica in the tournaments. I knew this would be my Court and what I was meant to do with my life. So, I spent the last decade creating the perfect Gladiator—the perfect member of The Court of the Vanguard.

Now that I was here, it was clear that this was the right choice. There was never a question. I was made for this Court. And it was made for me.

With midday upon me, the urgency to gather the materials required for patching my roof before nightfall compelled me to head to the market. Descending the hill, I set my pace at a soft jog, making my way toward the bustling market situated in the center of Creedence. As I approached the lively city center, the sounds intensified. In The Living Lands, we had a few blacksmiths who managed simple requests, but the skilled artisans here operated on an entirely different level. Their work was meticulously crafted, intricately detailed, and stunningly achieved. It seemed like there was a shop on every corner.

I hastened toward one of the carpentry shops, reluctantly parting with a significant portion of my already diminishing finances to acquire spare wood, tools, and supplies. Today, that roof was getting fixed.

"Thanks, Charlie," I offered, gathering my items in my arms as the shopkeeper nodded. When I first arrived in town and asked about finding work, several people pointed me toward Charlie. But they said he only sent jobs to people he liked. Right now, I wasn't sure where I stood with him. He got all my money, and

I tried to make myself seem valuable. "You'll let me know if you have anybody who needs an extra hand around here, yeah?"

Charlie looked me up and down in silence. His weathered face was the kind that told stories. I wondered if he had been a Gladiator at some point or if the scars on his face had been garnered from other sources. Either way, it was clear he was not a man to be messed with. "Yeah, kid. I'll keep ya in mind."

I smiled brightly. "You won't regret it!" I hurriedly moved across town, heading towards the small hollow where my worn-out home was situated. The door was slightly ajar, its hinges in need of a good tightening, and the porch steps had wholly caved in. However, hopping up without the steps wasn't too challenging, so their absence didn't pose a significant obstacle. Upon entering, I discovered my two bags still unpacked, resting near the old bed frame nestled in the corner of the space. Although it was one large room, I saw beyond its current state and recognized its untapped potential.

"First, let's get this roof patched."

I spent the evening, well into the night, patching and reshingling the roof. Hard work never bothered or scared me. Hard work meant the outcome would be worth it. Being here in this Court was proof enough of that.

It was pitch dark outside when I fell onto my mattress and into a restless sleep. I dreamt of my old home, of Riley and Oliver, the three of us joking around in the hallway of the Verihdian Institute. Then my dreams shifted to Lexa, my twin, my best friend. She often starred in my dreams. Her smile, her laugh. The way she teased me. She was the best part of me.

I miss her.

The following day followed a familiar routine—I took my run, spent the morning observing my Court from a distance, and then headed to Charlie's to part with even more of my nearly depleted funds for additional repairs to my home. It was becoming increasingly evident that I needed to secure a job soon.

I stopped by his counter with an arm full of supplies.

His eyes scanned me as they did every day. "I got a job for ya."

My eyes widened in surprise.

"Charlie, that's great!" I attempted to reign in my excitement. He didn't need to know how desperate I was getting. He didn't need to know that I had sacrificed meals for two nights in favor of spending money on supplies for my home repairs. On our initial evenings here as honored guests of our Warden, we were well-fed at a small inn she owned near the Coliseum. However, once I found my home, which consumed a significant portion of my savings, I was left to fend for myself."Thank you so much!"

"Don't thank me yet," he retorted gruffly. "They asked for you by name and said it's a tough job."

I nodded, confusion filling me. Who in this Court even knew who I was and that I was looking for work with Charlie? "Of course…Who is it?"

Charlie laughed under his breath, his round stomach shaking with the movement. "You're to report to the Chaos Coliseum immediately."

My heart skipped a beat. "I was asked for, by name, for a job at the Coliseum?"

Charlie nodded.

I felt my jaw hang open, shock spreading through me. "Right now?"

"That's what immediately means, ain't it?" He rolled his hazel eyes before moving on to help the next customer.

Leaving my supplies there, promising to return for them, I dashed off towards the Chaos Coliseum.

I hadn't set foot inside since the night we first arrived, when the crowd's energy was electrifying, sending shockwaves to my very soul. Running towards the entrance, I pondered whether the empty arena would evoke the same sensation. Within minutes, I reached the towering stone gate, and the guards stationed outside cast their gaze first at me and then exchanged glances with each other.

"Name?" The tallest one, in dark leather armor, inquired. He had a sword at his side, and his Court Mark was proudly displayed on his bicep.

"Axel Cromwell, sir."

With a nod, the two moved aside and offered me entrance into the Coliseum. "We will let them know you're here. Wait just inside," he spoke again, and I nodded as I strode past him. It felt both inherently wrong and undeniably right that I had gained access to this sacred place with nothing more than my name.

Embedded into the ground, the Chaos Coliseum unfolded before me as I passed through the stone gate, leading me to the highest tier of seating, furthest from the sandy gladiatorial ring below. The expansive and profound arena seemed to pulsate with life, even in its emptiness. A smile unconsciously spread across my face.

I knew I belonged here.

"Ladies, gentlemen, and esteemed ones…welcome to the Chaos Coliseum!" I started, mimicking the voice that announced our welcome to the Court on my first night here. "Welcome to the arena, first-time Gladiator, Axel Cromwell!" Cupping my hands over my mouth, I cheered. "And in this corner, the returning champion, Vanguard favorite… Cassius Dawson. Let the fight begin! Newcomer Cromwell seems to be teasing Dawson. Light on his feet. Dawson lunges… ohh, but Axel is out of the way and offering a counterattack. Right to the back, Cassius takes a hit! The crowd is going wild!" I watched the empty sand pit at the center of the arena become the site of my first fight, imagining the words as I said them, coming true.

"Cassius gets a good swipe in, their strength a clear advantage over Cromwell." Even in my fantasy, I knew my strength was no match for Cassius. But I was faster. It's how I would beat them if I ever got the chance. "Cromwell gets behind them. Dawson doesn't know where he went. I can't believe it–Cromwell's taking advantage of Cassius's blind spot. He goes in for the winning blow! And he's done it! First-time Gladiator Axel Cromwell takes down Vanguard's favorite, Cassius Dawson. This is a story for the ages." I'm smiling at my fictitious fantasy when I hear a slow clapping build from behind me.

Spinning around, I came face to face with Avalin Earheart, the Warden of Vanguard, and next to her was none other than Cassius Dawson. My face burned hot in shame. Cassius' hands clapped together, and a wicked smile crossed their face.

"Good show, mate," they spoke with a slightly accented tone. It screamed charisma and confidence. "Utterly unrealistic, though."

"You do have a blind spot, Cassius. You're lucky the other Gladiators haven't found it yet." Avalin said. Her long red hair hung down to her waist, braids held by metallic clasps decorating her head. Her eyes were a bright violet, not unlike the color of the wildflowers on my hill. She wore a dark purple leather breastplate that hugged her form tightly. A metal band encircled her upper arm, and chains and various accouterments hung from her belt. But it was her scarred face that drew my attention most. Each thick, carved line symbolized her courage and commitment to a lifetime of honor. She looked like the perfect picture of a Gladiator and a leader all at once.

"I do not, " Cassius retorted defensively. "Do I?"

Avalin laughed as her companion's face fell.

"Well, Axel… do they have a blind spot?" Avalin asked me. My name on her tongue sent a burst of pride through me. The Warden of my Court knew my name and wanted my opinion. I was going to give it.

"Uh…well. You do. You've obviously spent a lot of time working on your shoulders, which are impressive and contribute to your success in hand-to-hand combat."

Cassius beamed proudly.

"However, you haven't spent equal time developing your neck muscles, so you have severely limited your range of motion. Anything within your peripheral vision requires a full-body turn to be seen because your neck lacks the necessary strength and flexibility."

Cassius twisted their neck one way and then the next, testing the theory. My theory. "Damn," Cassius exclaimed after realizing that I was right.

"Why didn't you tell me, Avalin!?" They whined. I couldn't help but smile at this massive Gladiator in front of me, spinning around and around in either direction like an animal chasing its tail.

"Why would I tell you when I can easily use it against you?" Avalin teased humorously, but I knew, as well as Cassius did, that she was not joking.

"My Warden," I expressed, bowing my head towards her. We hadn't spoken since she personally gave me my Court Mark. And even then, we exchanged no words other than those that were expected of the Pledging Ceremony.

"Stand tall, Cromwell." She tossed dismissively. "I don't want your praise until I earn it." She smiled, and I couldn't help but admire her beauty. Of course, I knew it resulted from her Mythica and that she looked this way to me because that is what she wanted me to see.

"You've earned every ounce of praise I can give you, My Warden," I spoke honestly. I meant it. Stories of her gladiatorial exploits spread far and wide.

"Please, she doesn't need any more inflation to her already monumental ego," Cassius cautioned, rolling their eyes.

"You'd do well to watch your mouth, Cassius." Avalin jested, and the two of them laughed. "Axel, I'm sure you're wondering why I've asked you here today."

My body tensed, and my breath hitched. "You were the one who asked for me?" I spat out incredulously.

If she noticed my disbelief, she didn't mention it. "Yes, follow me." She turned on her heel, Cassius close behind, and approached a stone doorway past the gate. It looked like it would lead outside the arena again, but when she opened the door, it revealed a large spiral staircase that led directly down.

My eyes widened.

"You're about to become one of the only members of The Court of the Vanguard to have stepped foot in my personal quarters," Avalin promised, a smile gracing her solid and angular features.

"You live under the Coliseum?" It came out as more of an exclamation rather than a question, and both Avalin and Cassius laughed.

"Of course I do. No other place would be good enough." She began the descent, and as the door closed behind us, the darkness overwhelmed me for the briefest moments before the stone itself illuminated a faint purple light.

I must have gasped because Cassius' hand clapped me on the shoulder as they exclaimed, "Pretty impressive, right?"

I nodded because I couldn't find the words. I had seen plenty of artificial light before. There was an Instructor back at the Institute who could light his palms like beacons. But something this intricate and massive was new. Each brick glistened as if individually imbued with Mythica, a feat that probably would have taken a lifetime.

The entire space was basked in that calming purple haze. "How did you…" I asked as we continued down.

"You'll find soon, Axel, that what you were taught in The Living Lands is only a fraction of my Court's wonders," Avalin spoke proudly.

I smiled because it was all I could do.

We followed the spiral steps for several minutes until we reached solid ground again. Sprawled out in front of me was a wide-open reception area. It looked like a standard common room, similar to some we had back at the Institute, but instead of a few chairs and couches haphazardly set up to offer minimal comfort, this room was filled with plush carpets, decadent furniture, and dazzling artwork. It was a stunning display of lavish things. Several doors led from this main room to places unknown.

"Welcome to my home," Avalin smiled before venturing forward. "Let me show you where you'll be staying."

Her words surprised me, and I stumbled, losing my balance and falling forward. I managed to get my hands in front of me just in time to prevent a full-blown tumble. My nose hovered mere inches above the ground, and I silently thanked the Gods that I had avoided further embarrassment.

Cassius held a hand out for me. I took it sheepishly, returning to a standing position.

"I apologize…My Warden. Did you say, 'staying'?" I stuttered.

She nodded, averting her gaze. Either she was ashamed to look at me after my fall, or she was preserving my pride. Either way, I was thankful not to have her watchful gaze on me as I attempted to recover my dignity. "Yes, the job I have for you will take quite some time, and I need you to be accessible to me at all times." Her eyes found mine again, and I couldn't help but notice that her irises were even more vibrant in the glow of the amethyst lights.

I didn't respond, not because I didn't want to, but because I couldn't believe what I was hearing. Not only was I being tasked with a job at the Chaos Coliseum, but it was a job directly under Avalin Earheart, the Warden of Vanguard. And she wished for me to live here, in her personal quarters, for the duration.

"Unless you would rather I find someone else to do this job for me?" She asked tauntingly. She knew that nobody said no to a Warden's request as well as I did.

I shook my head. "I'd be honored, My Warden," I said as I bowed my head.

"I'll see you tomorrow, Avalin," Cassius said before heading towards a door on the far side of the room.

"You off to train that neck of yours?" Avalin teased. Cassius offered a crude gesture before disappearing behind the door, leaving me alone with the unrivaled Warden before me.

We stood silently for a moment as I took in the room around us. Marble statues stood in each corner, depicting famed Gladiators of old. I found myself gravitating toward them.

"You seem to know a great deal about our Verihdian Gladiators," Avalin spoke from behind me. I nodded, scanning the statue of Helia the Gallant. "And fancy yourself a champion in your own right."

I felt my body tense. I had hoped my little show for them earlier had been forgotten. I should have known not to hope for such futile things.

"I should apologize, My Warden. I never intended to claim I could best your favored Gladiator. Not even in jest." I turned to see her, and she crossed her muscular arms in front of her chest.

"You need not apologize for that, Axel. All of my favored gladiators began as eager Pledges once."

I felt a flutter of anticipation build within my core, but it faded as quickly as it began. "My Warden, may I speak freely?" I asked, knowing that it would haunt me if I did not ask the question that came to my mind.

"You have thus far. I hope you don't plan on restraining your honest tongue now," my Warden replied, raising one eyebrow.

"Does this treatment have anything to do with my sister?" I was not jealous. It wasn't in my nature, but I'd be lying if I didn't admit that the idea of getting this attention from my Warden simply because of my familial ties would wound my ego.

"What if it did? What then?" She asked, plopping down onto one of the spacious couches.

"I would be grateful for the opportunity but hesitant to accept a benefit that I did not deserve," I answered honestly.

She pursed her lips and narrowed her eyebrows at me before patting the cushion on the couch next to her. I moved across the floor slowly, then lowered myself onto the sofa near her. Her eyes tracked the movement.

"Did you know that the Final Compatibility Trials often give students two or three results?" She asked. I shook my head. I had not heard that. No one I've ever known has.

"Only the Wardens and the Seven are privy to that information, though." She finished. I took a slow breath and waited for her to continue. "Many of your classmates who Pledged to this Court could have easily fit in elsewhere. Four of them showed nearly equal aptitude in at least one other Court."

My heart rate quickened. Was it that close? How could they be sure they picked the correct one? How could they not give that information to us?

"You, Axel." Her eyes found mine and held me there. "You belong here, unquestionably. You were more compatible with my Court than any other Pledge has been in years."

Warmth bloomed in my chest. Pride.

"I would have been interested in you, sister or not."

She didn't strike me as the type to lie so freely, especially about something this impactful. I nodded, accepting her explanation.

"Thank you, my Warden."

She tilted her head in acknowledgment, then quickly stood from her spot.

"My Verihdian Gladiators need you." She leaned on her back foot casually as if she hadn't just offered me the world.

My jaw fell open. "You want me to be a Gladiator?" I asked in an anxious whisper, nearly jumping to my feet.

"Don't get ahead of yourself, Cromwell." She smiled. "You wouldn't be a Gladiator. You'd train them," she confirmed. "I am overhauling my training protocols. I would like you to assist in creating and implementing my new program." The realization of her offer quickly thawed the sting of rejection. "You need to understand I must be very selective with my recruitment. You are talented. That much was clear from your file and your result." She laid a hand on my shoulder. "But when I look at you, I don't see the fire inside that my Gladiators need to become the best." She indicated the statues.

I nodded, ignoring the hollow ache that formed at her words. How could she so expertly build me up and tear me down in the same breath?

"So, do you accept?" She inquired, and I weighed the advantages and drawbacks for a moment.

Being near the job I had devoted my entire life to securing was a significant achievement. Yet, it also meant remaining just beyond its grasp. I pondered whether it was preferable to be so distanced from your dream that you couldn't even see it or to be close enough for a constant reminder that it was unattainable.

The answer was clear.

"Of course, I accept, My Warden," I said confidently.

She offered me a pleased smile and led me to a room just off the central common space. It was a small but luxurious dwelling compared to my new cottage. "I look forward to seeing what you can do, Mr. Cromwell." She said before she took her leave, leaving me to settle into the aftermath of her offer.

Only an hour had transpired since I received the message from Charlie that I was needed at the Coliseum, yet it felt like a lifetime ago. The news that I would be working alongside my Warden to train her gladiators was almost surreal. I couldn't help but feel a sense of disbelief and questioned if I genuinely deserved such an opportunity. Nevertheless, deep down, I knew I did. While part of me wondered if this was some ploy to persuade my sister to Pledge, I was determined to make the most of it. Whether my role was seen as a potential gladiator or merely a bargaining chip, if this was as close as I could get to the Verihdian Gladiators, I was ready to embrace it.

Soon, she would recognize the fire within me, and I'd make sure she saw it–even if it burnt me.

Five

The walk to Lysander's library was not as long as I would have liked. I was at the double doors before I had even fully recovered from my goodbye to Chandler. What was I supposed to say to him? What did one say to a killer with whom you've shared a profoundly intimate moment? My heart raced at the memory of his strong fingers moving within me as if they knew exactly how to wring every ounce of pleasure from my body. Heat pooled between my legs as I shook my head, banishing the memory to the corner of my mind where I kept the other things I didn't dare think about.

Placing my bags down near the door, I pushed my palms against the wooden surface. Lysander's personal library was smaller than the one on the lower level of the Forsaken Quarters, and not many were invited to set foot inside. My mind flashed back to a conversation earlier this week when things were easier.

"You have a personal library? What do you keep in there that's so secretive? Are you reading inappropriate books, Warden?" I teased. He smiled while rolling his emerald eyes. I tried not to think about the ache in my core that built at the thought of him reading sensual, provoking words alone in that room.

"I keep my favorite titles there," he said as if it explained everything. I shook my head.

"So you keep them locked away? Wouldn't you want to share them if they're your favorites?"

He turned his head towards me, exhaling quickly through his nose.

"Oh wait, that's right, you don't share," I responded, truthfully but with a playful tone. He chuckled slowly.

"You're right, Miss Cromwell. I don't share what's mine," he promised, his eyes holding mine, sending a jolt of heat directly to my center. "But I do have other copies of those titles in our main library." He winked. "I'm not a total monster."

He had told me then that he wasn't a monster, but wasn't he? Or was he simply a man who had done monstrous things? How can you tell the difference? And when does the difference not matter? I stepped into the small library and immediately felt relaxed. This room wasn't the same as the luscious and spacious Forsaken Quarters I had gotten used to. The charming wooden bookshelves held hundreds of worn and deeply loved copies of books. The white floor was dotted with cozy rugs, begging me to sink into their promised comfort. The wall directly ahead consisted entirely of floor-to-ceiling windows that overlooked the side of the mountain range, showing the golden-flamed leaves of the eternally autumn trees.

The sight was one of such captivating beauty that I didn't even realize I wasn't alone.

"It's beautiful, isn't it?" The Warden of Shadows asked from his seat on one of the dark green upholstered couches. He had a book closed around his fingers. His dark hair was pulled back, but a few loose tendrils of hair hung around his eyes - eyes that hadn't yet met mine. His bronzed skin looked even more luminous in the sunrays spilling through the windows. A white shirt hugged his torso, unbuttoned just enough to show the hollow of his neck. He looked comfortable. Ready for a long day of travel, but only he could make comfortable look so *enticing*. He slowly moved his hand up and down, his fingers sliding between the pages he had been reading.

Oh, to be that book.

I shook the thought away and nodded my head. "Your Court is stunning, Warden." While I meant the words with every fiber of my being, they were lifeless, devoid of passion. It was all I could muster while fighting the ongoing battle inside.

He nodded, grabbing a small bookmark from the table and sliding it into the book, removing his fingers from the pages slowly.

I watched them like a feral beast, my thighs pressing together to relieve the tension there. If he noticed, he didn't acknowledge it.

"Are you prepared to begin our journey?" He asked, standing from the couch and sliding the book into a bag that sat open next to him.

"I am."

He nodded, avoiding my eyes. The silence continued for a few long moments as he finished packing his things. I watched his back as he worked. His muscles tightened and tensed with each movement.

He's a murderer.

I reminded myself again, but my traitorous inner voice spat back this time.

So are you.

"How are you feeling today, Miss Cromwell?" He asked, still diverting his eyes.

I swallowed, the dull ache in my throat still present, but the pain had subsided. "I'm doing much better today, thank you." Pleasant. Docile. Fake. That's what this conversation was. Gone was the raw honesty I had often felt brave enough to share with him. Gone was the biting wit and intensity we had grown to employ in each other's company. Whatever this new dynamic that was forming between us was, I hated it.

"I'm glad to hear that." The man before me didn't look like someone capable of doing what I knew he had done. He looked ashamed. Embarrassed. Not guilty. I watched him from my spot as he moved about the room, avoiding me.

I took the opportunity to move to the window. As absurd as it sounded, I wasn't sure I was ready to leave this Court. I had genuinely fallen in love with the culture, the sights, and the town of Everwatch. I couldn't contain the deep, heart-wrenching agony that filled me when I thought about how I would never be able to experience the Harvest Festival. I drew my eyes from the windows, if only to save my heart from the pain.

"Who's this?" I asked, approaching a portrait on the wall.

His footsteps paused behind me, and I heard his deep sigh fill the space. "My mother," he answered with a kind, somber remembrance. The dark-skinned, plump woman wore a black and white gown. Dozens of thick, black tresses twisted into ropes were piled into a loose coronet atop her head, and a few loose strands trailed over her shoulders. A silver circlet sat gingerly among the braids. The closer I looked at her, the more I saw the resemblance. Strong jawline, sharp features, and piercing green eyes. Despite her complexion being a few shades darker than Lysander's, there was no doubt that they were related.

"She's stunning," I whispered. My eyes studied the gorgeous woman in the portrait before me so intently that I barely noticed the soft steps approaching from behind.

"She was." His tone was a mixture of admiration and pain. I mourned for my family every night, the family I never knew, the family I so desperately needed, but that pain was abstract. In Lysander's every word, I felt a type of sorrow I had never before experienced. I nearly did, with Axel, but Gods be thanked, I was spared from the torment of losing him.

A torment that Lysander had not been so lucky to avoid.

"When did she pass?" My eyes remained trained on the woman in front of me, but I heard the sharp intake of breath from behind me, the same breath I often took to regain or maintain composure.

"A long time ago now." His tender voice wasn't more than a whisper. "But it burns as if it were yesterday." His faux confidence wavered, and I heard the slight crack in his voice. My heart begged me to turn around and embrace him, screaming at me to protect and help him. It was a strange sensation, as if my very soul lept to comfort him.

Despite that, I stayed put.

A million things ran through my mind, a million comforting phrases, things that you said when someone died, but they all felt too impersonal, too stale. Nothing was enough.

My eyes focused on the woman before me again, analyzing every detail while I avoided expressing surface-level sympathy. My heart skipped a beat the moment I recognized the dress she wore. The dress Lysander had gifted me to wear to the Welcome Ball. His mother's dress.

Tears welled in my eyes, and my breath caught in my throat. I opened my mouth to speak, but words evaded me. I turned quickly without thinking, tossing my arms around his neck and pulling him into me. He remained rigid under my touch briefly before slowly relaxing into my hold. The tears fell, trailing down my cheek and dropping onto his shoulder. For a moment, we just found comfort in this hold. I didn't see him as a murderer, and he didn't see me as a prize to win. We were just two people who had experienced pain and needed to feel the comfort of an embrace.

The reality of my actions hit me roughly, and I pulled away, avoiding his eyes. Turning back to the portrait, I wiped the tears from my face. He didn't say anything momentarily, his breathing ragged and forced. I stared at the dress in the painting.

"I'm sorry," I lamented. I wasn't sure exactly what I was apologizing for, but I knew I needed to say the words.

"I've come to terms with a life without her. As hard as it was." He was not close enough for me to feel his breath on my neck, but the rich timber of his voice still had my hair standing on end.

"Did she have to Pledge to you? Or was she automatically a legacy of your Court?" Countless accounts of the First Trial existed, including books, songs, and art about the fourteen commoners that competed for the title of Warden and the seven that won- although most of our histories exclude information about the mysterious eighth Court and its Warden. However, so little was known about the transition. What happened after they were crowned? What about all the people who were there before the Courts existed?

"Back when I was named Warden, every citizen of Verihdia resided in The Living Lands." It made sense, but it still shocked me. The Living Lands used to feel stifling to me. I could only imagine how it would feel if the entire world shared the small patch of land. "So when the Courts were created, and the Gods opened the gates, they allowed the citizens of The Living Lands to make their choice in a hasty and rushed event that came to be known as the very first Pledging Ceremony."

"It must have taken all day for every Uncourted person in all of Verihdia to make their Pledges."

He chuckled. "Luckily for all of us, that's not how the first one took place."

I fought the impulse to look at him.

"They simply told the citizens of The Living Lands that they should be standing at the gate of their chosen Court at sundown. When the sun disappeared beyond the horizon, the gate was opened, and my members got their Court Marks and crossed the veil into their new home."

I wondered why they changed the format of the ceremony. That seemed like such a simple and efficient way to make your Pledge.

"My mother was not only the first person in line to join my Court but she was also named the first Dean of Shadows." I could hear his smile. I couldn't help the tug that pulled at the corners of my mouth. "She helped oversee the inception, building, and running of the Verihdian Institute, along with the other Deans." He sounded so proud. It was impossible not to smile. "She was the hardest-working person I've ever known. She refused to do anything halfway. She was a tradesperson, a quality one at that. Her work was sought after, coveted." His voice sang as he recounted his mother's best qualities.

"What did she make?" I heard him inhale deeply as if searching for the right words.

"She was a blade spell." He answered matter-of-factly. What did their last name have to do with a profession? I narrowed my eyes, waiting for him to elaborate. He didn't.

"I don't understand," I offered truthfully.

I heard him run his hands through his hair and clear his throat.

"Her Mythica was blade-spelling. Imbuing weapons and armor with charms… and sometimes, although rarely, curses."

I racked my brain, trying to find another mention of a blade spell in my studies. There wasn't one. I didn't respond for a few long, quiet moments.

Then, under his breath, Lysander uttered a single word.

"Vahlach."

Abruptly, as if my feet had a mind of their own, I turned to look at him.

His green eyes were wispy, clouded with unshed tears. His arms were crossed across his chest as if he was holding himself together.

"What does that word mean?" I asked, my hand instinctively feeling the dagger against my thigh. The small word carved into the blade was the same word Lysander spoke now.

"It's a charm for protection. For safety." He spoke, averting his eyes. "It's an old word from a language long forgotten. It simply means…" he paused, his eyes trained on the ground. "Stay safe, my love."

My chest tightened as my heart rate quickened. My fingers clutched the hilt of Lysander's dagger through my skirt.

"My mother gave it to me before the First Trial. I have no false notions that I would have survived without it."

My body tensed at the thought of Lysander being killed at the Trial. Suddenly, the dagger at my side felt heavier.

"You shouldn't have given me this," I lamented quietly.

"Yes, I should have." He didn't meet my eyes. Instead, he glanced over my shoulder at the portrait of his mother, smiled briefly, and then returned to his packing. It didn't evade me that he hadn't looked directly at me for the entire conversation.

The powerful, selfish, manipulative, charming Warden of Shadows was not one to avoid eye contact. Not one to flit about the room awkwardly. Something was happening here. Some emotion, something keeping him from relaxing.

When the thought came to me, I asked it before I could stop myself.

"Are you afraid of me?" It was barely more than a whisper, but I know he heard because his anxious footsteps had ceased.

The quiet was potent, deafening.

"Is that what you think?" He asked calmly. His voice was also a mere whispered question.

Was it? On one hand, it made sense. He had seemed so taken aback when my Mythica worked on him. I was, too. I didn't know what I was thinking. I knew Mythica didn't work on Wardens. But the anger and the fear built up, and I couldn't stop myself. I never would have dreamed that it would work. And yet, it did.

If I was told my entire life that nobody could use their powers against me, only to find some ordinary girl who could…I think I'd be cautious too.

"Yes," I answered truthfully.

I heard a low sigh, almost imperceptible. Then, slowly, he stepped toward me. His eyes still didn't meet mine. Instead, they traveled along my frame like he was seeing me for the first time. He stopped a few feet before me, and I could feel his presence like a looming storm. His energy radiated around me, sending shockwaves of pleasure and pain in equal measure to my heart.

"The only thing I'm afraid of, little storm- " an involuntary moan escaped my mouth at the return of my nickname, "-is that I've lost you forever. I'm afraid I'll never get to hold you again or touch you… I'm afraid that you'll never trust me again. But above all, I'm afraid that you will disappear when these next six months are over, and I will never see you again."

His words bore into me with a type of heat I'd never experienced. For a moment, I would have gladly let the flames engulf me. I saw the internal battle he was fighting. He wanted to close the space between us almost as badly as I wanted him to. His eyes landed on my neck, the bruise that blossomed darkly there, peeking out from behind the high-neck dress. I recognized the guilt that flashed across his expression. His hand lifted slowly toward my throat. I didn't pull away, although I knew I should have. My body erupted in chills as his fingertips brushed the tender skin there.

"If you're not afraid, why won't you look at me?"

I heard a sigh rumble from deep within his chest. "Because when I look at you, I see my failure." His eyes finally met mine, and just like the first night at the Courting Ball, I felt entirely entranced by his gaze. "Your skin is covered in bruises that I couldn't prevent you from receiving." His eyes seemed to almost gleam with unshed tears. "I have not protected you the way I promised I would, and that guilt now outweighs anything else I've ever done," he spoke slowly, deliberately. His gaze and fingers traced the bruised flesh. I felt his guilt, and my Mythica itched to rush forward to latch onto it.

"You couldn't have known this would happen," I answered breathlessly.

He nodded, but the expression on his face remained steadfast. I let him continue his slow exploration of my throat and observed his emerald eyes. My chest heaved with heavy breaths. My body's reaction to him was a mixture of lust and fear. A terrible thought crossed my mind as I watched his eyes survey me. A chill ran from the base of my spine up to the back of my neck, sending the tiny hairs along my skin standing on end.

"Are you going to have me killed?" I whispered.

His hand fell from my throat, and I was simultaneously thankful and dismayed about the loss of his touch. His eyebrows furrowed, and anger flashed across his face, but somehow I did not feel threatened. He tried to speak, his words getting caught in his throat. I had rarely seen this flustered side of the Warden of Shadows. "Lexa…I.." He started. I put a hand up to stop him, and his mouth snapped shut as he observed me.

"If you respect me, you won't lie to me."

He nodded emphatically. "Lexa, the decision that was made concerning the Forgotten Warden's fate is…more nuanced than you believe. We made the best choice we could with the information we had." He spoke delicately, deliberately choosing each word.

My mind flashed back to the night before, Lysander and I sitting across from each other, my Mythica surging through his mind, ripping his darkest guilt from him. "I used my Mythica on you," I countered, ashamed.

"So did I," he responded calmly. "Lexa, what the Forgotten Warden did was not as simple as learning my secrets. It's what he did with them."

That caught my ear. My eyes trailed down to his hands, now anxiously tangled before him.

"Was his Mythica similar to mine?"

For a moment, Lysander looked as if he might avoid the question, but then his shoulders sagged, and his eyes trained on me.

"Not just similar, Lexa. Your Mythica is exactly like his."

I stopped breathing. By the time my brain could communicate with my lungs, I had already felt the effects of lightheadedness begin to creep in.

"But please, I can't say anymore."

"So, that's why you all want me?" I whispered.

He shook his head.

"We didn't know the extent of your Mythica. I'm the only Warden who understands it completely, having wielded it." He flashed an apologetic look in my direction. "We saw the similarities, and with your Final trial result, it was an easy conclusion to come to."

"Did you all think my Mythica would work on you?"

Again, he shook his head.

"Not at all. It should be impossible. It should have been impossible for him, and it should be for you." He ran his hands through his hair, pulling a few strands loose.

"Why did you do it?" I asked, unaware that I had started to cry until the salted liquid slipped across my lips.

"I wish I could tell you everything. Gods, I wish I could. But I can't." He seemed genuinely distraught by that. "If you have one ounce of trust left for me, can you trust that there is more to the story?"

Could I do that? Did I have any trust left for this man after stealing my Mythica and seeing what he'd done? I was ashamed to say I did. He had saved me twice and showed that he genuinely cared about my well-being.

"I can do that," I stated.

His shoulders visibly relaxed, his eyes softening at that.

"But, I cannot trust you."

His face fell.

I continued,"We have a long six months ahead. It will be better for both of us if we are cordial, but we need to keep things strictly professional between us. Our…uh, previous lapse in judgment can not be repeated."

He pursed his lips and nodded slowly. If I didn't know any better, I would have said he looked like I had offended him. But I knew well enough that I could never do such a thing.

"Lapse in judgment," he repeated quietly, as if he was appalled by the choice of words. As if qualifying our moment of passion as such was a personal slight against him.

"And we can't…" I started, but my words trailed off as his fingertips brushed my cheek, earning him a soft moan. My eyes fluttered closed at the sensation. Gods, I wanted nothing more than to lean into his touch, but that was precisely what I couldn't do. "You can't touch me, Lysander."

His fingers stilled before they fell from my face. His face searched mine for the lie, but he wouldn't find it.

I nodded, unable to find my voice.

He stood straighter, then. His muscles went rigid and stiff. The mask of Warden firmly fell into place. "I'm glad we agree, then. My skin won't touch yours again."

I suppressed a whimper, forcing myself to be satisfied with the ground rules I'd set. He took a step back.

"Good. See to it that it doesn't," I added with attempted ease despite the growing disappointment in the pit of my stomach.

"Well, not unless you ask for it, of course." He didn't smirk, and his eyes didn't light up as I expected. I scoffed at his presumptuous promise, waiting for him to tease me, to do what he could to get me to say those words. Instead, stone-faced, he turned to grab his belongings and made for the door. "The carriage leaves in ten minutes," he tossed over his shoulder before disappearing into the hall without so much as a glance back in my direction.

I watched after him for a long while, ignoring the gnawing guilt building in my chest.

I had done the right thing, placing a professional barrier between us. We had grown too close, and I became too dependent on his comfort. I couldn't swap one man for another when I needed support. I couldn't indulge with him physically while feeling this way emotionally. Anything physical between us was nothing more than a distraction, something to fill the void. Right?

With each step toward the carriage, I tried to convince myself that those words were true. And with each step, I believed them less and less.

Six

If I were a prideful man, I would have fought for her. Instead, I watched quietly as Lexa Cromwell carefully placed brick after brick on top of the growing wall between us. I didn't fight back when she denied gripping my purposefully gloved hand to climb into the carriage. I didn't fight back when Lexa poked her head through the window to get one last glance at Everwatch as we rode out of town. I didn't fight back when she shed a tear as the Forsaken Quarters disappeared behind us. I didn't fight back because I have long since learned the best way to covet is not to fight but to charm. Somebody else had power over me for the first time in a long time. Not in the sense that her Mythica worked on me, although that is something I desperately needed to wrap my head around, and soon. No, Lexa Cromwell's power over me had nothing to do with her Mythica.

I wouldn't fight back because she would learn in time, as I have, that she belongs in my Court - with me.

Something changed within me after the moment we shared in my quarters. With each burning kiss and each sensual thrust of my fingers, she became my obsession. She was mine.

I didn't fight back because there wasn't a doubt in my mind that she belonged to me, and I her. She would figure it out eventually. Until then, I would give her the space she pretended to need. I would prove to her that she could trust me. I was going to court Lexa Cromwell. But this time, it wasn't my Court that needed her. It was me.

She was quiet for the entire ride to the veil. Luckily, we started early enough in the day that we didn't need to stop until we got to The Court of Passion, so by the time the sun began to set, we had arrived at the gate of Shadows.

"Say goodbye to The Court of Shadows, Miss Cromwell," I implored softly. She wanted me to play the part of a professional guide. I would do it for now.

I willed my head to remain forward, but I couldn't resist. I turned slightly, just enough to see her shrouded face fall with sorrow. She had fallen in love with my Court exactly how I knew she would. I fought the urge to tell her not to worry because we both knew she would be back.

She has to.

The sky above was painted a bright pink with delicate stripes of orange, blanketing the area in a warm glow. Purple clouds hung low over the tree-covered hills. Sunsets in The Court of Shadows were something of beauty. It was a stunning masterpiece that used to capture me in awe but now paled compared to the woman admiring it. I memorized her expression. It was solemn like she genuinely believed this was the last time she would see these colorful trees or feel this cool autumn breeze against her perfect face.

It wouldn't be if I had anything to say about it. In a way, this feeling was familiar. Coveting. I was used to wanting things that were not mine to possess, but Lexa was not like any other thing I had ever coveted. I wanted her, not her Mythica, not her unique connection to The Forgotten Court, her, the dark-haired, blue-eyed goddess with a spiteful tongue and reckless convictions.

I couldn't explain it, but I knew, without a doubt, that no one would ever measure up to my little storm. And so the plan remained the same, although the intentions had shifted. Lexa Cromwell will Pledge to my Court, and I will convince her to do so. The countdown began now.

As we pushed through the veil, I braced for the secret it would pull from me. It had always been the same, the very secret the woman in the back of the carriage now knew as well. But as we crossed the shimmering Mythica, my mind was not clouded with my usual image. Instead, I saw her. Lexa. And the secret I was keeping from her. If I were to tell her the truth, she would believe and forgive me, but it was not within my capacity to reveal that truth to her. I deal in secrets freely given, and this was one secret that could not be given to her. No matter how desperately I wished it could.

The warm air and the pale blue sky were the bland reminders that we had left my Court behind. Six months. This tour would be the longest I'd ever been away from The Court of Shadows since I became Warden. I had prepared Lilith and Gregorio the best I could in the short time we had. I didn't expect any issues, but that wasn't going to stop me from worrying. I may have become less hands-on in the last few years, but I'd be lying if I didn't admit that Lexa's evident admiration of my Court made me fall in love with it all over again. All I had to do was look at it through her eyes.

I tossed a glance over my shoulder at Lexa. Her face contorted with a profoundly wrinkled brow. Whatever secret the veil had ripped from her had left her uncomfortable.

"How are you feeling?" I asked. Her head snapped toward me, and she nodded, carefully disguising the emotion I had witnessed on her face.

"I'm fine," she claimed, a little too eagerly. I knew I shouldn't push. I should remain the 'professional' guide she requested, but I couldn't refrain.

"Each of the veils requires something for entry," I started. "Some are easier to give than others," I spoke from experience. It had been decades since I'd been to some of my sibling's Courts, but I distinctly remembered their veils and the demands they asked.

"I can't say I'll miss that part of your Court," she joked. I chuckled lowly. I didn't necessarily disagree.

"But you will miss everything else?" I turned my head until my eyes were able to lock with hers. She briefly smiled before her face fell again.

"I will." She confessed.

It was enough for now.

We rode silently along the outer edge of The Living Lands with the shimmering veil on one side and the only world Lexa had ever known on the other. We would need to stop soon, but I had hoped to make it through the veil of The Court of Passion before nightfall. There was a small inn just on the other side that I had stayed at the last time I visited Korzich's Court, which was pleasant enough. The paraphernalia and atmosphere of The Court of Passion would undoubtedly be a welcome reminder of the way Lexa's body reacted so beautifully to me in her moment of unbridled pleasure.

We'd be there in an hour if everything went according to plan. And I had to admit I was excited to pass through the veil. There were many things about my sibling's Court that I found crude and inappropriate, but I was more than eager to give what this veil required, especially with my little storm in the backseat.

Seven

It had been a long and quiet ride thus far, and we'd barely exchanged three sentences. I couldn't help but feel a slight sting at the lack of spiteful banter, but wasn't this precisely what I had asked of him?

I wasn't allowed to regret it since it was my idea.

And yet.

We had been riding non-stop since early this morning, and I felt the sting of exhaustion threaten to take me, but a dark fear took hold of my mind and refused to let go.

Now that I was back in The Living Lands, would my nightmares return? They had only stopped once we crossed the veil into The Court of Shadows. A part of me knew that the nature of my nightmares had shifted, and I wasn't sure what that meant for me anymore.

So even though my eyelids grew heavy and my head began to sway, I refused to let sleep take me. Not here.

We traveled along the border of The Living Lands. Sitting between The Court of Shadows and The Court of Passion was the dark-red, shimmering veil of The Court of Echoes. Vicious energy radiated from it as we rode past, and I felt my anger toward Lysander, at all he did and kept from me, bubble up to a near-explosive degree. I could only imagine what fury I would be subjected to once I crossed through. I was thankful that we were not crossing the ominous border to that Court yet, although a slight panic gripped my heart, knowing that we would soon enough.

I visibly relaxed once we passed the red veil and ventured near The Court of Passion's territory.

We arrived at a large stable, and moments later, Lysander pulled our carriage into an open stall and hopped off the driver's box. When he opened the door and offered his gloved hand, I took it, telling myself that it didn't count as touching because of the thin leather gloves he had adorned.

While my mind was still far from offering clemency, my body had already forgiven him—traitorous thing.

"What are we doing?" I asked groggily.

"Our horse is unsuitable for The Court of Passion's terrain." He moved to the back of our carriage to grab our bags. My eyes landed on those gloves that hid his smooth hands and deft fingers. He has been wearing them since he promised his skin would not touch mine. My chest ached at the memory of my demand. "Neither is the carriage." He held the several bags easily in his arms. I couldn't help but be impressed at his sheer strength. My mind flashed back to the moment he held me up with ease, my legs wrapped around his waist, my bare core pressed against him…

Stop that.

I silently cursed The Court of Passion and their stupid veil for sending these improper thoughts to my head.

"So, we walk from here?" I asked, worried I would fall to my knees if I were expected to stay awake any longer.

"No, we just need a new ride." He gently brought his forehead to rest on our horse's long snout, whispered thanks to the old girl, and then led me out of the stall.

"Let me carry my bags," I demanded.

"No," he replied casually.

"Warden, I am perfectly capable of carrying my own bags," I insisted, trailing after him. He was quick and four of my tiny strides equaled one of his.

"I'm well aware of what you're capable of, Miss Cromwell." He continued, ignoring my request.

"Give me my bags," I beseeched, reaching for them in his hands. He pulled them just out of reach. "Lysander, give me my bags right now!" I called loudly, a force behind my voice that I had not often used with anyone.

He stopped, and a deep sigh traveled through his chest. He didn't turn to face me, but my bags dropped to the ground beside him before he continued.

I nodded to myself, proud that I could exert some semblance of dominance over him, as I gripped my bags and followed him.

We continued through the stable until we reached a holding area of some kind. From here, I could see the veil clear as day. It shimmered darkly, like the stars in the night sky. A thick, sensual air radiated from it as if beckoning me near, begging me to touch.

"Warden!" I heard a shrill voice call, drawing my eyes away from the veil. The woman was tall and beautiful, and her bright white hair was curled and styled in a bun atop her head. Her slender body was draped in a dark black dress that flowed effortlessly down her tan skin, hugging her thin frame. She ran over, her plump breasts bouncing in their fabric cage, and wrapped her arms around the Warden of Shadows' neck.

Envy.

It hit me harder than I had expected. The dark tendril of jealousy took hold of my heart as I watched this stunning woman embrace the man who had drawn every last bit of passion from my body just last night. The fingers he now used to curl around her neck and pull her into his body were the same fingers that had me crying out in ecstasy.

I think I hated her.

I couldn't stop myself from what I did next, even if I wanted to. My left foot lifted and slid down the calf of my right leg, taking the sandal straps with it. The straps pooled loosely around my ankle.

"Damnit," I emphasized. Lysander quickly turned, his hands falling from the woman's frame. I made a show of attempting to hold my bags while reaching for the straps on my sandals. An actress, I was not, but it must have been convincing enough because, in a flash, Lysander was in front of me, his emerald eyes shining.

"Allow me, Miss Cromwell." He sank to his knees at a torturous pace; his eyes remained glued to mine, but his gloved hands found my ankle. Heat pooled in my core at his covered touch, burning, even through his gloves' thick leather. His fingers made quick work of the straps, bringing them to their rightful place below my knee and tightening them. Once my straps were secured, his covered fingers trailed up just enough for the soft leather at his fingertips to graze the tip of the dagger cinched to my thigh. A fire lit in his eyes, and the corner of his mouth pulled up in a sinful smirk, one that simultaneously made me want to smack him and devour his lips with mine.

He was standing upright far too soon for my liking. Without drawing his eyes from mine, he spoke again.

"Elisa, we will need a new transport, please." The beauty behind him smiled. If she was upset at my interruption, she didn't let it show. There was a sort of heat in her eyes that told me she might have enjoyed our little show.

"One or two?" She asked, a wicked twinkle in her dark eyes.

"One," Lysander replied before I could even interject.

Ten minutes later, our bags were safely secured to each side of a massive camel, and Lysander was climbing onto its back.

The creature stood incredibly tall, yet the Warden moved to sit atop it with such grace and elegance, I nearly scoffed.

"I cannot get up there," I exclaimed to whoever would listen.

"Take my hand," he offered from his perch. He stretched his gloved hand toward me, and I simply glanced at it, dumbfounded.

"You will not be able to lift me up there." I was not insulting my size; I had learned long ago to love my curves, but I was a realist, and there was no chance that this Warden, no matter how strong he may be, could lift me onto a seven-foot-tall camel with one arm. I scoffed.

Lysander rolled his eyes and reached for my hand. Electric energy surged through me at his touch, even with the leather barrier. He pulled, and with his assistance - who was I kidding, he didn't assist, he did it all himself - I was seated in front of him on the massive animal within moments. His open legs straddled me, pressing into the outside of my thighs.

I felt his breath on my ear as he leaned forward. "When are you going to realize that I am perfectly capable of possessing every inch of you, Miss Cromwell?" He whispered. My eyes fluttered closed as I inhaled long and deep. I captured my bottom lip in my teeth, begging the moan that threatened to escape my lips to remain hidden.

This damn veil's influence was making it near impossible to maintain the same level of professionalism I demanded from him.

"You promised not to touch me again," I whispered. He chuckled behind me. The vibrations of his laugh on my back nearly had me leaning into him.

"I'm wearing gloves." He smirked. A fact that I was acutely and unfortunately aware of. "It doesn't count."

I rolled my eyes as the blonde beauty approached from the front of the camel, offering a welcome distraction from the budding need at my center. She smiled up at us from her place below us.

"Warden, you are all set. Your horse and carriage will be well cared for until your return." Her words were so mundane, yet the way she said it as if each word was a proposition, a promise, had my skin heating where Lysander pressed against me.

"Thank you, Elisa. We shall return in a month." Lysander offered the animal a slight kick of encouragement with his heels, and the creature jolted forward. His arms caged me in, holding the reins on either side of my body. Heat expanded over every inch of my skin, lighting me on fire. But this burn did not bring pain. Instead, it brought pure, unbridled desire. His breath on my neck had me pressing my thighs together as much as I could.

"Are you ready to pay the toll?" He asked into my ear as we approached the shimmering wall.

"Not at all," I answered as we passed through.

My eyes closed tightly against the strange sensation. Every nerve ending in my body tingled as we pushed through the Mythica border. Arriving on the other side, I sighed, thankful that whatever the veil took from me in payment had been taken silently.

Lysander's hand landed on my thigh, but I couldn't push it off. I didn't want to. Instead, a dark moan escaped my lips.

"If you make that sound again, little storm, I cannot be held responsible for the things I do to you." He spoke against my neck, his lips grazing the skin selfishly. I should have put an end to it there. I should have locked my lips and thrown away the metaphorical key. But instead, I tilted my head, giving him more access to my bare neck, and when my moan came, I did not stifle it.

Slowly, he removed his dark gloves, finger by finger, a torturous display. He growled against my skin, and suddenly, his hands were ripping at my skirts, dragging them up my thighs until his skin met mine. My head fell back against his shoulder.

"Let's be reckless, little storm," he commanded before his lips crashed to mine, and his fingers found my center. He moaned against my mouth at the wetness he found there. Ready and waiting for him. Always. He slid two fingers directly into my heat, drawing a cry from my lips but swallowing it with his mouth. His thumb raked over the bundle of nerves at my apex, applying the perfect amount of pressure to send me into a frenzy. Forgetting the reins, his other hand traveled up my stomach to palm my breasts, and I arched into his touch. His fingertips pinched at the swollen bud beneath the fabric of my dress, and suddenly, I hated the skirt and wanted it gone. His teeth found my earlobe, and he bit down at the exact moment that his fingers thrust up into my center. His fingertips pinched the eager peak of my breast, and I exploded into a cloud of ecstasy.

"Turn to face me, little storm." He spoke against my neck. His voice was unrestrained, feral. "I'm not done with you."

I didn't stop to think about the implications of what we were doing. I couldn't. I was lost to the passion, the desire– how he made me feel. With his arm guiding me, I turned until I faced him. My legs draped carefully over his, and my skirt bunched up around my waist, baring my core for him. His eyes filled with a dark and foreboding lust as he took me in.

"I need you, Lexa Cromwell." My hands instinctively found the waistband of his pants and started slowly loosening the ties there—the evidence of his desire strained against the fabric.

I began to pull the band open, nearly able to touch and capture him the way I so desperately wanted to.

Then my eyes opened.

I was facing forward, my back to Lysander's chest; the veil to The Court of Passion was just behind us as we finished passing through. My skirt was still in place, draped over my legs, and completely covering my center. The center that now eagerly throbbed.

The veil hadn't taken something from me. It showed me what I desired.

I felt a deep blush of shame crawl onto my face. My entire body felt like it was on fire, and I couldn't seem to catch my breath from the veil's fantasy. Lysander didn't speak, but his shallow breathing and the hard length now pressed against my back told me he, too, had experienced a fictitious, passionate moment. I wondered briefly if I was the star of his fantasy the way he starred in mine.

Neither of us spoke, but his heated breath and his hands tightening on the reins acted as a reminder of what we had shared once and might never share again.

What a shame that would be.

No. I couldn't think of that. Not only did I not trust him anymore, but we had promised to keep things cordial and professional. We couldn't do that very well if I kept fantasizing about wrapping my hands around his…. Stop.

As my breathing slowed and my heart rate returned to normal, I could finally take in the sight. Spanning out before us for as far as the eye could see was a dark black and silver sand desert. It glistened like the night sky. Out on the horizon, I could not tell where the ground ended, and the starry canvas began. It was dark, but a grey moon hung bright in the sky, painting the world in a noir palate. The heat was vicious and stifling. Humidity gripped my skin as if it were a physical thing. I couldn't tell if I felt suffocated by the warm, moist air around me or by the strong, tempting Warden behind me.

Our camel traveled across the uneven sand quickly for a few quiet minutes. A small town sprung up ahead of us. It was relatively tiny, consisting of only four buildings, but the exhaustion weighed on me at the promise of sleep.

"We're staying there tonight. You'll be able to sleep soon, Miss Cromwell." His voice was dark with an unreadable emotion.

I smiled wearily at the thought of my head falling against a pillow and drifting off into the night, but the looming threat of my nightmares soon snuffed out the pleasantry. I still wasn't sure if they would return, and if they did, would they be as harmless as they were back at the Institute, or would they continue to be a more physical torment?

I allowed myself a moment of uncertain fear as we arrived in front of the small inn. Its entire facade screamed 'lust.' From the dark black curtains drawn over each window to the sensual red lighting pouring from the lobby to the echoes of passionate moans bouncing through the air. I blushed, avoiding eye contact with Lysander as we dismounted the camel.

He grabbed our bags from our ride, and this time, I did not complain that he held mine, too. I wasn't sure I had the strength to carry anything.

Lysander led me inside, and I followed him in, my eyes widening at the occupied couches that took up the lobby. Naked bodies writhed beneath each other, and moans filled my ears. I averted my eyes instantly, swallowing the lump that was forming in my throat.

Lysander hadn't glanced toward the couches but instead greeted the half-naked man behind the counter.

"Good evening," the man whispered in an alluring tone, his dark eyes scanning our bodies appreciatively.

"Good evening, we need some rooms," Lysander spoke, his voice strained, and I tried not to notice that he, too, was wearing a deep crimson blush.

"Rooms?" The man asked, an eyebrow shooting up.

"Yes, two, please. We're not here to indulge in…" he paused, "the activities."

The man behind the counter nodded. "Suit yourself." He smiled and turned to grab the keys off the hooked wall behind him.

"Wait," I blurted out before I could stop myself. Lysander and the man both turned to watch me. The symphony of sex behind me had me feeling entirely exposed. "We only need one room, please."

The man smiled wickedly, knowingly, and Lysander's eyes narrowed at me in question. As the man reached for the key, I whispered to the Warden, "Last time I was alone at an inn, I was attacked." I explained as if that was the only reason I had requested a single room.

It was. Obviously.

He offered a tight nod and reached for the key from the man's outstretched hand.

"Enjoy your stay," he cooed the innuendo. As Lysander and I moved past the lobby, I heard the man from the counter walk to the group of naked bodies and ask where they wanted him.

I'd never felt more embarrassed – and entirely electrified.

Lysander and I disappeared into our room, and once the door was closed, the sounds of ecstasy ceased. I studied the wooden door. Black velvet padded the inside of the room entirely, from the walls to the floor beneath our feet. It served as an insulator, keeping the sounds of other activities from entering our space.

And keeping other sounds in.

I shook my head and turned to face the Warden behind me.

The dark room was lit only by a single lamp that gave off a sensual red glow. The large four-poster bed sat directly in the center of the room, and along the velvet-lined walls, there were various…accessories.

"Oh my," I muttered. Lysander let out a chuckle.

"Welcome to The Court of Passion," he offered in explanation before tossing our bags onto a dresser. "We should get some sleep, and if we leave early enough, we can reach the – the Pleas– we can reach the tower by dinner time."

I stifled a laugh at his reluctance to speak the name of his sibling's home. Although a wicked part of me was disappointed that I didn't get to hear that word roll off his tongue.

He disappeared into the restroom, and I took a moment to explore the room. My skin was heated, the memory of the bodies in the lobby replaying in my mind. Mouths and hands traveling over every inch of exposed skin–I would need to get comfortable with this sort of display, or it would be a very awkward month.

My hands grazed along the plush wall, stopping to trace the items hung there. I'd never seen anything like this. I couldn't even imagine what some of these things were intended for, but the thoughts that crossed my mind had me pressing my inner thighs together.

"What are you thinking about?" Lysander's voice was low, grave. I hadn't heard him return from the restroom. I turned to find him shirtless, a pair of soft pants hanging low on his hips. In the red light, his dark skin looked even more smooth and delicious. I captured my bottom lip in between my teeth.

"Sleep," I lied.

He nodded, his eyes scanning me from head to toe before he moved to the bed at the center of the room. He slowly pushed the silk sheets and slid into the bed's warmth. His eyes remained trained on me.

Perhaps it was the atmosphere or the lingering effects of the veil's fantasy, but I moved to the dresser, brazenly reaching into Lysander's bag to find another oversized shirt, this time a dark black cotton billowing shirt, with crisscrossed ties at the neck. I turned back to find his green eyes still on me, watching my every move.

My hands slowly reached for the clasp at my neck, and once it was undone, the grey chiffon dress fell down my body, pooling on the ground. I had no idea why I was doing this. I wanted to blame it entirely on the veil, and maybe part of it was that, but the veil only amplified what I already wanted. The logical side of my mind that told me to be afraid of this man was securely locked away for the night.

Lysander let out a deep possessive growl as he took in my naked form, but he didn't move, didn't say a word.

I slipped the black shirt over my head, and it fell just above my knees. The ties at the front were loose, and the opening offered a sensual glimpse of my cleavage. I swear I saw Lysander lick his lips, but I couldn't be sure in the darkness. I climbed into the bed, tearing my eyes from his and curling up so that my back was to him, but I still felt his eyes on me.

The bed groaned under him as he adjusted his position, and I heard him release an agonized sigh.

I knew I shouldn't say anything to him. He still hadn't explained what I saw when my Mythica tore into his mind, and we had agreed to keep things professional. I couldn't cross this line with him.

So why was I tempting him?

"Something wrong?" I asked, doing my best to feign innocence. I heard his muffled groan as if he had hidden his face in his palms.

"You know damn well what's wrong, Miss Cromwell," he frustratingly exclaimed. I smiled, amused that he was as affected as I was by the influence of this Court.

"I don't think I do…" I pushed. Why did I do that? What was I saying? And why couldn't I stop myself from saying it?

"You're making it very hard for me to keep my promise to you." He warned, and the collected facade of Warden was slowly breaking with every second we spent in this bed.

"What promise?" I teased. He sighed.

"I said I wouldn't touch you again until you asked me to."

I nodded, appreciative that he had made that vow to me while I simultaneously hated the thought of his hands never claiming me again. "Yes, you did," I answered, breathlessly. I turned over until I was on my side, facing him. He was lying on his back, the crook of his elbow draped over his eyes and his other hand somewhere underneath the dark sheet. My eyes trailed his chiseled chest.

What am I doing?

I sighed in embarrassment and frustration and moved so that I, too, was lying on my back, looking up at the dark, velvet-covered ceiling.

I felt like I was on fire, like every inch of me was begging for satisfaction, for release. I silently prayed that this had everything to do with this Court's influence and that it wasn't me that had become so feral for this man.

My fingers dug into my thighs, trying to distract me from the budding pain in my core. My eyes drifted closed, and my fingers trailed higher, closer to my center. Moving slowly, I let my hands trail featherlight touches along my inner thighs. My mouth fell open, and my neck arched. All I needed was a little bit of release.

I opened my eyes to find he had turned to look at me. His emerald eyes were full of heat, and he observed my face.

"I promised I wouldn't touch you… but you and I both know that I don't need to touch you to make you explode, little storm." My body tingled at the sound of my nickname on his lips.

Heat pooled in my core, and I felt my muscles tighten in anticipation. "Prove it."

His lips curled into a wicked smirk. "Touch yourself for me."

My eyes widened at his tone, his gaze full of dominating heat. I shook my head despite the way my fingers began to follow his command. "Do it now, little storm." His voice was low, guttural, filled with lust and reckless abandon. I dragged my fingers closer and closer until my index finger brushed against my wet folds. I had to bite my lip to keep from crying out.

I couldn't believe I was doing this with Lysander right next to me. I held his gaze and ran my finger through my slit again, ignoring the urge to stifle my moan.

In a flash, Lysander drew back the sheets, exposing me and the intimate action I was performing, but I didn't pull my hand away. The lust was more potent than my embarrassment. His eyes found my center, and watched as my finger slid up and down along my opening.

"Push a finger in, Miss Cromwell. Slowly. Let me see you." My core throbbed at his words as I followed his command. A long, drawn-out moan rumbled through his chest as I slid a finger into myself. His eyes darkened, and I could see the evidence of his arousal straining against the fabric of his pants.

"Show me," I commanded. The words slipped from my lips in a cry. I desperately needed it, and I wasn't sure I would survive without it.

He climbed to his knees, moving until he was perched at the end of the bed, his shadow looming over me as he watched my hands tease my core. He gripped the band of his pants and pushed them down until his erection sprung free. My mouth watered at the sight of him, and I felt the room begin to spin.

"Show me how you like to be touched," he whispered, his hand closing around his length and pumping in time with my fingers. I nearly exploded at his words, but I wasn't ready for this to be done, for us to return to how we were. Not yet.

I pressed another finger into my heat and drew out a strangled cry from my lips. I brought my other hand down to circle the bundle at my apex.

"Just like that, Lexa," he praised. His breath came in ragged spurts as he stroked himself, his eyes locked on the show my hands were putting on. "Tell me you wish it were my hands touching you." It was less of a command and more of a pleading. My heart constricted as the pleasure began to build in my stomach. "Tell me you wish that I was the one claiming you, making you feel this way," he begged, his hand continuing its rough trail along his length.

Did I want him to be the one touching me now? Of course, I did. Could I let him? Not yet.

I moaned, arching my back as my hands dragged the passion from me.

"Tell me you want it to be my fingers pushing you towards the edge, that you want it to be my tongue tasting you and making you mine. Tell me now, Lexa," he demanded, his own pleasure ramping up to a climax as mine did the same.

I sped up my movements as I reached a boiling point, "Gods, yes. Yes!" I cried at the height of my passion. My entire body was trembling as I readied to fall over the edge.

"All you have to do is ask," he exclaimed, tumbling into his release as mine fell over me in a thunderous explosion. My vision blurred, and I arched into the bed, pressing my fingers into my center as I rode out the last bit of my orgasm.

In the moment's bliss, I didn't have it in me to feel the weight of what we had just done. Instead, I smiled, pulled the shirt I borrowed from Lysander to cover myself, and turned until I was lying comfortably on the silk sheets.

The smile remained plastered on my face when I felt Lysander get up and move to the restroom. The smile was there when I felt his weight return to the bed. And it was still there when I heard him whisper, "I told you, I could do it," before exhaustion finally won, and I drifted off to sleep.

Eight

Is this what contentment feels like? Lexa Cromwell had managed to turn my world upside down without laying a single finger on me. Her words, 'Show me,' echoed in my mind as I drifted off to sleep, and they were the first thing that ran through my head as I awoke. The sight of her delicate fingers at her center was one I would relish for the entirety of my long life. She had been so eager, so sensitive. After our distant conversation before departing from my Court, I hadn't anticipated this turn of events. However, as we crossed the veil, it became apparent that things were about to take an intriguing turn. I braced myself for uncomfortable silences and diverted gazes. I anticipated her retreating to her own room, seeking refuge from the lively - and naked - commotion in the lobby and, perhaps, from my presence.

I don't know what the veil showed her as we crossed, but if it were anything like mine, I understood the impulse to chase the phantom physical pleasure the veil promised. The sight of Lexa bent forward on the camel, her skirt pooled around her waist, utterly bare to me, flashed across my eyes. I had tasted her, and although I knew it was nothing but a fantasy drawn from the deepest recesses of my desires by the Mythica-shrouded border, it was the most delectable thing I've ever had on my tongue.

She hadn't let me touch her last night, but this was enough for now. Something she would soon realize about me was that I was willing to wait as long as she needed me to. I had an endless lifetime, and I would sacrifice every second of it if it meant she would be mine.

She stirred gently, and I turned to admire her. Her pitch-black hair was splayed across the silken pillow like an intricate design, a prelude to the work of art. Her face was smooth and pale. I'd never seen someone's skin so untouched by the sun's influences before. It offered her a near-glowing aura, and I resisted the urge to reach out and caress her cheek to see my dark skin contrasted against hers.

I rose carefully from the bed so as not to disturb her. We needed to begin our final leg of the journey soon, but she could sleep for a few more minutes. She was in for a shock when we arrived at Korzich's Tower, and she needed to be well-rested. I made quick work of bathing, dressing, and packing my things. When I sat my bags by the door, I heard a soft groan from the bed at the center of the room.

The silk sheets had slipped off her legs, exposing them, and as she stretched, her shirt - or, I guess, my shirt - rode up, nearly giving me another look at the main attraction from last night. I turned my head. If I looked at her now, we'd never leave this room on time.

"Good morning, Miss Cromwell." I slipped up last night. I had intended to withhold my little nickname for her until she realized her 'professionalism' plan was pointless between us. Gods, the sound she made when the nickname tumbled from my lips in a moment of passion, I could survive on it.

"Good morning, Warden," she bit back. Her hoarse and tired voice was doing something impure to my mind and prompting me to take deep breaths to center myself.

"We should leave soon. Do you need any assistance?" I heard the bed whine under her movement. Her feet padded across the floor towards the bathroom, and I turned to face her. She had stopped at the entrance, her shoulders rising and falling quickly with panicked breaths. I was at her side in an instant.

"I can help you," I whispered to her, actively attempting to hold my arms at my side.

"No, I can do it." She spoke with faux confidence. If I hadn't come to understand her intimately, I might have believed it. I repressed a sigh. "But will you…be in there with me?"

I nodded my agreement, my heart fluttering.

She crossed the threshold into the washroom, and I followed closely behind, planting myself near the vanity counter. I slid onto the surface, letting my feet dangle below me. I watched her in awe as she bravely approached the basin and turned the spout, filling it with a warm liquid.

She stood above the filling tub, watching the swirling water stake its claim inside the vessel. When the rising level reached the top, her hand slowly turned the spout, and the trickling water slowed to a stop. She didn't move to enter it. Instead, she studied it for a minute, maybe more.

Then she turned to me.

"Turn around." She demanded with the same zeal I remember from the Courting Ball.

"It's nothing I haven't seen already," I teased. She scowled deeply, her forehead creasing, but I saw the deep blush heat her skin.

"You're just as charming in other Courts as you are in your own." Her sarcasm rang through her words. My lips pulled into a grin.

"And you're just as stubborn. No one could ever claim that we're not consistent." I beamed proudly at her.

She scoffed, placing her hands on her hips. "Turn around." She commanded again.

"How will I be able to help you if I can't see if you're in trouble?" I feigned innocence, and I could practically feel the indignation radiating from her.

"How will you survive as Warden if sight is the only sense you bother to utilize?" She tossed back, tilting her head and pouting her lips.

I lifted an eyebrow, giddy joy blooming in my chest as our quick-witted banter continued. I didn't realize how much I had missed our dynamic and how fond I was of her venom-laced tongue. I never wanted to lose it again.

"Turn around," she replied again, spitting each word. Tossing my hands up in surrender, I smiled before following her command. Lifting my feet until they were on the surface, I spun my body so that my back was to her. Satisfied, she turned back to the water basin. I knew that because I watched her in the small mirror before me. Her shoulders relaxed, and she reached for the hem of my shirt.

I could have watched and kept my eyes trained on her the way I desperately desired to, but I had betrayed her trust enough for a lifetime.

Damn.

"Wait, stop," I bellowed, exasperated, a sigh falling from my mouth. I may have decided to be a good person, but I didn't have to be happy about it. She turned back to me with fear and panic in her eyes, and I quickly realized my mistake.

"You're ok. It's ok. I'm sorry, I didn't mean to scare you," I rushed. She relaxed at that. "I just, there's a mirror here. I can still see." I pointed, and her eyes darted over my shoulder to the mirror and met my emerald eyes in the reflection. A dark pink blush crept onto her porcelain skin.

"Then close your damn eyes," she spat, and I laughed. She offered me a crude gesture, and I laughed even harder. "You want me to trust you, right?" She spoke it like a threat, a promise. My laughs subsided.

"Of course I do," I vowed. I watched her in the mirror's reflection as she pursed her lips.

"Then close your eyes." She shook her head a few times before returning her gaze to mine. "Show me that I can place my faith in you."

Show me.

The words she uttered last night immediately affected me, stirring desire within, yet I sensed a need to demonstrate something crucial. If I couldn't be entirely honest with her, the least I could do was prove that I was worthy of the trust she seemed reluctant to bestow upon me.

I closed my eyes.

They remained closed as I heard the rustling of fabric and when the shirt hit the ground. They remained closed as she sank into the water, tentatively. They remained closed because I refused to break my promise to her.

Never again.

I listened closely, prepared to rush to her rescue should she need it.

There was silence, and panic seized me. "You're going to need to make noise, Miss Cromwell. How will I know if you need my protection if you're silent?"

She sighed. "What noise would you prefer I make?"

My mind flashed my favorite sound in the world, her soft, pleasure-filled moans. If that were the last sound I ever heard, I'd die a happy man. The water splashed, and something light smacked me in the back of my head.

"Don't you dare say what I know you're thinking," she warned, though her tone was laced with humor.

I laughed, keeping my eyes shut. Her melodic laugh filled my ears, and my skin trembled. "What did you throw at me?" I asked, between my laughter.

"A sponge," she replied, deadpanned as if that was an entirely normal thing to throw at someone else. We both erupted into a fit of laughter again.

As the sounds died down again, I heard the soft trickle of water as she moved within it.

"Whatever sound you choose, Miss Cromwell."

She didn't respond, but I heard soft hums of relaxation a few moments later, and immediately, my worry was soothed. A few torturous minutes passed, utterly aware that Lexa Cromwell, the stunningly frustrating woman, was utterly exposed behind me when I heard the disruption of the water again. My shoulders straightened, and fear prickled against my skin. My ears focused on the movement. Did she need me? Was she finished? Where are her Gods-damned hums? I very nearly opened my eyes, turning to fend off whatever thought it could steal her from the water, but then I felt her presence behind me.

"Thank you, Lysander," she whispered, her voice laced with appreciation and honesty. I opened my eyes to meet hers in the mirror. Her ocean-blue irises held mine captive. I couldn't look away if I wanted to.

"I'll be ready soon," she finished before exiting the washroom.

I sighed, letting my head fall into my hands.

I've never wanted anything as much as I want her.

Ignoring that inconvenient and frustrating truth, I rushed out of the room, avoiding Lexa's gaze, and down to the front desk. The naked bodies were still present, but instead of being joined in various displays of pleasure, they were slung haphazardly across the couches in various states of rest. They looked peaceful, entirely comfortable to be on display in such a vulnerable position. I admired that. And thought they were completely idiotic.

I returned my key to the half-asleep man behind the counter, who merely grunted his recognition before moving to the stables.

The sun was vicious, entirely too hot for my liking, the air was humid, and I felt like I was walking through condensed water with each step I took. It was still early, so I could only imagine how awful it would become midday. No wonder everyone enjoyed wearing so little clothes here. I wore a thin shirt and breeches and felt like I might sweat through it all. I bribed the stable attendant to supply me with an umbrella for the trip. I had no doubt my skin would take the sun's harshness in stride, but the thought of Lexa's blemish-free skin being tainted by the red sting of this sun was enough to draw a growl from my chest.

Several minutes later, our camel was secured, my bags were attached, and Lexa exited the inn. Some of her black hair was pulled back in a braided crown while the rest tumbled elegantly down her back in soft waves. She wore a dark green dress that I had bought her before we left The Court of Shadows. It was a sleeveless keyhole-shoulder dress with an upwards-scooping corset that hugged her frame, the thin skirt draped delicately down to the ground. My eyes landed on her sandals, and I smiled as I remembered her display of jealousy yesterday.

"You look lovely in green, Miss Cromwell. Good choice." She did not respond but moved past me to secure her bags for our ride. She moved to the front of the large animal and gave it a tender pat. The creature seemed to appreciate it and leaned into her hold. The familiar envy stirred within me as I watched her provide this creature with affection. The affection that I wanted.

I shook my head and took a deep breath.

Was I just jealous of a damn camel?

I slid on my gloves, a barrier between my skin and hers, and helped her mount our ride. It was not lost on me that she shimmied as far forward as she could get on the saddle to get away from me. I smiled and moved back, giving her the room she thought she needed from me.

The first few hours were quiet. Whether she was lost in thought or still half asleep, I couldn't tell. The dark black sand glimmered with a luminous sheen beneath the pink sunrise, and the heat had begun to ramp up again. Small scaled creatures that called this barren wasteland home skittered across the sand before us, leaving trails in the dunes. Sweat was plastering stray hair that escaped the tie at the back of my head to my skin. As we continued our journey across the vast expanse of desert, we found ourselves in comfortable silence.

Hours into our journey, we passed by the most enchanting - in my opinion - part of my sibling's Court—the Dreamer's Gift Oasis. As Lexa's eyes latched onto the stunning display of nature's gifts, I led our steed toward the edge of the oasis. The transition from the black sand to the vibrant oasis felt like stepping into another world. The landscape unfolded before me, revealing a breathtaking scene of running water and lush foliage that were in stark contrast to the harsh desert surroundings. A subtle fragrance of blooming flowers drifted through the air, carried by a gentle breeze that rustled the leaves overhead. The oasis was a refuge of serenity amidst the arid expanse, offering a desperately needed respite from the relentless sun beating down on the desert. Even with the umbrella, the heat was stifling, so the temporary cover of the canopy of palms was a relief.

The camel's slow, rhythmic steps added to the soothing atmosphere, allowing me to absorb the beauty surrounding me. The oasis painted a vivid picture of life amid the barren sands. I couldn't help but marvel at the oasis's ability to make the black desert sand disappear, giving way to this unexpected haven of tranquility.

The beauty of the surroundings paled compared to how Lexa's eyes illuminated with joy upon taking in her environment. Excitement adorned her face, and she beamed radiantly as her eyes swept across the natural paradise surrounding us.

I would stop and let her explore in an instant if there was anywhere else to sleep nearby, but if I wanted to get her safely to my sibling's tower by nightfall, we had to keep going. The best I could do was ride through.

"You're awfully quiet," she pondered, her voice hoarse from hours of inactivity.

Clearing my throat, I replied. "Should I hum?" I didn't need to see her face to know that her eyes rolled in her head. "Is there something you'd like to discuss, Miss Cromwell?" I watched her shoulders tighten at the formality.

"No," she replied after a long while. I adjusted the reins and wrapped them around my gloved fingers. She inhaled a quick breath, preparing to speak again, but released it in a sigh twice. "Are you…" she started. Her body tensed. The space between us felt like a wide cavern of uncertainty. "Are you going to have me killed?" She finished in a tone so quiet I had to strain to hear. My heart skipped a beat, blood drained from my face.

"What would make you think that?" The words tumbled out at an uncontrollable pace, nearly incoherent. The thought of anyone hurting her sent an unfamiliar and unrelenting spike of anger through my chest.

"That's what happened to him, right? The Warden of Forgotten?" She toyed mindlessly with the ropes and pads beneath her. My breath caught in my throat. "He was more powerful than you, and he could use his Mythica on you, so you all..." Of course, that's where her mind would go.

"Nobody is going to hurt you, Lexa," I spoke clearly, trying to restrain the budding fear. It was a promise I knew I would keep, no matter the consequences.

"Are you going to tell them about what I can do?"

Was I?

I knew I would have to tell my siblings something, but I couldn't bring myself to think about revealing the entire truth.

"They're not monsters," I whispered. I know what she saw, and I also know what I would think if I had only that as context, but I needed her to know that my siblings were not the vindictive people they seemed to be. At least not entirely.

"I know that."

I released a breath at that. If she didn't see them as monsters, perhaps there was still hope for me. " I don't think they need to know. Not about this," I confirmed. She sighed, relief flooding her body. She nearly slumped back into my chest. I would have let her.

"I don't want to lie to them," she retorted weakly. "And I don't want to make you lie for me, either."

"I'd do a lot more than just lie for you, Miss Cromwell." The words were out before I could stop them. It's not that I didn't mean them, but I understood that my determination to have her could be a source of contention for her.

I waited for her to respond with ire or fear, but instead, she leaned into me, her back curving perfectly against my chest. The rise and fall of her steady breathing and the rhythmic beating of her heart calmed my own until they were beating together in perfect harmony. Lexa Cromwell was already mine; she just needed time to come to terms with that.

I kept my gloved hands tightly wrapped in the reins to avoid cradling her into me the way I so desperately desired to. We traveled in our familiar and comfortable silence for a few hours more. The heat from the midday sun burned my skin, but the heat that bloomed inside me had nothing to do with the desert heat and everything to do with the stunning woman in front of me.

She had fallen asleep at some point, her head lulling periodically to each side, her head dangerously close to nuzzling into the crook of my neck and breaking our 'no skin-to-skin contact' promise. I let myself get carried away in imagining a future where holding this beautiful woman in my arms wasn't a singular experience. Her tour of Verihdia truly started today, and the chances were high that she would fall in love with one of the many beautiful Courts. I knew it was foolish to think that my Court still had a chance, but I saw how she looked at it, how she smiled in Everwatch, and how she sighed as we left it behind. Call it foolish or hopeful, but I believed I still had a chance to have her. I was going to make sure of it.

Cresting over the sandy horizon was a massive tower. The tiered structure was constructed of entirely black brick. The setting sun reflected off of it, sending the light fractals dancing across the dark sandy dunes. The sky had turned a soft purple as the sun began to wane. I whispered into Lexa's ear, careful not to press my lips against her skin. "Wake up, Miss Cromwell." She stirred, moaning softly as she regained consciousness. She sat forward, and my body instantly missed her warmth despite the heat of the air. Her eyes scanned the small town just outside the Pleasure Tower's confines. Decorations were hung, and lights had been strung across the streets, illuminating the area in a soft glow. People in various states of undress wandered through the streets, embracing others as they seductively danced to the sensual music played by the musicians posted on every corner.

I had never been to The Court of Passion during their annual Endless Night festival, but tales of the debauchery and sensual *activities* had traveled widely. As we rode through the streets, groups and couples scattered across the area, in and outside the inns and pubs, their lips locked in heated passion or even indulging in public intimacy. I was not a prude in any sense of the word, but the idea of being so public with my passions had always concerned me, although the thought of sinking into Lexa as others watched her cry out in ecstasy and knowing that they couldn't have her did seem appealing.

I turned my gaze from the passionate displays to look at her. She did not turn away the way she had in the lobby last night, but the expression on her face was still somewhat unreadable.

I watched her as she watched them until we reached the gate to the Tower.

Even Korzich's guards had been indulging in sins of the flesh, and their nearly naked forms were on full display as they assisted with removing our bags and boarding our steed. The only indication of Lexa's embarrassment was the slight pink tint in her cheeks.

Lexa's eyes remained trained on the ceiling as the guards turned to lead us to the grand ballroom. I wasn't sure if she was avoiding looking at the exposed derriere of the guard ahead of us or if she genuinely was taking in the architecture of this stunning building. It was darker than I usually liked, but I guess that was all part of 'setting the mood,' as Korzich had once called it. The floor was entirely covered in plush velvet carpeting, and the walls were draped with elegant silk tapestry. If there were windows in here, they were thoroughly covered. The only light illuminating the space came from the sconces that lined the hallways and the fire burning from the deep black candles. The only color in the room came from the painted mural that took up the entire ceiling. Depictions of thousands of bodies, pleasuring each other, immortalized just above us. I had to admire the craftsmanship. It was incredibly detailed.

We approached large double doors, and I heard loud and enthusiastic moans from the other side. I cleared my throat and stopped, calling out to the guard before he pushed through the doors. "Could you tell the Warden we are here and will wait to meet them until they are…finished?" Although we were not siblings by blood, I had been able to avoid seeing Korzich in such compromising positions thus far and intended to keep it that way.

The guard nodded before disappearing into the ballroom. The sounds of pleasure drifting from the room crescendoed as the doors opened. I averted my eyes until the door closed again, leaving Lexa and me alone in the hallway.

"This is…" she started tentatively. "A lot." A laugh escaped me, and she joined me, chuckling nervously.

"You mean to tell me you aren't used to Court-wide orgies?" I teased. Suddenly, her hesitations slipped away, and she doubled over laughing. The sound carried through the hallway and rang deliciously in my ears. The sound of her amusement is a thousand times more arousing than the moans drifting through the hallway.

"Can't say I am," she admitted, calming herself down. I looked her over. Remembering what it felt like to have her curves melting into my body, to feel her warmth against me, to see her please herself. My eyes trailed her, inch by inch, and I felt her eyes on me, burning into my skin.

My throat suddenly felt dry, and I had to clench my gloved fists at my side to avoid reaching to touch her. Our eyes locked, and once again, I was entranced. Frozen in place, unable to tear my eyes from her even if I needed to.

Then, the door swung open, and my sibling stepped out to join us in the hallway. I could only look away from Lexa when she turned her head. Korzich wore a black silk robe, cinched so incredibly loosely that it didn't leave much to the imagination. Their long dark hair was braided down their back, and their pale chest was peppered with their Court Mark. They looked flushed and satisfied.

"Lexa! You made it!" Korzich moved to rush forward and embrace her, but the tiniest of growls rumbled in my chest, and they stopped short, smiling knowingly at me, before offering Lexa their hand instead. Lexa shook it timidly, her smile bright in the dark room.

"No hello for me, sibling?" I teased. Korzich smiled and embraced me. I laughed and quickly pushed them off of me. "Forgive me, but I prefer the people I hug to be fully clothed." Korzich made a tsk sound before looking at me with profound pity in their eyes. "Most of the time," I added with the quickest of glances towards Lexa. Her eyes darted to the floor.

"Your hugs must be so boring." They pouted. I rolled my eyes, but the smile remained plastered on my face. Korzich turned to address my little storm again. "So, Lexa, first time in The Court of Passion, I hope you're enjoying the view."

She nodded slowly. "The tower is beautiful, and I've never seen something so…" She searched for the right word. "Sensually decorated." She shrugged nervously, and Korzich chuckled.

"Love, you know that is not the view I was referring to." Their eyes twinkled with anticipation. Lexa blushed, a deep red.

"I will admit I'm not exactly used to this type of…display." She sheepishly blushed.

Korzich nodded and gripped her hand in theirs. "By the time I'm done with you, you will never take your passion for granted again." They nodded as if to accentuate their point. She swallowed at that, her throat bobbing with the movement. A look of recognition flashed across her face.

"You do plan on showing her more than sex while she's here, right?" I interjected, and Korzich feigned outrage, gasping loudly and placing their hand on their chest.

"What kind of a host do you think I am?!" They exclaimed.

"Well, your robe is hanging open, and you are exposed. Can you blame me?" Korzich glanced down at their exposed body and smiled but made no move to cover themselves.

"I suppose not." Korzich smiled, clapping their hands in front of them. "Well, you're in luck, Lexa. Tonight is the festival's first night, so it tends to get a little more intimate than the other nights."

Lexa sighed nervously.

"Take tonight to explore and visit the different floors of the Tower. There's a little bit of everything for everyone here. Do you enjoy bondage?" Korzich asked, and Lexa coughed, choking on the air that flooded her lungs. I rolled my eyes at my sibling's crassness, although the thought was not unappealing. A quick image crossed my mind, Lexa's pale skin turning pink under the pressure of dark ropes holding her in place as I worshiped her.

I shook my head, letting the image fall away. This Court and its influence was going to be the death of me if I didn't get a handle on these urges.

"Never mind, you'll find displays of just about everything here. Now, you should know that on most floors here, participation is encouraged, but don't worry, nobody will touch you without expressed consent." They winked, and I watched Lexa's already pale face drained of color. "But I have a feeling that you would enjoy the seventh floor the most. Explore tonight, Lexa, and not just the Tower. Explore yourself. Tomorrow morning, we will meet, and I'll show you what else my Court has to offer." Korzich kissed each of Lexa's cheeks before disappearing again behind the double doors.

Lexa stood, shocked and silent for a few moments.

"You know you don't have to go anywhere or do anything you don't want to do, right?" She nodded, her eyes still wide in surprise. "We could go directly to your chambers and avoid this entire night if you'd prefer that." Part of me wanted her to say yes, for her to choose a night alone in the chambers over a night of debauchery with strangers. And yet, a small part of me wondered what she would do when exposed to that environment. What secrets of her desire could I discover?

"I'm here to see if I belong here, right?" She shrugged, unconvincingly. I smiled at her as my answer. "Then I think I'd like to see the seventh floor."

Nine

"Get up!" I called out to the bulky man who had collapsed onto the sandy ground at my feet. His wheezing filled my ears. I had to remind myself not to show the apparent disappointment on my face.

Some Gladiator you are.

"If you cannot run five miles, then you are not Gladiator material." I raised my voice authoritatively. I directed the claim at all the Gladiators-in-training sprinting around the Coliseum in pathetic displays of exhaustion. They were improving slowly, but we were still only a few days in.

The first day of implementing my new training regime did not go well. Just about every single one of them had vomited and prayed to Kamatyan to subject me to a slow and agonizing death.

Today wasn't much better.

Raul, the strongest of the trainees, panted on the ground. His blonde hair was pulled back into a loose hold at his neck, and various flyaway hairs were plastered to his skin by the thick sheen of sweat that poured from his tan skin.

Avalin had called him her most prized trainee. I was anything but impressed.

"Raul, keep running, or I'll add another mile," I commanded. While I had never led a training regime like this, I knew what type of motivation worked for me. Raul nearly growled.

"Madilliam knows why you have us running like little sissies. We ought to be mastering our weapons," he spat. The eyes of the other soon-to-be-Gladiators watched us as they continued their run around the perimeter.

"I'm sorry. Who is running this training exercise?" I asked, looking down at the heap of muscles heaving on the ground.

"Nobody important. You think you're so special because Avalin asked you to train us? If you were special, you'd be training with us." He slowly stood, his frame towering over me, but I did not back down. I wouldn't. Even though deep down, I thought he was right.

"You're telling me you don't understand why I am making you run?" I rested my hands on my hips.

Raul scoffed. "Probably because you don't understand what it takes to be a real Gladiator." The others had ceased their workout to watch the unfolding argument - a decision they would pay for with more laps.

"You're strong, Raul," I started slowly.

He grunted. "I know that, Cromwell."

"You didn't let me finish," I stated evenly. He crossed his bugling arms across his thick chest. "You're strong, but until you have some endurance, you will always lose."

The others had gathered closer, their faces red from exertion, but the expressions on their faces told me precisely who they believed held the power in our scenario.

They were wrong.

"Prove it." Raul lowered his arms, bringing his fists together in front of him in a performative display of strength. It was on my training plan to avoid skirmishes until next week. There were foundational things that needed to be fixed first, but if these Gladiators were going to respect me, they needed to see that I knew what I was talking about.

I nodded at Raul, and the bloodthirsty smile on his lips curled as his peers cheered their approval. Walking to the weapons cart, Raul gripped the handle of a massive hammer. I had heard that this was his weapon of choice, and seeing him swing it wildly, testing its weight, I could see why. He was undoubtedly formidable. I made my way to the cart and gripped the hilt of a small dagger. It was all I'd need to make my point.

"You trying to get yourself killed, Cromwell?" Klover spoke breathlessly from her position in the crowd of trainees. The blonde female stood nearly five inches taller than me and had the most defined muscles I'd ever seen on another human, yet she was out of breath from running just two miles. This group had a lot to learn… things I could teach them. If they would let me.

That is why I stood my ground now against the ravenous Raul and his hammer. I did not doubt that he would kill me during this fight if given the chance, which is why he wouldn't get it.

"Lead us in," I tossed to the crowd without tearing my eyes from Raul. Klover cleared her throat, and Raul's muscles tightened as he prepared to rush me. I eyed the placement of his feet and smiled. I'd have plenty of time to get out of the way if that were his idea of a kick-off.

"On your honor…" Klover started, her chest still heaving, "fight."

And he was off. Raul's bulky frame came barrelling towards me, a sight that might have frightened a lesser-trained Gladiator. His feet struggled to gain traction in the sand, as I knew they would, and I smiled before ducking out of the way just as his hammer came swinging through. His grunt of exertion echoed through the Coliseum.

Our small audience erupted into cheers and encouragement. "Come on, Raul." "Harder!" "Don't let him get away."

As Raul's body spun from the weight of the swinging hammer, I moved to a new spot behind him, my feet dancing across the sand with ease and silence. The dagger in my hand rested idly by my side.

If all went according to plan, I wouldn't need it.

Raul had centered himself once again and twisted his head to lock me in his sights. His dark eyes widened with rage, and a scream tore through his throat.

A showman, yes. A Gladiator…no.

He rushed toward me again. This time, his hammer was hoisted high above his head. I bounced on the balls of my feet, readying myself for just the right moment and dodged his second attack. By the time his hammer made contact with the ground, sending vibrations across the surface and up through my feet, I was on the move again.

"Raul!"

"Come on!"

"Stop missing him!"

"Shut up!" Raul yelled back at our spectators. They continued their shouts and calls as Raul lifted his hammer again, his chest rumbling with a loud growl.

I saw it then, his determination, his fury. This was it. I bent my knees, lowering my center of gravity and keeping myself poised and ready to dodge as Raul gathered every ounce of his energy and stomped forward. His hammer pulled off to the side, and he swung before reaching me. I could easily step back. The whoosh of air from his swing felt cool against my skin. He screamed but wasn't ready to give up just yet. He brought the hammer back without slowing the swing's momentum, and I saw it coming a mile away. I spun out of the way, landing just off his side. His chest was heaving, and the determination was nearly gone from his eyes.

"Stay still and fight me!" He panted through ragged breaths as he threw an elbow in my direction. I was several feet away in seconds.

The other trainees cheered and taunted, but this time, their jests were not at my expense but Raul's.

"He's gonna pass out."

"He didn't even land a single hit!"

The teasing from his peers spurred Raul. I knew he had one last burst of energy in him, and he was about to use every little bit he had left.

The following sequence came in rapid succession. He swung the hammer towards my left side, but I pulled back, dodging it easily. He let the hammer slide from his hands, and he made a move to send his fist flying at my face. I ducked. His grunts filled the arena, and the wild shouts from our audience motivated me..

For a moment, just a moment, I pretended this was an actual match. That the stands were filled with thousands of fans cheering for me. That I was a true Verihdian Gladiator.

I kept light on my feet, dodging and ducking as Raul's fists swung aimlessly in the air, his breath coming in ragged spurts, his motions slowing.

Soon, he fell to his knees, catching his breath.

The trainees cheered for me. It was interesting how quickly they changed their allegiance. Although that was the unfortunate reality of being a Gladiator, you're only someone's favorite until you stop winning.

Klover and the others surrounded me, patting me on the back.

"You didn't even use your weapon," Klover exclaimed excitedly.

"You were like a blur," shouted another.

I nodded to acknowledge their praise, but this was not a fight. This was an exercise. So, I brushed past them and made my way to Raul's heaving form.

I extended my hand to him, waiting expectantly for his response. Had I wounded his pride or garnered his respect? With members of The Court of the Vanguard, it could go either way.

His dark eyes looked up at me as he sat, dejected, on the sandy arena floor. I simply waited, keeping my eyes, free of judgment, trained on him. He reached his arm out to grip mine, and I helped him to his feet. He kept my arm locked in his, in a warrior's embrace. A strange, stern depression was etched on his face. The others had quieted down, watching the exchange anxiously.

"You've gotta show me how you did that," he joked, and the other trainees chimed in with their agreement and began discussing the battle play-by-play. I couldn't help the bloom of pride in my chest as they recounted my skill and prowess.

"If you want to be able to do that…" I started, and the others quieted down, listening eagerly. "Start running." And this time, they didn't argue. They took off towards the perimeter of the arena floor and resumed their workout. Raul offered a curt nod of acknowledgment before joining his peers.

I watched them run, a smile plastered on my face, examining their form and calling out corrections for a few minutes. A flash of red in the stands caught my attention, and I turned to see Avalin and Cassius sitting among the stone benches. My eyes locked with hers, and she beckoned for me to approach.

"Alright, three more laps, and then we're done for the day," I called out as I sprinted up the steps toward my Warden.

Stopping on the row of seats below her, I bowed my head. "My Warden." I turned and offered the Gladiator a nod. "Cassius."

"You weren't supposed to fight with the trainees," Avalin's voice was matter-of-fact, not laced with disdain or anger.

"I assure you, it was necessary to get them to trust me," I replied in my defense. Avalin pursed her lips and turned her head towards the running trainees, watching them momentarily.

"And did you?" She turned her eyes back to me, the blazing purple color cementing me to my place. "Did you get them to trust you?"

I nodded. "Yes, my Warden. I believe I did." Her stoic face slowly slipped into a smile of appreciation, and my entire chest warmed at the sight.

"Impressive work, Mr. Cromwell," she praised, and I glanced down at my Court Mark, fully on display on my forearm, appreciating how right it felt on my skin, how perfectly I felt like I belonged here.

"My trainer tried to get us to run during my first season, and we nearly killed him," Cassius laughed. The deep, throaty sound was joyful and intoxicating. I laughed along with them. "I would have enjoyed having an instructor like you, Axel." My breath caught in my throat as I tried to accept this compliment without breaking into a million happy pieces.

My eyes stung as tears of pride threatened to fall. "Thank you, Cassius. That means the world to me."

"I gotta take off. I've got a hot date tonight." They slapped their hands down onto their knees as they stood, towering over me from their vantage point. "Seriously, good work out there, kid." As they walked away, I felt myself struggling to contain the smile that formed on my lips.

"They're right, you know," Avalin's voice brought me back to reality. I turned to face her, and she leaned forward so that her elbows rested comfortably on her knees. Her hands were clasped together in front of her as she surveyed the arena. "One of our trainers rarely gains their respect this quickly. Sometimes it doesn't happen at all."

I shifted on my feet, comfortably soaking up every ounce of praise she was willing to give me. "You said it yourself, my Warden, I belong in this Court. I intend to prove that fact every single day."

She glanced at me, her eyebrows furrowing slightly as she examined me. Maybe she was seeing the fire that burned within—the one she couldn't see before. "Have a seat," she insisted, patting the open spot beside her. I took a deep breath before settling into Cassius' empty seat. Sitting next to Avalin, I acknowledged her Mythica-induced beauty once again. Her long red hair had been decorated with braids and beads, and her amethyst eyes nearly glowed. Her bright skin was smooth and soft yet decorated with tiny scars that told her story—the story of a warrior—a Gladiator.

"Raul's been a vile trainee, hasn't he?" She asked, looking out over the individuals running below us. I followed her gaze and locked on Raul's form, slowly trudging along, painfully attempting to keep up with the others. He would not enjoy coming in last during these training exercises, but that is precisely how he will improve.

"He's a Gladiator. I believe hard-headedness is required," I teased, and Avalin chuckled.

"You're not entirely wrong." She ran her hands through her hair and sighed. "You're going to be good for this program, Cromwell."

Pride swelled in my chest again. "Thank you for the opportunity," I eagerly replied.

She nodded her head once before retraining her eyes out on the arena. Her face fell slightly, and her tongue darted out to wet her lush pink lips.

"Is something troubling you?"

She exhaled through her nose as her eyebrows darted up. "Observant," she mused. I sat quietly, waiting for her to continue. She released a deep sigh, her eyes closing. "I have something else I need to ask of you."

"Anything, my Warden," I replied quickly. She shook her head.

"I assured you that your appointment in this training program was entirely to do with your skill and not regarding your familial connection to Lexa," she started, her eyes meeting mine.

My heart sank. Of course, that wasn't true. Why would I ever think I could receive this kind of attention and praise just by being myself? Any ounce of fulfillment that had been building within me shattered as she watched me. "I should have known that was not exactly the case," I whispered in an attempt to find my voice again.

"No, that was the truth, Cromwell. I do not lie, especially in matters of pride." She reached out for my hand and held it in hers. They were warm, strong, and calloused. "However, I would be lying if I said I did not have a second, far more selfish position to offer you today."

She must have seen the look of confusion on my face because she quickly continued.

"I am creating a committee purely focused on planning for your sister's visit to this Court." She watched the figures below us as she spoke. My chest tightened at the thought of my sister. I missed her so desperately already. How has it only been a week? "I want you to lead it."

"Lead this committee?" I asked. She nodded.

"We have something that no other Court has," she began.

I inhaled long and slow, trying to sort out how this offer made me feel.

"You."

"You want me to convince my sister to Pledge to this Court?" I asked, although I knew the answer. I knew Avalin would try to use me to get to Lexa. I wasn't daft. I knew why Avalin personally had been the one to give me my Court Mark at the Pledging Ceremony.

"No, I want you to train me so that *I* can convince her to Pledge to this Court." Her eyes were pleading. There was something the Warden of The Court of the Vanguard wanted, and I was the only one who could get it for her. It felt odd to have this slight bit of power. A dynamic I'd be willing to bet not many experience with this Warden or any Warden for that matter.

On one hand, I wanted my sister here with me. To be together the way we always had. On the other hand, I was enjoying this new experience, settling into my new life…alone. She stared at me expectantly. I attempted to form words a few times but couldn't solidify a phrase that properly encapsulated my feelings about the offer.

Instead of responding, I studied her face, noticing the long pink scar carved from just above her eyebrow to below her eye, creating a gap in her hair. "How did you get that scar," I asked, my fingers hovering a few inches from her face. She turned to face me, her eyebrow cocked in question.

"You see my scar?" She asked, incredulously dropping my hand from hers. I already missed the warmth. I nodded.

"And others, too, but this one looks like it has the best story." She laughed once, her face contorting in an expression of disbelief.

"Nobody ever sees the scars," she mused, almost to herself. It was my turn to look at her questioningly. Shaking her head, she continued, "People only see what they want when they look at me. Scars are imperfections."

I frowned. Avalin was confident, brushing off the admission as if it didn't matter. Pride.

"I disagree." Her purple eyes met mine, and for a brief moment, I didn't see my Warden, one of the most influential individuals in all of Verihdia. I saw a woman who's had her guard up for far too long.

She tilted her head, offering me a knowing smirk. "Your flattery will get you many things in this Court, Cromwell," she stood then, straightening her skirt of leather strips that hung from her waist. "Please think about my offer."

Before she could get very far, I stood up, calling after her. "I don't want to coerce her into making a choice that does not benefit her. She may be some prize to you, but to me, she is my sister."

Avalin paused her back to me, gone rigid. I watched as she took a breath and turned. "Tell me what I need to know about Lexa, prepare me to be her guide, and I promise you that if I don't think she'd be happy here - if there truly isn't potential for her to enjoy her life in this Court - I won't pressure her."

I smiled, nodding. "Then I accept."

Her head tilted, and a smile spread across her face.

"We'll talk soon then, Mr. Cromwell." With a slight bow of her head, she strutted off. I watched her depart, savoring the second task entrusted to me directly by my Warden.

Ten

"Here, let me help you with that," I called out, jogging forward to grip the edge of a large bench as two individuals carried it out. They had been cleaning up The Forsaken Quarters for several days, removing any excess furniture or decorations brought in for the Welcome Ball. The two gentlemen craned their necks around the bulky piece to smile at me.

"Thank you, sir." The shorter of the two said. I nodded and began walking backward through the halls.

"You all certainly put on an incredible event," I offered.

The taller man's face lit up, a smile taking up his entire rounded face. "That's very kind of you…" He extended the final word, expecting me to fill in my name.

"Chandler, sir." I smiled.

He tipped his head slightly, adjusting his grip on the leg of the bench. "I am Evan, and this is Kline." The taller man, Evan, replied. I nodded and acted like this was my first time hearing their names. Pretending that I had not spent the last two days observing them, deciphering their place in the hierarchy of the Court, and determining if they could be useful to me. It took minimal effort to get the staff to tell me about the two event coordinators and their influence here in The Court of Shadows.

"It's an honor to meet you both," I offered sweetly, allowing my carefully calculated charm to seep through. We slowly traveled through the halls of The Forsaken Quarters, and I helped load the bench onto the waiting cart at the entrance to the ballroom.

Wiping his hands, Kline held out a hand for me. "Thanks for the assist, Chandler." I shook his hand eagerly.

"Please, I'm happy to help." They began the trek back into the ballroom, and I followed behind. "Do you plan many events throughout the year?" I knew the answer to this question already.

"We used to," Evan said, a twinge of sadness in his amber eyes. Kline mirrored the expression.

"But not anymore?" I feigned empathy.

"My Warden has grown weary of these events in recent years," Kline responded.

Evan quickly covered any indignation as he tacked on, "Of course he is. He's so busy protecting us."

Kline nodded at Evan's interjection.

"I'm not sure I've ever seen quite so many happy faces all in one place as I did at your Welcome Ball," I said. They beamed in pride. "It's a shame that we don't offer events more frequently. I think people could use a little joy, especially since we will be Wardenless for quite some time."

Evan and Kline mulled over my words as they gripped a second bench. Wordlessly, I assisted. "It is a shame." Kline lamented, a grunt of exertion escaping his lips as he lifted the bench.

"I sure hope morale doesn't plummet." I watched as Kline and Evan took in my words. "I heard The Court of the Vanguard holds weekly extravagant events. Rumors say they couldn't be happier."

Kline's eyes narrowed, and Evan scoffed. "Please, Vanguards wouldn't know a good party if it bit them in the arse," Evan grunted as we walked towards the cart. "Those prideful jackasses can't throw an event to save their lives."

"Have you been?" I asked earnestly.

"No, but I have met a Vanguard member, and they're too busy looking at themselves in the mirror to plan an extravaganza," Evan replied.

I turned to Kline, who was moving his head in agreement. "Maybe…" I started slowly. "No, never mind. It's not possible." I turned my head, avoiding their questioning gazes, feigning disappointment.

"What's not possible?" Kline asked as we loaded the second bench onto the cart.

I stood, brushing off my vest before retraining my gaze on the two of them. "I was going to suggest that we reintroduce these events to support our Court as we navigate this time without our Warden," I replied sheepishly. The two glanced at each other as I continued. I watched the silent conversation pass between them. They were about to say no.

It's time to play dirty.

"But I understand that managing that many events would be a challenge. Keeping up with The Court of the Vanguard could be quite demanding."

Done.

I didn't need to look at their faces to know that my words had done their job. It would have worked on me.

"Nonsense, perhaps we could bring back some of our most favored events during our Warden's absence," Kline began, his fingers resting comfortably on his chin as he mulled over the possibility.

"Is there a reason you have not yet finished, gentlemen?" I knew intimately who the silky voice behind me belonged to. I had heard it for the majority of my final years at the Institute, in her office, with my head between her thighs.

I closed my eyes and took a long breath to steady myself. I could still get what I wanted, but her presence meant my tactic had to shift.

"My apologies, My Dean," Kline offered, bowing at the waist. Evan followed suit, lowering himself in a show of respect.

My eyes passed over the two men, bent before this woman, this Vacant woman, and I felt the familiar twinge of envy crawl up my spine. My eyes met hers, and I plastered on my most charming smile. The one that got her into my bed in the first place.

"Mr. Mills. What can I do for you?" Lilith spoke without raising her eyes to meet mine as I strolled into her office in the Dean's Wing of the Institute. It was a modest room with dark brick walls and cozy leather furniture. Her desk was deep mahogany, and her pale skin contrasted with her dark green robe.

I sunk into the dark black chair, feeling its unforgiving material against my back as I leaned back. Crossing one leg over the other, I settled into my seat, waiting for her to look my way.

"Call me Chandler, please." I smiled, letting every ounce of seduction I've learned from Bellamy Vicious and their Court of Passion lessons influence my tone. Her eyes flitted up to meet mine, and while I found her a beautiful woman, I can't say I was particularly attracted to her. But she was my ticket to a life in The Court of Shadows, and that was a life that I had long since decided I would do anything to achieve, even if it meant seducing the Dean of Shadows.

"Chandler," she mused. I observed her mouth as she said my name, careful not to smile, but I saw the shadow of amusement as it crossed her face. "Why have you come to see me?"

"You know exactly why I'm here, Lilith," I replied darkly. Her eyes fell closed, and the sweetest moan escaped her lips.

"And you know exactly what I'm going to say…"

I stood then, abandoning the cool comfort of the armchair, and took slow, torturous steps toward her. Her gaze tracked my every action, akin to a predator observing its prey. Unbeknownst to her, the dynamic was entirely reversed.

I stopped behind her chair, letting my hands drape along the headrest. I leaned forward until my lips were inches from her skin. She sighed, and I knew that today, the months of flirtatious banter and subtle glances would pay off.

I wrapped a single curl of bright white hair around my index finger, tugging slightly until her head fell back, exposing her neck to me. My lips made contact just as her willpower shattered beneath me.

"We can't," she whispered, but even I could tell she didn't believe it.

"We can," I replied. I felt her chest vibrate with the groan she was suppressing.

"You aren't Pledged yet. We can't…influence the Pledge," she whimpered as my fist knotted in her hair and pulled gently.

"Lilith," I crooned, working my way down the column of her throat to the slopes of her breasts that threatened to spill from her corset. "I've spent months coveting you, doing everything I had to so I could finally have you." I let my tongue dance along the swell of her breasts. "Isn't that exactly what a member of The Court of Shadows would do?"

I slid my hands down from the headrest of her chair to cup her breasts and worked carefully at the ties of her corset. "Doesn't the fact that I would do anything to have you make me perfect for your Court?" The ties of her top loosened, and her breasts tumbled out of their confinement. I gathered them in my palms quickly, my fingers finding the eager peaks and beginning a delicious exploration. She arched her back, pressing herself into me. "I think of you every time I'm with Lexa Cromwell." It wasn't true. In fact, I didn't think of much when I was with Lexa other than chasing my own pleasure, but Lilith didn't need to know that.

"Don't you dare say her name when your hands are on me," Lilith growled, the last thread of her resistance snapping as she reached her hands up to slither around my neck and drag me down to kiss her lips. I indulged her eagerly.

Our kiss was a violent display of possession; her tongue swirled with mine as if she was marking every inch of my mouth, and I let her.

She was the key to what I deserved. I needed a backup plan to ensure I was where I belonged one day.

Feeling the final piece of the puzzle fall into place, I walked around the chair and lowered myself to my knees before her. Pressing her thighs apart and lifting her skirt, I feasted on her with reckless abandon.

It felt so good to get what I wanted.

We had spent dozens of passion-filled nights together throughout my final year at the Institute. Each joining was as desperate as the next. I wasn't naive. I knew Lilith was carrying a torch for her Warden. She would spend long bouts of time away in The Court of Shadows and return to the Institute a mixture of sexually satisfied and emotionally starved. It seemed our Warden was quite the lover but not exactly the comforting type. So, he would leave the heavy lifting for me. I was happy to do it if it meant I was securing my place in my Court. My Warden didn't even know it, but we were already the perfect team.

One night, only a month before the Final Trial, Lilith and I were tangled in her sheets, a layer of sweat on our bodies. I told her my biggest fear.

Or at least the biggest fear that she needed to hear.

"I'm afraid I won't receive a Shadows result…and I'll have to leave you." It was a carefully crafted plea, and she had eaten up every word as if it were a fine meal. Her hands caressed my bare torso as she whispered.

"I won't let that happen."

She didn't say it outwardly, but I knew that if the time came and I needed to Pledge against my result, she would accept me. That was what I wanted all along. That was the entire point.

I wasn't a prideful man, but damn, if I were, that moment would be the one with which all future moments were measured against.

Once I received my Trial results, my relationship with Lilith became moot. I had gotten what I needed, and my backup plan wasn't necessary. But maybe that connection could be used again for a different outcome.

I smiled at her, letting my eyes trail her slender frame appreciatively, hungrily. Taking my bottom lip between my teeth, I titled my head and let her see how much I wanted her.

Her eyes met mine as she spoke. "Please see to it that you are finished by sundown," she ordered the men, never taking her eyes off me.

"Of course, of course," Kline replied, flustered.

"It was my fault, My Dean." I stepped forward. Evan and Kline's jaws fell open as they looked at me. I simply stood, lowering my head as a sign of submission.

"Is that true?" Lilith asked the others without removing her eyes from me.

"Um-" Evan began, but I stepped in again.

"I was simply proposing that we host more frequent events to boost morale and promote community as we navigate these next six months without our Warden." I kept my gaze trained on her. Her eyes narrowed, and I pretended to admire her body again. When my eyes returned to her face, she was smirking, proud that she caught me red-handed, as if I didn't paint them red myself for the sole purpose of being caught.

"And why do you feel like it is your place to suggest such a thing, Pledge?" To anyone else, Evan and Kline included, it would look like I was being scolded, but I knew the dangerous game she liked to play—the power dynamic she enjoyed exploiting with me.

"I'm simply acting as someone who cares about this Court and its survival." I smiled again, feigning innocence as best I could. "Perhaps we can create a committee dedicated to maintaining morale. In fact, I'd love to be a part of that process in any way you see fit."

Her tongue darted out to wet her bottom lip, and I knew I had won. "You want to start a committee?" She asked, tilting her head to the side, but I didn't miss how her gaze traveled along the front of my body.

"I do."

Evan and Kline stood quietly, watching the scene unfolding with anxious worry. I sent them a quick smile and a nod.

"Then you should come to my office today to discuss your intentions." Lilith turned on a heel and disappeared into The Forsaken Quarters.

It was time to solidify my place in this Court.

And nobody was going to stop me.

Lexa

Eleven

My whole body burned with intensity. Every nerve ending seemed hyper-aware, registering every gentle brush of my skirt against my thighs as I ascended the stairs. Just a week ago, the idea of a life in The Court of Passion would have been inconceivable to me, but it didn't appear to be an entirely unfounded notion after last night.

The partner might have had something to do with it.

I couldn't help but think about the consuming heat that licked at my body as Lysander gave me commands last night while his eyes devoured me. Did I enjoy that because I was a sensual person destined for this Court, or did I enjoy it because of the man who had me crumbling under his gaze?

I still didn't understand the vision I had ripped from him. He seemed so confident that I wouldn't be afraid of him if I knew the whole story. Call me naive or foolish, but I was starting to believe him. The eradication of an entire Court was not exactly something to easily forgive or forget, and I'm not sure I ever could. However, I conceded that there was a context I lacked, one he couldn't provide.

But could I, in good conscience, let him touch me with the same hands after seeing what he has done with them? Why was this Warden challenging my feeble morals so relentlessly?

I was contemplating this as I arrived on the seventh floor of the Pleasure Tower. The air smelled faintly of sweat and citrus, and sounds of passion echoed through the halls. Directly in front of me was a large ornate door. Sitting guard was a slender woman with dark black skin on full display. She only wore a thin layer of gossamer, which very well could have been forgotten, given how much I could still see.

She smiled sweetly as I approached the door. Her eyes trailed to the figure behind me, and she bowed her head. "Warden, I was hoping we would see you out tonight." Her seductive voice was alluring, and I nearly swooned at the melodic tone.

But then, the envy came. Not wanting to alert Lysander to my fit of jealousy, I took the slightest step to the left, effectively blocking this woman's view of the Warden.

She pursed her lips and retrained her eyes on me. "Has my Warden informed you of what this floor entails?" She asked. I shook my head, a few strands of my long black hair falling loose into my face. "This is Voyeur Hall. Beyond this door, you'll find a hallway that stretches the length of the seventh floor. There are several stages set up along the walkway where performers and volunteers will be engaging in their activity of choice. All for your viewing pleasure." She drew out the word 'pleasure' as if it tasted divine in her mouth.

My heart rate quickened. Observing others in intimate moments had proven to be an unexpectedly intriguing experience. It left me with the feeling of being exposed and vulnerable, even though I was the one entirely clothed.

Then, I thought about watching those intimate acts with Lysander, and all of a sudden, my body was engulfed in flame. I felt my core tighten with the prospect of standing so close to him, feeling his heat while we watched others do what I wouldn't allow myself to indulge in with him.

"Oh…" I whispered. I felt Lysander's breath on my neck.

"We do not have to do this, Miss Cromwell." It wasn't a taunt, and it wasn't full of unspoken pressure. Instead, he saw my hesitations and offered me a way out.

Again, I found myself thankful for his presence.

"Perhaps another night," I proclaimed to the woman at the door, who simply smiled. If she was judging me for my prudish manner, she didn't make it known. I appreciated that. I turned on my heel and faced Lysander. His features were shrouded in darkness, and I suddenly felt very bare.

"Can you show me my room, please?" I focused on keeping my voice steady and calm, but the furrow in Lysander's brow told me that he didn't believe my performance for a second. Thankfully, he didn't bring it up. Instead, he nodded once and returned to the steps we just climbed. I followed behind him, trying to shake off the feeling of failure that plagued me with every step.

I was here in this Court for one reason. To experience all it had to offer and learn all there was to know about this Court before making my life-altering decision. Instead, I walked away from the passion behind that door as if I were a scared little girl. The most frustrating part wasn't that I was afraid of entering the room. It was the apprehension of doing so with Lysander.

I was so close to breaking every rule I set for myself last night. Something about how his body calls for me, makes me feel like I am unbound by the world's laws. I was too caught up in my thoughts to notice that we had stopped before a set of double doors. Dark-black paint covered the delicate filigree designs. My fingers instinctively ran along the swirls.

"This is your room." He pushed the doors open, unveiling a breathtaking chamber nearly twice the size of the room we had stayed in the night before. Plush black carpets adorned the floors with soft, pillowy shag that enticed me to bury my bare feet within. The walls were adorned with velvet curtains the color of blood, while a small crystal chandelier hung from the ceiling, radiating a dark red glow that bathed the room in a vibrant hue.

In the center of the room, a circular bed stood. It was a unique sight with no head, foot, or poster frame. The sheets, seemingly silk, exuded a sleek black allure, inviting me forward with a sensual promise. Just beyond the bed, the door to the assumed washroom caught my attention, and the briefest moment of panic seized my heart. However, my gaze shifted to another door on the right side of the room before I could succumb to the haunting memories of water beyond the washroom's door. Moving toward this mystery doorway, I stood before the unassuming door, captivated by the allure of its dark black handle.

"That's my room," Lysander said from the doorway. He hadn't followed me in. I turned to analyze him.

"Our rooms are connected?" I asked, shock lacing my tone.

He nodded, taking in my reaction.

"Why?" I prompted.

He leaned against the frame, arms crossing casually across his toned chest. "I wanted to be accessible to you at all times," he responded, but then his eyes widened in horror. "I'm sorry, I didn't mean in *that* capacity." He stumbled over his words. "I simply meant that I wanted to be there in the event that you needed me. Not *need* me, but need my assistance. Or protection." He shook his hands in front of him. "Not that you need protection-" He buried his face in his palms. I had not seen this Warden quite so flustered before. I wondered if this Court affected him the same way it affected me.

And why did I hope it did?

"Does this door lock?" I asked, running my hand over the handle. The metal felt cool to the touch.

"It does. I expressly requested that it lock from your side and your side alone," he sheepishly added. My heart constricted at the thoughtfulness of the gesture. Truthfully, I was glad to know he was close by should I need him. Should anything else happen, in the water or out. I toyed with the lock on the door before twisting the handle and revealing the room beyond mine. It was nearly identical, strange circle bed and all. I smiled at the thought of Lysander trying to find the proper way to sleep on it.

His footsteps approached from behind cautiously. "If I keep the door locked, then how will you be able to assist me?" I asked, knowing the answer. He can't.

"It's your choice, Lexa. It's always your choice." He slipped past me into his room, turning once he was safely on his side of the frame. "I'll be here when you need me."

When.

As much as I hated the idea of being in danger again, knowing that the threat on my life had not been resolved yet and very well could reappear at any moment. The prospect of having Lysander at my side, prepared and eager to confront and combat this threat alongside me - and for me - fueled a sense of solace and reassurance. I nodded, closing the door slowly, struggling with the thought of shutting him out but knowing I needed to.

Once the door was shut, I twisted the latch, locking it.

I padded across the floor to the door that led to the hallway, locking it as well. Once I felt secure in my new space, I moved to my bags that had already been brought up. I dug through my packs, searching for comfortable sleepwear, and my hand paused, hovering over the shirt I stole from Lysander last night.

I told myself that I only wore it because the weather in this Court was incredibly warm, and I didn't have anything light enough, but in truth, I found his fiery scent comforting. Like that night I went without a nightmare, it was his scent that blanketed me, that lulled me to the first peaceful sleep I'd had in far too long. His scent meant safety and comfort, which was so strange to me because his scent also reminded me of that vision. The dark, cold room. The other Wardens and the way their Mythica danced around their intimidating frames. Their discussion about the Warden of The Forgotten Court. Their decision.

He insisted that there was more to the story, and though I accepted it reluctantly, doubts lingered. How could there possibly be more to what I witnessed? I saw what they did. It's not like I could simply ask the other Wardens when I saw them either without alerting them to my unique predicament and revealing the delicate truth that my Mythica had influence over them risked restarting the cycle, potentially sending me tumbling into the same fate the Forgotten Warden faced.

Lysander said he wouldn't let that happen to me, but surely he couldn't stop the other six Wardens from eliminating me as a threat. Perhaps they'd eliminate him too for even trying to stand in their way, for keeping this secret from them. Lysander was risking a lot by holding this information confidential for me. Perhaps even jeopardizing his own life. That carries weight for me.

For now, all I knew was I needed to keep a tight grip on my Mythica, remain vigilant for any indications of The Forgotten Court's influence, and somehow discover if I belonged in The Court of Passion.

Judging by how I ran from the Voyeur Hall today with my metaphorical tail between my legs, I don't see that as a significant possibility, but I was determined to put in the effort. I would speak with Korzich, and starting tomorrow, I would be more open to having experiences here.

Maybe not experiences with Lysander… no, I didn't need any more of those to complicate matters further. Still, experiences of some kind were necessary.

I shimmied out of my travel wear and slipped Lysander's shirt over my head, letting his scent invade my senses. My eyes trailed to the locked door where Lysander sat alone on the other side. Was he looking at the door, too? Was he waiting for me to unlock it? Would he come in if I did?

I stood there, scrutinizing the barrier that separated us with cautious temptation. Despite our shared performance the previous night, I had made it clear to him not to cross any lines, and to his credit, he had kept that promise. His skin hadn't touched mine since that moment in his private library—a fact I was desperately trying to appreciate.

However, there was a genuine, dangerous threat out there. While I had demonstrated my ability to defend myself with my dagger and Mythica, I acknowledged that there might be a moment when they wouldn't be enough. It was reassuring to know that if that day ever came, Lysander would be there.

The acknowledgment of that truth was why I made my way across the room and unlocked the door.

Twelve

There was a bittersweet reverence to Lexa being the only person in my life that I've ever dropped to my knees for. The first time it happened, that morning at the inn, her Mythica surrounded me, pushing me down to the ground before her as if it knew that my rightful place was at her feet. I didn't have the capacity to disagree. What undoubtedly seemed like such a simple gesture to her was ground-shattering for me. And yet, something about the action felt right, perfect. So perfect, in fact, that I couldn't stop myself from dropping to my knees for her again, with no Mythica to blame my uncharacteristic behavior on. The more time I spend around my little storm, the more confused I become. I don't understand why I feel so drawn to her. I don't understand why my aversion to submitting to anyone other than myself seems to dissipate when I'm around her. But I know I've fallen to my knees for this woman before, and I would eagerly do it again. The irony is that the only person in the world I'd fall to my knees for is the only one who doesn't seem to want that of me.

I found myself lying on my back, fully dressed in this absurdly shaped bed, restraining my breath to an almost painful degree to keep the sounds to a minimum so that I could hear every movement, every breath of hers beyond the wooden door that separated us. She locked it, of course. I expected as much, especially if she felt this Court's effects as strongly as I did. Gods, her every movement was intoxicating to me. Although, as much as I'd prefer to blame my inappropriate thoughts regarding Miss Cromwell on this Court and its influence, that would be a blatant lie. She's affected me this way since I saw her at the Courting Ball. I just wasn't willing to admit it.

Every fiber of my existence begged me to be near, protect, and worship her.

I was behaving like a lovesick child. It was infuriating.

My lungs burned as I listened to the soft footsteps beyond the door. The sound of fabric rustling permeated my senses. I tried not to imagine how her travel garment would fall slowly from her shoulders, revealing her creamy skin. I tried not to think of the way her soft curves and wide hips would look as she stepped out of the ring of clothes on the floor at her feet. I tried not to picture her long black hair trailing down her back and falling over her shoulders as she reached into her bags for a shirt to sleep in. I definitely tried not to think of her grabbing my shirt, the one she stole last night, and draping it across her naked form, brushing against her unblemished flesh the way my fingers begged to.

I tried not to think of any of that. And I failed miserably.

My obsession with Lexa Cromwell was reaching an unavoidable inferno. This Court's influences would be nearly impossible to navigate while keeping my promise of abstinence from touching her.

I tossed in the bed, nearly toppling off one of the rounded edges. Cursing at the horrendous person who decided that sleeping on a circle was a favorable idea, I sat upright, letting my feet hit the floor just as I heard footsteps near the door.

My body stilled, and my heart pulsed with eager anticipation.

Open the door, Lexa.

I watched the golden handle with unrelenting hope. Honestly, it was a foolish emotion, but I couldn't seem to stifle it the way I had for most of my existence.

Not where Lexa was concerned. Unbeknownst to me, I had risen from the bed and positioned myself directly in front of the connecting door. My hands came to rest on the wooden frame, and my gaze fixated on the handle. The footsteps ceased, and the glorious sound of a lock disengaging echoed through the chamber. My breath hitched.

Let me in, Lexa.

I waited for what felt like an unfathomable amount of time, my breath coming out in disjointed spurts as I fought to listen. I could hear her breathing on the other side of the door. Her soft, even breaths were like a siren song, beckoning me to cross the threshold. But I stood still. My forehead came to rest on the wooden barrier as I closed my eyes.

Open the door, little storm.

My subconscious clamored for her, urging me to fling the door wide open and sweep her away to the superfluous circular bed to prove our connection, to show her where she truly belonged and how intensely I belonged to her. Yet, my rational mind held fast to my emotions, anchoring my feet in place. Her trust in me was shattered, rightfully so, after what she saw. The only way to win her back was to demonstrate that I could deserve her trust again. That single conviction restrained me from crashing through the door and illustrating that unbridled passion was not exclusive to members of The Court of Passion.

Eventually, I heard her retreating footsteps, and each step away from me was a piercing dagger to my chest. Through the pain pulsed a wave of relief. She had unlocked the door. And while the barrier remained and my hands were still too far away from her, she unlocked the door. Even if it was minuscule, the trust I must have managed to regain was enough for her to feel a sense of security rather than fear in my presence. And for now, that was enough for me.

As I sulked back to the pathetic excuse for a bed, I found my mind wandering to the tightness in my chest. The rush of emotions I've felt every time I've even glanced her way since the moment our lips first touched. The confusing and overwhelming connection had my mind in a twist. One thing was obvious. I needed to speak to Korzich.

The morning light woke me early, and my left arm felt heavy from its position hanging over the ledge of the farcical bed.

Seriously, why was it a damn circle?

I quickly dressed for the day, donning a pair of lightweight black pants and a thin green tunic before taming my wild mane.

As I turned to bound out the front door, my eyes involuntarily raked over the conjoining door to where I knew my little storm was sleeping just beyond. I reached for the handle, promising myself that I was simply checking on her, ensuring her safety as was my duty. Still, my hand paused, hovering over the golden knob, and I released a sigh. Pressing my ear against the wooden door instead, I felt instant relief at the soft sounds of her even breathing from the other side.

Once satisfied with her safety, I exited my room, ensuring my door was locked, and left to find my sibling.

Although it had been years since my last venture to The Court of Passion and the obnoxiously named Pleasure Tower, I still found my way around reasonably quickly. The halls were lined with remnants of the festival's first night—discarded undergarments, empty vessels of drink and mirth, and the occasional naked participant snoring away.

It was a quick journey to my sibling's private chambers. After briefly listening at the door to ensure I was not interrupting anything I desperately did not wish to witness, I pushed on the ornate double doors.

My sibling's chambers could only be described as an oasis. Leaves and greenery covered nearly every inch of the walls and ceilings, running water trickled across the space, cutting through the makeshift spring. A small path of dark black sand, lit on each side by small torches of Mythica, led me through the bewitching surroundings. I followed the trail, feeling the coarse sand beneath my boots give way with each step until the path ended at a bridge. A bridge that led to a floating platform over water where Korzich laid on a bed - another round one, although this one was nearly thrice the size of mine. Their chest was bare, and the only thing keeping their lower half modest was the mass of bodies that lay atop them. Limbs and torsos tangled to create a web of sated frames.

The wall behind my siblings' bed was not a wall at all but instead a massive waterfall. The running water rushed down to the pool below the platform.

I want a floating bed.

Filing that design choice away for later, I cleared my throat. When the pile of people did not stir, I attempted again, louder this time. My second attempt garnered some attention. Groaning with frustration, some of the guests began to untangle themselves from my sibling, shielding their eyes from the already minimal light in the room.

"Lysander," my sibling greeted me, although they did not move. "Have you come to join us?"

I ignored the rising bile in my throat at the thought of joining them in that bed. "You know I haven't." Was all I said.

"Then go away." Their arms flailed in a lazy attempt to shoo me off. I rolled my eyes and took a step forward.

"We need to talk," I bellowed. My sibling let out a deep sigh as they shifted in their bed.

"You heard my guest, it's time to take your leave." Grumbled annoyances rang from their sleepy mouths as they slid from the floating platform and hurried past me, revealing the very naked form of Korzich beneath them. I averted my eyes.

"Well, do I have a few minutes to get dressed? Or are we doing this now?"

I scoffed. "Meet me in your office when you're decent." As I turned to leave, I heard their laugh behind me.

"You'll be waiting a long time for that, brother." I heard the telltale sounds of their body creaking with movement as they stood, so I decided not to poke the proverbial bear a moment longer.

I made my way to their office, which I knew was across the hall, and helped myself to the amber liquid on the bar in the corner. Korzich's office was similar to my own chamber, with dark walls, dramatic drapes, and lighting. A red leather lounge couch sat in the center of the room, just in front of the large wooden desk. I dared not sit on it. I was going to operate under the assumption that most surfaces in this tower had been utilized during an activity I'd rather not focus energy on imagining.

I had taken three burning sips of the alcohol before my sibling threw open the doors and stepped into the room. They had draped a gossamer robe across their shoulders, and it was tied loosely at their waist, thankfully covering most of their form. Their obsidian hair elegantly hung down their back to rest just above their waist, and their expression was one of pure satisfaction. The dark black cloud of their Mythica encircled their neck and draped over their shoulders like a necklace of jewels, sensually caressing their skin as they walked, leaving a wisp of shadow with each step they took.

"Brother, welcome back to The Court of Passion." Korzich embraced me, and I jolted momentarily before settling into their hold. "How are you enjoying the Endless Night Festival?" They glided across the floor to their bar and poured themselves a drink from their decanter.

"Your Court's shamelessness never fails to surprise me, sibling," I smirked as they laughed before lying down on the chaise, their body twisting suggestively. I rolled my eyes. "Although knowing you, it shouldn't."

"How is our dear Miss Cromwell?" They asked, and I couldn't stop the possessive growl that rumbled in my chest at the word 'our,' as if my sibling had any right to stake a claim on my little storm. Logic returned to me as I reminded myself that I, too, had no claim on her. I released a sigh. Korzich watched me knowingly, raising an eyebrow. "I trust you've found your accommodations satisfactory? I made arrangements for everything you requested."

I nodded. "I appreciate that."

They smiled silently, waiting for me to continue.

"She's been through a lot these past weeks. Things I need to share with you."

Korzich nodded tentatively, taking a sip from their drink.

"Alright, I'm listening." And to their credit, they were.

I glanced around the room, desperate to sit but anxious that I wouldn't find an unsoiled surface. Instead, I remained standing. Gripping my drink in my hand, I paced. "What is it, Lysander?"

"Miss Cromwell was attacked. Twice." Four times, if you count the strange occurrences in the fountain and the bath. However, I hadn't decided if I was ready to tell them about that. Korzich sat upright at the edge of seriousness in my tone.

"Attacked? By who? Was she harmed?" They set their drink down as their eyes flashed with worry.

"She was injured, but nothing that won't heal."

Korzich placed their forehead in their hands.

"You're supposed to be protecting her," they accused.

I nearly rushed forward and gripped their throat as anger bubbled over."I have protected her every time. Do not question my ability to care for her," I snapped. My eyes burned into theirs, and I saw a slight upturn in the corner of their lips.

"Who is responsible? I assume you questioned them?" They prompted. I shook my head, ashamed that I had let the first assailant get away. Had I known then that the attack would turn into a persistent and ongoing threat, had I known it was targeted and not some random thief in the night, I would have given chase. I would have gotten answers. I would have protected her better.

"I fought the first man off, assuming he was simply a looter, and let him go. It wasn't until I saw what he painted on the side of my carriage that I realized he was anything but a simple thief." My voice was low, full of regret.

Korzich had to have noticed because they stood and placed a comforting hand on my shoulder. "What did he paint?"

I breathed cautiously, knowing the following few words had the potential to change everything.

"The symbol of The Forgotten Court." Silence permeated the air.

Korzich's eyes widened, and their hand dropped from my shoulder. "Impossible," they claimed.

I shook my head. "I wish it were, Korzich."

It was their turn to pace now, and they moved across the space slowly, their hands rubbing at their temples.

"And the second attack?" They prompted.

"Another man, presumably the same as the first attack, although I have no way to know for certain." I downed my drink, the amber liquid burning my chest on its way down. "He defiled her quarters with painted symbols of The Forgotten Court and nearly managed to steal her away. Had it not been for the dagger I gave her, he might have succeeded." I shuddered to think of that possibility. The thought of losing her, how close I had been to failing her…

"She killed him?" Korzich interrupted my spiral.

I nodded my answer.

Korzich's eyebrows furrowed, and they studied the floor at their feet. "This attacker was a member of your Court?"

I inhaled sharply, knowing that the next facet of information was something that was not only dangerous but could alter everything we've ever known about the Courts and Verihdia as a whole. The careful security we've crafted and upheld since eradicating the Forgotten Court hung in the balance.

"He had my Court Mark." I swallowed the lump in my throat and avoided their eyes. Korzich observed me, their black eyes scanning my face. "And he had the Mark of the Forgotten Court." The air in the room felt as if it stilled. A cold, creeping dread made its way through my bloodstream as I surveyed my now pale-faced sibling.

"That can't be.." they whispered, although the apparent fear in their expression and the way their Mythica trembled told me they knew it to be true.

"I fear our past missteps may be coming back to haunt us," I spoke quietly, although, in the room's silence, even my gentle whisper resounded like a scream.

"No one should remember that Mark, Lysander."

I nodded. "I know, but someone does."

Silence. Fear.

The unknown.

"Looks like we were mistaken," Korzich finally broke the quiet. "It's not simply the seven Courts of Verihdia that are interested in Miss Cromwell. It's all eight."

I lifted my eyes to them. "They will not take her," I growled, and Korzich raised their hands in mock surrender.

"You've taken your role quite seriously, Lysander."

"I am responsible for her safety during this tour, am I not?" I replied.

They nodded.

"Isn't it in our best interests that I take this position seriously?" I continued, attempting to keep my voice even.

"Of course." They moved away from me, refilling their drink at the bar cart in the corner. A slight hum of amusement escaped their lips. I rolled my eyes.

"Say it."

"Say what?" They asked innocently but did not turn to face me.

"Say whatever it is that has you acting like you're a schoolgirl with a secret."

They turned, placing a hand on their chest, and scoffed emphatically. "Whatever do you mean?" They winked at me while taking a sip of their drink. I stared at them with an expression I hoped told them how little I believed in the charade they were putting on.

"I'm simply noting how attached you seem to be to our-" They paused, noticing the involuntary rumbling in my chest again. "Apologies. *Your*, Miss Cromwell," they corrected.

"She is not mine," I stated, although what I attempted as a declaration sounded more like a plea.

"Yes, well." They returned to their seat on the chaise lounge. "If she were, it would certainly have made this entire tour more complicated, wouldn't it?"

I didn't need to tell them just how complicated it had already become.

A knock sounded at the door, and instinctively, I turned to it and braced myself. Korzich didn't comment on my paranoia, something I was thankful for, but instead called out to the door.

"Enter."

As the double doors swung open, I felt my chest tighten at the sight of our guest. Her long black hair had been combed and hung freely down her back in loose waves. Her curvy form was draped in a red dress that hugged her breasts tightly and flared out at the waist. Her blue eyes shone from the sunlight pouring into the room from the windows. Each step captivated me. Each movement drew me in.

Korzich cleared their throat, and I pulled my gaze from her to see that my sibling had a curious look on their face and an eyebrow raised at me in a challenge.

"Miss Cromwell, you look positively ravishing this morning." Korzich danced across the room and gripped Lexa's hand in theirs, kissing it gently. I had to dig my fingernails into the palm of my hand to keep myself from throwing them off of her for even thinking they were permitted to touch her. I watched the place where their skin touched hers and tried not to think about how long it's been since my own skin grazed hers.

"Thank you, Warden." She bowed her head, a flush creeping onto her perfect skin.

"I trust you found your accommodations -" they glanced over their shoulder at me - "suitable."

She nodded. "Your Tower is gorgeous, and the room was very comfortable. Thank you." She glanced at me, a soft smile on her pink lips.

"Lysander and I were just discussing your unfortunate encounter."

Fear crossed her expression, and her chest heaved with unsettled breaths. The cloud of Mythica that followed and protected her constantly seemed to beat in time with her rapid heartbeats.

"I informed Korzich of the attack in the carriage and the man from your chambers," I quickly added. I saw the worry slip from her face, and her breathing settled.

"Right, of course," she responded, turning her attention back to Korzich.

"You must have been so afraid." They brushed a finger against her shoulder.

Lexa's head fell forward, and her eyes trained on the ground.

"I'm glad that you were able to defend yourself," Korzich continued.

She nodded but did not respond.

"Did you use your Mythica?" They asked.

Her head snapped up again, guilt plaguing her expression. "What?" She gasped, her Mythica lashing out in violent swipes above her head.

"Your Mythica, did you use it on your assailant?" Korzich clarified, an inquisitive look on their face. They were trying to make sense of the way she reacted.

She released a breath, sighing. "Right, yes. Uh, I did."

I raised an eyebrow. She didn't tell me that she had used her Mythica on him. However, we hadn't really discussed the event in detail. I wasn't sure she wanted to. Maybe I should have asked.

Damn, my selfishness.

"And what did you discover?" My sibling prompted. I leaned in, mentally cursing myself for not discussing this with her earlier.

She glanced over at me briefly before continuing. "He said, 'We need you to save us.'"

My heart rate quickened.

Korzich rubbed their chin in their hand, doing an excellent job of hiding their internal monologue that was most likely matching my own. "Us?"

She shrugged, tossing a look in my direction. "I don't know who he was referring to."

Korzich's eyes met mine in a knowing glance. I tried to maintain my expression, not letting the shock I felt show on my face. Lexa saw the symbol in her room. She knew the Forgotten Court had something to do with it but kept it close to her chest for now. I silently thanked her for thinking so quickly. If my sibling had known I had told her what the symbol meant, things could have gotten out of hand.

"Anything else?" They asked. She nodded, taking another breath.

"He said that if I wasn't good enough, they were out of options."

My mind was swimming. Out of options? Good enough? The thought of The Forgotten Court aiming to use Lexa as a pawn brought bile to my throat. A dark thought crossed my mind. There were a few reasons someone in The Forgotten Court might want someone with Lexa's abilities. I hoped to the Gods that I was wrong. Maybe that wasn't it. Perhaps they were hoping to kidnap her and use her for ransom. Or use her to force the Wardens to admit their sins against the Forgotten Warden?

The most concerning part of this scenario is that I would admit to everything for her—no matter the consequences. I'd do it if it meant she was safe.

"Interesting," Korzich mused. They glanced at me again before moving across the room to their desk. We needed to uncover what these Double Marked individuals wanted with Lexa and their connection to the Forgotten Court. And soon. "I want to assure you that you are safe in my Court, Miss Cromwell, and if you'd let me, I'd love to show you around."

Lexa nodded cautiously without glancing in my direction.

"I hope you understand, Lysander, why I'd like to accompany Miss Cromwell alone." Their eyes met mine, a sort of challenge glistening in them.

"But I should-" I began, but my sibling raised a hand to cut me off.

"I'd like Lexa to experience my Court on her own, without the influence of you and your opinions."

It made sense. Logically. I guess. But I couldn't help feeling entirely helpless at the prospect of her falling in love with another Court. "Of course." I nodded my head and slowly went to take my leave, stopping just beside Lexa. My shoulder nearly brushed against hers. The minuscule space between us felt charged. I leaned down to whisper to her, relishing how her breath caught in her throat at my proximity."If you need me, call my name. I'll be there." I promised.

She nodded, her crystal eyes locked on mine, words and emotions unspoken passed between us as our eyes conversed more openly than I had with anyone in my entire life.

"She will be safe with me," Korzich spoke from their spot behind their desk. Their eyes surveyed us, and I knew they had picked up on the somewhat confusing attraction that took root and was budding between us. Spotting lust was just one of their many talents. They were the Warden of Passion, after all.

I had another question for my sibling that I believed I knew the answer to but simply needed confirmation. Yet, I wasn't prepared to hear the response, and I sensed they might not be ready to divulge it either. So, instead, I sauntered out of Korzich's office and left my little storm behind.

Thirteen

The Court of Passions was hot. I knew that before venturing through the veil. But spending some days in Oliver's class sweating through my shirt was one thing, and actually being here, feeling the sticky heat caress my skin from the bright sun above, or feeling an unexpected rush of euphoria at even the slightest brush of cool wind was another thing entirely. It seemed my body was perpetually overheating, and I'm sure my forehead was on the verge of perspiring profusely.

On Korzich, the unfairly stunning Warden in front of me, the sweat basked their already beautiful skin with a glistening sheen that glimmered like starlight across their face, whereas I'm sure I looked like a drowned creature with my hair unfortunately plastered against my forehead.

Although, perhaps the haunting emptiness of my dreams last night had something to do with the flames that licked against my skin moreso than the Court's heat. The nightmares hadn't returned in full, but they felt closer somehow. Like they were poised and ready, just on the outskirts of my consciousness, fighting for a way into my mind again.

"At last, we're alone." Korzich smiled an almost devious grin. I fingered the light fabric of my blood-red dress awkwardly. "You don't need to be afraid of me, Miss Cromwell."

I shook my head, swallowing the lump in my throat. "I'm not afraid," I spoke clearly. "And please call me Lexa."

Their eyes lit up, and a small chuckle escaped their painted lips. "Lexa it is then." They glided across the floor of their study toward the desk, their dark robe billowing behind them, offering a dramatic flare to each movement of their body. I followed behind at a comfortable distance. They stopped just before the large wooden structure and turned back to me, a mischievous look playing on their features. "How are you liking my Court thus far? I sincerely hope you've enjoyed yourself." They asked simply, a hint of innuendo in their tone.

"Your Court is beautiful, Warden," I offered truthfully. They smiled sweetly. "Thank you for being such a gracious host."

"You're uncomfortable," they mused, raising an eyebrow.

"Not at all." I stammered unconvincingly. They eyed me with a knowing look. "Is it obvious?"

A laugh escaped their lips as their head fell back. "Not to everyone, love, but I've spent most of my life reading people and understanding their desires…" They paused for a moment and scanned me with their eyes. "Which, I guess, is something you can agree with?" They prompted.

I nodded, swallowing the lump in my throat.

"How does that work?" They asked.

My blood ran cold, and I forced myself to maintain composure. Did they already know? Did Lysander tell them about my Mythica working on him? Was this a test? Uncomfortable heat bloomed in my chest as my breathing became shallow.

"My Mythica?" I confirmed.

They nodded.

Taking a settling breath, I smiled shakily. "Right, well, what do you know about it already?" I could convince myself that I asked it because I wanted to gauge what they had been told, to see if they'd show their hand…but in reality, I asked to give myself a few more moments of preparation.

"I know you have a talent for finding the things people tend to hide." Korzich made their way to the chaise lounge and sunk into the leather. Their body settled into a sensual position, and I fixed my gaze on their eyes to avoid looking at the space where their robe fell open. "Is that a fair assumption?"

"Essentially, yes," I answered carefully. Dropping my eyes to the ground at my feet, I continued. I wasn't necessarily a lousy liar. I just hated the feeling of guilt that often accompanied a lie. That was the part that I tried to avoid when I could. "It's like a silent question, a thought. All I have to do is imagine the question I want the answer to, and I can determine a person's fear, desire, or… guilt."

Korzich leaned their head back onto the chaise, pondering my words. I took the moment free from their burning gaze to venture across the floor to the window. I could see for miles from this vantage point in the Tower. The town surrounding the tower's base was quiet, with very minimal activity. Clearly, the residents were still sleeping off their eventful evenings. Beyond that, dunes of black glistening sand framed the bottom of a purple morning sky. I had not spent much time in this Court, but it wasn't hard to notice the difference between how I felt looking out over this expanse of the desert and the way I felt riding through Everwatch in The Court of Shadows.

I couldn't possibly belong in The Court of Shadows, not after everything, but I certainly felt more at home there than I do here. I could acknowledge that. Although, I had a month left in this Court to be sure of it. I heard faint footsteps behind me. Bare feet on wood. Their presence was magnetic behind me.

"You are fascinating, Miss… I'm sorry, Lexa," they corrected themselves. I turned to find them a few feet behind me. "Join me today for a tour of my Court?" They extended their hand to me, and I rested mine in theirs.

We journeyed in comfortable silence for a time. We started at the very top of their Pleasure Tower and worked slowly down floor by floor until we reached the ground floor that emptied onto the main street of Lustrada. The citizens of this Court did not smile eagerly at Korzich as we passed. They did not offer welcoming pleasantries, unlike the treatment Lysander earned from his people. Instead, the crowds parted and watched Korzich pass with quiet admiration and lust-filled expressions. These gazes had no familiarity but rather a desire for their body, not the person inhabiting it. For the second time in many days, I missed the comforting warmth of The Court of Shadows.

Hours passed while Korzich regaled tales of the many lascivious events that had graced their Court, and there were many. I listened intently, determined to give this Court a fair and honest shot, but the longer they spoke, the more the feeling of being misplaced settled in the pit of my stomach.

We had arrived back at the Tower just as the sun crawled toward the horizon in search of its evening rest. Korzich turned their black eyes on me, and I was reminded instantly of how exposed a simple pair of eyes can make a person feel and how much I enjoyed Lysander exposing me.

"This is where I must end our tour for the day. This evening's festivities will begin shortly, and I am nothing if not a prompt host." They chuckled, and I couldn't help the blush that crept onto my skin at the thought of another night filled with writhing bodies and sinful deeds. "Please feel free to participate or watch . . . but most of all, feel free to stay put in your quarters if that makes you feel most comfortable."

I wasn't able to hide the shock in my expression.

"I may be the Warden of Passion, and while I enjoy seeing and participating in the culture here, I understand not everyone feels the same. I believe in pushing boundaries, and discovering yourself, but above all, I believe in consent. Don't feel pressured to do anything you do not wish to do while in my Court, Lexa."

A weight I hadn't previously known was pressing down on me, lifted at that. A small comfort that I desperately clung to. "Thank you, Warden." I bowed my head slightly in thanks.

A finger gripped my chin and lifted until my eyes met theirs. They were close to me, and their warm breath tickled my lips. My eyes widened as they held my gaze.

"Something tells me, though, Miss Cromwell, that you've already sampled the life you could have here in the Court, haven't you?" Their nose hovered inches from mine before slowly trailing down to my neck, their closeness leaving a trail of bumps on my skin. "You've given into a desire, haven't you?"

My breath caught in my throat as the memory threatened to surface. "Maybe…" I responded meekly, perplexed by this Warden's attention. I was equally perplexed why my body was not having the same reaction to their advances that it had the night of the Courting Ball.

"You know," they started, their chest nearly touching mine. "There's often a misconception that people have when they think of my Court." My skin warmed under their heated hold. "They think that because we are passionate, because we indulge in our lustful fantasies, we must be immoral. They think that our desires are sinful." A mischievous light glistened in their eye, and their hand gripped my shoulder.

"Aren't they?" I asked breathlessly, my cheeks heating at the memory of Lysander's eyes watching me as my fingers drew passion from my body like his own personal marionette. It felt pretty sinful to me.

"Do you believe falling in love is wrong, Miss Cromwell?"

Did I?

I titled my head, my eyes scanning their sharp, angular face. They waited patiently for an answer. "Of course not, but I'm not-" they lifted a finger and placed it across my lips, effectively silencing me.

"You will not be pressured to indulge in any sins you do not wish to partake in. However, I encourage you to acknowledge that it's okay to desire them." They lingered momentarily, their dark eyes watching me before winking and taking off.

I allowed myself only a moment of confusion before returning to my room. I was feeling the slight caress of exhaustion, and no matter what Korzich said, I wasn't ready to partake in the activities of the Endless Night Festival.

As I trekked through the elegant hallways of the Pleasure Tower, I pondered their parting words. Was I holding back because I didn't belong here, or was I holding back because I felt like I couldn't? Was a person ever truly suited ideally for just one Court? Just one sin? Or was I right to assume that we are multifaceted individuals who cannot and should not be placed into tiny boxes?

I turned the corner down the corridor where my quarters were when I caught a glimpse of a handsome young man leaning against my door frame. Like many people in The Court of Passion, he was shirtless. His lower half was wrapped in dark black pants. His bright red hair was shaggy, but his waves landed just above his reddish-brown eyebrows. My heart skipped a beat, and my feet stilled. Was this another attacker? Was he here to proposition me? The possibilities were never-ending, and each theory was more nerve-wracking than the last.

Just as I decided and gathered enough courage to turn and retreat, the man noticed my presence. His eyes flicked up to meet mine, and I noticed they were nearly golden in color, with dark flecks painting his irises. His mouth spread into a deep smile, revealing straight white teeth. His friendly demeanor slowly went to work at melting the frigid nerves that held me captive.

"Lexa, right?" He said as he kicked off the wall and made to approach me. My fingers slowly went for the hilt of the dagger at my side. "Whoa," he said, lifting his hands. "The name's Kael. We were at the Institute together, remember?"

I studied his face. I did recognize him now that he mentioned it, but he was a few years older than me, so I didn't know much about him.

"I've been assigned to train you during your stay with us." He crossed his arms. My eyebrows furrowed. "My Warden informed me that your guide, the Warden of Shadows, requested it." He spoke tentatively as if my reaction had him rethinking his previous excitement.

Something dislodged in my chest. Like a section of the cracked wall I had begun to rebuild between Lysander and me had come tumbling down.

"That was thoughtful of him," I replied. To myself primarily, but Kael chuckled in response.

"Well, let's not forget who he is. Chances are, he will require something in return. Isn't that how he operates?" The angry part of me wanted to agree, to launch into a tirade about how selfish my guide was and how evil he could be. Still, the part of me that had been unwillingly exposed to the private side of this multi-layered Warden, the side I was beginning to understand, knew that it wasn't true. I didn't, however, have it in me to argue.

"So, you will be training me?" I asked, expertly moving the subject away from Lysander and into a safer topic, like fighting.

"I will." An eager smile painted his mouth. I glanced down at their hands, wrapped in a piece of white fabric.

"When do we start?"

He shrugged, and his muscular shoulders seemed even heavier as he tried to lift them. He did not have quite the same physique as Chandler, but it was impressive nonetheless. "That depends," he said, leaning back onto the wall behind him, crossing his arms casually.

"On?" I prompted. He smiled, a sort of cocky lopsided smile that was handsome but in the kind of way that made me think of Chandler, not Lysander.

"Do you want to be weak?"

A shocked grunt escaped my mouth. Kael didn't turn to watch me but instead looked down at his bandaged hands, which, upon further inspection, were covered in deep purple bruises in varying states of healing.

"I'm tired of feeling weak," I answered honestly.

"Then your training starts now." He kicked off the wall and started down the hallway, calling over his shoulder. "Follow me."

"I'm in a dress!" I yelled out after him. In a flash, too quick for me to comprehend, Kael had moved back into my space. His leg swept mine out from under me, and my entire center of gravity shifted until I was falling backward.

Panic didn't have time to register, though, before his arms caught my fall, cradling me against his bare chest. I gasped when I registered that his face was nearly inches from mine.

"If someone wants to hurt you, they aren't going to wait until you're dressed appropriately," he whispered to me, and I felt his fingers tighten their hold on me as if to drive home his point.

I pressed my palms against his shoulders and pushed off of him until he understood what I wanted and helped me stand. I took a few steps away from him, staggering back to regain the composure I didn't have.

"Come on then," he responded gleefully, a hint of amusement in his golden eyes as he turned on his heel and disappeared around the corner. I schooled my expression, ignoring the feeling of worthlessness and embarrassment that flooded me, and followed him.

He led me to the second floor. Despite the Tower bustling with activity as its inhabitants prepared for another endless night, the room he led me to was empty. The walls and floor were the same dark color as the rest of the Tower, but the vast open space looked like a training facility of some kind. The Verihdian Institute also had one, much smaller in size but similarly equipped. I'd only accompanied Axel one time before deciding never to return.

A mat lay in the center of the space, covering most of the floor, while along the walls were various objects used for what I assumed was strength training. Weighted plates were stacked against the dark wall near the single window. A large sack hung from the ceiling. From my time with my twin, I remembered that people would hit this object with their fists. I recall cringing every time the sound of flesh hitting weighted fabric echoed through the training facility.

Kael sauntered into the space, leaving me by the entryway to absorb the sight on my own. He crossed the mat and stopped just before a bench, taking a seat. I moved slowly toward the bench and stood cautiously beside it, watching Kael for instruction.

I am so incredibly out of my depth here.

"What's our first lesson?" I asked him as he went to work, tightening and securing his bandaged hands.

"Normally, we'd start slowly, build up your strength and endurance." He stood and made his way to the center of the mat. I followed him with my eyes but remained in my spot. "Normally, we'd work our way up to self-defense and combat only after you've mastered control of your own body." His eyes scanned my frame at that, and I tried to fight the urge to throw my arms in front of me in cover. "Normally, I'd have months, even years, to craft you into a skilled fighter. But we don't have months, do we?"

It was rhetorical, but I felt the need to shake my head anyway. He was right, and not even in the way he intended. I had one month here in this Court, yes, but The Forgotten Court could send someone else at any time. For all I know, the water could try to claim me again tonight. No, I didn't have months or years. I had minutes. Minutes I intended to spend preparing myself to fight back.

I slid my shoes off, and my bare feet plotted across the room until I stepped onto the slightly raised mat. It felt softer against the souls of my feet than the hardwood floors but solid enough that it would still be painful to be slammed onto it.

"Ok, I'm ready." I stood my ground. Kael smiled at me, his eyes alight with a sort of anxious thrill.

The next hour passed in a flash of sweat, pain, and anger.

By the time Kael lifted his body off of mine after pinning me to the ground for the nearly twentieth time, I was panting, and I felt the strain of our training already claiming my muscles.

"That's good for today," Kael said, reaching a hand down for me. His tan skin was glistening with a slight sheen of sweat, not nearly as embarrassingly red as mine, though.

He helped me back to my feet and chuckled lightly at my groan. "Now, when you can't walk tomorrow, be sure to tell everyone that was my doing." He didn't withdraw his hand from mine as his gaze traveled my body again, and I rolled my eyes. "You did well enough today. But if you're going to be halfway decent by the time you leave this Court, you need to go harder." His hand tightened its hold on mine, and he leaned forward. Just a foot remained between us.

"When are we meeting again?" I asked him between labored breaths.

"Whenever you want us to." He smiled again, but this time, his eyes showed a hint of flirtation. "While you're in this Court, Lexa, I'm yours. You call, I come." He winked at the innuendo, and I felt an unwelcome blush creep onto my face. I pulled my hand from his and turned to retrieve my shoes. I heard his dark chuckle behind me.

"Not comfortable with being so sexually open yet?" He teased, following closely to put his shoes back on.

"I'm sorry, were you trying to flirt with me? I thought you had something in your eye."

His laugh vibrated deep in my chest. I slipped my shoes on and quickly made for the exit.

"See you tomorrow?" He strolled past me towards the door, leaning on the doorway and waiting for me.

"If you're lucky," I shot back, annoyed by his teasing. I heard him laugh as I bounded past him and left the room.

The evening's festivities were in full swing as I made my way through the corridors of the Pleasure Tower. I was sweaty, and my skin showed that red tint of exertion, which was not entirely unlike the people I saw gleefully exploring the Tower, so I didn't immediately feel out of place. Curiosity bit at the back of my neck, hair standing on edge as I took in my surroundings.

Blatant and graphic sexuality was indeed the most inherent quality of the night, but beneath that, there was an air of excitement, of freedom. Before it registered, my feet had taken me down the main steps and out the front door.

I had seen most of what Lustrada had to offer today during Korzich's tour, but something told me that this Court thrived in the dark, and the charged energy I felt the moment I stepped outside instantly confirmed that theory. While there had been shops opened and joyful citizens roaming around in the daylight, now, under cover of night, in the pool of moonlight, I felt it. The Court of Passion.

The air was chillier than it had been during the day, no doubt due to the lack of blistering sunlight, but still warm. Like a comforting embrace, it licked at my sweat-covered skin. This town felt different down here on the ground than it had from my perch atop the camel last night as we arrived, but no less exhilarating. From this perspective, I saw more than just the naked forms and writhing bodies - which were still present, of course - but as I walked among them, I noticed a different kind of Passion. The bizarre was a glorious collection of shops, all seeming to be filled with crafted creations. Woven silks, forged jewelry, hand-baked loaves of bread and treats, and art. So much art.

My eyes didn't know where to look as I walked along the main thoroughfare of Lustrada. Mythica-lighted strings hung above the walkways in a crossing formation, casting ample but sensual lighting over the citizens below. The buildings and huts lining the path were adorned with sumptuous drapes and cascading vines of fragrant flowers. Soft, charged music filled the air, played by skilled musicians using exotic instruments like the harp, lute, and sultry flutes. The moon and stars cast a soft, romantic glow over the proceedings, enhancing the atmosphere of seduction.

I saw things differently now. Where last night, I had only seen the kissing forms, locked at the mouth, I hadn't noticed the exchange of thoughtful gifts that led to pure moments of intimacy. Where last night I'd only seen bodies joined recklessly and haphazardly, I hadn't noticed the devotion to safety and consent that I was seeing now that I was among it. Every booth was decorated with silk ribbons and gossamer fabrics in rich, deep shades of crimson, black, and gold. Candlelit lanterns and fragrant incense burned brightly at each station, diffusing intoxicating scents that teased my senses and beckoned me to follow it further into the heart of seduction.

Statues and sculptures depicting graceful, entwined lovers stood as towering works of art as I wandered through the streets, adding to the sensuous ambiance. We were not taught these things at the Verihdian Institute, and yet these were the things that made a Court what it was.

How are students expected to choose when they'll never see this?

That evening, I learned more about The Court of Passion than I had in all my years of schooling. That thought weighed heavy on me as I continued my exploration of the shops and activities. I felt more comfortable around such public displays of intimacy, despite what the perpetual blush that found residence on my face might have said to the contrary.

By the time I arrived at a minor stage nestled in the center of Lustrada among the stalls of food and art, I was feeling invincible. Musicians in various states of undress played a joyful tune. Their flutes and stringed instruments combined to form an almost gleeful melody. Patrons stood at the base of the stage, dancing happily and suggestively with partners, with groups, even alone. It was addictive. The energy. The excitement. The freedom. I wanted to soak every ounce of it up.

As the night continued, the festival-goers progressively lost themselves in the intoxicating atmosphere of The Court of Passion. The air was filled with laughter, desire, and whispered confessions of love. I understood the appeal instantly. This Endless Night Festival was where passions were ignited, and memories were made, leaving those who attended longing for the eternal pleasures that The Court of Passion promised. I now understood why this night was so important and why Korzich was so adamant that I attend their Court this week. The Endless Night Festival is a celebration of sensuality, desire, and indulgence, offering an escape into a world where pleasure knows no bounds and the night is alive with irresistible temptations.

I stood for a moment, mesmerized by the music and how it invited its listeners to let go before my feet began to move on their own accord. Slowly, at first, as if they were unsure how to complete the movement. I took careful steps in time with the tempo of the music that was seeping into my ears and vibrating inside my chest timidly. Still, by the time the musicians seamlessly transitioned into a second song, I was swaying with the swell of music. My hair tossed haphazardly around my face, my arms stretching in every direction as I spun and spun. A laugh bubbled out of me, erupting from the deepest part of myself. A part of myself I hadn't let myself ever truly embrace. At that moment, the strain in my muscles was forgotten, and I welcomed it.

My vision began to blur as I spun, smiling faces, twinkling stars, dangling lights. With each rotation, I noticed something new. I let my arms fall out, fanning out wide with the force of my spin as I watched the world around me become a mess of colors. I felt a pair of eyes on me, and before I could panic, I caught a glimpse of him. His dark skin seemed to glow under the lights, and he wore a light sage shirt, unbuttoned low enough to be obscene for his Court but high enough to be modest for this one. As I continued spinning, I thought I saw a smile on his face. I felt even more alive now that I knew his emerald eyes were on me. I wondered briefly if he thought my display was childish or if he could tell how desperately I needed this moment. I allowed myself to make eye contact with him as I spun, watching him as intently as he seemed to be watching me. I found myself momentarily ensnared in the electric current of a passionate connection as my eyes locked onto his for a brief moment on each rotation. His deep, dark skin was a captivating contrast to his irises' vivid, enigmatic shade. The green of his eyes was reminiscent of lush, untamed forests, and they seemed to hold the secrets of countless whispered desires. His arms were crossed nonchalantly across his broad chest as he stared. His smile was prominent now. I saw his shoulders shaking with laughter on one of my spins as he took in my display. I didn't stop. I couldn't. It felt like with each rotation, another piece of stress fell away. And despite my body feeling heavy with the weight of gravity, I had never felt lighter.

In that instant, a fire ignited within me, a slow and smoldering heat that coursed through my veins, starting at my core and spreading across my body. It's as if an invisible thread was binding my soul to his. At that moment, an unspoken understanding of the magnetic attraction that had been pulling us together was licking at my skin like the flames of an all-consuming blaze. In that shared gaze was a wordless promise of sensuality and adventure, an invitation to explore the depths of whatever connection this was.

It's too much.

I ripped my eyes away from Lysander to scan the crowd, taking in each face, the blur of color, and the flash of light. The sights and sounds of the festival became a cacophony. The music, the laughter, and the arousing atmosphere all seemed to intensify, creating an overwhelming sensory overload. It was disorienting. The weight of his stare was too much to bear. A sense of urgency swelled within me as I desperately scanned the crowd, seeking any distraction that could spare me from the heat of his gaze connection. My heart quickened, and the festival goers appeared as fleeting, blurred faces. As I turned my head in search of an escape, my eyes inadvertently landed on something. Amidst the revelry, I caught a glimpse of a taunting symbol on the periphery of the festivities. An eerie feeling washed over me, forming a pit in the depths of my stomach. My joyful spinning abruptly stopped when my eyes focused enough to comprehend what I was seeing.

My heart was racing, and my breath came in ragged spurts as I stared at the side of the tent through the bustling energy of the festival. I could only see it briefly through the eager crowd as they walked past, unaware of this symbol and why it was haunting me—the painted Mark of the Forgotten Court.

Lysander was at my side in an instant.

"What's wrong?" He pleaded with me over the music and the loud crowd that seemed dull to me now. His eyes surveyed me. "Did you make yourself dizzy?" Now that he mentioned it, my head felt like it was swimming, and the pressure forced the world around me to tilt on its axis. However, I wasn't entirely sure if it resulted from my dance moves or this ghost that had once again found me.

I didn't answer. I wasn't sure I could. As I stood, my eyes locked on the white paint, the raven, the crocus…I saw the blood again. I felt it on my skin, the way it was warm but thick. The way it had crawled across the floor until the majority of the wooden boards had been painted with the stolen essence of his life. The one I ended.

Lysander tore his eyes from me to follow my gaze. His body stiffened next to mine when he saw what it was that had caught my eye. I felt him prepare to take a step toward it but stop when he glanced back at me. I envied how he was able to rip his eyes from the Mark. I certainly couldn't.

"Miss Cromwell..." he called, but still, I couldn't bring myself to look away. I feared even if I had, the images of that man's lifeless body would remain. Suddenly, Lysanders's large frame came into view, effectively blocking the Mark, and I took a breath for the first time since seeing it. "Don't look at it, look at me. Right at me." He demanded softly. He stood close to me but was careful not to let his skin touch mine, still keeping his promise. I focused on him then. Worry painted his expression. His stare grounded me the way it always seemed to. He breathed, and my shoulders rose and fell with his as oxygen filled my lungs.

"That's it, Miss Cromwell. Breathe."

I nodded, listening to him without injecting my usual level of argument but slowly feeling more like myself in his presence. My hand found the hilt of my dagger between my skirts.

"We need to get you out of here," he whispered.

Again, I agreed.

Lysander did not grip my hand or hold my body close to his the way he had after finding me kneeling over that body in the Forsaken Quarters, but his tone was no less comforting. I felt the concern lacing each of his movements as he ushered me back through the crowd, carefully keeping his body between myself and the Mark. His eyes scanned the area with a quiet fury, no doubt attempting to catch sight of the macabre artist. With each step, I regained the pieces of myself that the haunting memory threatened to steal from me.

"I need to see it," I said, my voice coming out low, restrained, but no less full of the fire that was burning within.

"You do not have to subject yourself to that." Lysander had not torn his eyes from their survey of the crowd.

"I know."

His emerald eyes finally landed on mine again, and he nodded despite the concern etched on his face.

I pushed past him through the festive gathering to the offending tent. The paint smell hit my nostrils like a vicious serpent striking its prey. I shook my head, pushing the scent from my olfactory memory. Lysander was there, his head on a constant swivel, his body tense and prepared. I wondered briefly if whoever painted this was still in the vicinity. And if so, what were they hoping to achieve from this display?

I gently brushed the tips of my fingers along the feathers of the painted raven, pulling them away to reveal the cold, wet paint had transferred to my skin.

"This was just painted moments ago." The thought should have frightened me, but instead, I found myself pulling my dagger free from its holster on my leg and gripping it angrily between my now-painted fingers.

"They're still here," Lysander whispered, sending a ripple of goosebumps erupting along my skin. Although not from fear, surprisingly.

I glanced around the crowd, seeing faces differently than I had just moments ago. These smiling expressions could now be nothing more than a hidden truth, a mask.

"Let's get back to the Tower," Lysander said, never tearing his eyes from the surrounding crowd as he dragged his hand through the wet paint. The symbol disappeared in the smeared streaks, but the image was burnt in my mind. "Stay behind me." He urged, and then we pushed through the eager audience, my heart pounding with each step.

My heart pounded, and a sense of dread washed over me. We made a quick but discreet exit through the crowd, the festival's enchantment replaced by a gnawing sense of unease. As we retreated from the festival's enticing allure, I couldn't help but wonder about the mysterious artist. The Court of Passion, which was just a few moments ago, a realm of passion and desire, now held a darker and more threatening aura. I felt my body tense at the thought.

I was being watched. I could feel it in every fiber of my being. At first, it was just a subtle feeling, an inexplicable discomfort that made my skin prickle, but soon enough, I felt their gaze dance along my skin like a vicious wind, a taunting breeze. As the unsettling stare weighed on me, I felt vulnerable. The festival's music, laughter, and seductive allure now felt like distant echoes, drowned out by the ominous presence. I didn't know what direction the presence was coming from or what they had hoped to see when they looked at me. Were they hoping to see me break? To see the fear they were trying to plant etched clearly on my face? That thought forced me to take deep, steady breaths and stand tall with shoulders back as I followed Lysander, snaking through the crowd to the Tower. If they wanted my fear, they were going to be disappointed.

Lysander must have had a similar thought because he was the picture of unbothered strength. Together, we navigated the labyrinthine pathways of the festival, putting distance between ourselves and the unsettling presence that had watched me. The festival's atmosphere gradually returned to its alluring and enchanting state the further from the Mark we got. Still, his eyes continued to scan the surrounding area as we got closer to what we would tentatively call 'safety,' but to any bystander, it would seem as if he was simply taking in the sights. A violent emotion-filled shake wracked my body when we stepped across the threshold, past the guards, and were safely behind closed doors. Anger, mostly.

Lysander turned quickly, looking me over with anxious eyes. "It's ok, you're safe now."

I nodded, although I didn't believe him. How could I? There was an active threat that kept arriving and showing itself to me. One that wouldn't stop until it got what it wanted from me. Whatever that was.

How could I ever feel safe? Even when I eliminated a threat, another would simply arrive in its place.

I brushed past Lysander, ascending the stairs toward my chambers. Exhaustion from the day was seeping into my consciousness like water being soaked up by a rag. He didn't move to stop me, but I heard his soft footsteps climb the stairs behind me. When I closed the door and locked myself securely inside, I considered locking that damn adjoining door as well but ultimately decided against it.

I heard him moving about on the other side restlessly before exiting his room and heading down the hall, and I only briefly wondered if I should have thanked him for being there with me tonight. It had been foolish of me to go into the crowd alone tonight, and it was even more foolish of me to assume that just because I killed that man back in The Court of Shadows, the threat was gone.

That night, when I finally managed to banish the memory of the bright white painted Mark from my mind and drift into unconsciousness, I dreamt. And for the first time since leaving The Living Lands…I had a nightmare.

Fourteen

"This event has been such a blessing to our people." The old man stopped in front of Lilith to express his gratitude. She smiled lightly but unfriendly as he kissed her hand. "Thank you for providing such comfort during our Warden's absence." The castle courtyard, nestled within the imposing stone walls of the Forsaken Quarters, was a sprawling expanse of cobblestones and ivy-covered arches. Tall, gnarled trees with crimson and golden leaves stood sentinel along the perimeter, casting long, eerie shadows in the waning light. As guests gathered in the courtyard, jovial melodies filled the air. Musicians played lively tunes, their music resonating with the season's mood. The courtyard was filled to the brim with citizens from Everwatch as they danced to music and ate sweet treats provided by local confectionaries. For such a last-minute event, I have to admit those planners did a phenomenal job.

"Hello, sir. Thank you for joining us this evening," I said, inserting myself into the conversation. Lilith did not seem annoyed by my consistent interjections but rather thankful for the reprieve from the pressures of hosting—a title she assumed for the time being but one I eagerly awaited stealing for myself. The older man turned to me, a sweet smile on his withered lips.

"We've missed these frequent events. It's been a long while since the castle doors were opened like this, and twice in one month, no less." He chuckled excitedly.

I forced my most genuine smile. "Well, you're in luck, sir. We hope to provide these events frequently for our citizens while we navigate this time without our Warden."

He nodded, soaking up every word.

"It's important that we remain steadfast together," I added.

The old man reached for my hand, which I gave him willingly.

"You're such a dutiful young man. I love to see such pride in our Court." His wrinkled hands cupped mine. "What's your name, son?"

"Chandler, sir," I responded with my best eager enthusiasm.

"Chandler, thank you for what you're doing for The Court of Shadows." And with one last pat of my hand, he walked away. My smile deepened, and a euphoric sense of accomplishment filled me.

"Careful," Lilith warned, her voice low and menacing. My eyes darted to her. She wasn't looking in my direction, as she rolled her neck back and forth in either direction as if working out some kink. Her white blonde hair fell in a cascade down her back.

"I know what I'm doing," I assured her.

"So do I. That's why you should be careful." Her eyes landed on mine then, searing into me with caution. I didn't respond.

"I would like to retire to my room." Lilith brushed past me and paused briefly to speak directly into my ear. "I am aware of what your goal is, Chandler. And it won't work." My stomach dropped, a pit forming where, just moments ago, I was filled with eager contentment.

She sauntered off, and I watched after her. My confidence faltered with every step.

I made nice and worked the remaining crowd appropriately before excusing myself and bounding the steps to Lilith's quarters. We were housed on the same floor, but she was on the entirely opposite side of the atrium. I ensured there were no guards, timing my steps perfectly to use their rotating assignments to my advantage as I stormed up to her door. I'd been here less than a month and had already discovered the holes and the inconsistencies. It wasn't a secret that my Warden had reinforced security on the upper floors of the Forsaken Quarters after Lexa was attacked.

Unsuccessfully.

When I was sure there wouldn't be any prying eyes, I twisted the door handle and slipped inside. Lilith was wearing a light green robe, nearly see-through. She laid back against the lush nest of pillows on her four-poster bed. Her white hair spread out across the silk fabric.

"Took you long enough," she taunted, slowly spreading her legs to reveal her bare center to me.

I wasted no time removing my clothes and joining her. Being intimate with Lilith was not unfamiliar territory for me. In fact, I spent more time in Lilith's office in recent years than with Lexa. So here, despite the new surroundings, it was easy to slide back into the routine we created together. I pressed her legs wide and sheathed myself inside of her heat quickly. She called out my name as I pumped into her. Her core clenched around me. Her body held mine in a vice grip and begged for me to come for her. I pressed into her, my mouth coming down to claim the creamy space on her neck. She cried out, her nails racking into my bare back as she shattered around me, toppling me into my own release as well.

I withdrew myself from her and redressed while she lay, sated, on her bed.

"Oh, I've missed you, Chandler." She was breathless, an arm tossed across her eyes as she lay sprawled on the mattress.

"I've missed you too, Lilith." I lied. Because the truth was, I didn't miss her. And I didn't care that she had been aching for me. The fact of the matter was I needed something from her when back at the Institute, and now I needed her again. That unfortunate thought is what had me crawling back into the bed, sliding in behind her, and holding her tightly to my chest.

"The Court of Shadows seemed to need a night like this desperately," I started, rubbing a finger along the exposed skin of her thigh. "How long has it been since these citizens were honored?"

Lilith mused, still in a haze of pleasure.

Good.

"A long while," She yawned. "My Warden hasn't spent much time going above and beyond his duties in recent years."

I had gathered as much from my conversations around the Forsaken Quarters this past week.

"Shame." I couldn't help the smile that formed on my lips.

"He's barely responded to the disciplinary needs of the Court. Not until his precious Lexa was threatened."

I froze. I knew exactly what type of threat she had faced, being the person who let them in the back door, but Lilith didn't know I knew.

"What do you mean? Is Lexa ok?" I feigned worry.

Lilith scoffed. I could practically hear her eyes rolling.

"She's fine." The 'unfortunately' was silent but present.

"What happened?" I prodded.

"She was attacked in her chamber by some man." Her sated state made for loose lips, and I made a mental note.

"Gods, how horrifying. Who was the man?" She turned around to face me, her eyes studying my face.

"We don't know. We couldn't find any records on him. Which isn't surprising."

"Why is that not surprising?" I asked, continuing the slow stroke of my fingers against her skin.

She paused and pursed her lips as if trying to discern if she should tell me the truth. I let my fingers travel higher against her thigh, closer to her still-wet center. Her breath caught in her throat as she eagerly arched into my touch.

"I think he was Double Marked," she said, letting her eyes fall closed as my fingers trailed light touches along her folds.

"Double Marked? What does that mean?"

She sighed, frustrated at my slow exploration of her center.

"He had the Mark of Shadows, and I think I saw another one too." My fingers stopped their slow torture, and my entire body paused in shock. Two Court Marks?

"That's possible?" I blurted out. Her eyes opened.

"Possible, yes, probable, no." She reached for my wrist and guided my hands back to her center. I slid a finger inside of her heat nonchalantly, my mind swimming.

"What do you mean you *think* you saw another one?" I pushed as my fingers pulsed inside of her.

She moaned, arching off the bed slightly. Her lips parted, and she spoke with a sultry sigh. "There was something there, but it had been carved off. Like Lysander was hiding something." She writhed against my hand at her apex as I pondered that possibility. The Court Marks grant the individual access to the different Courts of Verihdia. By being Double Marked, that man could cross the veil into two different Courts and operate unrestricted. Was he a Court of Shadows member who had gotten a second Mark after his Pledging? Or did he belong somewhere else first and then find a way to steal the Shadows Mark to follow Lexa?

Something was bubbling under the surface then. A nagging voice telling me everything I already knew. In my life, I've always known I was destined for greatness, destined to be the most powerful individual in all of Verihdia. My Mythica made sure of that. My strength was not just physical. It was mental. My mind had the kind of grit that was fit for a Warden. Soon enough, everyone else would agree. And now I know how to do it. When Lilith was coming undone around my fingers, I kissed her neck, a plan already taking shape.

"You deserve more than he gives you," I whispered against her throat as she panted. "You deserve the world, Lilith. And if you help me, I'll give it to you."

She turned her head to face me, her eyes searing into mine. For a long moment, I worried that I'd pushed too fast, but my plan hinged on her devotion. Her need to have it all. Her envy.

When the corners of her pink lips turned into a sinister smile, I knew I had won her over. I kissed her with eager excitement, a new kind of promise lighting the place where our skin connected.

As long as it took, I would collect the Court Marks like stamps of approval, like medals that I and I alone could wear.

If I couldn't replace the Warden of Shadows, I would become the Warden of Verihdia.

Fifteen

Three weeks and six days.

That's how long we've been in this Court, and although the Endless Night Festival has ended, unfortunately, that did not mean that the public debauchery displays would become less frequent. It took me two nights after the close of the Festival to realize that every single night in The Court of Passion is an endless night, just without the pomp and circumstance.

Three weeks and six days.

It's how long Lexa had been touring the tower and the surrounding city, always accompanied by Korzich and their personal guard. I made sure of that after the Mark sighting. She seemed to be enjoying her stay, but I didn't think she had fallen in love with this Court the way she fell for mine. She doesn't have the same glimmer in her eyes or the same eager expression. Not that anyone could tell. To everyone else, she looked elated, but I knew her better than that. She still avoided the seventh floor, and I can't decide if I was relieved about that.

Three weeks and six days.

It's how long I've gone without touching her. There's this fire deep in the pit of my stomach that burns for only her and begs me to break my promise. But I won't.

It's also how long Lexa had been training with Kael. I had peeked in on one of their early sessions, only to find myself furious with Korzich for assigning him to her training detail. Korzich had only chuckled as if they knew how that decision would affect me.

Since then, I found myself sneaking into the training room every single day, slinking into the shadows high up in the spectator seating, and watching her. She was getting stronger, minute by minute. Her body moved more precisely, her weapon handling more exact and accurate. It was impressive and complicated to watch for many reasons.

One was that Lexa Cromwell looked unfairly delectable with a thin sheen of sweat on her forehead, plastering stray hairs to her skin. The other was that Kael was sure to find any and every possibility to press his body against hers, melding his muscular form around her luscious curves or letting his hands roam against her perfect, unblemished skin. I very nearly jumped off the balcony where I was hidden to pummel him to the ground. My fists itched to find purchase against his jaw so that he could no longer whisper innuendos into her ear or break each finger so that he would never again be blessed with the opportunity to touch her.

But I didn't do that.

Because despite the jealousy that was running rampant in my chest at his stupid and obvious advances, I had a secret advantage. A direct line to her emotions.

Her Mythica hated Kael's advances nearly as much as it hated Chandler's. It flicked with annoyance at his words, shied away at his touches, and acted as a barrier between the two when he pressed himself against her. Lexa could blush all she wanted, listen to his sultry whispers, and let him hold her closely, but I knew the truth.

She doesn't ache for him the way she aches for me.

That truth alone was enough to keep me silent in the shadows, watching her grow stronger each day.

We've exchanged a few short conversations since the night at the Festival. Still, when I wasn't sitting in the stands above the rafters during her training sessions, I coordinated with Korzich and their security detail to ensure the painted symbol was an unfounded threat.

Together, we exhausted every avenue to track the elusive 'artist.' Korzich was positively distraught to hear that this threat followed us into the safety of their Court.

When I wasn't working with Korzich, I was watching her. She had still not indulged in the physical nature of the Court's customs and traditions, but I had found her observing on more than one occasion. There had never been, and there would never be, anything more captivating than watching Lexa discover herself. At night, when I was sure she was safely secured in her room, I would rush off to the library, the town, or anywhere to continue searching for the answer I was missing. Each night, I'd exhaust my efforts and come up short, only to return to my chambers in the early morning hours tired and ashamed.

It was obvious that someone who knew of the Forgotten Court's Mark was behind these attacks. To my knowledge, there were only seven people alive who knew of its existence. The more I thought about it, the more I worried that these attacks were originating from within the inner circle of Verihdia. I couldn't fathom any other option right now. Although, the smallest threat of a darker possibility echoed in the back of my mind. I would blame it on a fellow Warden, before I could blame it on a ghost.

As the long, hot, tempting days ticked by, I seriously questioned my capacity for restraint. I wasn't sure how many more early mornings I'd be able to hear her restless tossing and turning, how many more days I'd be able to watch her delicious body exerting itself without ripping this gloved barrier off of my hands and holding her the way I know she burns to be held. She can lie to everyone else, but she cannot lie to me.

"You're getting better," Kael exclaimed breathlessly. He used to be entirely unaffected after a sparring match when they first began their sessions. Now, he was sporting a trickle of sweat on his temple, and his chest rose and fell with panting breaths. She had done that. She slid the dagger into the holster at her thigh, and I felt my core tighten at the memory of sliding that leather strap onto her skin, pulling it with my teeth, my mouth so close to her center. Her scent, her breath as it hitched. The way her body and Mythica begged for me. The way I fell to my knees for her.

The way I'd do it again if she allowed me to.

"I know." Lexa's comment shook me from the memory.

I couldn't help the smile that bloomed on my lips at her confidence. There's something that happens when you feel secure in your body and safe; it makes you feel bold. Brave. But it also opens someone up to the possibility of being reckless. That's when mistakes are made, and confidence becomes your downfall.

I hoped she understood the difference.

"What say you and I get a drink after this? My treat." Kael had taken a seat on the bench next to Lexa, and his leg brushed against hers as they slid their feet back into their discarded shoes. My teeth ground against each other, and I felt my fists ball on my lap.

"You ask me that every day," she mused, laughing at him like he actually made her happy. I hated that he was able to elicit that beautiful sound from her. Her Mythica was cautious above her head, not quite aiming to push him away but rather posed for action.

"And every day, you reject me. You're breaking my heart." He feigned falling over, clutching his heart as he toppled to the ground. She giggled again, and I had to pinch my thigh to keep from swooping in and stealing her away. "So what do you say, beautiful? Is today the day you finally say yes?"

I rolled my eyes, waiting for her answer. She finished stringing her boots and securing them to her feet, then leaned forward, her elbows resting on her knees.

Say no, little storm.

"I leave tomorrow," she said in response, and my breath caught in my throat. That wasn't a no. Kael knew it, too. He saw it for the opportunity it was. As I watched her, I noticed the dark circles under her eyes. She looked exhausted, and not just from the training session. I spent most of my free time in the library with Korzich. I rarely slept in the adjoining room these past three weeks, and when I did, I was so lost to exhaustion that I was very nearly dead to the world. Has she been sleeping well?

"You could come back," Kael said, the teasing tone absent from his speech. I sat forward, straining to hear her response.

She smiled, wiping her brow bone with the sleeve of her grey tunic. "You and I both know I don't belong in this Court."

I released a sigh. One step closer to her being mine.

"You could." Kael's voice was soft. I could barely hear it over my pounding heart. The flirtatious, fiery redhead was gone. In his place was someone with genuine feelings.

I was going to kill him.

I felt the overwhelming urge to steal Lexa's Mythica just to find what Kael was most afraid of and exploit it until he promised never to even look in her direction again. I promised not to be her villain anymore, but that promise did not extend to frustrating redheads trying to steal away the woman who belonged to me and me alone.

"You're a sweet guy, Kael. Handsome, too."

Kael smiled, sitting up on his knees in front of her.

"But…" he finished for her.

"But," she repeated. My heart settled to a comfortable rate, and I forced myself to breathe.

"There's someone else, isn't there?" Kael asked, his hand gripping hers. I ignored the physical contact for his sake because it seemed entirely platonic to her.

I leaned forward even more, eager to hear her answer, and the wooden bench beneath me creaked. Not loud enough to cause concern but loud enough to draw Lexa's eyes upwards. The brilliant crystal orbs landed on me, and I was frozen. I was always utterly helpless when it came to her. Her eyes were a mesmerizing shade of blue, like the tranquil depths of the clearest body of water. In their gaze, I could see endless depths of emotion, a vast expanse of fear, understanding, and vulnerability. Those blue eyes were like windows to her soul, where every feeling and desire is laid bare. I didn't need her Mythica to understand her desires when her eyes held me like this. I knew her as intimately as I knew myself when she looked at me.

Without pulling her gaze from me, she spoke, "I thought there could have been."

"Well, he's an idiot if he lets you get away," Kael commented, drawing Lexa's attention back to the redhead before her.

"What if I want to get away?" She asked in a teasing tone, but she and I both knew she wasn't intending any humor with her words.

"Do you?" Kael asked. Lexa's eyes flicked back up to me, telling me that every word she said had been for me and me alone.

"I don't know yet."

That's enough for me.

I stood up quietly, feeling her eyes watching me, tracking my movements as I took the stairs down to the main floor of the training room. I crossed the floor to the two of them in several large strides. All the time, my eyes remained locked on hers.

"Miss Cromwell. Kael," I offered without glancing at the redhead on the ground. "I trust you had a good training session?"

"I was wondering when you would stop watching us from the shadows and join us down here," Lexa said, her lips curving into a smirk. Kael turned to me and scampered to stand.

"You were watching?" he asked anxiously.

"It is my responsibility to ensure that Lexa is safe," I replied, still avoiding giving Kael my attention.

"Of course, Warden." He lowered his head slightly in a respectful gesture. I resisted the urge to roll my eyes at the false presentation.

Lexa was watching the two of us with a humorous expression. She enjoyed seeing my jealous side. I knew she did. Well, I was happy to oblige.

"Miss Cromwell, I'd love to escort you back to your room," I said, tossing a challenging glance to Kael.

Lexa stood, smoothing out her tunic, and turned to me. "Actually, I was just about to accept Kael's offer for a drink."

My eyes snapped to her, and I watched her face brighten with a mischievous smirk.

"Was that what you were doing? It certainly sounded like you were intending to reject his offer," I teased with a slight tilt to my head. She furrowed her brows in mock confusion.

"Your people skills must be getting rusty because you are not reading me the way you think you are."

"Aren't I?"

Her eyes burned with a familiar glimmer. She loved this game we played so expertly together as much as I did. There were moments of shared laughter and teasing smiles between the teasing barbs and sarcastic retorts. It's as if we have our own secret language, where humor was the bridge between our conflicting words.

A spark was burning between us as we stood in silence, facing each other in challenge. Our eyes locked. The stare was charged with a mix of amusement, frustration, and desire. There was an unspoken understanding that beneath the antagonism lay a deep attraction that neither of us could possibly attempt to deny. I had forgotten Kael's presence until he cleared his throat. I didn't tear my gaze from her as Kael began to speak.

"Perhaps we can have that drink another time, Lexa," he offered, and she turned to him, an embarrassed blush claiming her perfect skin.

"Oh, yeah, of course. That's fine. I'll see you later, Kael." She smiled sheepishly. Kael nodded solemnly at Lexa, a twinge of dispiritedness on his face before he glanced at me and sauntered off.

"You scared away my date," Lexa responded eventually, once we were alone.

"If you're hoping for an apology, you will be gravely disappointed."

She scoffed, rolling her eyes and grabbing her bag from the ground. "I've never expected an apology from you, Warden. I wouldn't be so naive." She pushed past me toward the entrance to the training chamber. I smiled brightly before following after her.

"Can I help you?" She asked over her shoulder after a few moments.

"No need, Miss Cromwell. I'm perfectly content watching you walk away."

Her steps faltered as she not-so-subtly pulled her tunic down to cover the soft curve of her backside.

"You've been pleasantly silent for three weeks. To what do I owe the unfortunate return of your opinions?"

I chuckled and caught up to her, walking side by side. It felt right to be at her side. Did she feel that too?

"You can say it, you know."

She glanced at me with as much 'contempt' as she could muster. "Say what?"

"That you missed me," I whispered, leaning into her shoulder. I felt the heat rolling off her body, and her sweet scent was so delectably strong after her training session.

"I don't make a habit of lying to Wardens." She pushed me off, her hands curling slightly around my bicep, and I desperately wanted to feel her skin against mine again. My restraint faltered more and more each time I was in her intoxicating presence. My palms itched under the leather gloves I had adorned.

"I have," I admitted quietly, the teasing tone still firmly in place, but the deeper undercurrent of emotions was present.

"Have what? Lied to Wardens? Yes, we've established that." It was intended to be a scathing accusation, but on her lips, it felt like an inside joke that only the two of us shared. I shook my head.

"Missed you," I clarified.

Her face fell slightly at the admittance, but she continued, turning down the hall toward our adjoining rooms. Her face contorted with unreadable emotions as we arrived at her door. I thought she might disappear into the room without another word, but she faltered and turned to face me.

"Why have you stayed away?"

Was that sadness in her tone? Did she feel my absence the way I so achingly felt hers?

"You *have* missed me," I teased, flashing a smirk.

She shook her head, trying to hide the smile that threatened to play on her lips. "One who has an infectious disease would certainly notice the symptoms receding, but that doesn't mean they would miss the pain," she retorted playfully.

A chuckle escaped my lips."Korzich and I have been looking into the appearance of the symbol. Trying to decipher who might have known of its existence and how they got here."

She nodded.

"But make no mistake, Miss Cromwell, I've never been far."

Her gaze locked on mine as I took a step forward. Her back pressed against the wooden door as I crossed into her space.

"Did you find anything?" She asked in a shaky voice, attempting to hide how her body reacted to me.

I shook my head, disappointed in myself. Lexa's safety was not only my job but also my obsession. Nothing would come to harm her as long as I lived. And yet, I hadn't found a single trail or clue as to where the Double Marked individuals were.

"You are safe with me," I assured her when I saw the glimmer of fear cross her expression.

"I know."

I nearly reached up to caress her cheek, but I willed my gloved hand to remain at my side, denying it the primal urge.

"You look tired. Have you been sleeping alright?" I asked, clenching my hand into a fist to restrain myself from reaching for her.

She cast her gaze down to the floor as her entire demeanor shifted. "I'm fine." Her wall was back, but she had revealed the crack to me and offered me a glimpse of the woman inside. The one who fell apart in my arms. That was enough for me.

"But are you ok?" I asked, and her deep sigh was enough of an answer for me. "Why haven't you been sleeping, lit-" I stopped the term of endearment from rolling off my tongue just in time. "-Lexa."

"It's nothing," she said, sliding out from the wall, escaping my presence. "Really. Don't concern yourself."

She was shutting down, and I would let her, for now. I nodded, and she thanked me before slipping inside the room and taking her captivating aroma with her.

I felt a tightness in my chest that told me something was wrong. I'd been so focused on the dangers outside that I hadn't been looking for the dangers within. One thing was absolutely sure… I would be sleeping in the adjoining room tonight.

Sixteen

One of Korzich's maids said I was invited to join them for a private dinner tonight. I'd attended all of the feasts and dinners Korzich held during my stay thus far - and there were many - but never had we been alone since that first day.

Honestly, I had come to enjoy the feasts. Korzich would invite a dozen or so of their advisors and friends to join them in the dining hall, a large circular room with red drapery hanging from the ceiling in decadent waterfalls of silken fabric. The stone circle table was nearly as large as the room itself, filled to the brim with the most delicious fruits, vegetables, and meats that The Court of Passion had to offer. The feasts all followed the same formula. The guests arrived and greeted each other with affectionate kisses and embraces. During that first hour, they would delve deep into their drinks. Then, the food was served, and everyone would eagerly claim a spot at the table. They devoured their meals while filling the room with satisfied moans. Then, for 'dessert,' several of the guests would choose to engage in sexual activity on one of the several plush velvet couches and daybeds that were scattered about on the edges of the room. The other guests who didn't participate usually watched.

Lysander attended these feasts often, but he kept his distance, choosing to converse with some of the other guests instead of crossing the space to me. I would frequently catch him glancing in my direction with a hungry expression. I tried not to think about how his eyes on me made my core tighten and the heat pool between my legs. I tried to convince myself it was the influence of the Court and nothing more.

Korzich made it quite clear that I was not expected to stay for the…dessert portion of the evenings. And most nights, I did not. Although I can admit that the more time I spent here, the less ashamed and embarrassed I began to feel about witnessing others in the throes of passion, that didn't mean I felt comfortable watching *with* others. Lysander never followed me out when I left before the evening's performances. I didn't want to admit the sting of jealousy in the pit of my stomach at the thought of him watching other women, beautiful women. Thin women.

I stayed once, for a few sinful minutes, curious about whether Lysander was enjoying himself, but I couldn't seem to keep my eyes on the group. When I glanced at Lysander, he wasn't watching the performance. Instead, his gaze was on me. I didn't confront him about it, but once again, he didn't follow after me as I retreated. No doubt he got his fill of watching once I had left the room.

Despite the tiny flood of unwarranted jealousy, I loved the atmosphere. Every night, I met a new set of people from the Court with new experiences and opinions that no one felt shy about sharing. Korzich would watch me from across the table as I eagerly listened to their tales and exploits. More often than not, the tales elicited a deep blush on my face.

Tonight, though, I was informed that it would be only the two of us. I hoped Korzich wasn't expecting any sort of 'dessert' after this evening's meal.

Florence, Korzich's maid, helped me dress as she had for every other evening, bringing me increasingly decadent and indecent gowns. Tonight's was a dark black gossamer dress with a short skirt overlayed with a single layer of mesh that flowed to the floor. The neckline plunged to below my breasts. The straps connected around my neck in a halter, leaving my upper back on display. The fabric fit my body like a dream, accentuating my curvy frame, not hiding it.

My hair was curled, and a braided crown of moonstone and flowers in the shade of midnight was placed on my head. My eyelids were darkened with kohl, and my lips were painted dark red. One thing was true about The Court of Passion, their clothing had an almost mystical ability to make me feel more beautiful than I'd ever felt in my life.

Well, maybe one other time.

My mind only briefly flashed to the emerald green gown I had worn to the Courting Ball over a month ago and how Lysander's eyes had scanned my body appreciatively. The way I had hoped Chandler would look at me.

I let my hands run over the fabric, closing my eyes and imagining that it was Lysander's hands that were grazing across my skin. Despite being the one to put it there, I hated the distance between us. It was for the best, of course. I knew that. However, I couldn't seem to ignore the ache in my chest when I thought about the time slipping away.

Time I could spend indulging in him.

But I couldn't.

A knock at the door shook me from my daydream. A kind older gentleman smiled and complimented me as I opened the door. My face blushed a dark red as he led me through the hall toward the dining hall.

Pleasure Tower - I had finally started feeling less trepidation in calling it such - was quiet this evening. Surprisingly, I didn't hear the tell-tale moans of pleasure as I followed the man through the winding halls. It was odd. However, what was perhaps the strangest of all was the fact that when I wasn't hearing people in the throes of passion, *that* was considered odd to me. So much has changed.

I couldn't help but wonder if that is what this entire tour of Verihdia would be like. Would I change so much, be so influenced by each Court, that the person

I was when this began will be a distant stranger? Did I want her to be?

We passed the wide double doors I usually would walk through for these dinners, but the gentleman kept going.

"Are we not eating in the dining hall tonight?" I asked, rushing to catch up with the gentleman.

"My Warden has prepared a feast for you in their private chambers," the gentleman expressed, and I felt the lump in my throat go rigid. I hadn't expected to be a guest in Korzich's chambers. According to rumors, the guests who are customarily invited inside are not there for dinner alone. My fingers anxiously tangled before me as the gentleman ushered me into the Warden's chambers.

It was gorgeous.

As I stepped across the threshold, I was immediately greeted by a lavish display of opulence. The entrance was framed by sheer, gauzy curtains that swayed gently in an artificial breeze, hinting at the lush paradise beyond. Immediately, I was transported into an oasis. Hanging gardens of lush trailing plants decorated the space, creating an abundant and verdant backdrop. The scent of blooming flowers filled the air, adding an intoxicating element to the atmosphere. The room was softly lit with a warm, golden glow that emanated from concealed sconces and lanterns. The lighting was designed to create an intimate and inviting ambiance, casting soft, romantic shadows along the sand-covered walkways. The bedroom's centerpiece was a network of meandering, manufactured streams crisscrossing the space. These streams were lined with smooth, polished stones and adorned with floating petals of fragrant flowers. The gentle, babbling water added a soothing and romantic soundtrack to the room. To cross the streams, there were arched bridges made of intricately carved wood and adorned with vines of passion flowers. I couldn't help but smile as I crossed one of the bridges, taking in the beauty of this makeshift natural hideaway. It reminded me so much of the greenhouse back at the institute, with the overhanging plants and that fresh scent that felt like home.

Home.

I didn't have one of those anymore. The thought invaded my mind just as a scantily clad Korzich approached. Their torso was on display, showcasing the dozens of Court Marks that decorated their tanned skin. They had silken drapery hanging from their waist, brushing against the sandy ground as they walked. Their long black hair was braided and slung over one shoulder. I was starting to love the way that their robust features drew you in. Where once it was intimidating, now it felt welcoming.

I bowed my head in slight recognition. "Good evening, Warden."

They smiled a bright, cheery expression.

"Lexa!" They reached out, offering their hand to me. I took it happily. That was something I had come to appreciate and love about how The Court of Passion operated. The residents never shied away from touch, but there was always a level of consent, of respect. It was a positively safe environment. Something this Court has taught me was that touch wasn't inherently sensual. Intimate, yes. But we need not shy away from that touch when we desire comfort from anyone. A friend, a loved one, family. "Welcome to my humble abode," Korzich gestured to the expansive jungle of a room.

"I did not expect this," I teased, and Korzich nodded.

"There must be an oasis in every desert," they responded. The loaded phrase landed hard on my consciousness.

"Do you consider your Tower a desert?" I asked. They seemed to ponder that, pulling at my hand to lead me further into the room.

"Being a Warden is oftentimes a burden. I'm sure your guide has said as much." They glanced over their shoulder at me for a moment.

"I can imagine," I replied. Korzich released a soft hum before turning down one of the sandy paths and leading me to a circle of plant life. A footbridge reached over the pool of water below and led to a small gazebo hovering above the shimmering water. Dark black flowers hung from the ceiling, giving the impression of a shining night sky. Sitting on the platform above the water was a table and two chairs. A decadent feast sat waiting. I gasped, and Korzich chuckled.

"Your time in my Court has come to an end, and I wanted to give you the proper send-off you deserve."

I smiled and followed them onto the platform. I forgot I was indoors for a moment as I smiled over the railing at the small fish that danced through the water below.

Korzich held my chair for me, and I happily took a seat. They sat across the small table from me and held their goblet up. I followed suit, and as soon as the glass was lifted, a waft of enchanting floral fragrances filled the air. The aroma reminded me of a blooming garden, with notes of fresh petals, gentle breezes, and the subtle sweetness of greenery and budding flowers in their prime. I couldn't wait to indulge.

"To you, Miss Cromwell. To your time in The Court of Passion."

I clinked my goblet against theirs before taking a languid sip. The first sip was an overwhelming symphony of flavors. The floral notes were delicate and captivating, with a natural sweetness that was both soothing and invigorating. I knew I would miss it when I was gone.

"How has your training been going?" They asked, diving into the food in front of us.

"It's been fantastic. Kael is a great teacher," I added, a soft bloom of shame cresting in my chest.

"He's taken a liking to you," Korzich offered with a soft glint in their eye. I blushed deeply, taking a few pieces of the meat from the center of the table and placing them on my plate.

"Oh?" I feigned ignorance, unsuccessfully.

"He came to me this morning after your training session. Practically begged me to ensure that you pledged to my Court."

I took another sip of wine awkwardly.

"Don't worry, I don't intend to get on my knees and beg for you. I only do that on special occasions." They winked.

I coughed, choking slightly on the sip I had taken. "My apologies," I mustered, composing myself. Korzich simply watched with a humorous expression.

"Have you enjoyed your time in my Court, Miss Cromwell?" They asked carefully. The light and airy tone was present, but there was a deeper eagerness behind the words. They dug into the delectable feast before them, and I wasted no time indulging.

"I've loved it," I answered truthfully. Korzich sighed, losing the breath they had been holding. It baffled me how this powerful Warden was so desperate for my approval. "Not only is it gorgeous, I mean…I've never seen a sky so vibrant and lively before."

They nodded their agreement.

"But it's the people too. They're so -"

"Unashamed?" Korzich offered. I shook my head, biting off a piece of meat.

"Unafraid," I clarified. "Shame has nothing to do with it. Everyone here is so positive about what they want, and they're not afraid to go for it, to ask for it. To beg for it," I added cheekily, earning a full belly laugh from Korzich. "I envy that. To be so steadfast in their decisions." I saw a twinge of disappointment cross their face.

"Envy…" they repeated to themselves.

"I didn't mean to," I started but stopped as they raised a hand to me.

"Not at all. Your honesty is what makes you a powerful asset, Lexa."

I frowned. The image of my brother lying in an infirmary bed flashed through my mind in a brief but unrelenting reminder of my dishonesty.

"Trust me, honesty does not come easily to me," I admit, swallowing a bite of food.

"Me either." We sat silently for a moment, letting our confessions hang in the air. "Can we make each other a promise here tonight?" They prompted.

I nodded tentatively.

"Let us be honest with each other." Their dark eyes bore into mine.

"I can do that," I said, finally.

"As can I." They took a sip of wine and leaned back in their chair. "So, Miss Cromwell," they began. "Do you have any intentions of pledging to my Court?"

My heart raced as I contemplated their question.

"There are a lot of things to love about your Court, Warden," I started. A knowing, sad smile played on their lips as they took another bite. "But-" they prompted coyly, trying to hide their distress as they swallowed their food.

"But," I repeated. "I don't see myself belonging here." The admission burned my throat but relieved a weight on my heart.

"I can't say I'm not disappointed, but I also cannot say I'm surprised."

I raised an eyebrow in question.

They leaned forward, resting their elbows on the table in front of them. "You've offered me honesty, so I will do the same." Their tone had an edge to it. "Your Mythica is powerful, Lexa. You know that. So do we."

I swallowed, fear gripping my heart. Do they know what I can do?

They continued. "Some Wardens would rather jump to drastic measures than see you in the care of another Court."

"You mean like…"

"I mean, that power like yours has the ability to corrupt even the best of intentions." They observed me. My chest heaved with labored breaths. "There are people eager and willing to do anything they have to in order to have a power like yours in their grasp. A Warden of lesser confidence might go to incredible lengths for it, or even further lengths to keep someone else from having it."

"Are you implying that a Warden has been sending the attackers?"

Korzich didn't answer, which said enough.

"I just want you to understand, Lexa. This world does not favor those who stand out. As unfortunate as that fact is, it is the truth." They reached for my hand across the table. "Do not be as honest with the other Wardens as you have been with me tonight. Some may not take lightly to your dismissal."

I nodded, filing away the advice. "You don't think that Lysander…"

Korzich waved their hand quickly. "Not at all. He is reduced to a schoolboy in your presence. You'll be safe with him."

I furrowed my brows.

"He's done a poor job of making himself seem harmless in my presence," I added.

"Because he's not harmless. Not by any stretch of the word. You have witnessed his ability first-hand. I said you will be safe with him, not that he is harmless."

I shivered at the memory. The way his vicious mind grabbed ahold of the Mythica that thrummed within me and dragged it to the surface for his own selfish use. However, the sting of the memory wasn't as harsh as it once had been.

"But he will be honest with you the way many of my other siblings will not be. With some, it will not be intentional. They simply can't help but twist the truth. For others, it will be a carefully calculated attempt at manipulation. You should be prepared for that."

I let that thought ruminate. I wasn't daft enough to think that these Wardens would spill their every secret or offer up true and utter honesty to me as a guest in their Courts, but the thought of one of the remaining five Wardens being behind the attacks against my life sent a chill down my spine. Was there any way to determine who it was? How was I supposed to last an entire month in their presence when they hoped to eliminate me from the playing field?

"I don't mean to frighten you, Lexa, but I believe you deserve to know the truth, or at least what Lysander and I believe to be the truth."

My head snapped up.

"Lysander thinks one of the Wardens is behind it too?"

"Vehemently," they responded. "It took me nearly a full day to convince him to let you complete the tour. He almost rushed off to take you back to The Court of Shadows."

My heart warmed at the thought of that Court and its Warden.

"He cares greatly about your safety." They watched me closely.

"He can be rather confusingly duplicitous," I admitted sheepishly.

Korzich simply raised their glass. "Show me a Warden who isn't, and I'll show you a liar."

I smiled and took another sip of the wine. The sweet taste danced along my lips.

"You, too, seem to have taken a liking to him."

"What gave it away? How he has avoided me for three weeks, or the way he hasn't been within five feet of me since arriving?" I teased, and Korzich simply smiled.

"The way you can't stop blushing at the mention of his name." It wasn't an accusation, but I might as well have been completely exposed.

"I don't-" I stopped, watching their face. We had promised to be honest with each other tonight. Maybe being honest with Korzich would be easier than being honest with myself.

"It's inappropriate," I finished. It was not quite a vast declaration, but the whispered words held all the longing I was denying myself within their confines.

"Perhaps," Korzich mused, leaning back into their chair and crossing their legs.

I took another sip of the wine before me, draining the glass and feeling the warmth from the liquid spread through my chest. "It doesn't matter though," I continued. "At the end of this tour, I'll be pledging to a Court that isn't his. That is if I'm even still alive at the end." The admission of my fears nearly stole the breath from my lungs.

Korzich studied me for a long moment, fighting an internal battle. Finally, they spoke. "How much do you understand about mates?"

The jump in conversation was jarring enough to cause me to stumble over my words. "I'm sorry- you, what?"

"Mates, what do you know about them?" They urged.

"Very little, considering how rare they are. They're not really taught in classes at the Institute."

Korzich hummed.

"Why?" I asked.

"We're being honest with each other tonight," they started quietly. "How do you believe mates are created?"

I couldn't quite understand the purpose of their questioning. "You gift certain children with mates when they are born," I replied.

"That is what you've been told," Korzich continued.

I shook my head. "I don't understand," I responded.

"My Mythica cannot create a mate bond."

A gasp fell from my lips. "What do you mean?"

"As flattering as it is for the public to believe that I have the power to do so, even I do not have power over fate itself." They took a drink, looking contemplatively over my shoulder.

"I'm sorry, I don't think I-" I stopped. My mind swirled as pieces of history came rushing back to me. How much of what I learned at the Institute was fabricated?

"I assume you understand how important the Court system is to the order of Verihdia?"

I nodded, ignoring the twinge of fear that began to crawl up my spine.

Korzich sighed deeply before leaning forward and resting their elbows on their knees. "And you know the creed, of course, the one my sibling Vander just loves to toss around at any given opportunity."

"Let no single thing influence the Pledge," I repeated. The phrase was often recited to me when I would complain about having the information about my family withheld from me.

"A mate bond is a pretty heavy influence, isn't it?" They asked slowly, enunciating each word as if they were willing me to see the meaning behind them.

My breath caught in my throat as their half-admission settled in my mind.

"You don't create mate bonds…" I started slowly, my shaky voice coming out as a pained whisper.

Their face twisted into a frown.

"You hide them."

Their silence was all the confirmation I needed. As the information settled in my mind, an initial wave of disbelief washed over me. It was as if the world around me blurred, and I struggled to comprehend the enormity of what I'd just heard. My mind raced and desperately searched for some way to refute or dismiss the information.

"Why?"

"My siblings agreed that it would be best for the Court system if the bonds were no longer complicating matters." They sounded defeated, as if their very soul was being ripped into shreds. There wasn't a doubt in my mind that Korzich disagreed but was simply outnumbered.

I wondered only briefly which side of the argument Lysander had found himself on.

"Why are you telling me this?" I asked, wiping away a stray tear that had escaped my eye and was trailing a moist path down my cheek. "So, there are mates out there who will never know that they have a second half out there somewhere?"

Korzich flinched but composed themselves quickly.

"Yes."

"How many?" I asked, unsure if I even wanted to know the truth. When they did not respond, I repeated my question with more force. "How many?"

"Countless," they responded finally, and the pit in my stomach deepened.

"How do you live with that?" I spat, a feeling of betrayal bubbling beneath the surface of my skin.

"Because there is a delicate balance of hierarchy in this world, Lexa Cromwell," they whispered hurriedly, leaning forward again until I could feel their warm breath on my face. "And I think you understand better than anyone that in order to survive the game, you must play it."

I let those words sink in. It's all a game. Everything. And I am nothing but another prize to be won in this childish tournament of power and corruption. Nobody tells you that there's often a profound sense of loss in the wake of life-altering news, as if a cherished part of your identity or history has been taken from you. They don't tell you how you will grieve for the life you thought you knew, mourning the innocence of ignorance.

"Why did you tell me this?" I asked, forcing my anger to the bottom. Despite how furious the thought made me, seeing the pain on their face told me they hated this fact almost as much as I did.

They thought momentarily, their tongue darted out to wet their bottom lip. Eventually, they exhaled sharply. "I like you. I think you are a kind-hearted, extraordinary individual. I think you might be capable of doing something good in Verihdia. But if you're going to survive this tour, I need you to know that there are so many secrets." They paused, taking another breath. A glossy sheen misted their eyes. "I need you to understand what the Verihdian Wardens are capable of."

Their hand gripped mine tightly, and I let their cool touch calm my frantically beating heart.

"I'm afraid," I whispered.

They nodded. "I know."

Suddenly, this room, despite its size, felt far too small for me to breathe in. I stood from my chair and took a few steps away, and I pressed my palm to my chest, hoping to calm my breathing. I looked over my shoulder and found Korzich sitting still, waiting for me to regain some semblance of control over myself.

"I think I need to call it a night, Warden," I offered with a bow of my head.

"I understand," Korzich said, standing and stopping before me. They reached for my hand and kissed it gently. "Thank you for dining with me this evening. And thank you for being honest with me."

"You too," I replied, dazed.

I pulled my hand from theirs and staggered backward. Their words swirled through my mind, every truth, spoken and unspoken. I had learned so much about these Wardens during my short time in their presence. The unblemished mask of solemnity they wore in their public personas was cracking and dissolving with every second I remained in their circle. What would they do to me if they knew I could see beneath the masks? Would they hurt me? Would they give me the same treatment they offered the Warden of Forgotten?

Could I trust Korzich? Could I trust Lysander?

Could I even trust myself?

With fear coursing through my veins, I began the torturous walk away from the Warden of Passion, but my feet stilled as I crossed the bridge. The cool blue water rushing beneath my feet seemed to taunt me with the ease of its departure from this scene. There was a question, one I knew that I could not leave without asking, but one I did not want the answer to. That vicious dichotomy held me frozen in my spot. I turned over my shoulder, and despite every nerve ending in my body begging me to turn around - to leave without adding another secret to the ever-growing list of things that could get me killed - I asked the question I needed to.

"Do I have a mate, Korzich?"

Their face was calm and did not betray their emotions. I watched as they furrowed their brow. They opened their mouth to speak a few times only to close it again. I only briefly debated accessing the truth from their lips by using my Mythica, but that was one line I knew I couldn't cross - even with Korzich.

Slowly, after what felt like hours, they nodded.

My heart constricted, and tears fell freely from my eyes. I glanced down at my feet and sucked in a few steadying breaths before turning my gaze to them again.

My mind flooded with images of one man in particular and our stolen moments in time. His hands on my bare skin, his eyes lighting with desire, his lips claiming mine, his soul calling to mine, his breath giving me life. The nearly suffocating draw I feel, the pull between us. How infuriatingly he understands me. How expertly he can calm me. I remembered those moments like fragments of a cherished dream that I tried so hard not to succumb to. He was the one I shouldn't have fallen for, the man who was never meant to occupy the tender spaces of my heart. Yet, against my best intentions, he etched himself into my memories with a force that couldn't be denied. As if there was a tether wrapped around our souls, burning with a fire that only fate could light or extinguish.

"Is it him?" I asked in a volatile whisper. Watching the Warden before me, I saw the truth in their expression, but they did not respond. "I thought we were being honest?" I snapped. Again, they did not respond, but they did not have to.

I turned on my heel and rushed out of the Warden's quarters, bursting through the doors and nearly sprinting down the halls of the Pleasure Tower on my way to my room. Tears flowed steadily down my cheeks as I ran. A few people stopped and watched me in my distressing retreat, but I couldn't give them a moment of my time. The pounding of my heart in my ears and the sound of my thoughts were too loud. Too terrifying.

A few feet from my door, Kael stepped into my path.

"What's wrong, Lexa?" he asked, attempting to put his hands on each shoulder, but his touch felt like a prison. This whole place felt like a prison. I couldn't breathe. I couldn't see.

I tried to pull back from him, but he held on.

"Are you ok? Are you hurt?"

I shook my head, but sounds did not come out of my mouth. He squeezed, and I nearly screamed.

"Get your hands off of her." The voice was deep and commanding. I felt the tone of it travel down into my soul as if it belonged there. Which I guess it did.

Kael rolled his eyes but dropped his hands from my shoulders. Without turning over my shoulder to look at the source of the other voice, I rushed forward into my chambers and threw the doors closed behind me. Once I was safe behind the locked door, I tossed myself onto the bed and cried.

Sobs wracked through my body as the gravity of the unspoken confession hit me fully. Breath came raggedly as I hugged my knees to my chest, hoping the pressure might keep my heart from bursting through my skin.

Hours slipped by like seconds, but eventually, once my eyes had dried out and my heart slowed its racing, my eyes fell closed, and sleep took me.

*

In the depths of my subconscious, a nightmarish vision took hold, casting me again into a chilling realm of terror. My eyes were forced open by the immense pressure of the water. Already, I felt the limited supply of oxygen in my lungs running desperately low. I once again found myself trapped in my unfortunately familiar, endless, dark ocean, the weight of the water pressing down on me with suffocating force. My hair danced around my head in whisps as I thrashed in the dark blue ocean. The water was darker tonight, and something felt different. More volatile. I pushed forward, swimming toward the safety I knew was not there. All around me was nothing but an inky blackness, as if I'd been plunged into a void that even light could not penetrate. The water was cold and unforgiving, a relentless abyss that wrapped around me like a shroud of doom. My lungs began to burn against the lack of oxygen, and my skin felt raw as the salted liquid displaced around my thrashing form.

An eerie sensation washed over me, familiar and yet also so foreign. In the depths below, I sensed a presence, a shadowy figure lurking in the darkness. It moved with a sinister, unnatural grace, its form distorted and monstrous. The terror it evoked was primal, as if it embodied all my deepest fears. I struggled against the weight of the water, pushing in the opposite direction, but I couldn't move. No matter how hard my limbs tried, the shadow grew ever closer. The figure's presence sent tendrils of dread crawling up my spine. I could feel its eyes on me, even though I couldn't see them. It's as if it was studying me, relishing my fear and vulnerability.

My eyes tracked the movement as the shadows neared. My hair danced around my head, and I struggled to swim away, trying to escape from the secrets of the deep that were threatening to consume me. My lungs cried out in pain, and I gasped. A scream died on my lips as the water rushed in, claiming every inch of me as its own. My strength waned as I continued to struggle against the relentless pull of the ocean. My limbs grew heavy, and I could no longer distinguish which way was up or down. The water closed around me, filling my throat, nose, and ears, suffocating me.

Weak and alone, I tried to fight against the pain, tried to back away from that shadow, but I wasn't strong enough. As I sunk further into the abyss, I knew the darkness would eventually consume me. There was no escape from this nightmarish, watery grave, and the helplessness felt overwhelming. By the time the shadowed creature reached me, I was already dead.

*

"Lexa! Please, wake up!"

I woke up in a frenzy, my heart pounding in my chest, gasping for air as I emerged from the harrowing nightmare that had held me captive. At that moment, the reality of my bedroom felt like a sanctuary, a stark contrast to the drowning torment I had just experienced. My lungs ached, and my breath came in ragged gasps, coughing up the phantom liquid as if I were still struggling for air beneath the weight of the dark, suffocating water. The sensation of drowning was so vivid that it lingered, haunting my every gasp. I touched my face and arms and felt the reassuring texture of my skin, reassuring myself that I was back in the safety of my room. My eyes adjusted to the figure that sat above me. His hands hovered above my shoulders without making contact. His dark skin was illuminated by the moon's soft glow that spilled in from the window. His green eyes scanned my form with worry and fear. My chest heaved, and anxious sobs ripped through my lips.

"Shh, little storm, you're ok. You're safe. I'm here," Lysander whispered, his face painted with worry and an emotion I wasn't ready to acknowledge.

My blurred vision focused on him. His hair hung freely around his face, and his bare, toned chest moved up and down rapidly as he watched me.

At that moment, I didn't see the Warden who had lied to me. I didn't see the Warden who had conspired with his siblings. I didn't see the contentious, stubborn man I had traveled with. I saw Lysander. The man behind the mask he wore. The man who saved me. The man who protected me.

There was nothing I needed more than to be in his arms, and I needed his comforting embrace like I needed air. I leaned forward, aiming to throw my arms around him, but he quickly slipped off the bed, awkwardly stumbling to his feet. A pit in my stomach formed. Of course, he wouldn't want this moment with me. He didn't owe me comfort in these moments of vulnerability any more than I owed him. How foolish I was to think he would.

"No," he whispered, shaking his head back and forth. The dark black tresses of his hair fell in a glorious frame around his face. "No, I'm not- damnit. Lexa, I…" he stumbled.

"It's fine, I understand," I offered, feeling my cheeks heat with embarrassment. How quickly I had been willing to toss my own rules aside for just one moment of his comfort.

He doesn't want me.

"No, you don't," he urged, drawing my eyes back to his. He leaned toward me but was sure to keep enough distance between us. "I made a promise to you, Lexa. And I don't want you to think I'm taking advantage of this moment of vulnerability to go back on my word."

My eyebrows furrowed as I studied him. His face was strained, and his hands were balled into tight fists at his side as if he were restraining himself from reaching for me.

"I swore to you that I would not touch you again," he whispered, his tone filled with shame.

My heart leaped, raging against the cage of my chest. I inhaled sharply. I felt wet, hot tears continue to slide down my face.

When I was younger, Axel would wake me up during my nightmares and hold my hand until I fell back asleep. I felt so much guilt surrounding that, so I pushed him away instead of indulging in his support again. I told him I was fine. I told him I didn't want him to see me in that state anymore. It was the same reason I never told anyone about the nightmares. I didn't want to be a burden. Instead, I suffered the nightmares in solitude. Alone in the darkness of my room at the Institute, I would cry myself to sleep while remembering the terror of them like a lingering specter that refused to fade.

I didn't even realize how desperately I missed the feeling of someone grounding me until I was close to experiencing it again.

Resolved in my decision, I reached for him. His eyes tracked my movement, remaining just outside of my radius.

"Please," I pleaded quietly. His eyes met mine then, burning into my soul. "Please, hold me."

He pressed forward, and the moment my fingertips brushed against his smooth, unblemished skin, I gasped. Something akin to a charged shock jolted through my body, sending a warmth rushing to my core. But it was not desire that I felt. It was safety. It was devotion.

The bed shifted under his weight as he climbed carefully onto the mattress. When he brought his hands up to hover above my shoulders, I nearly cried out for him again. Our breathing mingled, and our hearts beat in perfect unison, but still, he did not touch me. His eyes broke their connection with mine just enough to glance at the air around my head.

"What is it doing?" I asked, knowing he was watching my Mythica dance around me.

He smiled softly. "It's wrapping around me," he answered, dumbfounded. I bit my bottom lip and let my other hand grip his arm. His eyes snapped back to mine. Something unspoken passed between us, quiet and gentle, and then he brought his hands to rest on my shoulders.

The first touch had a relieved sob escaping my mouth. I pressed forward, tossing my arms around his neck and pulling him into me. His body was tense under my hold at first, but slowly, he relaxed into my embrace, and finally, the reservations slipped away, and his arms circled my waist. He didn't ask me to explain or describe the terror I had just endured. There was no need for words. He simply pulled me into his arms, wrapping me in a protective embrace that felt like a shield against the darkness. He held me there, grasping onto me as if I were the most precious thing in his world. The pressure of his hold felt unlike anything I'd ever experienced. It was like I was finally free to breathe. I wanted nothing more than to lose myself in the safety of his embrace. If I were to drown again, I hoped it would be in his arms.

I clawed at him, pressing our bodies closer until his flesh was flush with mine. Just the thin fabric of the dress I wore acted as a barrier between us, but even then, it felt like there was nothing between us at all. No walls, no barriers. No secrets. He sighed quietly, a sound of disbelief and relief, before lowering us onto the mattress so that we were lying facing each other, and I was folded into his embrace. I didn't care to acknowledge the intimacy of the new position we found ourselves in, with my head cradled onto his chest and his arms circling me, idly tracing lines across my bare skin.

His presence was all that mattered. There in his protection, the nightmare's aftershocks returned, and I cried into his chest. Clinging to him. He pressed a kiss to the top of my head, and his hands explored the bare skin of my back as he held me tighter. For now, I would selfishly give my soul what it so craved.

I sobbed into his chest till the early hours of the morning, but he did not complain, he did not move, he did not question me. He simply held me. Just as exhaustion began to whisk me away to slumber again, he placed another comforting kiss on my temple. "I've got you," he promised, and this time, I believed him.

SEVENTEEN

The atmosphere in the gladiatorial arena was overwhelmingly charged with anticipation as the crowd gathered for the first match of the season. I was among the thousands of spectators who had come to witness this grand spectacle, and the air buzzed with a mixture of excitement and tension. However, I was not merely a spectator. I held a position of importance here that I was so proud of. I could barely contain my own eager excitement. The stands were a sea of faces, a mosaic of impatient and hungry expressions. The warm, gleaming afternoon sun cast long shadows across the arena floor, creating a dramatic interplay of light and darkness. The sand, a pale golden expanse, stretched out like a canvas awaiting the artistry of combat. People from all walks of life had gathered, their voices rising in cheers and shouts.

The sound of thunderous applause was deafening. I was sure they could be heard from miles away, but standing in the tunnels beneath the Chaos Coliseum, the sound vibrated through my body like a rush of Mythica. If I closed my eyes and pretended hard enough, I could imagine those voices cheering for me, calling *my* name as I stepped out onto the golden sand, feeling the sting of the hot sun and a thousand pairs of eyes watching me. My exposed skin would be painted in the traditional way, with dark streaks of honor and valiancy. The sword at my side would feel heavy against my hip, begging me for the chance to prove its worth. Same as me.

If I pretended hard enough, I could almost imagine I was a Verihdian Gladiator.

"Do you think they're ready?" Avalin's rigid voice broke me from my daydream.

As my eyes popped open, I saw the dozen Gladiators preparing for their first fight of the season. They moved about the tunnel system, stretching their limbs and securing their armor. Their eyes locked in focus, as I taught them.

There was a chance that some of them would not survive this fight tonight. Death was never intended to be the goal during the Verihdian Gladiator tournament. These warriors fight to the concession, not death, but one wrong hit, or a fighter who refuses to concede, and well - anything could happen. Death is an integral and inevitable part of being a warrior, and these Gladiators understood that. I just hoped none of them would be too proud to concede if the time called for it, but I couldn't say with any amount of certainty that I would be able to surrender, if I found myself in the same situation.

"I do," I answered without turning to face my Warden. She had become a frequent presence at our training, and as I shared her quarters, I sometimes saw her around the living space. I never thought I'd get comfortable with having a Warden of Verihdia standing over my shoulder, watching my every move, but now, when she wasn't there, I found myself missing her presence.

"You've done well with them, Cromwell," she mused, patting me on the arm. Hearing her utter those words sent a powerful euphoria rushing through my chest, warming me from the inside out.

"Thank you." I turned my gaze to her. She was dressed in a ceremonial set of leather armor. Her long red hair was braided back and decorated with golden gems and charms. Her striking green eyes were framed by dark black paint, consisting of two long lines on either side traveling from hairline to cheek over each eye.

Her scars were on display, stunning reminders of her well-fought battles. I didn't know what my Warden looked like beneath her Mythica, and often, I find myself trying to remind myself of that fact. I should not lose my head because I found her physically attractive. After all, that was precisely what she wanted.

"The First Trial Festival begins tomorrow," she stated, retraining her gaze on the group of fighters before her.

I nodded. It was my first Festival since pledging my life to The Court of the Vanguard. I used to look forward to the celebration because it would offer me the slightest glimpse into the life I so desperately wanted in this Court. And now, here I was. Another bloom of pride blossomed in my chest.

"Are you planning to attend?" She asked.

Now that I was happily Courted and had no one in the Living Lands to visit, I didn't see much reason to attend. My sister would be in this very Court in just over two months. I haven't yet had time to miss her, not with all the planning for her arrival.

Avalin and I have spent several evenings discussing my sister. I admit that I found myself frustrated with the arrangement at first. Still, after I got past feeling like I was being used for my information, I immensely enjoyed sharing all the things I loved about my sister with my Warden.

Something that people who are not members of The Court of the Vanguard do not understand is that we feel pride not only for ourselves, but also for those we love. Regaling her exploits in school and her incredibly powerful Mythica to my Warden reminded me how proud I was to be her brother.

"Probably not. We have a lot to do to prepare for Lexa's visit."

She nodded. "That we do."

The crowd above our head stomped, and dust fell from the tunnel's ceiling to the ground below. The roaring crowd was so loud I could barely think. It was exhilarating.

I heard a soft chuckle next to me.

'What?" I asked, turning to see Avalin smiling at me.

"Your eyes are full of wonder," she mused.

I lowered my head shyly. "It's an incredible sight," I confessed.

She smiled solemnly, nodding her head briefly. I watched as she took her bottom lip between her teeth. "It gets old," she whispered, and I had to strain to hear her above the noise from above our heads. "After a while, it becomes something you must do. Not something you care about."

"Respectfully, I don't understand how that's possible," I began. "This is all I've ever wanted. This Coliseum, this crowd, this rush. This is the most euphoric feeling in all of Verihdia." As I spoke, I stepped forward, invading her space, but like the true Gladiator she was, she did not retreat. Instead, she stood her ground, breathing in the same air as I did. "Close your eyes," I commanded. She cocked her head and raised a brow in question. "Please?" I added.

She shook her head with a slight smile playing on her lips but ultimately followed my request.

"Listen to the crowd. Hear them cheering."

"It's all just noise," she tossed, shrugging her shoulders.

"Noise? Avalin, they come here for a tournament, for a display of courage and integrity," I started.

"They come for a show," she interjected.

"A show maybe, but one filled with honor and a true display of chivalry. The Verihdian Gladiators are not performers in the menial sense. They are a spotlight on who we all should aspire to be. Those screams are for the honor, the bravery, the person they want to be, and the person they deserve to be. It is not noise. It's the most beautiful sound in the world." I took deep breaths, calming myself from my impromptu passionate speech. Avalin opened her eyes and studied me carefully.

"It's refreshing to see someone care so much about the things I've taken for granted for so long."

I smiled at her.

"Let's go give them what they want," I offered, waiting for her to lead the charge.

She nodded once before fixing the mask of Warden back onto her face and striding down the tunnel toward the arena.

"Alright, Gladiators. Circle up," I called out to the fighters. They quickly gathered around me. I saw Cassius file in behind the others. They were not in the fight today, but their presence was enough to have the others on edge. "The tournament begins today, and I expect a fight worthy of The Court of the Vanguard. There is no shame in concession, and there is no pride in pushing past your limits. Fight as you live. Raul and Klover, you're up first."

Raul was the first to let out a guttural scream, and the others joined in a chant of support. The two Gladiators shook hands and descended the tunnel together toward the arena. I followed behind them closely, watching as they shared a single nod. The crowd erupted in loud cheers above us as Avalin breached the entrance to the tunnel and raised her arms above her head.

I watched her claim her rightful place at the center of the arena from the shadowed entrance to the tunnel. She commanded the attention of every single patron with her fluid, confident movements. It was not lost on me that everyone who stared at her now saw something different. Different hair, different eyes, different build. They saw what they wanted to see. She was giving them the show they so desperately longed for. Her hands rose, beckoning the cheers to cease, and they did. Silence fell on the arena, and somehow, the stillness of it all felt so alive. She glanced around the stands in silent anticipation, and the crowd awaited her introduction.

"You should all consider yourselves very lucky," she started, the timber of her voice deep and resounding. The sound bounced off of the stone throughout the arena. I'm sure there was some Mythica influence, allowing her voice to carry that way. "Today, you get to witness what so few in all of Verihdia have ever had the privilege to. This tournament has been a show of pride and valor for my

Court for years. This tournament has displayed what we are capable of here in The Court of the Vanguard!" She raised her hands, prompting the crowd to cheer in eager agreement.

She lowered her hands and waited for the crowd to settle into silence again before continuing. "These champions have been hand-picked, rigorously trained, and brought here to prove to you their merit."

My heart leaped at the briefest mention of the training I had put her Gladiators through. In just over a month, I've crafted these individuals from muscular brutes into warriors. Pride, pure and unbridled, flowed through me.

"To the Valor!" She called out and was met with a deafening echo of the crowd repeating the sentiment. "Welcome, everyone, to the tournament of the Verihdian Gladiators!"

Cries of admiration and excitement flooded the space, and I could barely breathe through it all. How anyone could ever feel stagnant in an environment like this was beyond me. This is what life was supposed to feel like. This was what being a Gladiator felt like.

I cast my eyes toward my Warden and found her eyes closed as she soaked up the sounds of her Court cheering. When her eyes opened, she turned to meet my gaze and nodded once, a small smile on her lips.

A hushed anticipation settled over the crowd as the massive gate at the end of the Chaos Coliseum creaked open. From one gate emerged the gladiators, their armor gleaming in the sunlight, weapons in hand. They marched with a measured, confident stride, their faces hidden behind ornate helmets. With a final, thunderous cheer, the match began. The clash of metal, the thud of fists, and the shouts of combatants filled the air. The gladiators danced across the sand, their movements a blend of skill, strategy, and brute strength.

Raul and Klover were one hell of a fight to witness. I knew they would be. Which was why I suggested they go first. You want your best fight either first or last, and in this case, since it's the first day of the tournament, I knew I wanted to start off with the best we had. That, and I think Raul would benefit from the slight check to his ego about not closing the first tournament. He's come a long way, but you can't unlearn an entire lifetime of favoritism in a month.

Klover had a lot of power in her form. Truthfully, the only thing I really had to focus on with her was her aim. During training, she had the speed and the strength, but I noticed that during the sparring matches, she'd often get lost in the fight and wield her weapon aimlessly. It tired her out quicker, making her an easy target. She didn't win a single spar for the first three weeks, but I knew she had the potential to be one of the best. Now, as she held her own against Raul, she nearly was.

As the first match of the season unfolded before my eyes, I couldn't help but feel a sense of awe and wonder. The gladiatorial arena was where heroes were born, legends were forged, and the spirit of competition burned brighter than ever. It was a season of challenges, of battles to come, and I was privileged to be a small part of this grand spectacle of ancient combat.

"You did some impressive work, Cromwell."

I turned from the battle in front of me to see Cassius leaning against a pillar next to me. I took a moment to soak up the accolade before replying. "Thank you."

"I tell you what, I thought this crop of recruits was going to be a lost cause." They chuckled to themselves. "You've got a future in this Court as a trainer." They meant it as a compliment, but the words pierced my heart like the sharpest blades. I did not have time to school my reaction before Cassius noticed the shift in my demeanor.

"Did I say something wrong?" They asked carefully.

I sighed deeply and considered lying, but eventually, I responded. "I don't want to be a trainer," I admitted. "Not yet, at least."

They looked at me inquisitively as the crowd roared at the impressive dodge Klover had made out of the way of Raul's swinging weapon. I momentarily watched the action in the arena, formulating my response.

"I have wanted to be a Verihdian Gladiator for nearly my entire life," I started slowly. "I want the honor of the title, I want the thrill of the fight, I want the glory of the challenge. I don't want a future as a trainer until I've had a present as a Gladiator."

When I had finished, I waited for them to respond by watching the final moves of the current battle. Raul was gaining ground and had more endurance, but Klover was quick. The evenly fought battle was edged out by one quick sweep of the legs by Raul, bringing Klover down onto her back and sending her weapon clattering across the sand. Raul aimed the tip of his sword at her throat and waited for her concession.

My heart caught in my throat as I willed her to concede.

Don't waste your potential.

She begrudgingly tapped his leg twice, and Raul's demeanor shifted. He smiled and raised his weapon above his head in victory. The crowd cheered for him, chanting his name. Klover rose slowly, the look of defeat clear and present on her bruising features.

Raul reached out a hand for Klover, who took it and shook it. The crowd erupted in more cheers, and I let myself, for just a moment, consider what it would feel like if those adoring calls were for my benefit.

As Avalin announced the winner and called forth the second round of contenders, Cassius remained quiet. It wasn't until the next two fighters began their slow circle of each other that they spoke again.

"Have you said any of this to Avalin?" Cassius asked, and I had to restrain myself from scoffing aloud.

"Have I told the Warden of my Court that I don't want the job she personally appointed me to?"

Cassius flinched away slightly at my tone.

"No, I haven't told her. And I can't." I crossed my arms across my chest and watched the fight.

I saw Cassius nod a few times out of the corner of my eye.

"I'm sorry, Axel," they whispered. I could barely hear it above the shocked gasps of the crowd. "For what it's worth, I think you would make one hell of a Verihdian Gladiator."

The compliment felt bittersweet to hear in the context. Knowing that it was most likely a fool's wish. "If the closest I ever get to that arena is you saying those words to me, then I guess that's ok." I smiled sadly at them, and they brought a hand down onto my shoulder.

The matches continued with minimal bloodshed, much to the audience's dismay, but still, they cheered. Avalin seemed to be soaking up each burst of exhilaration, and it was a beautiful sight, to say the least. There was something so powerful about how she stood, with shoulders square and arms still and poised at her side. Her posture was so rigid and stoic that I would have thought her a statue if it weren't for her vibrant red hair blowing wildly in the wind.

When I pulled my eyes away from her frame, the final match had concluded, and Avalin dismissed the crowd.

Shaking off the momentary distraction, I assisted the Gladiators with their gear. I escorted the few who needed it to the healer's quarters at the heart of the tunnel system beneath the arena.

"They did well today," Avalin's voice startled me. I turned to see her leaning against the rocky wall of the tunnel. Her eyes glinted with an air of amusement. "You should be proud."

"I am," I replied, not even bothering to mask my pride. She smiled brightly at me.

"So, you really don't want to attend the First Trial Festival?" she asked, pushing off the wall and crossing the space toward me.

I shook my head. "I don't need to," I answered honestly, returning to the housing quarters I shared with her. She fell in step with me.

"Not fond of it?" She guessed.

"No, it's not that at all. I love the Festival, actually." Aside from the singular Gladiator fight I saw once a year, the First Trial Festival was the closest I could get to The Court of the Vanguard. I'd wait all year for the Festival where I could taste the cuisine, meet the people, and ask them questions. " I just don't think I need it anymore."

If she didn't understand what I meant, she didn't let on, opting to continue our walk in silence. When we reached the entrance to our abode, I stepped aside, gesturing for her to lead. As she brushed past me, the scent of her invaded my nostrils. Wildflowers and leather. I inhaled deeply, barely muting the groan that threatened to escape. I followed behind her, begging my mind to get a grip on whatever little infatuation was budding with each step down the illuminated staircase.

When my feet hit the landing, I rushed past her toward my chambers. "Congratulations on a successful first round of the tournament, My Warden." Without glancing back at her over my shoulder, I pushed into my room and closed the door behind me.

I could not jeopardize my future with this Court by allowing my mind to be clouded by childish attraction. I wouldn't. I've worked too hard and overcome too much.

I had a Gladiator season to prepare for and my sister's visit to plan. All the while, I needed to prove to Cassius and the Court that I deserved a spot on the arena floor.

Avalin would not distract me from showing her the fire within me.

I can't let her.

Eighteen

I awoke with a distinct awareness of the woman who was fast asleep in my arms. Her skin pressed against mine was like a balm on the painful burns her absence had left behind. I was so desperately lost to her. There was no hope for me. There was no chance I could spend another moment without her. As far as I was concerned, the rest of this tour was simply for show because there was not a doubt in my mind that Lexa Cromwell would be returning to The Court of Shadows by my side.

Her eyelashes fluttered gently, brushing against the smooth skin of her cheek. Her raven hair was sprawled across the pillow and hung over my arm that was wrapped around her. I was the farthest I'd been from my Court in years, but I never felt more at home.

I am hers.

She stirred slightly, and I tried to remain still, bracing for the regret. She made a concession last night, one that I was so desperate for, but I needed to be ready for the possibility that in the light of a new day, she would regret what transpired in the comfort of darkness.

Her eyes fluttered open, offering me a clear look at her bright eyes. Those blue eyes were the color of a midsummer sky, a shade that danced with flecks of cerulean and hints of ocean depths. They were a vivid contrast against her creamy skin and dark, lustrous hair, a mesmerizing portrait of elegance and grace. In that instant, as I locked eyes with her, I realized something profound. The shade of blue that graced her gaze was, in fact, my favorite color. It was the hue that had always brought me solace and comfort, the color that had been a constant thread in the tapestry of my life. In the sky above my head, in the calming waters of the bath, which would relax me after a difficult day, in the moonlight that blanketed me when I felt alone. It was a serendipitous discovery, an echo of fate's design. Like a mirror to my heart, her blue eyes revealed a profound and undeniable connection. In that moment, I couldn't deny that the universe had conspired to bring us together, weaving our stories into a symphony of shared love and destiny.

A brief moment of foggy clarity occurs in the liminal space between sleep and consciousness where your dreams feel like reality and reality is a waking dream. At that moment, Lexa looked at me as if I had been the answer to every wish she ever had. It was at that moment that an emotion I could only call trust slipped into her gaze as she watched me. And at that moment, my heart cracked wide open, not as if it were breaking but as if it were rearranging the walls I'd been so delicately crafting for decades to make room for this blue-eyed beauty before me.

And then the dream ended.

Realization crossed her face quickly, shattering the briefest of glances at what I was sure would be our future. She quickly slipped off the bed, a deep red blush painting her cheeks. I remained still, watching her as she smoothed out the fabric of the dress she had fallen asleep in.

"Good morning," I offered softly, unable to keep the smile from my voice. She didn't turn to acknowledge me.

"I'm sorry," she whispered before shuffling across the floor toward the washroom. I swung my legs over the side of the bed and got up to follow after her. My hand reached out, gripping her arm. The feeling of her skin beneath my fingertips nearly had a moan escaping from my lips. She stopped but didn't pull her arm from my grasp. I didn't have to see her Mythica to know how my touch affected her.

"What are you sorry for?" I asked, stepping closer until her back was nearly pressed to my chest. Her breath caught in a gasp.

"You know what," she argued. I couldn't help but lean into her scent. As my breath danced across the column of her throat, she sighed, and her eyes fluttered closed.

"Tell me anyway," I urged her, letting my lips hover just above her skin.

"I shouldn't have asked you to cross that line last night," she admitted breathlessly, barely keeping herself from leaning back into me.

"The line was there for your benefit, little storm, not mine," I began, whispering my words into her ear not unlike I had at the Pledging Ceremony. "You are the only one who gets to decide who crosses it and when."

I couldn't restrain my lips any longer. I pressed the softest of kisses to her bare shoulder. The moan the action elicited from her was so delightfully sinful. "Tell me to cross the line."

"Lysander," she whispered, her head resting on my shoulder.

"I love the sound of my name on your lips." I pressed another quick kiss to her skin before slowly stepping back. She righted herself and turned to face me. Her flushed skin and messy hair made this already stunning creature nearly irresistible. My eyes scanned her body hungrily. When my gaze returned to her face, her shy smile told me she knew exactly how I felt. Her Mythica was moving around her in slow circles, just as lively as usual but calmer, more relaxed.

"When do we leave?" she asked, shifting awkwardly on her heels.

I smiled and ran a hand through my hair. "As soon as you're ready."

She nodded to herself a few times before turning to finish her trek to the washroom. She paused at the doorway and looked back at me over her shoulder.

"Do you want me to sit in there with you?" I asked, seeing the fear etched on her face.

"I'm pathetic," she whispered.

I crossed the space to her quickly. "Don't you dare speak about yourself that way again, Lexa."

Her eyes widened as she took in my face. "I can do this. I need to do this," she whispered.

I gripped her hand, suddenly intoxicated by the feel of her skin against mine, and squeezed once before she turned and disappeared into the bathroom alone. I instantly missed her touch. I wasn't sure I'd ever have my fill of her. I could hold her for the rest of my days, and still, I'd crave more.

I stood just outside the bathroom door, my heart heavy with conflicting emotions. She was in the bath, and my instinct was to be there with her, to provide comfort and reassurance. But I couldn't bring myself to enter, even knowing that her fear of what lurked within the water ran deep. The gentle sound of running water filled the air. A soothing cascade that was meant to relax had the opposite effect on her. I knew the bath was a place of vulnerability for her, where her fear hid in the shadows. My desire to protect her was overwhelming. I wanted to be by her side, to hold her hand and assure her that she was safe. But I also knew that my attention might only intensify her anxiety. As I waited, I whispered a promise to myself – that I would always be there for her, ready to hold her hand and face her fears together, even if it meant standing just outside the bathroom door, waiting for the moment she was prepared to emerge, stronger and braver than before.

Once she was finished, I heard her bare feet pad across the marble floor, and then the door creaked open in front of me. She had covered herself in a thin towel, and my heart rate quickened to a dangerous degree.

A gentleman might have looked away and averted his gaze from a woman in such an inappropriate state. I was not a gentleman, not with her. As my eyes raked over her body, watching the droplets of water fall from her hair to crawl across her perfect skin, gliding over the perfect curve of her breasts, I let out a low groan of approval.

"The very stars envy your shine, Lexa Cromwell."

She blushed deeply and lowered her gaze from mine. "I'm done. I just wanted to thank you."

I knew I should have stepped back from the doorway and allowed her to pass, but instead, I remained fixed in her personal space, feeling her breath on my chest as I towered over her.

"You're welcome," I offered, leaning just close enough that she could press her lips to mine if she chose to.

For a moment, I thought she might have.

With a slight shake of her head, she stepped back, once, twice. The distance between us was even more charged the further she got from me.

"I'll be ready in a few moments. Should I meet you in the stables?" She whispered, shame coloring her expression.

"Yes, I'll wait for you there."

She nodded and brushed past me. After a few moments spent trying to desperately - and unsuccessfully- erase the taunting curvature of her breasts from my mind, I left to ready our camel for departure.

In the calm stillness of the desert stable, just outside the shimmering Pleasure Tower in The Court of Passion, I began the task of packing our belongings onto the sturdy camel. The cool, pre-dawn air promised adventure, and the anticipation of the journey ahead was palpable. The camel stood there, an unwavering companion in this vast sea of sand. Its large, expressive eyes regarded me with calm wisdom as if it understood the significance of our departure. Beyond the stable's threshold, the desert stretched endlessly, a mesmerizing landscape of rolling dunes and shifting black sands. The first light of dawn painted the horizon with hues of the deepest black and shimmering sparkles.

I felt my siblings' Mythica before I heard their footsteps in the sand behind me.

"Come to say goodbye?" I asked, turning to greet them.

Korzich wore a melancholic expression on their sun-tanned face. "I fear you'll be angry with me when you hear of what I've done."

I pushed off of the wall and took a step toward them.

"What did you do?" I asked, watching their Mythica as they reacted to the fear in my tone.

They sighed deeply. "She knows."

My eyebrows furrowed for a moment as I tried to piece together what it was that they were talking about. "Knows what?"

They did not respond, but rather, their eyes softened as they met my gaze. Realization dawned on me, and suddenly, last night came into perfect focus.

"She knows?" I repeated.

They nodded, letting their chin fall forward, and their dark hair spilled over in front of their eyes.

"Did you tell her?"

"I may have given her the book, but she's the one who found the right page." Korzich shrugged and I groaned.

"Did she seem... happy about it?" I prompted selfishly. Korzich raised an eyebrow and glared at me.

"She ran off crying."

I winced.

That doesn't bode well for me.

"I just wanted you to know," they spoke with a clear warning ringing in their tone. "Some Wardens would understand the sanctity of that, but you know as well as I do that a few of our siblings wouldn't hesitate to remove the threat." They turned to leave.

"Wait," I called out, and they paused, looking back over their shoulder at me expectantly. "I'm sorry." I don't know why I felt compelled to say it. I'd never before felt the need to apologize for possessing what others only wished for, but even mesmerized by my affection for Lexa Cromwell, I understood the dangers involved.

"Keep her safe, Lysander," they added with a nod before retreating into the Pleasure Tower. I watched after them, allowing myself to process the new information about my travel companion. My heart leaped out of its chest.

She knows.

Lexa arrived at the stables a few moments later, and I couldn't help the low hum of approval that escaped my lips at her appearance. Her full frame was draped with a soft orange gown that rested just above her knees—one of the dresses I bought her in The Court of Shadows. Stunning. Sensual. Emerald. Warmth bloomed in my chest at the thought of claiming her so absolutely.

"Ready to go?" I asked, and she nodded her agreement.

"Lexa!" A voice interjected.

I groaned outwardly at the sound of his needy voice calling out for her. Turning, I saw Kael jogging up toward her. His red hair was messy and damp.

Lexa turned to face him.

"I didn't want you to leave without getting to say goodbye," he started, and I rolled my eyes.

"I'm sorry, Kael. I should have come to see you," she replied.

"I understand. I just… I hope I get the chance to see you again." His eyes scanned her frame and finally registered the color of her outfit. His eyes darted over to me with the slightest look of disgust. I smiled slyly back at him.

Lexa sighed, effectively dashing Kael's hopes. I saw the moment it registered on his face. It was beautiful.

"You're not coming back," he said as if he knew it was the truth. Which it was.

"I'm not," she whispered. I saw the guilt in her eyes and hated that Kael was making her feel that way.

"Well, in that case, it's been one of the greatest pleasures of my life getting to train with you, Lexa." He extended a hand for her, and I couldn't stop the tightness in my chest as she gripped and shook his hand. "Don't forget to protect your heart. That's where they'll strike if they really mean to harm you." His eyes flicked ever so slightly toward me as he issued the reminder.

Lexa nodded, her eyes glistening with the sheen of unshed tears. Her Mythica coiled around her as if forming a protective barrier.

Kael glanced at me. "Tell my father I said hello," he offered. Lexa looked back and forth between the two of us frantically.

"Your father?" She asked.

"Take care of yourself, and work on those core muscles," Kael said, deflecting the last question. He nodded and let one last longing glance dance over her as if he was burning her image into his mind, and then he turned and jogged off.

I turned my attention then to my travel companion, loving the way the humid climate in this Court had her cheeks in an almost constant shade of pink. When her eyes met mine, I held up the gloves I had been wearing around her for the last month to avoid physical contact.

"We crossed the line last night, but I want you to know that you can step back to the other side whenever you need to." I indicated to the gloves. Wanting her to know she had all the power here.

She looked down at the gloves in my hand and then back at me.

"Do you need to?"

She took a deep breath, and I studied her face as she weighed the options in front of her. I would never ask her to stick to a decision she made under the shadows of the night when in the light of the day. I just hoped she would.

She reached out for the gloves and took them from me. Holding them in her own hands, she hummed softly. "No." Her eyes flitted up toward me, handing the gloves back to me. "I don't need to."

My smile must have taken her off guard because she chuckled softly at my reaction. I tried to compose my joy and helped her up onto the camel. Tossing my gloves into my pack, I climbed up behind her, situating myself as close as I could possibly be, holding her back pressed against my chest. Her head lulled back to lean against my shoulder, and I pressed the slightest kiss against her hair. She sunk into the position, and I couldn't help but realize that I had never felt this intimate with another person in my life. The camel rose gracefully, its powerful legs carrying us away from the Pleasure Tower and into the heart of the desert. As we ventured into the endless sea of sand, I couldn't help but look back one last time, cherishing the memories we had created in The Court of Passion while eagerly embracing the adventure that awaited us on the rest of this tour. Her face contorted in sadness as she watched the Tower disappear over the horizon behind us.

"You look like you'll miss it," I commented quietly. She shook her head and averted her eyes.

"It's a beautiful Court with wonderful people." A flash of Kael's face in my mind had a sting of jealousy slicing at my heart, but it slowly receded when I remembered whose arms were around her body last night. "But it could never be home for me."

I barely avoided asking if my Court could be. Instead, I focused on leading our mount back toward the border of the Living Lands.

We rode in comfortable silence for a while, and I was growing to not only appreciate but crave these moments of silence with her. We did not need to speak in order to communicate. She'd shift in her seat, or I'd see her Mythica moving about, and I would know exactly what she needed—handing her the canteen of water when she was thirsty or producing an apple from our pack when she was peakish. I was learning everything about her, and she had to see that. She had to see how perfectly crafted we were for each other. She may have known it now, but I needed her to believe it.

"Who is Kael's father?" She asked after a while, taking a sip from the canteen.

"Vander. Warden of Silence," I answered, and I heard her choke on the water.

"Excuse me?" She stuttered. I chuckled slightly at her shocked expression. She was so beautiful when she was surprised. "He's the son of a Warden?"

I nodded.

"That is… a very interesting piece of information." She chose each word carefully. "And to think, the Warden of Silence could have been my father-in-law," she added playfully.

I couldn't help the growl of displeasure that erupted from my throat. She leaned back into my chest, letting the vibrations travel through her.

"Do you enjoy riling me up?" I asked.

She shook her head innocently. "I don't know what you're talking about."

"You know exactly what I'm referring to, Miss Cromwell," I spoke quietly, enjoying how her breath quickened. "Are you trying to make me jealous?"

She shook her head, but the way her breasts rose and fell with her labored breaths made me groan.

"It's working," I admitted, and suddenly, her Mythica was wrapping around the two of us, shrouding us in privacy. Gods, I loved the way her magic welcomed me. Even when her vicious tongue was slighting me, she couldn't hide her affection. Not from me.

Many hours later, we were approaching the veil, and I could barely keep a hold of the lewd thoughts that were claiming my mental energy and making it nearly impossible to sit here so close to her and not indulge in one of the several indecent things I desperately wanted to. As we passed through the shimmering barrier, my mind crafted a glimpse at what it might be like to have Lexa sink onto my length and ride me as we rode our mount. As the vision slipped away, I groaned in frustration, hoping that I would soon get the chance to make my dreams come true.

Lexa shifted uncomfortably before me, pressing her core onto the saddle. I smiled slyly. Recognizing her wanton need.

"What did the veil show you this time?" I whispered into her ear, relishing the way her body reacted to my proximity.

She reacted, a brief flash of embarrassment crossing her features. "Kael would be a wonderful partner," she teased, and although I could see directly through her lies, I couldn't help the bloom of furious jealousy. My bare hand snaked up her midsection and between the valley of her breasts to grip at her throat. She gasped as I moved to expose her neck to me. I stopped just short of pressing my smirking lips against her skin.

"I would be envious if I didn't already know precisely who you shared yourself with within your vision."

She inhaled sharply, and I could feel her pulse quickening beneath my fingertips.

We rode further into the Living Lands for a moment, and I suddenly felt the difference in the air. A calmer temperature replaced the dry, humid heat. We stopped at the travel depot and exchanged our mount for our horse and carriage, and I immediately missed having her pressed against me. I didn't even spare the attendant a second glance, all I could look at was my little storm's flushed face, and I could only imagine the sinful things we did in her mind. Even the mere thought of her was more addictive to me than the stares of appreciation from other women.

She wordlessly climbed into the back of the carriage, and I claimed my seat at the reins. We had barely ridden for a few minutes when the bustling energy and colorful crowds drew our attention.

Lexa sat forward in her seat, glancing out the front window at the activity. "It's the First Trial Festival! I forgot all about it," she exclaimed, bright excitement beaming on her face. I smirked, intensely amused by her optimism. "Can we stop?"

I made a show of weighing the pros and cons, as if I hadn't already decided to allow her the night to enjoy the Festival. Her bright smile was enough to stop my heart. I pulled the carriage over and tied it off. She barely waited for us to come to a stop before she was out fully and excitedly moving about the Festival.

The Court of Passion's section of the Festival was a watered-down version of the sinful and sensual offerings we had just been surrounded by for the past month, but appropriately lascivious nonetheless. People from other Courts, as well as The Living Lands, milled about, indulging in the wares and delicacies of the Court.

I kept my eyes on her from a safe distance, enough to allow her to enjoy the Festival alone, but close enough to intervene should another Double Marked individual make a move.

When she was satisfied, we hopped into the carriage and continued into the next section, repeating the process from Court to Court, and with each one, she smiled, danced, ate, and drank. Lexa was a vision of radiance amid the splendor of the festival. Her creamy skin seemed to glow in the ambient light, and her dark hair cascaded like a waterfall, framing a face that could rival the most exquisite artwork. She wore a gown of rich, deep Court of Shadows colors that complemented her beauty, and the soft, flowing fabric whispered with each step she took. The First Trial Festival was a grand celebration of Verihdia's diversity and beauty, but for me, Lexa was its most breathtaking masterpiece. She embodied the Courts' allure, a living testament to the magic and wonder surrounding us. In her presence, I felt like I was truly seeing the Courts for the first time again, each reflecting a facet of her complexity and charm. The festival was a tapestry of colors, emotions, and experiences, but Lexa was its brightest, most enchanting star.

I didn't miss how her eyes lit up as we reached the section dedicated to my Court. She tried to hide it, but forgot how well I understood her.

I didn't miss the look of disappointment on her face as we walked around The Court of the Undying's section, and she didn't see the familiar face of her best friend. I assured her she would see them when we visited that Court in a few months. That seemed to appease her slightly.

The moon had replaced the sun in the sky, and the Festival came to life with Mythica-induced lights, twinkling and offering a warm, inviting glow. By the time we made it to The Court of Talisman's section, she and I were starving, so we indulged in some delectable food and found a seat among the joyful Festival participants.

She took a careful bite of her dinner and moaned her appreciation of the taste, and I couldn't help how that sound affected me. Everything she did affected me.

Her eyes met mine, as if she knew what she had done to me.

"Are you enjoying yourself?" I asked.

She took a moment to consider it, but the smile plastered on her face all night was enough of an answer. "I've always loved this Festival," she finally replied. "It was my favorite event of the year, every year. At the Institute, for so long, I never felt any connection to the Courts. I couldn't understand why all my classmates were falling head over heels for their chosen Court when I couldn't even understand them. It's like falling in love, I guess. How can you fall in love with someone you know nothing about?"

I smiled, watching her hands move with her expressive and passionate monologue.

"That's how I felt about the Courts. So, this festival made me feel like I was getting a little glance at the real Courts, not the watered-down textbook version. This festival was such a beautiful way to experience the Courts in the only way I could," she gushed. Instantly, her cheeks darkened with a blush. "I don't know why I'm telling all this to you. I mean, of course, you already know that."

"I've never attended."

Her eyes widened in shock. "Never?"

I shook my head.

"How is that possible? It's a festival in your honor. All of yours," she gestured her arms widely and I chuckled softly at her enthusiasm.

I sighed then, letting the decision I was faced with weigh on my mind. I could give her the same half-truth that I give everyone brave enough to ask the same question concerning all my Wardenly duties. All the festivals, all the events, all the requirements. Tell them that I have experienced it all before and that I've grown tired of the frivolity and monotony of it all. Or, I could do what I haven't dared to do with anyone, least of all myself, and tell her the truth.

The strangest and most concerning fact was that it wasn't even a hard decision. "The First Trial is not something I wish to celebrate." The truth was a whispered confession on my lips.

Her expression softened almost instantly from one of shock to one of concern. She nearly started to speak four different times before rethinking her response. A soft, melancholic smile played on my lips.

"I'm sorry," she said finally.

I nodded, accepting her sympathy.

"Do you want to talk about it?" She asked.

"It's not a pleasant story, despite the picture this Festival likes to paint," I warned, attempting to keep the playful air present despite the memories that were beginning to flood to the forefront of my mind.

"I don't mind."

And honestly, I believed her.

"There were twenty-four of us." I studied her face to gauge her reaction. She folded her hands on the table's surface and watched me thoughtfully. "Before the inception of the Courts, Verihdia was governed closely by the Gods."

"How close?" She asked eagerly.

My hand reached across the table and gripped hers before I could stop it. "This closely," I replied, staring into her gaze. Her chest rose and fell softly, and her lips parted ever so slightly. I held her gaze longer than I should have, then pulled my hand back. "The Gods had planned the expansion of Verihdia and knew they needed to find worthy successors to rule on this plane." It all sounded so diplomatic, but the reality couldn't have been more different. Flashes of blood and fear briefly shot through my mind, and I shook them off, closing my eyes tightly.

"How did they choose who would compete?" It was a question I'd asked myself as well. To this day, I wish I never got my answer.

"The Gods hand-picked which individuals would participate," I started, feeling sick to my stomach.

"They chose? I thought whoever wanted to compete was able to?"

I shook my head.

"The Gods did not want to leave this up to chance. They choose the twenty-four most powerful Mythica wielders in all of Verihdia."

"I guess that does make sense," she mused. Yes, it would make sense…if only that were all there was to it.

"It certainly served their purposes," I responded, ignoring the urge to curse the very Gods I spoke of.

"What do you mean?" She prompted, leaning forward. My eyes trailed to her chest, where her new position pushed her breasts up, and a salacious grin played on my lips. She cleared her throat and drew my attention back to her face, which was painted with faux fury but also present was just as deep a blush.

I sighed, knowing that I needed to continue the recount for her. "It was clever of them to choose the most powerful to compete for a chance at one of the elusive Wardenships. Because that way, their winners were guaranteed to wield Mythica, which would be incredibly beneficial to have to fight for their side."

She raised an eyebrow at that.

"And this way, the seven people that the Gods were puppetting could eliminate the other Mythica-wielders who were the closest to having the power to overthrow them."

A sound, almost like a strangled gasp, escaped her mouth. She recovered her composure quickly and narrowed her eyes at me.

"Overthrow the Gods?" She asked as if it were the most ridiculous claim.

"Things were a lot different when they walked among us." I let my gaze trail off into the distance, watching smiling people mill about the festival's booths, excitedly basking in the joy and extravagance. I was one of the few who survived that fateful Trial, though it was a victory tainted by survivor's guilt. I had made choices that had spared me, but those choices had come at a heavy cost. I had taken lives to preserve my own, and the weight of that burden is a darkness that lingers in the depths of my soul. "I bear the scars of that First Trial both seen and unseen. That day torments me like a specter that cannot be banished, a reminder of the bloodshed and death that still stains my hands."

She studied me for a moment, content to sit in silence. I hoped I had not scared her away or confused her with my rather brutal opinion on the way of the world. The Court of Shadows may be my domain, but it is also a prison of my own making, a reflection of the torment that dwells within my soul. The memories of that First Trial are a curse I can never lift and they serve as a painful testament to the price of survival in a world ruled by divine whims.

"The Institute has taught us so many wrong things," she lamented.

"The First Trial wasn't a celebration or even a competition," I continued. "It was a bloodbath of horrific proportions orchestrated by ruthless and terrified Gods who would sooner destroy the world they created than give up their power over it." I tried to contain the vitriolic tone of my voice, but there was a certain relief that came from sharing these secrets with Lexa. Secrets I hadn't been able to tell a soul. I never even shared these secrets with my mother, who was so proud of my ascension that the thought of ruining her image of my newfound position was too much to bear. Throughout the years, the memories of that First Trial remained a constant companion, a haunting reminder that I could never escape.

She sighed deeply, then spoke clearly, her eyes burning into mine. "Let's go."

I flicked my eyes back to her. She was standing from the table and smoothing out her dress.

"What?"

"Let's leave. I'm ready to go."

I glanced up at her Mythica, it was roaring around her head, thrashing in what seemed like anger.

"You were just having fun," I commented, trying to make light of her statement.

She waved me off with a single brush of her hand. "I've seen everything I need to and am ready to continue." She did a relatively good job hiding how my story affected her outwardly. I can see her more clearly than that.

"You're angry," I stated, standing to meet her gaze.

"No, I'm just done looking around."

I shook my head.

"I can see you, little storm." I didn't miss how her breathing hitched as the words slipped past my lips.

"I'm fine," she lied.

"Are you angry at the Gods?"

She shook her head as I took a step forward into her space.

"Then you're angry at me for what I had to do at the First Trial?" Another step.

She shook her head again.

I was close to her, feeling her warm breath against my skin. "What then?"

"I just hate that this Festival is bringing up memories you shouldn't have to relive," she exploded in a rushed whisper. The corners of my mouth turned up in a soft smile.

"Are you… concerned for my feelings, Miss Cromwell?" I teased. She rolled her eyes before she turned on a heel and started toward the cart. "Does this mean you don't hate me anymore?" I called after her. She scoffed dramatically as if it was the most absurd claim ever to be made, but I noticed the way her Mythica surged around her and felt an eager warmth pull at my chest.

"Just get in the cart," she tossed over her shoulder before climbing into the back of the carriage. I chuckled to myself and slid onto the front bench. We took off down the road, passing smiling faces, upbeat music, and bustling excitement.

I felt her presence as she leaned forward through the open window at the front of the cart. "Does it still hurt?" she asked quietly.

"Your mood swings? Yes, desperately. I don't know how I am expected to survive them," I feigned irritation, then fell into a loud, bellowed laughter as she playfully punched my arm.

"I was trying to have an honest moment with you, but I can see that was naive of me to expect of you," she spat back.

I held my hands up in mock surrender. "My apologies. You know I can't resist riling you up. It's quite possibly my new favorite pastime."

She scoffed.

"I cannot stand you," she exclaimed with a dramatic sigh. I turned over my shoulder to face her, my eyes meeting hers, and I could have sworn there was the briefest shock that ran through my blood as our breath mingled due to our closeness.

"You and I both know that isn't true," I breathed softly. I searched her eyes for a reaction. Wanting her to let the wall down again as she had last night.

She let her eyes drift closed, breaking the connection of our gazes and took a deep, steadying breath. I couldn't help but smirk at the way my proximity affected her.

When her eyes reopened, heat seared through them.

I very nearly closed the space between us to taste her lips again, but I couldn't make myself, not now that I knew what she had learned from Korzich. She needed to come to me when she was ready to accept the reality of what this connection was between us.

I broke the tension between us by returning my gaze to the road ahead.

"We were disillusioned to the so-called majesty of the First Trial fairly quickly," I whispered, ignoring the slight warning bells sounding in my mind. "It all became agonizingly clear when, after the welcome banquet, we were asked to kill our first competitor."

She gasped but otherwise remained silent.

"We all received a note at our quarters when we retired for the evening. It simply said that one of the competitors must be dead before the first round of the Trial commenced the following morning." I sighed, remembering the feel of the ivory envelope in my hand. The vile words were written so elegantly. The cruel juxtaposition still haunts me to this day.

"Her name was Sevia," I whispered, seeing the flash of her soft tan skin in my memory. She was kind but lethally potent. Her Mythica could freeze a person's very blood in their veins. She offered a demo at dinner that evening when we all were playfully showing off for each other. I almost participated, but I'd learned that not everybody appreciated their Mythica being stolen for however brief a moment it was. I decided not to show my cards just yet.

That showcase of her skill was her downfall. It could have easily been mine.

And I am not unaware of the fact that had I participated, it would have been me.

"The First Trial lasted for three months. Truthfully, sometimes, I'll have nightmares of my own and wake up without realizing it's over. That's why I understood your fear last night."

An almost impulsive shiver ran through my body. Her hand came to a rest on my shoulder.

"It is over. You won," she whispered. I shook my head.

"We didn't win. We survived."

"I don't understand something…" she started. "If you hate what the Gods forced you to do, why would you all agree to do the same to the Warden of Forgotten? I don't get it. Why hurt him?"

I heard the judgment in her tone. I would be shocked if it had not been present. She was still holding back from me, and what she had seen in her vision of my guilt was precisely the reason why.

"I once asked you to believe there was more to the story that I couldn't disclose. Can you still do that?" I felt her lean back and take a long breath.

"Yes, I can," she answered after a long while.

"If you take nothing else from this story, perhaps you can see how I wouldn't make a choice of such gravity lightly," I urged, hopefully.

"I'm sorry you had to go through all that, Lysander," her voice was soft, full of care. The depth of her empathy truly shocked me.

"If I had to do it all over again to arrive where I am today…" I paused, thinking about the implications of the statement I was about to utter. A little over a month ago, I would have given anything to return to the First Trial and lose. But now? Now, I thank my lucky stars for being strong enough to survive and make it to Lexa. I turned my face once more toward her. Our mouths were inches apart."I would," I finished. Her eyes flicked down to my lips before returning to mine. She sighed softly.

"Well, where to next?" She asked, leaning back from me.

I smirked, recognizing how her cheeks flushed in embarrassment at how much she enjoyed being so close to me.

"The Court of Talisman," I replied.

We rode through the bustling activity of the Festival, and I couldn't help but notice that the wonder and light were gone from her eyes. She was looking at this Festival and its origins in a different light. I couldn't feel guilty about that, although I should have. I couldn't help but feel a sense of solidarity, having her understand my aversion to the 'holiday.' She was angry *for* me. She was upset *for* me. She wanted to help me remove myself from a situation that would bring unwanted memories to the forefront. She cared about me.

Suddenly, a gasp of excitement caught me off guard.

"Stop!" Lexa called, and I found myself immediately feeling on guard. My fingers tingled with my Mythica that prepared for a fight. As it slowed, she hopped out of the carriage, and I cursed under my breath.

I pulled the cart to the side of the road and followed after her in a sprint. She was weaving through the crowd and stopped at a man in the crowd. Her arms latched around his neck, and she embraced the surprised gentleman. Jealousy rolled off of me in waves as I approached, only quieting when I saw the face of her professor from the Institute. The same one she was speaking to in the hall outside of the Greenhouse when she didn't know I was watching her.

I made my way back to the carriage ot wait and allowed them a few moments to talk privately, knowing how important this reunion was for her.

There was very little I wouldn't do for her.

After her conversation, she returned to the cart with a slightly more forlorn expression than before, and I could see her Mythica swirling in discomfort.

"Everything alright?" I asked as I sent the cart back into motion.

"What?" she said, distracted. "Oh, um, yes, I'm fine." As we rode past, the professor watched us with a gloomy gaze. Our eyes met and I felt an almost icy familiarity wash over me.

Shaking my head, I turned my attention back to the road ahead. Eventually, we arrived at the depot on the outskirts of The Court of Talisman's veil. After stocking up on warm cloaks and boots and preparing for the eternal winter just beyond the veil, we began the trek through the Mythica shroud.

As we approached, the shimmering pink veil glittered and reflected small fractals of light across the ground. It had been so long since I traveled through this veil that I'd forgotten what toll it asked of its travelers.

As we pushed through, the temperature dropped instantly, and I regretted not buying myself a third pair of socks and another cloak. You know, come to think of it, I could have used an entirely new wardrobe for this trip. Lexa, too. We could have stocked her up completely. She's probably hungry too. I know we just ate at the Festival, but surely she will need something else soon…

Shutting my eyes tight, I forced the gluttonous thoughts away. The veil brought forth the tempting thoughts of wanting in excess, and there was nothing I wanted more than Lexa Cromwell—all of her.

Glancing around I remembered why I avoided this Court. It was a vast expanse of white rolling hills covered in thick blankets of pristine snow. The setting sun cast an almost pink tint across the fields. Ice-covered trees glistened in the waning light. We would reach the Prism Library by early morning if we rode through the night, although the thick snowfall might prove challenging to navigate. The Court of Talisman did not have many widespread villages outside of Dedaria. So there would be no place to stop for the night even if we wanted to. I probably should have timed our voyage here more carefully, but I wanted her to experience the Festival for as long as she wanted to.

I could tell she was cold. She pulled the cloak I had given her back in my Court around her tightly, and I could see her breath in the air, but still, she looked around at the Court with a wonder-filled expression.

"Welcome to The Court of Talisman."

NINETEEN

I rushed past the excited Festival attendees and threw my arms around Oliver. He grunted as my body made contact, then chuckled softly and settled into the embrace.

"Hello to you too, Lexa," he offered warmly.

I had no idea how much I missed him until the warm tears were pouring down my face. I pulled back and wiped them away, shame coloring my expression.

"Are you alright?" He asked with an edge of worry.

I nodded, "Yeah, I just missed you so much." He tilted his head and nodded his understanding. "It's been a long month and a half."

His weathered face softened as his lips pulled up into a sad smile. "I agree." He seemed distraught about something. His usual bright attitude was dampened by something.

"What's wrong?" I asked, placing a comforting hand on his upper arm.

His mouth slipped open, and a sigh escaped. He avoided eye contact with me, and suddenly, fear clutched my heart. "What happened, Oliver? Are you ok? Is it Axel? Riley? Did something happen to them?"

He shook his head, dismissing the claims.

"No, no, nothing like that. I'm sorry. I guess I am just a little sentimental. I didn't know I was going to miss you this much." His light blue eyes glistened with unshed tears.

"See, I knew I was your favorite," I joked, feeling the sting of sadness in my own eyes.

He laughed and patted me on the back in a firm comforting way. "Don't tell your brother. He'll be devastated," he spoke with all the intentions of a joke, but it felt more loaded than that.

"How is your tour going?" He asked, changing the subject quickly.

I considered the question. Seeing two Courts of Veridia is something nobody besides the Wardens themselves has been privileged enough to do, so in that respect, it has been a dream come true. But at the same time, the budding relationship with Lysander and the unresolved secrets I've recently learned have complicated everything. Not to mention the Forgotten Court sending people to try and capture or kill me. "It's overwhelming," I finally settled on.

He nodded, understanding. His eyes flicked over my shoulder to where I had left the cart and Lysander. "Is he treating you well?"

The briefest flash of his fingers pressing into me and drawing out the most intense moment of passion I've ever experienced crossed my mind Quickly, I cleared my throat and forced the image back, embarrassment coloring my expression.

"He's…" I briefly looked over my shoulder at him. He was sitting atop the cart, keeping a watchful eye on me and the surroundings. "Surprising."

When I turned back to Oliver, his face was severe in a way I wasn't familiar with from my joyful professor. "You need to be careful with him," he warned in a low voice.

I stuttered for a moment, searching for a response. "I .. uh... I know. I am." That was all I could say.

"I mean it, Lexa," he continued, lowering his voice. "He may be one of the better Wardens, but he's still a Warden. You need to consider that the people who seem to be on your side are not acting in your best interests." He took a deep breath. "And maybe there are people who are on your side, but you don't know it."

I shook my head, trying to make sense of his words, but he just continued to stare at me with that confusing, serious expression.

"What do you mean?"

He placed both hands on my shoulders and lowered his voice.

"Just promise me that you'll reevaluate who you are putting your trust in."

The man I was looking at now did not look like the man I had grown to admire and trust at the Institute. His eyes were nearly wild, and his voice was almost desperate. I took a step back, and his hands fell from my shoulders.

"I should probably get going. We're expected at the next Court in the morning." I offered a curt nod and turned on my heel without saying goodbye. I knew I would probably regret that later, but at the moment, I felt like I needed some space from him. He tried to call after me, but I was already back at the cart and settling into the seat.

I replayed the conversation with him in my mind repeatedly as Lysander navigated us through the crowds toward the depot outside of the veil leading to The Court of Talisman. Once we had successfully bundled up to prepare for the eternal winter we were about to cross into, I decided to put all thoughts of Oliver and our strange conversation behind me. He was simply worried about me. He just wanted to make sure I was safe.

He's always wanted to make sure I was safe.

Crossing through the veil, I braced myself for whatever payment it would claim. As the temperature dropped and I felt the cool sting of winter air bite my nose, I realized that I had been going about this tour all wrong. I had been considering this a burden when it was a gift. A gift that I deserved to savor. By crossing this veil, I added yet another Court to the list of places I have been fortunate to explore. I would experience this Court and the others after it in its entirety. I wouldn't shy away from this opportunity.

It was a rather indulgent way of thinking and I couldn't help but note the veils' influence, but I was also thankful for it. My eyes drifted to land on the back of Lysander's head through the small window. The exposed dark skin on his neck had developed tiny bumps from the cold. At that moment, I wanted to taste it. To let myself get lost in his touch the way I had before. I wanted to feel his arms around me and hear his whispered words meant for my ears only. I wanted it all… and I wanted it from him.

"Welcome to The Court of Talisman," Lysander offered and I shook my head, letting the frankly concerning thoughts drift away.

"It is rather cold," I admitted, pulling his cloak tighter around me.

"Do you need another cloak?" He asked, unhooking the latch on his own. I reached forward, placing my hand on his.

I was fully prepared to stop him. I should have said no, but something about being this close to the veil made me desperate to accept everything he offered. Everything.

"Yes, please."

His eyes bore into mine as he slid his cloak off his shoulders and handed it back to me. I'd grown to cherish how he looked at me like he was discovering something new in my gaze each time his eyes met mine.

Did he know that I knew the truth behind what we were to each other?

Did I want him to?

"How long have you been having nightmares?" He asked softly.

I slid his cloak around my form, trying not to let the guilt eat me alive that he was now one cloak down in this frigid air and I furrowed my brow.

"I don't mean to pry," he added.

I bit my lip, finding it already chapped from the cool night air. In my entire life, the only person to ever know about the reality of my nightmares was Axel, but even he wasn't privy to the truth of their effect on me. He only knew that they had happened. He didn't know that I was forced to live out my watery death each and every night.

That reality had been incredibly isolating, but the idea of sharing that reality with someone else was almost too terrifying to face.

And yet. I found myself wanting to share it with Lysander.

"Most of my life," I admitted.

He exhaled sharply through his nose. "How often?" He asked.

"Every night," I whispered.

He nodded his head, looking out at the road in front of us. A soft winter storm was blowing wisps of white dancing across the paved road, covering it in a layer of dusted bright snow. The sun quickly descended behind the horizon and I already missed the minimal warmth it offered.

"Tell me about them?" He urged quietly after a while.

I sighed, willing my heart rate to slow so that I could get through this without breaking down.

"They always start the same way," I began, my voice low. "I open my eyes and I'm underwater in the middle of a wide ocean. Which is very strange, considering I've never even seen an ocean in person," I tacked on awkwardly.

Lysander was listening intently, remaining calm, but I saw his jaw tighten.

"I try to swim, but there's no surface. There's never any surface." I swallowed the lump that was forming in my throat and continued. "I can't find a way out, and I can't hold my breath much longer, so I drown. Every single night. I drown."

A tear slid down my cheek. "I feel it all. It's so real. I mean, I know that it's not, but Gods, it certainly feels like it. The water burns my lungs, stings my eyes, and claims my body. So I die, no matter how hard I try to survive, hoping maybe this time it'll have a different outcome."

Lysander gripped the reins tightly as he listened.

"For a long time, that's all it was, but recently…there's been something else."

I took a deep breath, pushing back the tears that were beginning to fall. "There's a creature. The one I thought I saw in the fountain. It's there, looming in the darkness of the waters. Waiting for the chance to take me."

He let out a shaky exhale and I watched as the clouds of breath danced in the chilled night air.

"I don't know what it is, I don't know what it wants with me, and I don't know why it's been getting worse." I was fully crying now. Wet, hot streaks fell down my cheeks, and when the cool air brushed against the paths, a sting of cold reminded me where I was.

Lysander pulled on the reins, bringing the horses to a complete stop and, in an instant, he was climbing into the back of the carriage with me, quickly wrapping me in his arms.

I didn't have it in me to protest, so I held on and accepted the comfort he was offering.

"You've suffered through that every night since we met?" He asked in a broken, almost pleading voice.

I shook my head, pulling back to meet his gaze. "For some reason, I didn't have a single nightmare when I was in your Court. It was the most well-rested I've ever been in my life," I tried to tease, unsuccessfully, because instead, it came out entirely sincere.

His lips curved into an almost blinding smile. His emerald eyes flicked down to my lips and back to my eyes. His breath was warm on my lips, and I felt the literal and metaphorical icy shell around my heart begin to melt with each brush of his fingers across my body.

There was this nearly hypnotic pull that was drawing me to this man. It had been at play between us from the moment I laid eyes on him at the Courting Ball and, despite the several times that he reminded me why he was the Warden of envy, I couldn't bring myself to ignore it anymore.

There were a million reasons why I shouldn't indulge in him, shouldn't indulge in this connection we have, but with his arms wrapped around me and his lips mere inches from mine, I couldn't bring myself to care about a single one of them. I wanted every inch of Lysander Bladespell. I wanted to claim his body and his heart. I wanted to be the only person in Verihdia who knew all his secrets. I was tired of fighting this draw that I felt toward him. I wanted him, and I was feeling just selfish enough to take him.

I leaned forward, ready to claim his lips with mine in a promise that I was fully prepared to make when the door to the carriage was ripped off its hinges.

The next several minutes were a horrific blur.

Lysander was caught off guard and the two figures who ripped the door open had gotten their arms around him, dragging him from the carriage. I think I might have screamed. A third figure grabbed my waist and pulled me into the cold night air. The horses whinnied and took off running, taking our carriage and belongings with them. I violently thrashed in the man's hold. He grunted in pain, as my elbow made contact with his temple. I saw the flash of his eerie white mask in the corner of my eye, and instantly, anger replaced the fear that was coursing through my veins.

I heard Lysander fighting off the other two figures and fear bloomed in my chest.

I can't lose him.

Not when I finally decided to let myself have him.

"We're not trying to hurt you," the man who held me around my midsection seethed as he struggled against my thrashing.

I turned my head toward the figure, feeling an overwhelming surge of Mythica burning within my core. It was there, bubbling just beneath my skin, and every ounce of my body begged me to indulge in the power. To let myself have what it was I wanted. Whether it was the veil's influence or my Mythica itself, I couldn't tell, but I lost track of where I ended and where my Mythica began. We were one. And we were powerful.

As my hand snaked down my side and reached for the dagger strapped safely against my thigh, I stared into the dark voids of the mask where my assailant's eyes would be, and I unleashed every ounce of my power in one silent question.

What are you afraid of?

He screamed as my Mythica sank its claws into his mind. I wasn't being gentle with him. I wanted it to hurt. It felt almost overwhelming and nearly sentient - my Mythica. It was as if it was making the decision to bring this man to his knees all on its own, but I didn't have time to worry about that. I had an assailant to destroy.

It was almost admirable how hard he fought against my power. Pathetic, but admirable. My eyes burned into his mask as he choked on the words I forcibly dragged from his lips.

"Fa-fai-" he struggled, trying to keep his secrets. That simply wouldn't do.

"Tell me," I commanded in a nearly unrecognizable voice.

"Failing my Court!" He cried out, falling to his knees in the white snow, cradling his head in his hands. A trickle of red blood fell from his ears down onto the blanket of white snow beneath him, and something about the stark contrast of color brought me back to my senses. The almost grey haze that had clouded my vision lifted and my breath came in ragged spurts. I pulled my Mythica back and it returned to me reluctantly, but not before ripping through this man's mind. He fell forward, his sobs of pain muffled by the mask.

What did I just do?

I pressed a palm to my chest and sucked in shallow gulps of freezing air.

I couldn't stop looking at him. He was writhing on the ground in obvious pain, holding his head like it might fall off if he let go. What I had just done was not self-defense. It was torture.

I stumbled back from him and I felt the dagger weigh heavy in my hands. Sobs wracked my body.

"Lexa!" Lysander's worried voice distracted me from the man at my feet. "Lexa, we have to go. Are you hurt?" His strong hands came down onto my shoulders. His face was stern, covered in a slight sheen of sweat despite the temperature. There were dark red specks of blood decorating his cheek and I tried not to look over his shoulder to the men behind him, but I failed. They weren't dead, but they were severely injured. The snow around them was splattered with their dark crimson blood.

"Little storm, please. Focus on me. We need to go."

My eyes snapped back to his, and I nodded, unable to form words. He grabbed my hand in his and we took off running. Our carriage was long gone. Even the tracks had been covered by a layer of snow as it continued to fall steadily from the sky. I kept up with him as much as I could, but the cold air burned my lungs. To my surprise, he didn't stay on the main road. Instead, he veered us off the path and into the thick woods. He expertly led us through the forest, dodging branches and carefully navigating in the dark. When my shock began to wear off, I noticed that he was doubling back and branching off in new directions. He was covering our tracks, changing the path. He was smart.

I don't know how long we ran through the woods before he finally slowed to a walking pace. I felt my lungs and legs screaming at me in pain, but it was my head that hurt the most from the almost fugue state of anger I had found myself in back there. My body was warm, but the freezing bite of the evening winter air was ferocious and would claim my flesh in no time.

"We have to get out of the cold," he muttered, reading my mind. He held my hand in his as we trekked through the trees in the dim moonlight. "There's got to be some kind of shelter around here somewhere."

As Lysander searched, I let myself finally think about what had just happened. I was attacked again. This time, they sent three. Next time, it'll be more. In the moment of fight or flight, my Mythica chose to defend. I always knew my Mythica was powerful, but never in my life had I ever felt like I didn't have a hand on it. Back there, it had made its own choices. It wasn't mine to control. I had often resented my Mythica growing up, how unpredictable it was, but for the first time in all my years, I was afraid of it.

Lysander's body began to shake and I realized that I still had on his cloak. Quickly, I slid it off my shoulders and wrapped him in the fabric. The loss of the extra layer was immediately noticeable. Still, I realized that Lysander had needed it because instead of arguing he wrapped himself up tightly and continued forward.

My fingers were aching and I tried to breathe warm air into my hands in an attempt to stave off the frostbite. Lysander was focused and determined. He hadn't relaxed his shoulders since the carriage doors were ripped open. He led us through the woods expertly and I admired his dedication to getting us to some sort of relative safety.

"There," he whispered, his voice cutting through the still night air. I followed his gaze to see the opening of a small cave. The cave's entrance was framed by a towering arch of ice and snow, creating a natural doorway to this hidden wonder. Long, crystalline stalactites hung like fragile chandeliers, catching the soft, diffused light of the winter moon that filtered through the frost-covered branches. We breached the mouth of the cave, and although the cold was still overwhelming, the reprieve from the biting winds was enough to calm my shaking nerves.

The world outside was silenced as we stepped inside, a hush of tranquility surrounded me. Within minutes, Lysander had somehow gotten a fire going near the back of the cave. The smoke was thick, but it mostly traveled up and out through minuscule holes in the cave ceiling where a few snowflakes fell through. The roaring fire danced along the ground, its flames were a mesmerizing blend of crimson, gold, and orange. The fire crackled and popped, sending sparks into the air that vanished in a swirl of steam. The radiant heat emanating from the blaze created a cozy oasis amidst the icy surroundings, warming both body and soul.

When he was satisfied, he turned to face me and I watched as the last few hours finally hit him. His stern and focused face softened and he rushed forward, embracing me. "Are you ok? Did he hurt you?"

I shook my head. "No, he didn't. I'm ok. I'm ok," I reassured him.

He sighed deeply, closing his arms tighter around me, but then he winced in pain.

"What's wrong?" I pulled back to look at his face, which was twisted in pain. "What happened?"

He shook his head, "It's nothing."

I scanned his frame, pushing the cloak off his shoulders to reveal a dark red stain on the side of his tunic.

How did I not notice?

"Lysander-" I whispered, reaching for the hem of his tunic.

He grabbed my wrist and held me off. "I'm ok," he stated, but I shook him off and grabbed his shirt despite his protesting. He had been wounded. The angry slash looked like it had stopped bleeding, thank Gods, but it would get infected if we didn't clean it soon.

"Sit," I commanded. He began to protest, but one look at my face and he knew I wouldn't take no for an answer. He settled down onto the ground and leaned against the wall of the cave for support, his torso flexing as he tried to overcompensate for his wounded abdomen. I rushed back into the cold and gathered a handful of fresh snow. Returning, I saw that Lysander had removed his soiled tunic and was sitting near the fire with nothing but his trousers on. His dark brown skin glistened in the warm amber firelight. I bit my lip to avoid licking it like some hungry fool and rushed forward.

"This might hurt," I whispered, kneeling next to him and pressing the first handful of snow onto the wound. He held it together as best he could, but I knew he was in pain.

"You don't have to do this, you know?' He whispered,

"It could get infected," I replied, meeting his gaze.

"I'm immortal, remember?" He teased.

I actually hadn't remembered. Not in the moment, at least. All I could think about was what it would feel like to lose him and I despised that feeling. "I'll be fine in a few more hours. Like it never happened."

"Oh." I sat back on my heels, pulling my hands back from his skin. Our eyes were locked together, and our shoulders rose and fell with matching deep breaths.

"I know that you-" Lysander trailed off gently. I looked at him in question. "You know about," he paused, sighing and switching tactics. "Korzich told me that you know."

My breath caught in my throat. He knew. And he knew that I knew. We both knew. I turned my eyes to the floor and tried not to focus on how his eyes still bore into my face.

"Say it," he pleaded, inching forward. I felt his body heat enveloping mine.

I shook my head, suddenly feeling much less confident in my choice this far from the veil's influence. " I can't."

"Can't or won't?" He challenged.

"How do I know I can trust you?" It was nothing more than a whisper. Tears streamed down my cheeks. "How do I know you wouldn't use me just to get me to Pledge to your Court? How can I be sure that you'll keep my secret? You hold all the power here, Lysander."

"Ask me," he challenged. My hands were clasped tightly in my lap, and my gaze locked on the ground. His fingers found my chin and lifted my face so I could meet his eyes. "You and I both know that it is you who holds the power and you have a foolproof method of discovering what it is I want."

Shock flooded me.

He couldn't possibly mean…

"So, Lexa Cromwell." He drew out each syllable of my name as if he savored how it tasted on his tongue. "Ask me what I desire."

"I...I can't." I stumbled over the phrase, and the overwhelming feeling that this was a trap consumed me.

"You have my permission, little storm."

My heart jumped, as it often did when he called me that. It was another reminder that he saw my Mythica for what it was and still did not fear me.

"Are you positive you want to do this?" I whispered. This ability that I had was the very same one that got someone killed. A Warden, no less. Not to mention the display it just put on when we were attacked. I had no idea if I could trust it not to go digging for more than I asked right now.

"I am many things, Lexa, but I am not a liar." He raised his hand to cup my cheek and his thumb rubbed circles on my suddenly sensitive skin.

I nodded slowly, inhaling a long and deep breath. And then I reached…down into the darkest parts of myself, into the inky well of Mythica that constantly swirled within me - around me. The Mythica now felt like more of a burden than a gift. I gripped onto the dark, smokey edges and pulled. It felt more lighthearted now, as if it hadn't just torn a man's mind to shreds just an hour ago. Once I was positive that I had a confident hold on the tendrils of magic, I slid my eyes closed and let the question whisper from my mind.

What do you desire, Lysander?

My silent question reached him with a gentle caress and my Mythica coaxed him seductively to provide the answers I required. He braced himself and I witnessed the moment it took hold. His eyes widened, his back straightened, and he opened his mouth involuntarily.

"You, Lexa Cromwell. I want you. Nothing but you…my mate."

That word on his lips was the sweetest thing I'd ever heard. Tears began to fall from my eyes, but this time, they weren't tears of fear, anger, or even regret. There was nothing but adoration and relief in these tears now.

"You and I are like fire and tinder, Lexa." His thumb ran delicate lines across my lips as he held me close. His eyes searched mine. "This heat between us is intoxicating, burning, powerful." His voice was barely above a whisper, as if it pained him to speak the words into existence. "It's also destructive, dangerous, it's…reckless." There was that word again. "My siblings still want you, and they're still going to force you to finish this tour. They won't stop pursuing you because of me. If anything, it paints a larger target on both of our backs." Those emerald eyes pleaded with me.

I saw it in his expression, that he felt the same way I did. All those moments when I wasn't sure I could trust my feelings were real. That he felt the bond between us, too. Suddenly, he felt all too far away. I leaned closer, testing the boundaries. When he didn't retreat, I swung a leg over his waist and straddled him. His eyes followed me with a lust-filled expression and his willpower shattered a little more as I settled my hot center just over his aching length.

I hovered over him, not quite making contact, our gazes locked in a heated standoff. His body tensed and his fists clenched at his side, as if he were resisting the urge to touch me. I was not as strong. My hands drifted up to rest on his muscular chest. I felt his heart pounding. It wasn't enough. My fingers trailed upwards to the bare skin of his neck, which then erupted in goosebumps under my touch, and his eyes fell closed. A warning in the form of a deep moan escaped from his lips. My fingers continued to explore the unblemished skin of his throat as his breath tickled my face. The familiar and intoxicating fiery scent invaded my senses, and before I knew what I was doing, my fingers had begun tracing the lines of his lips. They parted slightly under my touch, his breath slowly becoming more erratic with each passing, desire-filled second.

"You're right," I whispered seductively. "A pairing between the two of us is inconvenient at best. Destructive, dangerous, and yes, reckless."

His eyes opened narrowly, filled with lust.

"But I can't help how you make me feel, Lysander." It was true. I tried. Gods, did I try. I did everything possible to avoid this outcome, but he was an unavoidable force and I was tired of trying to fight against the inevitable.

"So, what do you want to do about it?" He replied in a playfully challenging tone. His emerald eyes darkened with so much desire that it should have scared me. Instead, there was a kind of heat only he could ignite in me, building at my core.

"I want to be reckless with you."

And then, finally, his lips were crashing against mine. His kiss was demanding and rough but full of everything we still had left to say. There would come a time when we said the words to each other, but right now, we would let our bodies do all the talking.

His hands grabbed my soft waist and pulled me down onto his lap. We groaned into the kiss the moment my core connected to his trouser-covered length. He took control of my movement, moving my hips in just the right way to create a delicious friction. I was blind with euphoria, feeling his touch in every nerve ending and every breath. His mouth trailed eager kisses down the column of my throat.

My head fell back to welcome his touch against my skin. I drove my hips into him, desperately chasing some relief from this white-hot burn of need and desire. His fingers claimed the flesh at my thighs and slid higher and higher, closer to the apex of my thighs and the center of my lust. His eyes flashed up at me in a silent question. One I was eager to answer.

"Yes, Lysander. Please."

He smirked, looking almost devious as his lips resumed their exploration of my throat, while his fingers pushed the fabric of my dress up over my waist to expose my core to him.

The moment one of his expert fingers slid through the slick arousal there, he moaned with appreciation. I watched him with rapt attention. His smooth brown skin and bright emerald eyes were so stunningly beautiful, I was transfixed. His long black hair hung wild and free across his forehead and shoulders. I'd known he was attractive, anyone with eyes could see that, but Lysander wasn't just beautiful…he was a work of art. Perfectly crafted for me and me alone.

He pushed a finger into my heat and I cried out, throwing my head back. The feeling of him inside of me in this way felt so intimate, like he was claiming me in a way that no one else ever could. "This is mine," he growled, thrusting a second finger into my core, his eyes burning with mischievous selfishness and I moaned at the exquisite intrusion.

I bucked my hips, pressing into his fingers with reckless abandon. I was so riled up, so completely lost to the sensation of him, that when he pressed a thumb against the swollen bundle of nerves at my apex, I detonated around him. My fingers dug into his shoulders and my mouth fell open as I rode out the wave of blissful euphoria.

When my body slowed its trembling, Lysander slowly pulled his fingers from my center, and I immediately missed the fullness. Just as I was about to protest, he pressed his fingers against his tongue and closed his mouth around them. I think I gasped as I watched him drink each drop of my arousal from his fingers. His eyes fell closed, and he moaned, a deep resonating sound.

I couldn't move if I wanted to. He was captivating. I was a prisoner to his passion. His hand fell from his lips and I couldn't look away from them. He leaned forward and pressed an almost chaste kiss against my shocked mouth. I tasted myself on him and was positive that I would never taste anything as perfect as the combination of us again. Fire and Rain. Water and Shadows. His lips once again trailed kisses down my throat, and I wanted to feel all of him against all of me. I threw off my cloak and tore my dress over my head. The biting cold nipped at my naked form, but the combined warmth of the fire behind us and the man beneath me made me feel like I was going to go up in flames.

His eyes scanned my body slowly. I didn't have a single moment to feel self-conscious about my soft, round center and thick hips being on full display because this man was staring at me like I was faultless. His gaze trailed across my every imperfection like they were just another gorgeous strand in the tapestry of my beauty.

"I never knew the definition of perfection before this moment," he whispered as his eyes continued their loving exploration of my exposed body. I felt a deep blush warm my skin. He pressed a single emotion-filled kiss against my throat. "I need to taste you," he whispered against my skin.

I felt the vibrations of his claim all the way to my very center.

He moved quickly, setting me down on my back on top of my crumpled cloak and positioning himself on his knees between my legs before I could even take my next breath. "Say yes, little storm," he commanded as he stared at me with eager hunger.

"Yes," I whispered and, within a moment, he was drawing his tongue through my wet, hot center. My back arched and a gasp fell from my lips at the sensation. He continued his hungry claiming of my arousal, lapping at me as if I was the most delectable thing in all of Verihdia. His lips closed around the sensitive bundle of nerves and sucked, sending a wave of pleasure wracking through my body. I was teetering so close to the edge of another orgasm I could barely keep my eyes open. The pleasure was so overwhelming, so consuming. My hands gripped his wild hair and held him to my center.

When he pressed the thickness of his tongue into my core, I was lost to him. Completely. My thighs pressed in on either side of his head as I felt my core clench and pulse with waves of pleasure.

My vision blurred as I rode his tongue through the last shockwaves of my orgasm. When my body settled, and logic returned to me, I glanced down at him to see him kneeling over me, licking his lips with an almost wild expression on his face. It made me feel like the most beautiful woman ever to exist.

Something about how he looked at me was almost enough to convince me to do anything, say anything, or give him anything.

With his eyes on mine, he slowly unlaced the front of his trousers and slid them over his hips, down his thighs, and eventually, he was rid of them altogether, and we were bare before each other.

His length was solid and eager. He settled his hands on either side of my head and leaned forward until I could almost feel him pressed against my center. I ached for it. He pressed the softest kiss against my lips. This wasn't just a kiss. This was a promise. A vow. I felt it as intimately as I could feel myself breathing. With this kiss, he told me everything we hadn't yet put into words, and I answered.

"You know what this means, right?" He asked against my lips in a breathless whisper.

"I do," I answered, waiting for the fear or apprehension to settle in but finding that it never came.

He lined his length up with my slick opening, and I nearly begged him to press his hips forward and claim me.

"Say it," he ordered.

I knew what he wanted to hear. He wanted to know that I was his. That no one else could make me feel how he makes me feel. He wanted to know that I was his mate and he was mine. I watched his verdant eyes as he hovered over me. The man who held my gaze now was Lysander. Not the Warden of Shadows, or envy, or the covetor. Although, I was learning that I appreciated that version of him just as much. But right now, in the darkness of this cave, alone and lost, I wanted him. Every version of him. The good, the bad, the devious, the selfish, the passionate, the caring, the teasing, the powerful. I wanted him. And I needed him to want me, too.

"I'm yours. I've always been yours, Lysander. I will always be yours."

Then he slid into my heat and claimed me in a way only he could. I felt my core tighten around him, throbbing eagerly at the fullness of him. He stretched me so deliciously that I nearly detonated around him again just from the first thrust of his length into me. He exhaled sharply as his eyes drifted closed, as if the feeling was all too much for him. I understood the sentiment. We laid there in perfect stillness for a moment. Only our eager breathing and rapid heart rates caused minimal movement. The feeling of him inside me was like finally learning the answer to a question I didn't even know I had been asking.

His eyes met mine and everything came into such clear and sharp focus. Suddenly, the thick and angry fog that had plagued me unknowingly was lifted. There was no barrier anymore. Whatever Korzich had been instructed to do to hide this connection between Lysander and I drifted away, and in its place was a nearly shimmering tether within my soul, tying myself to him. He must have felt it, too, because his eyes widened, and a gasp fell from his lips. Tears stained my cheek as I felt the full force of the magnificence of it - this bond between us. It was so pure, so vibrant. I wasn't sure how I was ever able to deny it. I lifted a hand to rest on his cheek, wiping away the single tear that slid from his eye.

"My mate," he whispered. It was like arriving home. His smile brightened the dark cave and I smiled back at him, feeling a sort of giddy freeness.

By latching my soul to his, I felt like I was finally able to share the burden of the load with someone else. I didn't realize how heavy it had become.

His eyes darkened then with lustful intentions. His hips pushed forward and I felt him hit the spot so deep within my core that I cried out.

"You're mine," he growled hungrily before he began thrusting with wild abandon.

My neck craned back and my mouth fell open in a breathless pant as he pounded into me. His deep grunts filled the space and his possessive hands found their way to my neck, holding me in place as he continued to hit the deepest part of me that craved him extensively. I ran my hands along his back, dancing across the inked Mark of Shadows that claimed his spine.

One of his possesive hands gently caressed my throat, while the other drifted down toward that sensitive bundle, just above where his length was claiming me. His rough finger rubbed delicious circles there, and I screamed out as a blinding light of ecstasy washed over me.

"Oh gods," I whimpered, feeling entirely submissive to the onslaught of passion that had overcome me.

Lysander leaned forward, his hand still delicately tracing the lines of my throat, and his lips found my ear. With a quick bite, he growled. "Call for the Gods all you want, but they can't make you scream the way I can."

I gasped with shock as he continued to claim me over and over. My cries echoed throughout the cave. There was nothing beyond this moment and nothing beyond the two of us in this space together.

I didn't care what came from this tour. I didn't care which Court I ended up Pledging to. I didn't even care about the masked figures and their pursuit of me. At this moment, with Lysander buried deep inside of me, I felt only him and only us. He sped his hips up, sending me tumbling into another orgasm, while he followed me over the edge with a satisfied moan and the faint shadow of my name on his lips. It was then I knew, beyond a shadow of a doubt, that even though I still had no idea which Court I was meant for, I belonged in his heart… and he belonged in mine.

Twenty

I strode through the bustling festival, a grand showcase of all the seven Courts of Verihdia, with an air of superiority that I couldn't help but wear like a regal cloak. The vibrant colors, enchanting music, and captivating performances were meant to enthrall the masses, but I couldn't help but feel like I was above such frivolous distractions. In my heart, I knew that I deserved to rule this realm, to reign supreme over the Courts of Verihdia. One day, there would be a festival in my honor. I would personally see to it.

The festival was a spectacle, with each court presenting its unique charm. The Court of Passion, with its sensual displays, was seductive and lewd. The Court of Silence displayed its 'honor' and 'righteousness' by hosting mock trials. The Court of the Undying showcased a display of healing magic. At the same time, The Court of Echoes offered nothing comforting, but instead, they opted to provide a clear look at the punishments the criminals of Verihdia had to look forward to.

Despite the grandeur of the festivities, I maintained an air of disinterest as if the wonders of the Courts were beneath me. I watched the revelry unfold with a cold detachment and my mind was focused on my goal.

In the intricate web of Verihdia's courts, I was a man driven by ambition who believed he could manipulate the threads of power to weave a tapestry of his design. My key to this clandestine endeavor was the connection I had forged with Lilith, and through her, I aimed to seize the Court Marks of the six other courts of Verihdia and discover their power for myself.

With her connections and intoxicating allure, Lilith was the linchpin of my plan. She had entranced me with her whispers of secrets, telling me things that only a Warden or their trusted inner circle should know, making me believe that I could ascend to a position of unrivaled power.

"Are you sure you want to go through with this?" She asked, turning to look at me over her shoulder. Her pale skin and bright white hair looked almost translucent in the waning light of The Living Lands.

"Are you having second thoughts about assisting me?" I asked playfully, raising a taunting eyebrow in her direction. She rolled her eyes, but I could see the almost guilty twinge in her jaw. It took some convincing that I wasn't making some sort of cruel joke when I first proposed my plan to her. For a brief moment, I thought perhaps she would turn me in for treason against my Warden and all of Verihdia and that would have been the end of it. She had that power. But the moment my promise of having her at my side through it all reached her ears, she was as receptive as any envious Court of Shadows member would be.

"If we don't succeed-" she started.

"I know," I cut her off. She had thoroughly explained the dangers and risks to me as if I hadn't already known them. The difference was that I was more than willing to take those risks. There was very little I wasn't willing to do when it came to getting everything I deserved in this life. "I don't plan to fail, Lilith."

She nodded a few times to herself, but I could tell my answer only temporarily placated her. I hated how weak she was. If I were Warden, I would never be caught dead with a Vacant liaison. However, her desire to prove her worth despite her defective upbringing certainly influenced my plans. Her need to be 'good enough' made her perfectly malleable to my needs.

"This will be a slow process, you know that, right? You're not going to leave here today with every Mark," she whispered. I wanted to argue, but she made a good point, as much as it pained me to admit that. While the liaisons were present at this festival today, there was no way we'd make the rounds fast enough, leaving enough time to trick them out of their Marks. Lucky for me, they often resided in the halls of the Institute, so whomever we could not meet with today, I would find there when I returned with Lilith for the school year.

Lilith was competent and well-versed in Court politics. I would give her that. I appreciated having the cunning creature on my side. I had to dampen the anxious energy that was eating me inside at the idea of following her lead on this, but even I could admit that she was the one who was best suited to get me what I wanted. Being a leader doesn't mean doing everything yourself. It means knowing who you can manipulate into doing it for you.

Lilith stopped beside the Dean of the Undying, Vance Darkwing. His pale blue eyes were bright and energetic as he surveyed the festival. His form was draped in a soft blue tunic with the Institute crest proudly displayed on his breast pocket. His eyes darkened when he saw Lilith.

"Ah, Dean Hargrove, a pleasure to see you," he responded, sounding anything but happy to see her.

"Vance, I hope you've enjoyed the Festival this year," she said with a slightly less scathing tone than he employed.

"I was," he said quietly with a sharp smile on his lips.

"You remember Chandler, of course," she said, turning to allow me to step forward and reach for Vance's hand. He shook it reluctantly.

"Of course, Mr. Mills, I hope you've enjoyed your first few weeks in your new Court."

I nodded, adding in a charming smile for good measure. "I couldn't be happier." A lie that I planned to rectify as soon as possible. I just need his Court Mark.

"Chandler!" The soft voice that had grated on my nerves for years back at the Institute sent a bolt of fury into my stomach. I looked past Vance to see Riley's familiar face. Their hair was slightly longer, and the color had recently been revived, so the faded blue they had been sporting just last month was now a bright electric cerulean.

I barely managed to contain the scoff that threatened to fall from my lips and plaster the fake smile I'd mastered. "Riley!" I rush past Vance and grab Riley in a tight hug. They tensed in my hold, obviously feeling as out of place in this affectionate embrace as I, but they patted my back a few times and pulled away only after an appropriate amount of time.

"Well, didn't think you'd miss me that much. Wasn't like I was the one you were sleeping with," they teased, and I had to dig deep to respond with a cheery smile.

"Look at you," I said brightly, gesturing at their attire. "An honest-to-God's Undying member right before my eyes. I never doubted you for a second, Riley."

They loved hearing that, damn-near preening at the praise.

"Thanks." They nodded appreciatively. I watched their expression shift slightly as their brows furrowed. "How.. how was she? She was there for the first few weeks, right?"

I managed to school my reaction and keep my composure at the mention of Lexa Cromwell. The 'little storm'. "She was fine, great even. We said our goodbyes, and it was nice."

Their brow rose in question, but they didn't press further.

"Sorry to bother you, Vance," Lilith interjected, demanding our attention again. "I just wanted to see if I could borrow your Institute Manual. I know you always seem to have it with you." She was laying the admiration on thick. She tossed a look my way as if to assure me that it was all for show as if I cared about who she chose to spend her nights with. As long as she got me what I needed, I couldn't care less whose bed she was in.

"Lost yours again?" He teased, slinging his pack off his back.

Lilith shrugged with a smile. "I just needed to check something and didn't feel like traveling all the way to the Forsaken Quarters for the answer." Then her eyes connected with mine, and looked over at Riley. Her message was clear.

"Riley, why don't you show me which Undying delicacy I simply can't live without." I offered them my arm, and they took it reluctantly before leading me to one of the nearby carts. They pointed out a few of the herbal remedies and gushed about the contributions they already seemed to be making. Apparently, Warden Miya Moonshackle had taken a personal interest in their training. I couldn't contain my scoff that time.

"Excuse me? Something you want to say to that?" They asked with a hand on their hip. I had put up with this annoying classmate for years because of their connection to Lexa, but I had no connection to preserve anymore.

"I'm just saying, if your Warden is taking an interest in you right now, it has nothing to do with your talents and everything to do with your friendship with Lexa. They're going to manipulate that bond in their favor, and if you don't see that, you're naive."

Their eyes burned with a type of hurt and anger that I almost admired. Almost.

"You're a vile person, Chandler. You always have been."

"Ah, I see the social niceties have been forgotten," I replied, running a hand through my tousled hair.

"Lexa was always too good for you and your jealousy," they seethed.

"My jealousy got me to where I belong," I retorted, barely containing my volume. They laughed, a chilling sort of sound.

"You hated that she was so powerful. You hated that she had Professor Thorne's ear and trust. You wouldn't let another person even get close to her, And Gods, the look on your face when you realized the Wardens weren't there for you…you looked deranged, Chandler. Sick with jealousy."

My jaw tensed, and I felt my fist clench at my side. "Envy is the trait that my

Court respects the most in me," I tossed back through bared teeth, unable to hide how their words had affected me.

"You weren't just envious. You were bitter. Resentful. Nobody could respect that," they nearly growled at me.

I chuckled softly, with a dark edge of the unhinged nature they had so cleverly observed in me.

"I look forward to the day you are forced to bow down to me."

Their eyes flashed with recognition like the veil had been pulled back, and finally, they saw who they were threatening and insulting—the monster behind the man.

"I would say it's been wonderful catching up, but I don't want to lie to you. I hope you get everything you deserve, Chandler."

"I will," I said quietly as they turned on their heels and stalked off.

I didn't allow myself to waste a single moment on the pang of loss that could have built within my chest. Instead, I turned to find Lilith approaching with an almost guilty look gracing her features.

She didn't speak as she grabbed my elbow and pulled me between some of the pop-up carts and booths, finding us a secluded space.

"Did you do it?" I asked, analyzing her face.

She nodded and I felt the smile creep onto my face like a serpent prepared to strike. Deadly.

"We need to be quick," she said as she pulled the patch from the sleeve of her cloak. I lifted the hem of my shirt and revealed my ribs to her. She sighed and for just a moment, as her eyes surveyed the clear patch of skin, I thought that she might have been second-guessing this endeavor. But then she placed the patch against my skin, pressing it with her chilled hands. Her eyes fell closed as she whispered Mythica-laced words. The enchantment danced in the air, and I felt a slight burn as the Mark was transferred onto my skin. When she finished and pulled the patch back, the Mark of The Court of the Undying was in its wake. I couldn't resist the gleefully wicked smile that spread on my face if I wanted to. And I didn't want to.

In fact, I never wanted to resist a single one of my desires again.

Lexa

Twenty-One

I awoke in the dim, cozy confines of the cave, nestled in the heart of winter's icy grip, and yet I didn't feel the sting of the winter's chill. My senses slowly stirred to life and I became aware of the warmth that enveloped me—a warm fire was crackling softly nearby. The memories of the night before flooded back and I couldn't help the content smile that claimed my lips.

As I opened my eyes to the soft, diffused light filtering through the cave's entrance, I was greeted by the sight of winter's embrace outside. The world beyond the cave was a pristine wonderland blanketed in a layer of fresh, powdery snow. It was as if the dark and dangerous Court we had fled through the night before had been transformed overnight into a realm of pure enchantment.

My gaze shifted to the source of the warmth—the crackling fire that had grown small in the night. Its flames painted patterns of light and shadow on the cave walls, casting a mesmerizing glow. Sparks spiraled upward, disappearing into the rocky ceiling like shooting stars. Memories returned to me in golden threads of happiness. The night that I had shared with my mate. The embers of our shared laughter still echoed in my ears. The night had been filled with shared stories, whispered confidences, and the music of our hearts beating in unison. Between the several times that he claimed my body in a burst of passion, we shared tender moments that would remain imprinted on my soul for as long as I lived.

As I sat up, I realized that I had once again had a night free of nightmares. Instead of spending my dreams in the dark oceans of death and despair, I slept comfortably in the arms of the man I loved. I was filled with an almost eager hopefulness that held the promise of a new day, a new beginning. My eyes drifted down to the sleeping form beside me. Lysander was peacefully dreaming, his body wrapped in the cloaks we had used as bedding last night, the flickering firelight casting a gentle glow on his calm features. I trailed my eyes along his exposed skin, determined to devote every inch of his indescribable body to memory so that I may be lucky enough to call upon the image of him should we ever be separated.

I couldn't help but feel a surge of gratitude for the warmth of the fire, the love of my mate, and the beauty of the winter world outside. It was a morning where everything felt right, where the chill of winter was met with the warmth of our connection, and where the promise of this new adventure held endless possibilities.

"You're staring at me," Lysander murmured, indicating his awoken state despite keeping his eyes shut tight. The softest smile played on his lips and I couldn't resist tasting that smile for myself. I pressed my lips against him, leisurely basking in his kiss. His hands snaked around my neck and held me in place as his tongue sought out mine.

I drank up his kiss with eager moans, which only seemed to propel him on. He shifted underneath me until I was forced to throw one leg over his hips and straddle him. With the cloak discarded to the side, nothing acted as a barrier between our bare bodies. His length was solid and eager beneath my heat, as my core pressed down onto him.

I rolled my hips, causing his tip to slide through the lips of my center and brush against the sensitive bundle of nerves. Our lips broke apart, only for him to release a husky groan.

"Claim me. Take all of me," he demanded, a wild, passionate gleam shining in his emerald eyes. All it took was the slightest shift of my hips and he disappeared into my heat. As my core slid down his length, I felt my walls tighten around him as our bodies joined most deliciously and intimately. His hands gripped my hips and directed my body in just the right way. We moved so easily together, as if in a perfectly choreographed dance. I sat up, looking down at the man beneath me, the man who had coveted me and claimed me so completely.

He pushed up off of the ground until he, too, was sitting up with me. Our eyes met in a locked gaze of desire and, interestingly enough, trust.

"I am completely lost in you, little storm," he admitted.

"That's funny because I think with you, I've finally been found," I responded in a breathless whisper. He exhaled sharply and I saw evidence of tears forming in his eyes as he gazed at my face.

His hands pressed my hips forward quicker, eliciting a gasp from my lips as the delicious pressure ramped up within my core. He leaned forward, claiming one of my bare nipples into his mouth. I leaned my neck back, pressing my chest into his lips. His tongue slid along the hardened peak and I felt that pressure build like a blazing inferno until I was moments from slipping into passionate oblivion. My fingernails dug into his shoulders as he pressed forward, working my body as if I were an instrument and he was the only person alive who could play it.

"I'm so close, Lysander," I gasped between ragged breaths. He released his claim on my nipple and brought his lips to mine in a fierce kiss as his hands spurred me forward.

"Fall apart for me," he whispered into my ear. "Fall apart *with* me."

And I did.

Stars erupted in my vision, as a wave of overwhelming ecstasy threatened to drown me, but not like in my tormenting dreams. And keeping his whispered promise, he fell apart as well with my name on his lips. As our bodies slowed and the heat of our joining subsided, I felt the soft bite of the cold air nip against my sensitive skin, but I couldn't bring myself to rise and break this intimate connection we had indulged in.

Once Lysander's breathing had returned to normal, he reached for one of the discarded cloaks on the cave floor and wrapped it around my shoulders, enclosing the both of us within the warm confines of the garment. He also made no move to remove himself from his position buried deep within my heat.

My still sensitive center was idly gripping him, chasing the same passionate feeling.

"Good morning to you too, my mate," he teased playfully, kissing my forehead. I blushed deeply, letting my hands rest on his bare chest.

"Will I ever get enough of you?" I asked, resisting the urge to roll my hips once more and chase that delicious oblivion that only Lysander could take me to.

"Not if I can help it," he wrapped his arms around my waist and held me tightly against his body. I'd never felt so wholly coveted and cherished.

"When do we have to return to the reality of the outside world?" I glanced wistfully at the entrance to the cave. A soft pink glow was filtering into the cave from the early-morning sun.

"Soon," he responded dejectedly.

"What does this mean, Lysander?" I whispered, avoiding meeting his eyes. "For the rest of the tour."

His fingers found my chin and tilted my head until our eyes met. "We don't have to worry about any of that right now." His words were meant to be comforting, but I couldn't help but feel this sense of dread looming and threatening to cast a vindictive shadow over my newfound happiness.

Would he expect me to Pledge to his Court now? Did I even have a choice anymore? Maybe The Warden of Silence, Vander, was right about the mate bonds being an unfair influence because right now, there was an eerie feeling blanketing me, whispering into my subconscious that I was sitting firmly in the center of a perilous game, one I didn't want to play anymore. I certainly did enjoy my time at The Court of Shadows and I could see myself there, but was that it? Was the choice made? What if I genuinely belonged elsewhere? Would I be able to make that choice if it were right for me? Did I even want to?

"So, we continue on the tour?" I asked sheepishly. He nodded.

"Some of my siblings would not react lightly to this development, little storm. We need to placate them. The tour must continue, and…" his voice trailed off as a pained look crossed his face.

"And no one can know about our bond," I finished. He nodded with a sad expression. I pressed a kiss to his lips. And the movement caused my hips to press down onto his length, which was still nestled deep within me.

He moaned softly, a sound that I would forever cherish. "Careful there, little storm, unless you're prepared for me to take you again?" He teased, the melancholic somber-ness long forgotten and replaced with a sparkling mischievous mood. He pressed his hips up, and the worries filtered back into the corners of my mind as pleasure took root once again.

I felt his hardened length, stretching my walls and lighting the fire within my core. "We should make the most of our privacy while we can," I offered eagerly before he turned us over until he was hovering over me.

"Yes, we should," he agreed before drilling his hips forward in an almost punishing thrust.

My love for him was front and center while he took my body to heights of passion I'd never dreamed of. And yet, that slight nagging dread threatened to slip inside and taint the experience. I didn't let it.

I just hoped I could hold it off forever.

TWENTY-TWO

After the most magical evening of my existence and an equally enchanting morning, I knew it was time for my mate and I to continue the venture through The Court of Talisman to the city of Dedaria and the Prism Library at the heart of the Court. And unfortunately, due to the violent attack we endured last night, we would be making the journey on foot. Leaving the cave was nearly impossible. As I reluctantly stirred from the warmth of our makeshift bed, I couldn't help but cast one last longing look around the cave. The dim firelight that had danced merrily the night before had dimmed to a soft glow, and the remnants of our shared moments seemed to linger in the air. With a heavy heart, I knew it was time to leave. Duty and responsibility called, and I couldn't ignore the world beyond the cave's entrance any longer. The warmth of our shared moments would have to be enough to sustain me as I ventured back into the chill of winter and continued our tour.

I held her chilled hand in mine as we ventured across the enchanting landscape. Snowflakes glistened like diamonds in the air and the ground was blanketed in a pristine, untouched layer of snow. The air was crisp and invigorating, carrying the scent of pine with it.

Something was bothering Lexa. I could see it in her eyes and feel it in her silence, which was not as comfortable as we had gotten accustomed to. I would discuss her reservations with her in detail once we arrived safely at Ivis' home, but her safety was my first priority now, and I needed my focus to be on this journey. The Double Marked might be out here still and, without our cart and horses, I needed to be prepared for anything.

We were bundled tightly in our cloaks, but despite the thick wool shield from the frozen winds, I felt my teeth threatening to chatter. I tensed my jaw and ducked my head into my hood as much as possible to soften the icy bite. Out of all the Courts to find ourselves stranded in, this one was undoubtedly the worst. I made a mental note to threaten Ivis with a little friendly murder for the trouble. But even as my anger simmered beneath my skin, I felt a soft warmth wash over me at the memory of our secluded cave, the bond, and my breathtaking, powerful mate.

"If we freeze, at least nobody will be fighting for my affection anymore," Lexa teased, but her voice was strained, and I could sense that the effort it took even to speak those words was grueling.

I growled at the thought of her death. Literally growled. I didn't even have the good sense to be ashamed of just how feral the idea of her in harm's way made me feel. I stopped in my tracks and turned on a heel to come face-to-face with her. She looked up at me with wide, blue eyes, her pale face colored in shock.

"Death itself couldn't stop me from fighting for your affection, little storm." I trailed an ice-cold finger across her trembling lips, but I knew this tremble came from her wanton need and not the cold. It filled me with an unrelenting satisfaction to know that I was the one who affected her this way. "But something tells me I won't need to fight so hard anymore. Isn't that right?" I taunted with an utterly seductive smile that I hoped showed her every ounce of my desire for her. She gasped, and her lips parted slightly, practically begging me to taste them. I leaned forward and pressed my lips to hers. It was a soft, gentle kiss, a mere fraction of what my body so desperately needed from her, but I couldn't afford to lose my head, not until we were safely tucked away at the Prism Library. When I pulled my lips from hers, she whimpered, and I had to groan and run a hand through my hair to keep from devouring the sound. She was looking at me with so much lust in those heavy eyes that her shivering body seemed to have been forgotten. I smiled again, this time to myself for being the one who could bring such warmth to her. I somehow gathered the resolve to turn away from her and continue my trek.

This time, as we walked, we fell into that particular kind of silence that I loved sharing with her. Something had shifted in her mind, and whatever had been bothering her was gone for now. Her soft breaths were shallow and labored by the second hour of our trek. I honestly had no idea how far we were from the Library at this point. I'd only spent a small amount of time in Ivis' Court. Not because I felt any sort of animosity toward her. In fact, she was one of my favorite siblings, but her Court's weather was utterly vile.

By the third hour, Lexa was breathing heavily, and I, too, felt the tight strain in my lungs from the frigid air that had been forced down our throats.

By the fourth, I had lost nearly all the feeling in my fingers despite their place hiding within the sleeves of my tunic.

When the fifth hour came around, I was considering finding those Double Marked and killing them for forcing us into this frigid hike when I saw the faint outline of the Library on the horizon. The sigh I released was Gods damned euphoric.

I pulled her into my side and we pressed forward eagerly. The village of Dedaria seemed like something out of a fantastical tale, where indulgence knew no bounds. Towering lampposts lined the streets, their soft Mythica-induced glow casting a warm and inviting light upon the snow-dusted cobblestone pathways. Frivolously decorated storefronts, adorned with intricate lighted trimmings and shimmering icicles, made the frigid air feel imbued with warmth. At the heart of the village stood the most remarkable edifice of them all, the Prism Library. I had remembered its beauty from my last venture to this Court, but something about it took my breath away. It glistened like a multifaceted jewel, its crystalline walls capturing the winter sun's rays and casting a dazzling kaleidoscope of colors that danced upon the snow. The building seemed to breathe with a life of its own, and its beauty left me in awe.

Lexa seemed less than eager to explore the wonders of Dedaria in our current state, so we pushed past the bustling villagers and made our way to the Library.

When we crossed the threshold into the opulent building, I sighed with relief, warmth immediately chasing away the bite of cold. Lexa's stunning eyes were wide and full of wonder as she took in the space. The interior of the grand repository of knowledge was a breathtaking contrast to its transparent exterior. It exuded a warmth and coziness that was unexpected, given the crystalline nature of the building.

Sunlight filtered through the countless facets of the crystal walls, casting a gentle, ever-shifting rainbow of colors across the spacious chamber. The light created a mesmerizing play of hues on the polished wooden floors, making it seem like one was walking on a vibrant, living tapestry.

The library was vast, with rows upon rows of towering bookshelves stretching endlessly into the distance. Each shelf was laden with an eclectic collection of books, scrolls, and manuscripts, their spines glistening with the same ethereal hues as the walls. The titles and bindings ranged from ancient tomes of Mythical wisdom to modern works of art and fiction. Amidst the shelves, plush reading nooks beckoned with their inviting comfort. Soft, oversized armchairs and loveseats were adorned with plush cushions and blankets in various shades of pink hues.

A crackling fireplace stood as the heart of this literary sanctuary. Its flames danced and flickered, basking Lexa and me in an almost sensual warmth. Nearby, a grand oak reading table with ornate wooden carvings and padded leather chairs invited scholars and visitors alike to gather and immerse themselves in the treasures of knowledge within these walls.

The Prism Library was easily recognizable as a haven of tranquility and intellectual exploration. It was a place where The Court of Talisman's insatiable appetite for indulgence met its intellectual curiosity, offering a blend of opulence and wisdom for all who ventured inside. It was cozy, remarkable, and captivating, and the look of awe etched on my mate's face had jealousy instantly curling in my chest.

"Brother!" Ivis's booming voice beckoned to me from the second landing of the library. I turned to see her descending the glass-like staircase toward us. Her extravagant pink robe, adorned with intricate embroidery and shimmering sequins, billowed around her like a regal cloak, hugging her thick curves expertly. The gown cascaded in luxurious folds, its vibrant hue contrasting beautifully against her black skin. Her braided black hair was pulled back to a tie at the base of her neck, and the tresses fell down the center of her back. Her soft Mythica trailed behind her like a wisp of smoke. Gentle and unthreatening.

I stepped forward to offer my hand for my sibling to shake. She scoffed at it as if it were the most treacherous thing to do and pulled me into an embrace. I chuckled briefly before folding my arms around her waist.

"Lexa, dear, I'm so glad you're here. Welcome to my Library," she gestured around her before pulling Lexa into her arms. Lexa let out a little gasp of shock before being smothered into my sister's plush bosom. I suppressed a laugh, only barely.

"Oh my, you two are positively frozen. Not used to the climate yet, I see. Let's get you to your rooms." She linked her arm with Lexa and led her to the stairs she had just descended. Lexa tossed a worried look over her shoulder at me, but I simply smiled at her and followed behind them. "We were expecting you last night. And where are your bags? Did you get lost, Lysander?" She teased.

"We have much to discuss, sister," I offered quietly, and the look on her face as she tossed a glance over her shoulder told me that she understood that what I had to say was not meant for lingering ears.

She pursed her lips and hummed softly before leading us up the stairs. Once we reached the second landing, she turned down an aisle of bookcases to a second staircase. The third floor was a much quieter space, and it was evident from the lack of loitering individuals that this floor was not open to the public. We passed countless large wooden doors until she found the one she wanted.

"Lysander, this one is yours." Ivis pushed the door open to reveal a stunning chamber. The glass walls, while glass-like and transparent, bore a subtle, translucent film that ensured my solitude was respected. From the inside, the world beyond was softened into a dreamlike, abstract panorama. The room was adorned with tasteful furnishings that exuded both comfort and elegance. And above all…indulgence. In a blatant display of maximalism, the room was littered with countless items of comfort and decor. A welcoming four-poster bed with a thick wool comforter sat near the glass wall. A deep mauve velvet chaise lounge sat against the wall closest to me, its upholstery inviting me to recline and relax.

Ivis began to lead Lexa away and I felt a pain in my chest. I wanted her to share this room with me. I wanted her to share every room with me for the rest of my existence, but we could not risk letting my siblings know about our bond. I knew that. It didn't mean I hated it any less.

"Ivis," I called after her. "Lexa will need to have access to me, and I to her. She is my responsibility to protect, and I don't particularly want to travel too far to do so." I prayed that Lexa could see through my act of disregard.

"She is in the room next door," Ivis answered, and thankfully, I did not see any signs of suspicion in her features.

"I will let you settle in, Miss Cromwell. Rest, relax, and see the library. Tonight, we feast!" Ivis laughed gleefully and helped Lexa into her room. I caught her eye as she disappeared across the threshold.

When the door shut, Ivis turned to me.

"You can settle in later, I'm sure. Come to my office, brother. Let's speak in private." She led me down the hall, her heels clacking against the floor, echoing in the quiet chamber. She stopped before a set of double oak doors and pushed them open to reveal what I assumed to be her office.

Crossing the threshold into the room was like stepping into a realm of wanton excessiveness. Beyond the transparent walls, I could see the vibrant village of Dedaria, lively and bustling with activity despite the frigid temperature. The room itself was a testament to extravagance, a lavish retreat within the hallowed halls of knowledge. The room was adorned with an eclectic mix of antique and contemporary furnishings, each piece a masterpiece of design. A massive mahogany desk stood as the centerpiece of the room, its polished surface gleaming under the soft, golden light of a dazzling crystal chandelier.

She led the way, and I followed, sinking into one of the plush armchairs. She settled into the chair next to mine and smiled at me warmly.

"You were expected yesterday," she began. "I had a welcome feast planned for my guest."

"I'm sure it did not go to waste, dear sister," I responded with a slight bite in my tone.

"What happened?" she prompted, ignoring any offense she might have found in my words.

I sighed and lifted my arms to pull my loose hair back into a bun. She watched me quietly.

"We have a situation regarding Miss Cromwell."

Ivis's eyes narrowed to slits as she watched me. "What kind of situation?" She asked, leaning her arms onto her knees.

Ivis remained silent as I explained the threats that had been following her through the last three Courts she had visited, including this one. Her sharp intake of breath at the mention of the Double Marked assailants was the only sound she made as she quietly absorbed the information.

Once I had adequately explained the threat to Ivis, excluding only Lexa's nightmares and the incident at the fountain, she sat back in her chair, a solemn look on her face.

"Do you think it's him?" She asked finally.

I shook my head.

"What we did to him was irreversible," I responded confidently, despite my gut's slight twinge of uncertainty. My head ached, warning me that I was too close to revealing something I shouldn't. "But I fear that we did not eliminate the concept of The Forgotten Court as we had intended."

She made a soft humming sound again, the sound she makes when contemplating something, I noticed. "What do you think they want with her?"

"You know what her Mythica is," I started with a shrug. Hating that this option, while the most logical, was also the most terrifying. "Isn't it obvious?"

She sucked in a sharp breath and nodded. "I suppose it is."

"An assailant told her that they needed her to save them." The words felt like ash on my tongue.

"What are you planning to do about that, Lysander?" She asked, without judgment and without making it feel like the burden fell solely on my shoulders, although it certainly felt as if it did.

"Keep her safe until she can make her Pledge. They will stop their fool's mission when they see she's claimed a home. They are only persistent because she's Uncourted."

That was naive wishful thinking. I knew that, and she knew that, but Ivis didn't voice the concerns aloud.

"How many do you think there are?" Her face was a mix of fear and anger.

"It could be ten… twenty."

She relaxed at that, but then I whispered the fear I've had swirling in my chest since I first saw that symbol painted on the side of the carriage.

"Or it could be thousands."

She took a long, calculated breath.

"We should have removed the threat entirely."

I shook my head vigorously. "No, that would make us no better than him. And be careful what you say."

She didn't seem to agree, if the indignant look in her eye was any indication. "If they plan on enacting the Trials, Lysander, nothing short of death will stop them."

My heart skipped a beat as flashes of blood, death, and fear spun through my mind.

The Trials.

"That may not be their goal," I spoke softly, knowing how weak I sounded.

"If they wanted her dead, they wouldn't waste time on threats," Ivis offered. And I knew she was right.

"So, is it really happening? After all this time." She whispered, her soft eyes glistening with fear and concern.

I pulled in a lungful of air and let my mind settle on the undeniable truth. "Yes," I started. "It appears The Forgotten Court refuses to be forgotten any longer."

Twenty-Three

The welcome feast at The Court of Talisman was a spectacle beyond my wildest imagination, a proper culinary spoiling that was as awe-inspiring as it was overwhelming. It took place in a dining hall nestled in the heart of the Prism Library.

As I entered the hall, my senses were immediately overtaken by a symphony of sights, sounds, and scents. The soft, multicolored glow from the glass walls bathed the dining hall in an inviting and enchanting light. The long decorated banquet tables were adorned with a dazzling array of dishes, each more extravagant than the last. Towering platters of succulent roast meats were surrounded by mounds of fragrant, perfectly cooked vegetables. Mountains of fresh loaves of bread and bowls of exotic fruits and cheeses added to the opulent spread.

The sound of laughter and conversation filled the air as guests indulged in the pleasures of both food and company. The clinking of fine crystal and silverware harmonized with the melodic hum of delighted voices. Servers moved gracefully among the tables, their attire as sumptuous as the feast itself. They wore lustrous silks in vibrant hues, and their trays were laden with delicacies that ranged from the decadent to the exotic. It was a spectacle of abundance, a true celebration of the sin of gluttony.

I didn't know where to look. My eye was drawn to every offering like some invisible force piloting my senses. It was stunning. It was exciting.

It was overwhelming.

The sheer amount of choices I was asked to make from the moment I stepped foot over the threshold into the dining room was insurmountable.

How many different types of wine does one party need to have?

Ivis moved about the room, commanding every ounce of attention from her guests. I could see why she was beloved in her Court from how she spoke to each person. She left them with bright smiles by making each of them the center of her attention for the briefest amount of time. It was admirable.

My chest warmed the moment that my mate entered the room.

My mate.

The thought was still so strange to me, so foreign, and yet it felt entirely right at the same time. He looked deliciously poised as he swept through the crowd, making small talk with the high-ranking members of the Court. It was obvious he felt my eyes on him because he had the most sensual of smirks gracing his lips, and I knew, without a doubt, that it was meant for me and me alone.

When his eyes finally landed on me, I inhaled sharply at the force of the connection there. Would I ever look at him without feeling like the rest of the world has disappeared?

Did I ever want to?

He bit his bottom lip in an attempt to hide his eager smile. I did the same. As the night continued, we avoided meeting eyes in any actual capacity in an effort to hide our bond from the prying eyes around us. He would brush his fingers against mine as he passed by me, holding an entirely separate conversation, and I would lick my lips while I knew his eyes were on me from the other side of the room so that he knew how much I missed his taste. How I managed to have a conversation with members of the Court while feeling his lustful stares might just be my biggest accomplishment. There was something so irritatingly thrilling about keeping our relationship a secret from those around us.

On the one hand, I hated that I was forbidden from telling every person who would listen about the magnificence that is my mate and our bond together. On the other, the stolen glances and brief touches were so charged and so full of desire that by the end of the night, my entire body felt heated and tense with wanton energy. I was so wound up that if he were to touch me where I so desperately wanted him to, he would find me wet and eager.

The night was winding down, and I was captivated by the heat in his gaze as he left the room. It said everything he couldn't. It was a feat to force my feet to remain planted and not run after him to give myself over to the primal need he elicited within me. But I stayed and counted.

Three-hundred seconds.

That would be long enough not to seem suspicious. If I could last another three hundred seconds, I could leave undetected and slip into his room to let his body claim mine.

Two-hundred and forty-five.

The man I had been speaking to was one of the curators of the Prism Library. He was single-handedly responsible for the weekly read-along events that occurred here. He hoped I could attend one while I was here. I agreed.

Two-hundred and ten.

There was a gaggle of women filling their bags with leftovers, of which there were many. I watched as they smiled and laughed with each other in a comfortable friendship.

One-hundred and thirty.

I excused myself from the conversation with the curator and milled about for a while, watching as people began to retire for the evening. Their arms link with their partners as they disappeared into the night together to indulge in something else entirely.

Eight-five.

I started directing my footsteps toward the door, focusing every ounce of my energy on keeping a steady and inconspicuous pace.

Fifty.

I heard laughter echoing through the hall as Ivis conversed with the few stragglers left at the table. The rich timber of her voice was warm and inviting.

Thirty-three.

I reached the threshold of the door, my core tightening at the promise of what my mate would do to me once I made it to his chambers.

Ten.

My nipples peaked, pressing against the fabric of the floral dress that Ivis had delivered to my room. My entire body was alight and ready for Lysander.

Five.

As I reached the threshold, I politely waved goodbye to the few people I passed.

One.

Just as I lifted a foot to cross into the hallway, I heard my name being called from behind me. As I turned, Ivis rushed toward me with a bright smile on her pink-painted lips. I struggled to hide the disappointment on my face and forced a smile in return.

"My dear girl, I'm so sorry we didn't have a chance to speak this evening. My attention was pulled in about a thousand directions tonight."

I nodded. "No need for apologies, Warden. I thoroughly enjoyed the feast. It was decadent beyond my wildest dreams." I didn't mean for the words to sound as bleak as they did. Thankfully, she didn't seem to pick up on it because she smiled again, the bright expression taking up her whole face.

"Just a portion of all the wonders my Court has to offer to someone like you, dear," she responded with a twinkle in her eye.

"I can only imagine," I replied, doing my best to stamp out the heat curling in my belly and begging to be stoked by my mate.

"I want to show you something," she gushed gleefully. The space in my chest where my bond with Lysander sat grew impatient, but I pushed back against the force of its eagerness until I was able to think clearly again without the cloud of lust.

"Of course," I said, taking her outstretched arm and letting her lead me from the dining hall.

We walked in silence, and I took that time to calm myself and extinguish the flame of desire that had been ravaging me for the last few hours. By the time we arrived at the Warden's destination, I felt as if I had returned to normal, and the disappointment over the sensual indulgence I was missing out on was tightly locked away.

Mostly.

I glanced around at our surroundings to find myself at the mouth of a long hallway. Portraits hung on the wall, showcasing pivotal members of The Court of Talisman. I glanced back at Ivis, and she nodded, encouraging me forward. I took slow steps down the hall as I appreciated the portraits. The faces stared back at me from the canvases with an almost judgemental glare.

"I hope you are not upset, but the Warden of Shadows informed me of your…issues regarding certain individuals."

My breath caught in my throat, and I paused my footsteps. I hated how vulnerable I felt in that moment, with what felt like hundreds of eyes watching me from behind their frames.

"He is worried for your safety. As am I." She stepped forward again, brushing past me gently to look at the portrait of a former Dean on the wall. His pale skin was decorated with dark freckles. She sighed softly before turning her eyes back to me.

"Do you know what they want from me?" I asked quietly, afraid to speak much louder than a whisper.

She shook her head, but a slight twinge of fear danced in her eyes. I very nearly asked her for the truth. Very almost stole it from her lips. My Mythica roiled within my chest like a sentient creature, and I had to take a deep breath to calm it. It listened to me, returning to a calmer state, but I was intimately aware of how close it remained to the surface.

"When was the last time you indulged in something forbidden?" She asked, her eyes drifting over to the portrait of a past Dean once more.

Thoughts of Lysander's dark skin, shimmering with a sheen of sweat beneath my palms as our bodies joined in rhythmic pleasure, crossed my mind. I swallowed the lump that formed in the base of my throat as I avoided her gaze.

"Recently, then, if your rising heart rate is any indication," she mused with a slight chuckle.

"I guess you could say that." I felt the dark blush heat my skin beneath her gaze.

"You feel shame about it?"

"No, not at all," I started. She smiled at the clear resolve in my tone.

"My Court often has a bad reputation. As I'm sure you're aware." She gave me an almost cheeky glance over her shoulder as she walked up to the portrait of the Dean. "Never satisfied. Gluttonous. That we will only be happy with what we have if we have it in excess."

I observed her, watching as her eyes shimmered with unshed tears.

"And perhaps there's a modicum of truth in those assessments," she said quietly. "We want in excess not because we're not satisfied with what we have, but because we carry so much endearment for them that we'd do anything for more. Just one more treat. One more song. One more story. One more day…" A tear slid down her cheek. "Just one more."

"I'm sorry," I whispered. Ivis cleared her throat and shook the tears from her eyes as she turned back to me.

"For what, dear?"

"Your loss," I replied, tilting my head toward the painting. Her lips upturned into an almost melancholic smile.

"It was a very long time ago."

I nodded. There was a soft warmth of endearment on her face. There was something so pure and profound in her gaze, and I felt my heart break for her and the loss of the man in the portrait.

"This hallway holds a lot of memories. I guess you could call it an abundance of memories," she chuckled to herself. "Tell me, have you ever denied yourself what you've wanted simply because you felt like you should?" She whispered, glancing back over to the portrait.

"I have," I answered. She waited for me to continue. I sighed. "I can understand the urge to have everything you want. To get what you desire. I've been following those impulses more frequently."

"I'm sure your time in The Court of Passion helped with that," she winked, but I could sense the probing question beneath her words. I chuckled sheepishly as she signed. "What a special kind of satiation you have been gifted."

"A large part of me is thrilled to be the only non-Warden in all of Verihdian history to travel to all seven of The Courts."

"But-" she prompted, her beautifully manicured brow was arched high.

"But I don't feel like I deserve it."

The truth of my confession hung heavy between us. I had voiced the concerns before; I meant it then, and now, after visiting three Courts, I was surprised to find that I meant it even more. What did I do to earn this?

"So many people in our world take whatever they want, and however much they want, without regard for others and feel no shame or regret about it. Why should you?"

I glanced at her through my dark lashes and studied her calm face.

"Life is too short to be unhappy, Miss Cromwell. Not mine, of course, but generally speaking." She shared another glance with the man in the portrait.

A long sigh escaped my lips.

"Regardless of the choice you make at the end of this tour, if you take one thing from your time in this Court with me, I hope that you will allow yourself to be a little gluttonous when it comes to the things you get. Deserved or not."

I smiled softly at her, not sure I agreed with her sentiment, but I could see the appeal of that line of thinking.

"Is this your family?" I asked, stopping in front of one of the portraits that showed a trio of individuals sporting dark skin and bright smiles. A stunning woman in a light cream dress was the obvious focal point. Her smile was wide and stretched her skin. She was sitting next to a taller man, his hand resting comfortably on the shoulder of the beautiful woman beside him. His smile was one of love, of comfort. Just in front of them sat a young boy no more than fifteen, his hair cropped short, his lips pulled back into a smile that didn't quite reach his eyes.

"Yes," Ivis spoke from behind me. I turned to study her. The resemblance was evident between her and the figures in the portrait. I wondered what memory this painting held for her. The father looked strong and proud, and the mother had a comforting smile that warmed my chest just to look at her. The young boy wore a tight tunic, stuffy and uncomfortable. He seemed so out of place, with an almost haunting look of loneliness in his eyes.

"Is this your brother?" I asked, unable to tear my eyes from the young boy's face. He looked so destitute, his smile purely performative. I didn't remember learning if the Wardens once had siblings, but I assume some of them must have.

"No my dear," she spoke slowly, joining me at the base of the portrait. Her pink eyes remained trained on the faces, looking back at us. "That is me." My eyebrows furrowed in confusion as Ivis' fingers began tracing the young child's face in the painting. It was apparent then that her eyes, despite their new pink shade courtesy of her Warden position, were the same eyes staring back at me from the painting. "Although, it is not who I am anymore. Truthfully, it wasn't even who I was then, either."

I nodded, understanding washing over me.

"Why do you keep this portrait if it's not who you are?"

She sighed, her shoulders sagging low. "Do you know what my Mythica is, dear?"

"Only what is taught at the Institute," I answered.

"I have the unfortunate ability to recall every piece of information I've ever learned or seen. It's always there, right on the forefront of my mind." She shook her head.

"Unfortunate? Forgive me, but that seems like more of an asset." I said.

She sighed, smiling sweetly. "That's true. I have certainly made the most of it. I remember every member of my Court's date of birth and their favorite foods. I remember every passage I've ever read, every person I've ever spoken to. I've won many a trivia contest, and made several people feel wanted and appreciated…and heard."

She pressed a hand to her heart. "But I also remember every horrid thing anyone has ever said about me. I can recall every word my parents, or my former Dean ever said. I remember their final moments like it was yesterday. The way the light left their eyes or the sound of their final breath. I remember every ounce of pain and suffering I've ever come across in my entire existence, which you know has been extensive."

I felt tears prickling my eyes. "You must be very strong to deal with that all," I admitted.

"It would be so simple for me to feel trapped by my past. To wallow in the pain and the mistakes that seem so raw and fresh. It's important not to forget where you come from—it's key to knowing why you're headed where you're going. This painting always reminds me that I am allowed to be who I am—every beautiful, tragic, gluttonous part of me, despite what was said, despite the hate and the fear. I will remember that for the rest of my existence, but I won't get anywhere if I lose sight of *why* I'm here, what matters to me, and how far I've come. I'll just end up wandering and feeling lost along the way."

As she spoke, I felt the sting in my eyes intensify, and she turned to face me.

"What is your 'why,' Lexa?" She asked. A quick flash of brunette hair and blue eyes crossed my mind.

"My brother," I whispered, trying to ignore the guilt that crept into my chest at the memory of what I've done to him, what I've taken from him. Twice now.

"I've made a lot of mistakes, Warden," I admitted, a tear sliding down my cheek.

"We all have, dear."

"He'd hate me if he knew what I did," I admitted, for the first time voicing my deepest fears aloud as if my own Mythica had pulled them from my tongue.

"Perhaps, but I also think he may be the one most likely to understand why you did it," she offered, placing a comforting hand on my shoulder. "Do you love the person you are?"

My jaw fell open as the weight of that question slammed into me. Did I? I've made selfish choices, hurt people, and kept secrets. But I've also found love and learned how to protect myself.

"I want to," I answered truthfully.

"Sometimes that means making a change," she glanced over my shoulder at the portrait of her family. "Sometimes that means not apologizing for the person you are." She met my eyes. "But most of the time, it means acknowledging our faults and growing from them."

"I wish it were that easy," I admitted.

"Easy?" She chuckled. "Love, I never said any of this was easy. Life isn't easy. And no matter how many years pass by, it doesn't get any easier. Not loss, not acceptance. None of it. Life hurts. But that is what makes it so glorious. And I don't know about you, but I want to feel it all. Every painful second of it. Even if it means I'll relive it over and over again." She put a comforting hand on my shoulder. "Don't ever forget your 'why,' Lexa. It's how you'll survive. He'll forgive you. If you learn to forgive yourself."

I nodded, a tear sliding down my face.

"Come, we're having dessert in my chambers, and you do not want to miss the first course."

I composed my emotions and smiled back at her. "How many courses are there?" I asked, smiling as she draped her arm around my shoulders.

"How high can you count?" She laughed as she led me out of the room, leaving the portraits and her history behind us.

Twenty-Four

"What's her take on blood? We can always host a free-for-all brawl in her honor," Avalin mused, leaning back in her soft armchair. Her red hair was pulled back into a messy tie at the back of her head, with soft strands falling from the hold and framing her smooth, heart-shaped face. The scars that decorated her skin like delicate tears in a canvas were more prominent in the lighting of her - or, I guess, *our* - living room.

Over the past two months, I had gotten over my shock at seeing her in such a casual setting. The first time she knocked on the door to the room I was given in her chambers, I nearly choked on the air I was breathing when I saw her in soft bed clothing. Silk purple shorts and a light and airy tunic. She pulled me into the living room, sat me down on the couch, and asked me to tell her about my sister. So I did.

She would knock on my door twice a week, and we would spend the night and well into the morning discussing my sister and how Avalin could win her over. Soon enough, she was knocking four times a week. Then, last week, it was five. Eventually, she didn't have to knock any more, but instead would find me waiting for her on the couch.

This week, we haven't missed a single night.

I told myself I was simply a means to an end for my Warden. That she needed me only until my sister arrived, and then I would go back to being a faceless member of The Court of Vanguard, and I should prepare myself for that.

But damned if I wasn't going to enjoy it while I could.

"Lexa has never been a fan of gore," I replied, smiling at the memory of the two of us in the stands at one of the Gladiator tournaments when my cheers could only barely drown out the sound of her hurling into a bag at the sight before us.

"Squeamish?" She asked.

I nodded.

She grunted a noise of acknowledgment and made a note on the piece of parchment in her lap. "An honor fight then, a show of strength, but one where violence isn't the goal." I smiled, watching the way the skin between her brows scrunched up when she was thinking.

"Do you think we could finish early tonight?" I asked sheepishly, hating how my chest tightened at the thought of disappointing her.

"Somewhere to be?" she teased with a glint in her eyes.

"I've been working on my house slowly, but I just got the paint I requested from the store, and I'd love to get a first coat on. I hate leaving work for later."

She nodded. "You and I agree on that." Her teeth caught her bottom lip as she thought it over. It took every ounce of my willpower to divert my eyes from her mouth. Spending this much time with Avalin has given me a very exclusive chance to see her Mythica-induced facade up close. Between the late-night Lexa information sessions and the days at training, I have studied every inch of her stunning face.

Because her Mythica is interesting and I want to know more about it. Not for any other reason.

I hadn't gotten the courage to bring up my desire to be a Gladiator with her yet, but Cassius has been trying to encourage me to. I just didn't see how it would help. If anything, it would make me seem ungrateful for the opportunities she's already granted me, and I couldn't bear parting with the rush I got from being there on the arena floor. If the only way I get that rush is by coaching, then that is something I would have to accept. I could accept that. I had to.

"You're renovating?" She asked with a smirk.

"Not as much renovating and more like rebuilding. The place was nearly unlivable when I bought it." I chuckled as her brows furrowed. "It was all I could afford, but I like the work."

"You know your place here is not conditional on your sister's choice."

I glanced over at her. Her face was a mask of earnestness. My heart rate sped.

"Right?" she finished.

Had I been waiting for the rug to be pulled out from beneath me? Was I waiting for the moment when my 'worth' had dried out and Avalin no longer needed me or my talents? Yes.

"Truthfully, I didn't known that was the case," I said softly.

"Then allow me to apologize for not being clear in my intentions here." She leaned forward, resting her arms on her knees, and met my gaze with a stare of honesty and respect. "I will not mince words with you. Your sister may have gotten you an invitation to my personal chambers, but your trial results earned you a place in this Court, and your pure talent and drive are what's awarding you these opportunities. Make no mistake, Axel Cromwell, you belong in this Court and this Coliseum. I've never seen instincts like yours, and I've lived a life longer than I'd care to discuss. When your sister leaves our Court - regardless of her choice - you will not be asked to vacate the room I've offered you. You will not be asked to leave your position with my Gladiators. You will not be tossed aside and discarded like an object. You are not a means to an end, Axel. You are an asset. And dare I say, a friend."

A calming warmth spread throughout my body as her words settled in my mind. Pride was bursting in my chest, and I nearly preened at the compliments she showered me with. I sighed, releasing the fear that had subconsciously been claiming my breath.

"Thank you, Warden."

"Avalin," she corrected.

"Avalin," I echoed.

She nodded, a sweet smile playing on her lips. "So you don't need to move out if you don't wish to."

I considered her words for a moment. Ignoring the way my lower stomach fluttered at the thought of sharing this space with her long-term. "That is an honor that I will spend the rest of my life in disbelief that I've earned. However, I love having my own place. It needs a lot of work, but I'm not afraid to get my hands a little dirty. I've never had something like this. Something that was just mine. Mine to fix, mine to protect, to care for. Other than my sister, of course, although with her Mythica, she didn't need a Vacant like me taking care of her."

Her lips pursed, and I once again struggled to avoid staring at them. "Well," she said, slapping her palms onto her bare knees. "Let's go."

She slid off the chair and began heading to her room.

"Um, go… Where?" My eyes tracked her every movement. Something I'd been doing more and more recently. Every time she was in the room.

"To paint your house. I'll help you. Let me just change so the townsfolk don't recognize me." She took a few steps toward her door before turning back to face me, a stern look painted on her face. "And Axel. Don't ever refer to your Vacant status as a negative aspect of who you are, ever again." With that, she disappeared into her chamber and closed the door behind her, leaving me dumb-struck in the living room.

My heart was beating at an uncontrollable speed, and not because of my proximity to her, which has had that effect in the past, but at the thought of having the Warden of The Court of the Vanguard see my tiny, one-bedroom shack of a home. I was proud of the work I had done on it since my arrival, but it was no Chaos Coliseum. There were no grand staircases or Mythica luminated walls. It was quaint. Perfect for me, but not perfect.

I was lost in my little spiral of self-judgment when her door creaked open, and she slipped back into the living room. Her movements were timid, almost nervous. Both were emotions I was not used to seeing her display. Her hair had been let down from its tie and was drifting around her shoulders in long, thick tresses, as she wore it for most of the fights. She wore an all-black outfit like I've seen her wear on the few occasions she's joined us for training.

Essentially, she looked like she always did.

"Are you ready?" I asked, gesturing to the stairs.

Her hands clenched at her side, and her head tilted as her eyes narrowed. "Yes…" she said in a near-question. Ignoring the confusion in her stare, I headed to the stairs and began the trek up to the top level of the Coliseum. Avalin and I walked side by side in silence toward the gate. I've walked through town with Avalin on only one other occasion - most of our meetings being reserved for the arena or our living room - and to say she was swarmed would be an understatement. People practically fell over themselves to offer her gifts and their praise. It was overwhelming, and I couldn't believe that she had to experience that daily. But as we walked through the town toward my small cottage, no one so much as glanced our way. It was late, and people were beginning to turn in for the night, but even the small number of people left walking through the streets were ignoring us like they had no idea who we were.

Well, they probably didn't have any idea who I was, but Avalin was their Warden. When I looked over at her with a question in my gaze, I could tell she was avoiding my gaze. Within a few strange, quiet minutes, we arrived at the isolated road that led to my home. She smiled brightly as the half-rebuilt home came into view.

"This is your home?" She asked, a bright smile on her lips.

"It is," I answered with a sigh. "It's not much, and it's taken a lot of work to get it to where it is now. You should have seen it when I started. There was a hole in the roof. The porch wasn't stable and there wasn't a door on the back. I'm nowhere near done, but at least I feel confident that it's structurally sound and I won't go falling through the floorboards." I was rambling, but I couldn't help it. An anxious energy was building in my chest, pressing down on my heart.

She pushed ahead, stepping onto the porch and studying it carefully. The evening light was beginning to fade behind the trees, but she looked like she was glowing in this light.

"It's beautiful, Axel," she said, finally. A sigh fell from my lips.

"Thank you."

Her eyes met mine, and we remained there for the briefest of moments. We were locked in each other's stares.

I brushed past her, ignoring the way my skin tingled as I touched her, and led her inside. I avoided meeting her gaze again while I lit a fire and prepared the paint. She stood behind me, watching with rapt attention. I felt her eyes on my every move and it was charged with something dangerous and unknown.

We began painting in burning silence. The acidic scent of the paint invaded my nostrils but wasn't enough to distract my mind from the woman beside me and the strange atmosphere that had so clearly shifted between us.

I avoided looking in her direction long enough for the sun to disappear behind the horizon and paint the sky with a soft purple glow as night took root. The wall I was working on was finished, and the fire had begun to die slowly, casting a low flickering light across the freshly painted walls. Finally, I turned to face her again; she was still watching me with a contemplative look on her face.

"What do I look like to you," she whispered, an air of self-consciousness in her tone.

"What do you mean?" I asked carefully, feeling the tenuous ground of our carefully constructed professional relationship shifting beneath me with each word.

"Describe what you see?" She asked, laying her painting supplies down onto the sheet at her feet and stepping forward. "Please."

"I… I don't think I understand," I whispered, taking a step back despite the urge to rush forward. Something about the vulnerability painted on her face made me feel like I was seeing past the mask of strength that she wore for most of her life.

She shook her head, breaking eye contact. Shame coloring her expression. "Never mind, it was nothing."

"No, I just don't think I-"

"It's fine. Please. I should probably just go-" She turned on a heel and began to rush toward the door. My heart rattled in my chest.

"I see long, red hair," I called out to her. She paused near the doorway, her shoulders rising and falling with her labored breathing. "It falls down your back like a waterfall of fire. Skin, the color of fresh cream, sweet and smooth. Dark scars decorate your face like tributaries on a well-worn map. They tell the stories of battles fought, struggles endured, and the resilience of your warrior's soul. Eyes the deepest purple, like the purest cut of amethyst. You are… stunning, My Warden."

She stood still for a moment more, taking deep breaths before turning to face me again. I couldn't read the expression on her face. "And what do you see when you normally look at me?" She asked in a whisper.

My eyebrows furrowed. "What do you mean? You look the way you always have."

Her eyes softened as tears began to glisten. She took steps forward slowly until she was just a few inches from me. Her eyes scanned my face. "You see me like this?" She said so quietly I could barely hear it above my beating heart. "You've always seen me like this?" A laugh bubbled from her lips as a single tear slid down her face.

"I don't understand-" I started, but I was cut off by her lips meeting mine. My first impulse was to shy away because there were so many reasons why kissing my Warden was a terrible decision. I couldn't get distracted, I had a goal in this Court, and I didn't want to lose sight of that. If I ever did accomplish what I set out to, I couldn't bear the thought of people believing I achieved that by having a relationship with the Warden.

Reasons why I should have pushed her away flooded my brain, but I couldn't focus on a single one. Not when she tasted like home.

My hands locked around her waist and pulled her close to my body. Her tongue chased mine eagerly, and I happily obliged, opening my mouth for her. She moaned into the kiss, and I felt my entire body light on fire.

The kiss ended far too soon, and I found myself panting and desperate as we rested our foreheads against each other while our breathing returned to normal.

"You kissed me," I whispered, unable to utter anything else.

She chuckled softly in an airy tone. "You kissed me back."

"Not that I didn't enjoy that, Avalin, I just… I don't understand." I said, putting my hands on her shoulders and putting a little distance between us. Just enough to think.

"I'm not using my Mythica right now, Axel," she admitted. "That's why nobody in town recognized me. I don't look like what they want or what they find most attractive and appealing. This," she said, gesturing to herself. "This is me."

The realization hit me with the force of a thousand winds.

"What does this mean," I asked breathlessly.

"I don't know," she replied with an incredulous chuckle. "But I do know that I am going to help you finish painting this room, and then I'm going to kiss you once more before I leave, and you are going to kiss me back. We're going to enjoy this moment before facing the reality of the world outside this house."

I nodded, not trusting my voice to remain steady. We got back to work, but my mind was racing. She did as she said she would, finishing the job and planting another longing kiss on my lips. I never wanted to forget her taste, so as her mouth latched onto mine once more in the dark seclusion of my home, I memorized her. She held me firmly and didn't melt into my touch like a submissive lover but met me with just as much power and passion as I did.

"I see it now," she whispered, pressing her forehead against mine.

"See what?" I asked, wishing I could prolong this moment.

"Your fire."

When we finally left my house, the stars twinkled above with a glittering but fateful promise. That whatever comfort we had found in each other in the cold night could not survive to see the light of day. We returned to the Coliseum, muttering inconsequential phrases to fill the strenuous void of conversation. All the while, my mind raced with the fact that I would never be allowed to indulge in my Warden again. No matter how desperately I may have wanted to.

One thought rang louder than the others as we said our goodnights and parted ways to retreat to our individual rooms. She claimed that I'd always seen her for who she was, the person behind the Mythica. And yet, in the soft glow of the evening, as sleep crept forward to claim me, it was her - I realized - who had always seen me.

Twenty-Five

I used to think The Court of Talisman was one of the more pointless of the seven in Verihdia. Not that I thought my sibling's Mythica was useless - although recalling everything you've ever learned is as much a curse as it is a benefit - but I never saw the advantages of over-indulgence. I never understood why someone would want to imbibe in something so heavily and frequently that it began to lose its appeal.

I used to think that too much of a good thing was a bad thing.

Until I found my mate.

Now, I can wake up beside her and still miss her. I can be touching her, feeling her skin against mine, and still feel the need to memorize every inch of her. I can be inside of her, wringing every ounce of pleasure from her body, and already desire to do it again. For three weeks, I did nothing but indulge in Lexa Cromwell.

Each night, she would slip into my room, and I'd returned only to find her waiting. Her eyes would be bright with wanton need. I'd satisfy her as she stifled her cries of passion. And when she would sink onto me and claim my body with hers, we'd silence our moans by pressing our mouths together in a punishing kiss.

She'd fall asleep in my arms to a nightmareless slumber, and we'd wake up to surrender to our salacious desires again. We fortified this bond we had each and every night within the bubble of safety in my quarters.

We were careful. We had to be. Nobody could know what she was to me. Not only could my siblings find this information a threat, but there was also the matter of the Double Marked to be wary of. There had been no other sightings since that night in the carriage. We made ourselves busy during the daylight hours to avoid arousing suspicion. Lexa continued training and became a more assured and skilled fighter with each session. She would accompany Ivis around the Court, experiencing the wonder of the eternal winter for herself. While Lexa was learning what being a member of The Court of Talisman meant, I followed trails.

Three days after we arrived at the Library, the horses and our abandoned carriage were recovered. Luckily, the horses seemed in good health and all of our things were still there. After realizing I wasn't going to get any answers from staring at our former transport, I took a carriage out to the place where Lexa and I were attacked, only to find that any evidence of our attack and the people who performed it was long since covered by a fresh blanket of pristine snow.

I knew that the individuals who came after us were harmed in their assault, so the following week, I ventured to the nearest village and asked to speak to the healers. Alas, none of them recall healing anyone with injuries like Lexa and I inflicted.

This week, I had spent the majority of my daylight hours searching the streets of Dedaria for any sign of the Forgotten Mark. The freezing cold bit at my nose, and my feet felt heavy from the layers of wool socks that I had on beneath my boots.

To say the last few weeks here in The Court of Talisman have been a harrowing ordeal would be a significant understatement. As the Warden of Shadows, it was my duty to protect the most significant asset Verihdia has seen since the Warden of Forgotten, but as Lysander, it was my obsession to protect my mate from the threats that plagued her. Unfortunately, the unrelenting grip of eternal winter has made that task all the more challenging. The frigid winds howled through the towering spires, and the snow drifted higher with each passing day. It's as if the very soul of the court had been frozen in time.

But my concerns ran deeper than the weather. I couldn't shake the ever-present worry that kept gnawing at my mind. The Double Marked individuals, those elusive and dangerously gifted beings, threatened to harm the one person who had made my ancient heart beat with purpose again. Their attacks have grown more vicious, and their intent increasingly sinister. It was becoming more evident what their plan was. If it were true, I would do everything in my power to keep her from that fate.

Every day, I ventured out into the biting cold, with my senses on high alert, tracking the signs that could lead me to these attackers so that I could finish this once and for all, but they remained frustratingly out of reach.

I knew where I needed to go to find the answers, but it was the one place I swore never to venture to again... I knew that time was running out, and the danger was only increasing. I could only hope that my efforts would be enough to protect Lexa and keep the Forgotten Court at bay.

Ivis informed us that the Court would throw a decadent showcase of artistry this evening. I had to bite my tongue to avoid asking if there was anything that wasn't considered decadent in this Court. She wanted to offer us a proper send-off as we would leave to venture to our next stop on the tour tomorrow.

Ivis and Lexa seemed to have found mutual respect and admiration for each other during her time here, a sight that should have made me jealous, and even last month, it would have. I wanted Lexa to enjoy all that Verihdia had to offer because she would feel confident in choosing my Court and me when the time came to make her Pledge.

She would choose me. Right?

We had carefully danced around the subject of her impending Pledge during our time together under cover of night. There were only four Courts left for us to visit before she would be required to make her choice. I wasn't afraid of losing her to another Court, not after the way she claimed me so wholly each night, but I'd be lying if I didn't admit that the thought of her picking someone else to be her Warden was enough to send my Mythica into a tailspin. I've become a more patient man with Lexa by my side, but my envious side would require some reassurance soon, or I'd burn down the other Courts just to remove the competition.

Lexa wore a light pink robe over a darker base. It was tied together at her waist and flared out to trail behind her as she walked through the party that evening. The event pulsed with life, a kaleidoscope of colors and sounds that echoed through the vast open space at the heart of the Prism Library. The crystalline ceiling mirrored the extravagance below.

"You watch her like a man in love, brother," Ivis' voice startled me, but I regained composure quickly. The pink cloud of her Mythica rested on her shoulders and traveled down her back like a regal cape of power.

"I watch her like a man who knows there are people who intend to hurt her," I retorted, hoping the feigned indifference in my voice was enough to placate her.

She watched me through hooded eyes and kissed her teeth. "Of course," she stated, finally. "You haven't seen anything else to indicate this threat, have you?"

"You'd know if I had, sister," I said.

She nodded. "Then why don't you enjoy your evening? She is safe here, and she is enjoying herself. You don't need to keep such a close eye on her." It was a trap. Ivis suspected that I harbored deeper feelings and was merely trying to fish them out. She was more intuitive than our other siblings gave her credit for. That's how she won her Trial, after all.

"I suppose you're right," I answered before gripping a glass off a nearby tray. The liquid was sparkling and bubbly, tickling my nostrils and tongue as I threw my head back to swallow the contents.

"I have a few lovely friends who have been dying to keep you company during your stay. If you wish to find comfort in their arms tonight, I'm sure they would be happy to oblige." She tilted her head in the direction of a few women who stood a good forty or so feet from us. Their bright eyes were trained on me, and they devolved into girlish giggles when my eyes met theirs.

"That is a tempting offer, sister, but seeing as it's our last night, I should get some rest for the journey to Echoes tomorrow."

Ivis' eyes narrowed as she tried to see through my lie but eventually sighed. We stood in comfortable silence for a few moments, shoulder to shoulder, overlooking the ballroom of bliss. The air was alive with laughter, the rhythm of music, and the clinking of glasses. Amidst the vibrant chaos, Lexa stood like a beacon of light, drawing my eye immediately. She was happily lost in the swirl of dancing bodies, surrounded by the intoxicating blend of music, art, and laughter. I leaned against the wall behind me, a silent spectator, content to watch her immerse herself in the festivities. Her laughter resonated with the infectious joy that permeated the room, and every movement, every twirl on the dance floor, seemed like a brushstroke, adding to the canvas that was the Prism Library.

"She's a marvelous creature," Ivis offered. "The Court that wins Lexa Cromwell's loyalty will indeed be a lucky one."

"They would," I relented.

"You are holding out hope that she'll choose you, aren't you?" She asked.

"I'd be a foolish Warden if I didn't hope for her power to be mine." Even as I said the words, though, they felt false. She meant so much more to me than what her power could offer, and lying, even to protect her, felt immoral. "I don't think you need to be worried, though. She's made her position quite clear."

I wish it were clear.

She nodded, finally seeming to relent her incessant probing. The atmosphere was electric, and the scent of food wafted through the air, mingling with the melodies that danced throughout the room. As I watched her, I felt warmth, a quiet appreciation for the simple joy of seeing her happy and carefree. Her Mythica danced around her head in a jovial display of livelihood, mirroring the smile on her face. I don't know if it was my imagination, but her Mythica had seemed like *more* lately. More prepared, more vicious, more alive. But in this moment, it seemed to let its guard down, to flow freely above her.

Then, in an instant, the harmony shattered.

The crash of breaking glass and splintering crystals cut through the music like a discordant note. Startled gasps erupted, and the lively atmosphere twisted into a frenzy of panic. I turned my gaze upward, searching for the source of the disturbance, only to witness the ceiling giving way. Sharp shards rained down, and chaos unfolded as people scattered, desperately seeking safety.

Amid the commotion, my eyes locked onto Lexa's, still amidst the swirling chaos. Panic gripped me, a visceral fear that transcended the crowd's cries around us. I pushed through the frantic swarm of retreating bodies, the urgency of reaching her heightening with every step. As I neared her, I could see the realization dawning in her eyes, the sudden shift from joy to understanding. The once vibrant celebration had transformed into a scene of turmoil, with people screaming and fleeing in every direction.

Amidst the chaos, a group of assailants descended through the freshly shattered ceiling. Their bodies were propelled down with the assistance of ropes amidst the falling snow that now began to dust across the ballroom floor without the barrier of the ceiling to keep it at bay. Revealing themselves from their space hidden within the shadows of night, their motive was clear. I had to get to my mate. Now.

Adrenaline surged through me as I raced toward her, intent on bridging the gap that separated us. But just as I approached, a figure dropped in my path from among the falling glass. The assailant's face was obscured by that familiar white mask with dark voided eyes, cold determination resonated through their body, and their Mythica -which encircled their wrists like bracers - was at the ready. Without a word, the clash began.

Their Mythica became clear immediately as they lashed out. Their hands moved at incredible speed and as their Mythica pulsed, packing a punch much more potent than they should have been able to deal. They managed to get two hits in before I could register the movement. Each blow reverberated through my body, the raw intensity of the fight drowning out the sounds of the crumbling party. The desperation to reach Lexa fueled my every move, but the assailant was relentless. We grappled in a frenzied dance, the stakes higher than the dizzying swirl of the ongoing battle. With a grunt of anger, I pressed my hand against their chest and called their Mythica to me.

I felt the power drain from their body and flood into my palms, and they vibrated with the additional boost. The assailant had just a moment to realize what had happened before my hand, powered by their own Mythica, slammed against their cheek. They fell to the ground, and I didn't bother waiting to see if they would stay down before I raced toward Lexa again.

My eyes found her Mythica before they landed on her. It was impossibly massive, a ferocious storm raging above her head. My steps faltered only slightly at the enormity of it. It lashed out at the assailants that were encroaching on her, and I watched them fall to their knees one by one as her Mythica surged through their weak bodies.

Across the expanse of the glass and snow-covered battleground, the frigid air was thick with the palpable essence of Mythica, swirling clouds of luminescent smoke around nearly every person. The sight of it was overwhelming, like witnessing the very soul of individuals dancing in radiant hues. Streams of ethereal energy intertwined and clashed, creating a visual tapestry that sent a sharp pain through my mind. For the last several decades, I have avoided large gatherings for this very reason. So often, in moments like this, I found myself unable to maintain composure when my senses were overloaded by the mystical energies of those around me. But now, her Mythica stood out like a beacon, my little storm who beckoned me through the magical mayhem. With every step, I navigated the intricate dance of energies, my determination to reach her unwavering.

Each wisp of Mythica in the room seemed to clamor for attention, yet I tuned them out, honing in on the one that mattered above all. I focused on her as she fought off the advancing figures. Her pale skin was flushed with exertion and fear.

Another figure stopped before me, and I didn't even break my stride before reaching a hand toward them, latching onto the Mythica that burned within their chest, and ripping it out. Their scream was loud, but the crack of their whip-like Mythica against their skin was louder. Lexa was holding her ground impressively well, and if I wasn't terrified for her safety, I might have been proud of her work in the last few months to prepare herself for an attack precisely like this.

I pushed past the writhing bodies on the ground at her feet and reached her side. Being within her proximity again sent a jolt of relief through me, calming my shaking hands. The swirls of her Mythica encircled us, welcoming me into its barrier of protection. The instant of relief didn't last long, however, because I quickly recognized the look of fear in her eyes and the energy that was so viciously powerful that I could almost choke on it. It took me only a moment to see that Lexa, my mate, was not in control.

Her Mythica raged above our heads, lashing out at the nearly lifeless bodies on the ground. Their eyes rolled back in their heads as they screamed in fear and regret. Lexa's eyes darted around their circle as if she was involuntarily drawn to their devastation like a moth to a flame.

"Lexa," I called out, but her attention did not waiver. The fight beyond her storm continued, and as more figures advanced on her, the more her Mythica lashed out and claimed their minds as its prize. Tendrils of dark Mythica branched out like the arms of a vicious creature, digging its claws into their minds. They spasmed on the ground, crying out in pain and fear. "Lexa, stop," I said forcefully, but again, my pleas fell on deaf ears. "Lexa!" She was killing them.

I had to stop her before she did something irreparable. My chest tightened as the screams continued, and her glassy eyes danced around the people on the ground at our feet. "Please, little storm, listen to me," I pleaded.

Her assault on their minds continued, and I truly saw just how little control she had. It was as if the vicious storm that raged above her was the sentient being and Lexa was simply a host for its abilities. Looking at her, I didn't see my mate. I saw a beacon of overwhelming power. Logic evaded me, and instead, fear gripped at my very core. I had to save her. I had to rip her out of whatever trance her Mythica had pulled her into.

The choice was clear, and despite the promises I made and the tumultuous nature of the cloud above our heads, I reached for her and latched onto the essence of her Mythica…then pulled. It was an instinctive act, a desperate attempt to shield her from the spiraling chaos that threatened to consume her. As her volatile Mythica poured into my veins, I felt the vibrating power sear beneath my skin, sending pinpricks of energy throughout my body.

Ash and venom.

This time, the poisonous snake of her Mythica didn't strike out at me but instead coiled around my body as if it was prepared to protect me. It was stronger this time, a feat I would have thought impossible given the sheer staggering potency of it the last time I stole it from her. My eyes glazed over as it flooded my body. Suddenly, my vision was being overtaken by the force of its rage, and with it came a flood of emotions and visions. It was as if I had opened a door to the innermost fears and guilts of the figures at our feet that she had unwittingly targeted in the heat of the attack.

The room transformed into a surreal panorama of fractured memories and haunting regrets. My eyes scanned the faces before me, contorted in pain and sorrow, each a reflection of the toll of Lexa's uncontrolled Mythica. It was as if I was witnessing a montage of the worst fears and regrets of those who had fallen victim to her powers.

One figure was writhing on the ground, screaming and brushing away phantom crawling creatures as the ghost of them danced along their skin. Another was sobbing painfully as he relived the moment he made the selfish choice not to return home to visit his mother, only for her to pass before he had the chance to see her again. Tableaus of guilt and fear circled me, filling my mind, and my knees nearly buckled under the weight of it all.

Lexa's crystal eyes had cleared in the aftermath of my Mythica pulling away the dark cloud of her power. She sank to her knees, a hand on her chest as she struggled to find her breath. Tears clung to her pale skin as she came back to herself.

In the midst of this torment of fears, I inadvertently saw Lexa's pain—her desperation to control the potent force within her, her guilt at unintentionally causing harm. Her eyes now mirrored the profound sorrow of the souls she inadvertently touched with her Mythica. A sense of responsibility weighed heavily on my shoulders. I had taken her Mythica to protect her, but in doing so, I had unwittingly opened a conduit to her innermost struggles. The gravity of her pain pressed upon me, and a surge of empathy washed over me.

I let out a scream, drowned out by the fierce storm of Mythica, as I recalled the tendrils of power that had sought to destroy her assailants. The magic reluctantly returned to me, as if it was frustrated at being ripped from its true purpose of destruction. It was a delicate dance, a balancing act between the power she held and the power I sent out to grasp it, and with each passing moment, I felt the ebb and flow of the energies slowly come to a more manageable resting position.

As the last echoes of the magical turmoil subsided, the room fell into an uneasy silence. A quick glance around told me that my sister and her Court had managed to subdue a handful of intruders, and those who had been lucky enough to escape were long gone into the wintery night. Guards were rushing forward, grabbing hold of the few figures at our feet who were slowly regaining consciousness after Lexa's Mythica's attack.

I fell to my knees as her Mythica slipped away from me. The force of it drifting away felt like running my hand across a rough surface. It burned, and the pain was constant and raw as her power returned to her. I threw my arms around my mate, ignoring the inquisitive eyes around us. Lexa, who sunk into my embrace, appeared drained, the weight of the unintended consequences etched on her face. The clarity behind her eyes told me everything I needed to know that stealing her Mythica when I did was the right move. However, the aftermath left me grappling with the realization that the line between protection and intrusion was a delicate one.

"Lysander." My sister's near frantic voice cut through the moment of relief and unease I shared with my mate. Despite every ounce of my soul begging to cling to her, I released my hold on her. I stood, helping Lexa to her feet and watching her regain strength with each passing second.

Turning toward my sister, I saw evidence of the fight on her body. I had been so focused on my mate that I hadn't bothered to assess the damage the attack had done to everyone else. Her ordinarily smooth skin had several cuts and was already forming bruises. She held her hand against her abdomen, and it took me a few moments to process the image of the deep crimson blood that was seeping through her garments beneath her palm and pooling on the floor beneath her.

"Ivis," I exclaimed, reaching out to hold her steady in my arms. "You're hurt." She waved me off but sunk into my hold nonetheless.

"Nothing I haven't survived before," she responded, effectively moving on. "Lexa, dear, are you ok?" She glanced over my shoulder at the shaken woman behind me. I followed her gaze to look at my mate. Her ashen face was hollow, and her vacant eyes were wide with shock. She cleared her throat and nodded her head.

"I will be," she responded, but it sounded off, like it wasn't quite her voice. I wanted to reach for her, to hold her within my arms where I could be sure she was safe, but even I knew that I was no match for the guilt that was eating at her. She met my eyes and smiled softly, but it didn't quite reach her eyes.

"How bad was it, Ivis?" I asked, glancing around at the few masked figures who were being restrained.

"Several of them got away, running like the cowards they are, but you can see we've managed to capture eight." The five that surrounded Lexa, the two that I used my Mythica on, and another who looked to be housing even worse injuries than my sister. I watched, satisfied, as their hands were bound and they were led out of the destroyed ballroom.

"They'll need to be interrogated," I said, watching them, knowing what Marks we'd find on their skin if I looked hard enough.

"You know we don't handle that here, Lysander."

I looked back at her, knowing what she meant by that.

"They'll be transported to The Court of Echoes, and since that is your next stop, my guards will escort you, as well, to ensure your safety," she said softly, grunting at the pain at her side.

"You need to see a healer," I exclaimed, preparing to guide her to the healer's quarters, but she brushed me off again.

"Don't worry about me. I'm harder to kill than that. But I will see a healer when you and Lexa are safely on your way to The Court of Echoes." She looked past me again to meet eyes with Lexa. "Words will never be enough to express my deepest regret that you've suffered not one but two attacks during your time in my Court. I can assure you, my dear, that your safety was always my priority, and I will lament the failure for as long as I live."

Something in Lexa's expression shifted at that, as if the expression of guilt, given freely rather than torn from Ivis' mind, shook her from the shocked state.

"You don't owe me an apology for the actions of others, Warden. This was not your fault, nor is it your guilt to bear."

Ivis smiled and reached her hand, the one not currently covered in her blood, out to hold Lexa's hand. She took it eagerly, cradling it.

"Your Mythica saved us tonight, Lexa. I saw it as plainly as I see your face now."

Lexa swallowed deeply.

"My Court owes you a debt of gratitude for your protection. And we will hold out hope that you choose to return to protect us again and allow us to return the favor."

I narrowed my eyes at my sister and her desperate attempt to sway Lexa's loyalty. I respected my sister, but I couldn't believe she was using the aftermath of this attack and taking advantage of our heightened emotions to plead her case.

"Thank you, Warden," Lexa responded, lowering her head in a slight bow.

"Go, both of you. Pack your things. The guards will want to prepare the prisoner's convoy and get on the road as soon as possible. You'll have to go with them, and I'll personally send my Dean, Vitrola, with you. Be careful, both of you. Take care of her, Lysander," she ordered.

It was an order I would willingly accept.

Ivis was guided away by members of her Court who intended to tend to her wounds, and guards led Lexa and me to our quarters to pack our things.

We walked in silence, side by side, through the library halls. The cold air from the ballroom seemed to permeate the entire building, and I silently wondered how long it would take them to repair the damage from the Double Marked attack.

Lexa and I didn't have a moment alone in the next few hours as we packed and prepared a carriage. Ivis's guards insisted on having an escort steer our carriage so Lexa and I could remain safely enclosed within the covered structure. I relented, knowing that the carriage would offer an air of privacy both of us desperately needed.

The enclosed carriage exuded an air of luxurious seclusion, a sanctuary on wheels designed for privacy and safety. The carriage gleamed in the soft glow of discreetly placed lanterns. The exterior bore the insignia of the Court, a rolled scroll bound by a twig of pine.

As the carriage door swung open, the plush, burgundy velvet curtain adorned with golden tassels parted, revealing the interior. I helped Lexa step up into the enclosure, and her hand gripped mine desperately for the briefest of moments. Which told me that she needed the comfort I could offer her the same way I needed her safely in my arms. The walls, lined with padded upholstery in a rich, deep shade, absorbed any stray sounds, ensuring conversations within remained confidential.

The large, panoramic windows inside the carriage were fitted with heavy, embroidered curtains, allowing passengers to control the natural light filtering in. The windows were made of tempered glass, ensuring insulation and discretion. Each detail, from the pink accents on the door handles to the discreetly placed crystal decanter, spoke of a commitment to providing a haven of privacy and decadence.

"We will arrive at the Veil of Talisman early tomorrow morning, and we will escort you and the prisoners to the Veil of Echoes," Dean Vitrola stated before I could close the carriage door.

I nodded.

"The prisoners are heavily guarded and their Mythica has been dampened. You can rest easy, Warden, Miss Cromwell." She bowed her head once more before closing the door and locking the two of us away inside the safety of the padded walls.

A few moments later, the carriage jolted as the journey began. The rhythmic sound of the wheels moving over snow-covered ground flooded the space, and for the first time, I finally felt like we were alone.

Our eyes met in the dim light from the single lantern. I reached out to cup her face, and my fingers traced the contours of her features as if reassuring myself that she was indeed unharmed. At least physically. I wasn't naive enough to assume that the encounter had not left a myriad of mental scars far too deep for my touch to reach.

Her eyes, still reflecting the intensity of the recent ordeal, met mine. In that silent exchange, the weight of worry and the echoes of fear seemed to melt away. The relief was palpable, an unspoken acknowledgment that we had weathered the onslaught together.

With a tenderness born of shared vulnerability, our lips met in a kiss—a kiss not fueled by passion but by the profound sense of relief that enveloped us. It was a gentle meeting, a fusion of emotions that spoke of survival, of overcoming the darkness that had threatened to engulf us. As the kiss lingered, time seemed to stand still. The world outside the cocoon of our shared moment ceased to exist. It was a sanctuary of peace amidst the storm, a moment where the memories of the attack faded into the background, leaving only the soothing cadence of our shared breaths.

When our lips finally parted, a quiet serenity settled over us. She slid down until her head could rest in my lap, and I cradled her torso in my arms.

"I'm so sorry, Lexa," I began in a tentative whisper. She glanced up at me.

"Why are you sorry?" She asked as if it was unthinkable for me to apologize.

"I used my Mythica on you again. I swore to you that I wouldn't do that. I just didn't know how to help you," I whispered, ashamed to even say the words out loud. Her hand lifted and pressed a gentle touch against my cheek. "I'm still that selfish Warden you met at the Courting Ball," I finished. I hated the way that voicing the concerns that had been weighing on my soul felt like acknowledging their truthfulness.

I haven't changed. I wasn't suddenly a better person because of our mate bond.

"Lysander, look at me," her gentle voice drew my focus back to her. "I need you to hear me when I say this."

I nodded, watching her crystal eyes well with tears.

"You saved me," she whispered. "When the attack started, I was so terrified. Seeing their masked faces, all of them there to take me away was too much. My Mythica lashed out." She paused, taking a deep breath before choosing to continue. "Recently, it's been... different. It's like it has a mind of its own, a will that doesn't always align with mine. I feel it, Lysander, and it scares me. It's as if I'm not in control, as if my Mythica is guiding me instead of the other way around. I'm... I'm afraid that I might do something terrible, something irreversible. I'm afraid I won't be able to stop it."

Her vulnerability hung in the air, and my heart ached for her. I reached out, gently taking her hand in mine. A thought became crystal clear to me at that moment. She was operating on the 'truth' she knew about what had happened to the Warden of Forgotten when his power seemed to become uncontrollable. Yet, here she was, admitting her fears, admitting the dangers of her power, to me.

She trusts me.

"I don't want to hurt anyone. I don't want my Mythica to control me. I don't want the Wardens to feel like they have to neutralize me as a threat. I want to find a way to master it, to bring it back under my control before it's too late."

I felt my chest tighten, and a growl escaped my lips at the thought of my siblings harming my mate. I don't care what she does or what her Mythica is capable of, and I would protect her from them until my last breath.

I pressed my lips against her forehead gently. "We'll figure this out, Lexa. We'll face this challenge just like any other—together. You're not alone in this. You'll never be alone again. I'm beside you."

"I was going to kill those people," she whispered. The pain etched on her face was almost too much for me to bear. The primal need to protect her was so deep, so incredibly potent. My heart ached in my chest. Her Mythica was calmer now but never silent. It danced around her, poised to strike should the need arise. I felt the looming power buzzing within it. Alive and awake.

"I know," I responded calmly, rubbing gentle circles along her cheek, brushing away the fallen tears.

"Thank you," she started carefully, "for stopping me," she finished. I felt the corners of my lips turn up in a half smile, proud that I could help my mate but furious that she was in this position to begin with.

"Do you think Ivis saw how out of control I was? Will she tell the others?" She asked, an eager nervousness to her tone.

I shook my head. "I couldn't tell until I was right next to you, and even then, I only knew because I know you, Lexa."

She nodded, seemingly satisfied by that answer. She was silent for a moment longer, and I watched as her brows furrowed with the thought that came to her next. "What if I can't hide it anymore?"

I didn't know the answer to that. When it came to the decision of what to do with the Warden of Forgotten, it had been a difficult choice, one we toiled over, despite the snippet that Lexa saw that made it seem like we were resolved. The outcome we settled on was born from decades of fear. In the end, we chose to remove the threat of him, but not after extensively considering other options. It would not be as challenging a decision for several of my siblings should they discover what Lexa was truly capable of. After all, she wasn't a Warden.

"I will protect you." Was all I could offer because while I didn't know what would happen or how powerful she would become, I did know that. I would give anything in this lifetime or the next to protect Lexa Cromwell.

My mate. My life. My little storm.

Until my dying breath.

Twenty-Six

The carriage ride away from The Court of Talisman did little to calm my nerves. Still, Lysander's gentle touch was a soothing balm against the burning memory of my Mythica's relentless assault. His cool skin brushed against the heated flesh of my face, and the chilled touch grounded me so effortlessly.

I don't know when things shifted between us - if it was the moment in the cave or long before - but when it came time to admit the truth about my fears to him, I didn't hesitate. There wasn't a second of uncertainty. I wasn't worried he would use the information against me or run off to his siblings with proof that I should be eliminated like the Warden of Forgotten.

I needed him to know because I'm brave enough to admit that I am afraid. I needed him to see that I was becoming volatile and dangerous because I couldn't handle this alone. It was humorous in a taunting sort of way to think that a monster like me, who could rip someone's guilt and fears from their very minds, could ever feel scared. What do I have to fear anyway? I'm powerful, I'm valuable…All seven Wardens of Verihdia want me. And yet, all I can feel is fear.

I've always been wary of my Mythica, even as a girl at the Institute. I was often led to see this power as a burden, not a gift, which I had recently been trying to disprove, and truthfully, I have. I never would have survived these attacks if it weren't for this storm inside of me. I would have died. I would have been taken. I would have lost.

But my Mythica saved me. Time and time again. It kept me safe. It protected me.

Maybe that's why it started lashing out all on its own.

It's an unfortunate contradiction, truthfully. To wield a power that should make me feel fearless, to possess the ability to stave off assailants and pluck at the very fabric of their fears and guilt, and yet, in its wake, feel even more unstable than I had before. It doesn't make sense.

I should be invincible, a being beyond the grip of fear or uncertainty. And yet, here I am, afraid of myself. Afraid of my Mythica.

And now, it feels different. Stronger, more restless. What if it's not satisfied anymore?

Maybe it's no longer content stealing the fears and guilt of others anymore. What if it's begun feeding off my apprehensions, even going so far as to amplify them? It's an insurmountable obstacle. Thinking that the very force that saved me was now intertwined with my fears and doubts. What would happen if I were to lose control? What if it becomes a force beyond my command? What if my Mythica, once my savior, becomes the thing that controls *me?*

How far can I push the bounds of this magic before the Wardens decide to step in and solve their problems by eliminating them? The very thought of my potential for destruction is suffocating.

I let my mind drift briefly to Oliver. When I was younger, and my Mythica had first reared its ugly head, he had taken me under his wing, determined to help me gain control of the raging storm within me. He would be so disappointed to see how little control I really had. As the thought of him crossed my mind, the sadness I had attempted to stave off gripped my heart. Thoughts of our last interaction floated to the forefront of my mind. What had he meant? Why was he so insistent that my trust may be in the wrong place?

My eyes drifted back to my mate. Lysander had sprawled out across the back seat of the carriage. He looked so peaceful as he slept that I couldn't bring myself to wake him so that I could fit in next to him. Instead, I laid down on the seat across the way from him and instantly missed his touch. It was cold and unforgiving in this Court, but the chilled air felt like an appropriate punishment for what I'd done.

When I finally drifted off to sleep, I found comfort in the soft sound of Lysander breathing. Oliver would change his mind about him if he knew what we were to each other. He wouldn't question his intentions, then.

Would he?

More importantly, why did I seem to crave his approval so desperately?

Sleep claimed me then, but I was not claimed by sleep alone.

*

The oppressive darkness of a familiar ocean surrounded me, a suffocating cloak that seemed to press against my every pore. I again found myself adrift in that same endless, unfathomable ocean where the inky abyss had swallowed the concept of a surface. Panic clawed at my chest as I struggled to stay afloat in the cold, silent void.

The bitterness of salt stung my lips and eyes, a vicious reminder of the desolation that stretched endlessly in all directions. My limbs moved slowly as if battling against an invisible force that sought to drag me deeper into the dark.

A primal fear clawed at the edges of my consciousness, intensified by the deafening silence that enveloped me. As always, there was no escape, no refuge from the unyielding darkness. I felt like a lone speck in the vastness of an ocean that knew no boundaries.

Suddenly, that eerily familiar presence emerged from the shadows below. Massive tentacles unfurled like serpentine arms, reaching for me with a sinister intent from the darkness of the sea. The creature, which seemed to feed on my fear, rose from the depths, giving me the first authentic glimpse of the monster from my nightmares.

The creature's eyes, if they could be called that, bore into mine with a malevolence that sent shivers down my spine. It was a grotesque amalgamation of nightmare and reality, a manifestation of the darkest corners of my subconscious. Its blackened skin was unnatural. It could only truly be described as an otherworldly behemoth. Its colossal form writhed with a fluid grace, revealing a body adorned with glistening black scales.

As the creature's eyes met mine through the murky and shadowed waters, I felt an unsettling connection—an inexplicable familiarity that defied reason. The creature's head bore a crown of sinister-looking tendrils that seemed to writhe with their own sentience. Massive tentacles, each lined with rows of serrated suckers, reached out with an evident awareness of my presence.

Panic surged through me like a charged shock as the creature's appendages closed in. I tried to scream, but the sound was swallowed by the salted water, which took the opportunity to flood my lungs. The tentacles coiled around me, tightening their grip, and a suffocating terror took hold.

I fought against the creature's grasp, a futile struggle against an entity that seemed beyond the laws of nature. The icy water closed in around me, and I felt the weight of impending death. Desperation clawed at my throat as the creature's tentacles constricted tighter, a relentless force intent on dragging me into the abyss.

Echoing through the water, in a muffled, amplified cacophony, a voice slipped from the creature. "It's almost time, Lexa."

The creature held me still, its eyes searing into mine as the edges of my vision began to blur from the loss of air. "If you will not find me, I will find you," it promised in that deep, vicious voice. "Soon."

My lungs filled, and my body writhed in the creature's hold as death came to carry me away.

*

With a sudden gasp, I jolted upright, and my heart was pounding violently in my chest like a trapped and threatened bird. The suffocating darkness of the endless ocean was replaced by the dim glow of the carriage, which still traveled on, but the residue of fear lingered like a haunting melody. I clutched at my chest, feeling the rapid rise and fall reminded me that I had just surfaced from the depths of a drowning nightmare.

"Little storm?" Lysander's sleep-riddled voice reached me through the haziness of my adjusting mind.

"I'm ok," I promised, unconvincingly. "I'm ok."

He sat up in the seat across from me and reached forward to wrap me in his arms. I sank into his hold and breathed in his comforting, fiery scent.

"I had a nightmare," I whispered into his shoulder.

"I'm sorry," he offered in a pained tone. "I'm so sorry."

It wasn't until I was safely in his arms that the pattern became clearer. The nights I'd gone without a nightmare were ones where I was in the protective embrace of my mate or his Court. His presence was enough to chase away even the worst threats. I held him tighter.

"I saw the creature again."

His hands rubbed idle circles on my back.

"It spoke to me," I finished. His hands paused their comforting strokes for just a moment before he continued.

"What did it say?" He asked, and I wasn't imagining the tenseness in his tone.

"It said it was almost time." I swallowed the lump in my throat. "It said that if I wouldn't find it, it would find me." My words trailed off as the memory of its almost familiar and eerie voice as it echoed through the water returned to me. My body trembled.

Lysander's arms tightened around me, and he held my head against his chest. The rhythmic beating of his heart was a comforting sound.

My hands trembled as I brought them to my face. As I pulled them back, they were slick with moisture. Panic rushed through me as I tasted the unmistakable bitterness of salt on my lips. The remnants of my ocean clung to me like a phantom residue that deliberately blurred the line between dream and reality.

Frantically, I pulled back from his embrace and wiped my lips with the back of my hand as if trying to erase the lingering taste of the dream. The ramifications settled on my soul like a weighted secret. The creature had revealed itself to me.

It spoke to me. And it was coming for me.

His lips pressed against mine in a gentle kiss. It was quick but grounding. I sighed with contentment as he pulled back and cupped my face in his hand.

"You don't deserve to suffer these nightmares," he spoke quietly, just barely above a whisper. There was more behind his sad eyes. Guilt. The same guilt I saw the night in his quarters when I knew he was hiding something from me.

"They're not just nightmares, Lysander. They haven't been just nightmares for a while." I wiped a tear from my cheek as it slid down my skin. "You taste it on your lips, don't you?"

His tongue darted out, briefly running along his bottom lip before he sighed and nodded.

"Salt," I whispered. "I don't think I will be able to survive them much longer. You can only drown so many times before your lungs give out."

He pulled me into his arms and held me there securely for what felt like hours. It may have been. Eventually, he pulled back and brought me over to sit on the seat next to him. Lysander reached for my hand and held it gently. I marveled at just how perfectly his fingers fit into the spaces between my own.

I was distracted abruptly by the feeling of the veil of Talisman claiming its toll. Once again, I felt the desire to indulge and take all that was promised and owed to me. I wanted to know the truth behind these nightmares. I wanted to know the secrets behind the guilt in my mate's eyes. I wanted to lose myself in his kiss until I forgot about the burning in my lungs. I wanted so much. I wanted it all.

Eventually, I settled for the one thing I could have immediately. My lips met Lysander's. He eagerly reciprocated. His tongue darted into my mouth and danced with my own. His hands snaked around my waist, and I slid my fingers into his messy locks and pulled him tighter to my body. It wasn't lust I was being driven by, but rather the desire to have one more kiss and one more moment with him that wasn't tainted by the fear that chased us. There was a lot of uncertainty in my future, and I couldn't help myself from indulging in this moment of peaceful clarity with my mate before the rest of the world caught up to us.

When I finally pulled my lips from his, the veil's influence was slowly drifting away, but I was thankful that it forced me to take that last moment with him before we faced our reality again. He pressed a kiss to my temple as I snuggled into his side. I didn't realize just how cold it had been until the warmth of The Living Lands began to seep through the windows and permeate through the carriage, chasing away any lingering effects of winter.

"How far are we from The Court of Echoes?" I asked, nervously clasping my hands together in my lap. I hadn't told Lysander about my encounter with the Warden of Echoes at the Courting Ball and didn't want to admit that this was the one stop on the tour that I most dreaded.

Warden Rein Mithroar told me precisely what he was going to expect of me. He wasted no time ensuring that I knew what my role would be in his Court. He was going to ask me to use my Mythica. I had considered that fact ever since this little tour was announced, but I tried to push it from my mind. I couldn't do that anymore now that we were almost there.

"A few hours, most likely. Undoubtedly, we will be headed directly through the center of The Living Lands," he responded, stretching his arms out above him.

"By the Institute?" I asked eagerly. It seemed like a lifetime ago that I last walked those halls.

"That would be the quickest route to Echoes from here. And I doubt they'd be willing to take any detours with the prisoners."

My stomach dropped at the thought of the prisoners, the masked figures who fell victim to my Mythica's rage.

"Rein will get to the bottom of the attacks," Lysander offered quietly. "He has a… talent for that kind of thing."

"By talent, you mean torture," I whispered.

Lysander didn't answer with words but nodded solemnly. That thought felt sickening to me.

"They've been attacking you, Lexa. These Double Marked terrorists are trying to harm you. I'm not particularly fond of the idea of torture either, but I also want Rein to discover what they are after so we can stop them."

I took a moment to process his words before something stuck out.

"Double Marked?"

His face twitched and he sighed, as his eyes drifted closed. He almost seemed disappointed that he had revealed too much.

"What does that mean, Lysander? What does Double Marked mean?" When he didn't answer, I gripped his chin and turned his face to mine. He tried to avoid my eyes.

"What are you hiding from me?" I demanded.

"I wasn't trying to hide it. It's just… it doesn't make sense," he stated, but I wasn't letting him off that easily.

"Tell me right now, Lysander."

He ran a hand through his messy hair, brushing it out of his face, and he shook his head.

"It.. I've been trying to figure it out," he replied.

"What is it?" I asked forcefully.

"The man who attacked you at the Forsaken Quarters had the Mark of Shadows."

I nodded. That much was obvious. He had been in the Court of Shadows, after all. He wouldn't have been able to pass through the veil without it or the Warden of Shadows himself helping him through.

"He also had the Mark of the Forgotten Court."

My lungs lost their ability to intake air. The smell of paint invaded my nostrils as the image of the white-painted symbol flooded my mind. That raven's silhouette was so stark against the dark ground, the hanging crocus dangling from its beak. The red blood was marring the delicate design. I felt faint all of a sudden. Leaning forward, I held my head in my hands.

"Lexa, are you alright?" His voice cut through the images, and they dissipated like clouds of memories that would never really disappear from my mind.

"Why didn't you tell me about this?" I asked, keeping my eyes trained on the floor of the carriage.

"Because it shouldn't be possible," he started in a low whisper. I glanced over at him through the curtain of hair that hung in my face. His posture was rigid, and his face was severe. His hands were folded in his lap, but I could see how tightly he held them together. "We destroyed the Court Mark patch when we…"

He stopped, sighing. I nodded, knowing where he was headed. "Destroyed the Warden of Forgotten," I finished.

Lysander lifted a hand to his head and rested his forehead in his palm with a deep sigh. "Don't do that. Don't paint me the villain now. Not after what we've been through. You still don't know the whole story, Lexa."

"Then tell me," I begged, sitting up to face him. 'Tell me the story, Lysander. Don't you think I deserve the truth?"

"Of course you do, but it's not that simple," he argued, his eyes softening as he looked at me. I took a composed breath.

"Why not?" I probed.

'Lexa," he warned.

"What aren't you telling me?" I commanded.

"The Wardens have sworn a vow of secrecy, Lexa," he unleashed in a forceful whisper. "I cannot tell you because if I did, I would die." His words stung me as they landed. The sharp pain jolted directly into my heart, reminding me just how much of my soul was tied to his and just how much of myself I would lose if he were to die.

"You already know more than you should," he finished in a soft, melancholic whisper. "When you saw my guilt that night in my quarters, the look of fear on my face wasn't due to your Mythica working on me. It wasn't even because you saw what you did in my mind. I was waiting for the vow to be broken. I was waiting for the promise I made to my siblings to come and collect my soul as a price for my failure." He didn't shy away when my hands reached for his. "You have no idea how badly I've wanted to tell you everything. Anything to get you to stop looking at me like that."

"Like what?"

"Like you still can't trust me," he finished, shame coloring his expression.

A tear slid down his dark skin, and I caught it with my fingers. Those emerald eyes glistened with the guilt that weighed so heavily on him.

"I had to choose between keeping secrets from you and staying alive. And perhaps I am the most selfish man alive because I would rather hide things than lose a single moment of time with you."

My heart nearly burst with just how full it was with admiration and love for the broken man before me. He wasn't perfect. He made mistakes and selfish choices but made them for me.

"I've been holding my breath, waiting for the moment when it all comes crumbling down. When the vow realizes that you know the truth or part of it, and it takes me from you."

"It didn't, it won't. You're here. You're alive," I whispered, bringing his knuckles to my lips to gently kiss them. He smiled softly at me.

"Perhaps it was because I didn't tell you willingly," he winced at the memory, but then another thought crossed his mind and reflected on his face as his eyebrows furrowed and he looked off to the side. "I didn't tell you willingly," he repeated.

"Yes, and I am sorry about that," I offered.

"I cannot tell you the rest of the story, Lexa," he said, eyes scanning mine. "But perhaps you can see it for yourself."

I dropped his hand. Shaking my head, I turned to face forward, ignoring how his gaze felt hot against my skin.

"Absolutely not, Lysander. I will not use my Mythica on you again. You saw how out of control it just was. I won't put you in harm's way."

He reached for my hand, but I pulled it away.

"Little storm," he started. "You were threatened and scared. You had to defend yourself." The words felt false even as he said them. "It won't be the same."

I took a mental inventory of my Mythica. The swirling storm within my soul felt calm but eager at the promise of being unleashed again. I shook my head again, stronger this time.

"No, I can't. It's too volatile right now. And I won't turn you into an experiment," I stated.

He nodded. "I understand," he started. "But when you're ready to try, I want you to know."

The time passed quickly after that. I drew the curtains to watch the familiar landscapes pass us by as we neared the center of The Living Lands.

The carriage rumbled along the dirt-covered streets, and I peered out from the window at the looming silhouette of the Veridian Institute as it came into view over the horizon. The gothic spires of the castle-like school building pierced the sky. Months had passed since I last existed amongst the shadows of the Institute, and as the carriage approached, a wave of nostalgia and uncertainty washed over me. The familiar sight stirred memories of my former self - the person who had walked those halls with a head full of questions and a heart brimming with anticipation for discovering where I belonged. But now, after months away, I couldn't shake the feeling that I had become a stranger to the very place that once felt like home.

The carriage slowed, and I strained to memorize every detail of the Verihdian Institute as we moved past it. Ivy tendrils clung to the ancient bricks as if trying to reclaim the building from the passage of time. I marveled at the intricate details of the architecture and the way the sunlight played upon the stained glass windows that adorned the towering façade.

There was a beauty to the steadfast structure that I wasn't sure I ever truly appreciated until I had to leave it all behind.

The arena where I sat and watched the people closest to me make their Pledge came into view, and I thought back to that day. If I had made a Pledge that day, would my nightmares still plague me? Am I being tormented by these Double Marked individuals because I'm Uncourted?

I tried to imagine a life where I had made a choice that day, but then my heart constricted at the thought of existing in a life without knowing who Lysander was to me. I'd suffer the nightmares if it meant he could belong to me.

I would never be the girl who walked those halls again. The sun had reached its midday peak as the Institute and its memories disappeared behind us.

Twenty-Seven

The carriage slowed as we neared the veil to The Court of Echoes. With each passing second, I grew more wary about visiting this Court and its entitled, torturing, villainous Warden. Who was he to expect such vile things of me? How dare he plan to use me as a weapon to make his castle of punishment more effective.

When the carriage came to a halt, I shook off the growing tide of anger that bubbled beneath my skin. A knock on the door made me jump and scramble as far away from Lysander as the seat would allow. Lysander, however, was calm and collected as he pushed open the door to reveal Vitrola, the Dean of Talisman. Her eyes were red-rimmed with exhaustion from the journey.

"We have arrived at the veil, Warden," she offered, slightly bowing. Lysander thanked her before stepping out of the carriage and turning to provide me with a hand. It took a moment for my legs to adjust as I set foot on solid ground again. My whole body was sore from the fight and the nightmare. I took a few moments and stretched out the aching muscles as Lysander spoke to the Dean and her guards.

The veil of The Court of Echoes shimmered with an almost suffocating influence as if woven from the threads of wrath and anger. I felt the tendrils of its Mythica dancing along my senses, begging me to give into the anger that had reared its ugly head before.

My eyes landed on the barred carriage ahead of us. I hadn't noticed it the night before. The skeletal frame of the carriage, stained with years of neglect and hardship, bore the scars of countless journeys, which made my stomach turn with guilt. Thick iron bars enclosed the wooden structure, creating a cage on wheels that seemed to swallow any hope of escape.

The carriage's exterior was coated in layers of grime, and the stench of confinement hung heavy in the air, a suffocating mix of sweat and despair. Small, barred windows lined the sides of the carriage, allowing only slivers of light to pierce through and illuminate the faces of those trapped within.

Guards adorned in dark crimson uniforms approached from the veil and headed for the prisoners. The enforcers of The Court of Echoes emanated an aura of severity as they neared the carriage of prisoners. Each guard bore the emblem of the Court—a symbol of warped justice and wrathful judgment.

As they drew closer, I noticed that the guards carried with them a searing iron, its tip glowing with a malevolent heat. The intent was clear - to mark the prisoners with The Court of Echoes brand. The sinister insignia would serve as both identification as a criminal and their ticket to the Sunken Province Prison. The prisoners, already ensnared in the shackles of the carriage, awaited their fate with a mixture of trepidation and silent defiance.

The guards seized the first prisoner, pulled them from the confines of the carriage, and held them in an unyielding grip as the red-hot brand hovered menacingly over exposed skin. The sizzle of flesh meeting metal resonated through the air, accompanied by the prisoner's stifled gasp and a pungent scent of burning. The brand left its mark, a burning flame design, with a violent raging storm within. The prisoner fought back. I wasn't sure whether it was the veil's influence or a reaction from the pain. A guard slammed a fist into the side of his head, and the prisoner crumpled to the ground, which only sent the other captives into a frenzy of anger that took a few minutes of brutal force to calm.

Once the situation had settled, the process repeated for each captive, and a palpable tension hung in the air. With each brand, each scarring of flesh, I felt a rising tide of anger and wrath within. With each branding, my fists clenched involuntarily, and the flames of indignation ignited within. The guards' callous demeanor and the systematic way they marked each soul fueled a growing fury. The veil, a crimson doorway to the world beyond, now seemed to shimmer with the tainted essence of injustice.

"They made their choice, little storm," Lysander whispered, his warm breath on my ear, sending a shiver through my body, coming in to wash away the wrath. "They tried to harm you. They stabbed my sister. They don't deserve your empathy."

I turned to look at him and saw the familiar glaze of anger in his eyes. I wished we were alone so I could kiss away the veils' influence. I settled for a brief touch as I pressed my shoulder into his. His eyes flicked back to mine, and we took a deep breath together.

"I'd like to get as far away from this veil as possible soon," I stated, and Lysander returned my sentiment with an eager nod of his head.

Footsteps drew my attention back toward the spectacle, and as I turned my eyes in that direction, they landed on a familiar foreboding figure. Damon Howden, the Dean of Echoes, approached. His hair was slicked back, and his dark brown skin was slick with sweat. He wore a more casual version of his red robes from the Institute, complete with the school's emblem.

"Miss Cromwell, Warden," he said as he stopped before us.

"Dean Howden," I said, tilting my head in greeting. "It's nice to see you." The lie felt like ash on my tongue.

"Thank you for meeting us at the veil," Lysander offered his hand to the

Dean, who took it eagerly. His respect for the Warden before him was evident in his face and actions. It was nice to see that despite his ties to The Court of Echoes, he still felt compelled to hold such a high regard for the Warden of Shadows.

"My Warden received the message from The Warden of Talisman late last night. We came straight away to escort you to the Prison and to ensure that these criminals are brought in to face their punishment," he spat, tossing the words over his shoulder toward the prisoners as if they were the most vile creatures he'd ever seen.

"We appreciate the escort. We'd like to get going as soon as possible. You can imagine the veil's influence is a lot to endure for long periods."

Damon nodded and promised to get us moving as soon as they could.

It took a significant amount of energy to keep the rising levels of anger at bay while we transferred the prisoners to their new barred carriage, and Lysander and I were also led to our new transport.

Its exterior was worn and weather-beaten, repelling any notion of comfort. Cold metal accents adorned its frame, their sharp edges promoting an unforgiving appearance. Upon closer inspection, the interior mirrored the inhospitable nature of the carriage. Stiff, rigid surfaces replaced any semblance of plush upholstery, offering no respite from the jarring motions of the journey. The seats, if they could be called that, were mere slabs of unyielding wood, lacking the cushioning that might provide solace to weary travelers. I immediately missed the plush comfort of the carriage from Talisman.

Lysander and I climbed in and sat silently as the anxious anticipation gripped me. I wasn't sure I was ready to pay whatever toll this veil would charge, but the time to worry was waning as the carriage jolted forward, and we began to move.

Lysander gripped my hand, both in comfort and as the key to my ability to cross through, and held it tight as we pushed through the shimmering wall. Instantly, the price of passage became clear. My mind suddenly became a battleground where anger, rage, and resentment waged war against reason and sanity. The veil seemed to amplify the darkest corners of my soul, dredging up buried grievances and nurturing them into malevolent entities that whispered poisonous thoughts into my mind.

Lysander lied to me.

My Mythica betrayed me.

Oliver doesn't trust me.

Chandler never respected me.

They are hiding my parents from me.

I'm being chased.

I'm being tormented.

I drown every single night.

The Forgotten Court wants me dead.

The Wardens killed them all.

The thoughts poured one by one out from the darkest corner of my mind to the forefront, and each word was just another degree added to the burning inferno beneath my skin. I gripped the hilt of my dagger and held it close, poised to attack the next object of my ire. The hilt felt cold against the heated skin of my palm, and it wasn't until I felt Lysander's gentle touch against my wrist that my grip loosened. I begged my mind to calm down as the veil slipped away behind us. The further we got from it, the more those vicious whispers retreated to the corners from which they came. I thanked Lysander with a squeeze of his hand before turning my focus to the new world outside the window.

The first thing I noticed was the heat. It was scorching, unbridled, suffocating. The journey to the Sunken Province Prison unfolded through a desolate realm, a landscape that seemed torn from the fabric of fear itself. A barren expanse stretched as far as my eyes could see, dominated by the ominous presence of fire and brimstone. The ground beneath us was cracked and scorched, and waves of heat had me concerned that the very floor of the carriage might combust into flames.

Rivers of molten lava snaked through the ashen plains, their fiery tongues licking at the lifeless sediment. The air itself shimmered with the heat, carrying the acrid scent of sulfur that stung my nostrils. The very ground seemed to writhe in agony as if the landscape itself bore the scars that the Prison intended to inflict on those housed within.

Above, a storm raged in the darkened sky. Forks of lightning cracked amidst the nearly red clouds, illuminating the desolation below with jagged streaks of light. The thunderous roars echoed through the carriage, sending shockwaves to my bones. How anyone could call this palace home was beyond me. The sheer energy in the air was unwelcoming and foreboding.

Lysander's attention was split between the desolate world beyond the window and me, waiting for me to fall apart. Frankly, I was too. I was considering making a premature Pledge just to avoid continuing this journey, but my mind drifted to something Ivis had reminded me of… My 'why.' As I pictured my brother's face, I felt the fear subside. I would make it through this Court and whatever Rein had in store for me because then I would be with Axel. And it will have all been worth it.

Along the journey, we passed through two villages, which seemed pleasant enough. The first was nestled in a small valley amid the ashen plains. The huts and cottages were constructed from charred timber and volcanic rock, a testament to the harsh conditions of the environment. Flickering flames adorned the entrances of these humble abodes, providing a feeble source of light in the perpetual gloom. The villagers moved about the town in a manner that I'd almost describe as haunting. Their careful steps amidst the charred ground and fury-laced stares told me everything I needed to know about the Court's inhabitants.

The second was perched on the edge of a vast expanse of cracked soil. A settlement born from necessity rather than choice, the town resembled a makeshift outpost carved into the parched ground. The buildings were constructed from salvaged materials, their facades weathered and worn. Dust-laden winds swept through the narrow streets, carrying the echoes of fear and anger.

This Court was so unbelievably unforgiving, and I couldn't imagine that anyone here felt at home amidst the death and destruction. Perhaps that was the point. Maybe the people who belonged here didn't care to feel safe and secure in their homes. Perhaps they preferred the discomfort so that they could convince others that their ruthless natures were necessary.

After a while, the hair on my neck stood on end, and my body tensed. I felt the ominous presence before I saw it. Atop a rocky cliff's edge, the prison loomed on the horizon - a dark, foreboding structure. The cold and rigid exterior seemed to meld with the shadows cast by the storm clouds. The Sunken Province Prison could only be described as a fortress of despair. It clung to the rocky, dangerous cliff like a dead man clinging to life. Its architecture was malevolence incarnate, with towering spires reaching into the storm-laden sky like skeletal fingers. One tower rose above all others. Its foreboding shadow stretched across the ground toward me as if it would devour me whole.

As we approached the Prison, I couldn't help but notice that it felt like we were embarking on an ascent into the heart of darkness. The path was uneven and treacherous as it led us through the imposing cliffs, jagged rocky edges, and toward the prison gates. The rocky cliff beneath seemed to crumble into an abyss, only emphasizing the isolation and hopelessness surrounding the Sunken Province Prison.

The carriage stopped just inside the large iron-wrought gates, and Damon opened the door and offered me his hand. As I stepped out and into the oppressive heat, I decided that I preferred the discomfort of the carriage to the threatening aura of danger that seemed to charge the air here. I tried not to let my eye follow the line of prisoners as they were ripped from their transport and dragged by their chained hands to their new reality.

"My Warden is eager to see you both," Damon said, giving me something else to focus on. "He requests that you join him for dinner in the main hall after you freshen up and settle into your rooms."

"Will we be staying in the Prison?" I asked, barely containing the fear and disgust in my tone.

"My Warden's home sits at the center of the Prison. He has rooms prepared for you there."

Surrounded on all sides by torture, death, and punishment?

Wonderful.

"Allow me to show you to your accommodations. Follow me. The guards will bring your belongings." Damon turned on a heel and led the two of us into the large and foreboding building. The interior of the Prison was just as welcoming as the outside. As we stepped past, the shadows along the floors and walls felt coiled and poised to strike. The space was illuminated by a warm red light emanating from Mythica-imbued bricks. Damon walked ahead, not bothering to check that we were still behind him. He knew as well as I did that there was no avoiding this stop on the tour. I was going to be here for a month, and there wasn't anything I could do to change that.

"It seems worse than it is," Lysander offered quietly, low enough that Damon could not hear from his position ahead of us.

"Doubtful," I replied, and Lysander let out a humorless chuckle.

"You're safe here. I will keep you safe. You know that, right?" He asked, and I could hear the promise within the words.

"I know," I said, a soft smile playing on my lips, but even that tiny symbol of happiness felt out of place amid the shadowed corridors.

"Think of it this way, if you continue your training here, you'll be getting a very… aggressive approach of self-defense," he offered, trying to calm my nerves. Still, the thought of learning how to fight from people whose demeanor is full of rage didn't seem like the safest option.

"Maybe you can train me while we're here?" I asked, and Lysander's face broke into a full, bright smile.

"I won't go easy on you," he teased, and the darkness of my surroundings seemed to brighten just a bit as if our levity chased away some of the despair.

"Neither will I," I taunted back, admiring how secure he had made me feel in just a few moments.

"Here we are," Damon called from ahead of us. He had stopped in the center of a hallway with a large iron door on either side, standing tall and menacing. "Your rooms."

Lysander thanked him, and with a reminder of our expected appearance at dinner, Damon was off. I smiled at Lysander before disappearing into the door across the hall from him.

The bedroom bore the unmistakable imprint of confinement despite its notable departure from a typical prison cell. The air in the room was heavy with a pervasive sense of isolation, and the sparse furnishings emphasized a stark lack of comfort.

The walls were muted, lifeless, and seemed to absorb any hint of warmth or vitality. Narrow windows allowed feeble rays of light to filter through with each strike of lightning across the sky, casting faint patterns on the cold, stone floor. Mythica-induced lighted bricks lined the floor, creating an eerie flood of red light that climbed toward the ceiling. A solitary bed, draped in coarse, gray sheets, stood against one wall.

Though not overtly restrictive in design, the room exuded a subtle but profound sense of captivity. The lack of personal touches or comforts made it feel more like a reluctant refuge than a sanctuary. My bags had already arrived, which I was thankful for because I desperately needed to rinse the journey off of me and slip into something that reminded me of any Court other than the one I was currently trapped in.

Avoiding the bath, I utilized the small basin of water to rinse my face and the layer of grime I felt built up from the day of non-stop travel off my body. I knew instantly which outfit I wanted to wear.

The bright emerald-colored fabric of the dress still smelled faintly of The Court of Shadows as I slid it over my head. This was one of the outfits Lysander bought for me that I hadn't had the pleasure of wearing yet, and the way the bodice clung to my curves felt like a comforting embrace. I tightened the holster around my thigh and let the cool metal of my blade calm me. With a deep breath, I stepped out into the hall and knocked on the door across the way.

Lysander had also changed into something that reminded him of home. A green velvet jacket and dark black pants. It looked very similar to the outfit he wore that night at the Courting ball. This jacket was less formal but no less elegant. He was firmly wearing the mask of the Warden of Shadows, but when he saw me and took in my outfit, the mask slipped to reveal my mate.

His eyes quickly assessed our surroundings before grabbing my wrist, pulling me into his room, and closing the door behind us. He pressed me back against the cool iron in an instant, and his lips claimed a spot on my throat. My head lulled back against the door as his mouth pressed delicate, passion-filled kisses against my heated skin.

"You're wearing my color," he exclaimed, muffled against my skin. His lips trailed heated kisses up my jaw toward my mouth. Waiting for his lips to meet mine was tortuous in the best way. My entire body pulsed with want as his hands slid down my waist to the hem of my skirt.

"I am," I whispered, lost in the haze of wanton desire. His fingers trailed up my legs, and my skirt began to bunch around my waist as he slowly revealed my body.

He peppered featherlight kisses against my cheek, then my earlobe, and I couldn't stop the frustrated moan that slipped through my lips. His lips pressed against mine, finally, just as his fingers found my center. Hot and dripping for him.

His kiss devoured me like a man who was starving for intimacy, and I willingly gave him everything I had.

He pulled away, breaking our kiss far too early, and I groaned in frustration. He chuckled darkly as he lowered himself to his knees before me. My legs trembled with anticipation.

His fingers found my center again, and I pressed my back against the door in response to the flood of euphoria. His hot breath dusted over my core, and I think I begged for him.

"You know," he started, then punctuated the words with a kiss to my inner left thigh. "I do not kneel." He repeated the kiss on the right side. "Not for anyone, at any time." His fingers spread open my center for him and one of my hands dug into his hair and tangled in his dark hair. "But, for you…" He leaned in, and I could feel the barest touch as he hovered over my most sensitive spot. "I belong on my knees at your feet, Lexa." Then his tongue met my core, and I nearly screamed from the intensity. His fingers and tongue worked in tandem to bring me blindly to the edge of euphoria and prepare to topple me over.

"Yes, Lysander," I moaned, pressing my head against the iron door, willing it to support me so I did not collapse.

"Tell me why you wore it," he demanded, pausing his pleasurable attack only long enough to speak the words before returning his attention to my slick opening.

"I…" I started, but a gasp caught in my throat as his tongue pressed deep inside of me. "I.. oh." I pushed him into me with the hand that was gripping his hair, and he willingly submitted, pressing deeper and letting his fingers dance along the sensitive bud at the apex of my thighs.

"Tell me," he commanded again, and this time, he thrust a finger into my core, and I folded over, knowing that I was nearing the point of blissful release.

"I wore it because it…" I forced out through labored breaths. "Because I miss your Court." I felt his smile against my core as he lapped his tongue furiously across the bundle of nerves and pressed his fingers deeper.

I had to bite down on my arm to avoid screaming as the orgasm claimed me and sent me shivering over the ledge into beautiful contentment. I felt my arousal drip down my legs as my mind slowly returned to my body, and my breathing returned to its normal level.

"Hmm," Lysander mused as he slowly lowered my gown and stood. "You taste even better than I remembered."

I laughed, a deep, full-body laugh, and pushed playfully on his shoulder until he joined me in a fit of levity. It felt nice to find a moment of comfort in a place like this.

"Come, we shouldn't keep Rein waiting long. He's hot-headed enough without reason." Lysander squeezed my hand once before letting go to open the door. He ushered me down the hallways. If we were traversing a new path, I couldn't tell. Each corridor was just as unwelcoming and desolate as the previous. It wasn't until we spilled into the dining hall at the heart of the prison that I felt like I had entered something new. Crossing the threshold into the hall felt like stepping into a realm torn between opposing elements - cold and hot, a disconcerting blend that sent a wave of unease coursing through my veins. The heavy iron door creaked shut behind me, sealing off any fleeting notions of escape.

The air within the dining hall carried an unsettling chill, a pervasive cold that seemed to seep into the marrow of my bones. Yet, amidst the biting cold, there was an undeniable heat reminiscent of the scorched ground outside the windowless room. The air pulsed with an unsettling fusion of elements at odds with one another.

"At last, my guests arrive," the chilling voice drew my attention to the massive wooden table at the center of the room.

Sitting at the head was Rein Mithroar. The Warden's presence was as imposing as the prison itself. He somehow looked even more menacing against the backdrop of his own Court's angular and inhospitable setting. His figure was shrouded in a dark, austere uniform that accentuated the jagged contours of his ashen skin and exuded an aura of authority. As he stood and began to cross the floor toward the two of us, I couldn't help but recognize that every movement he made was deliberate and calculated. His steps echoed the weight of the power he wielded within the confines of the Sunken Province Prison. His eyes were a striking contrast to the muted tones of his complexion, and they blazed with a vivid, bright red as he approached. Vicious and unyielding, his gaze held a predatory intensity, a hunger for power. My power.

The air thickened with tension as the Warden fixed his gaze on me. His expression spoke volumes. This was a man who saw not just an individual but a source of power to be harnessed, a potential pawn in his twisted game of dominance and punishment.

"Miss Cromwell, I have been looking forward to your arrival in my Court," he offered me a hand. I placed my hand in his, noting how my pale complexion seemed vibrant and lively against the backdrop of his ashen skin. He pressed a kiss that I could only describe as rigid to my knuckles before releasing his hold on me.

"Thank you for hosting me," I replied, hoping the apprehension in my tone wasn't as apparent as it felt.

"Let us sit. I can imagine you are both famished from your journey." He turned and led us to the table. As he mentioned it, my stomach decided that would be an excellent time to show its frustration by growling in the quiet of the room.

Thankfully, Lysander took the seat closest to the Warden and ushered me to the seat beside him. I was relieved to have my mate as a buffer between us. I prayed I didn't have to spend significant time alone with Rein during my time here, although that was a naive hope.

"Help yourselves." He gestured to the spread at the center of the table. The offering was nothing compared to the meals I had gotten used to in The Court of Talisman, but the soup had a pleasant enough aroma, so I eagerly filled my bowl. Lysander also filled his plate but in a much more composed manner.

"It seems we have much to discuss, brother," Rein began, and I felt my body tense. "Should we begin with the prisoners you accompanied back to my Prison or the several attacks against Miss Cromwell that you've failed to inform the other Wardens of?"

I swallowed a spoonful of soup quietly, willing myself to become as still as possible. Perhaps then, I wouldn't need to participate in this conversation.

"You weren't informed because I was assigned as Miss Cromwell's guide and protector. Her safety was my concern, so I handled the small matter. I shared the necessary information with the Wardens who needed to know it at the time."

Rein did not appreciate hearing that. His nostrils flared.

"So it was intentional to withhold this information? I assume you didn't believe we deserved to know about the Marks you found on their bodies either," he growled. The rising anger in his tone was unmistakable.

"Your anger is misplaced, brother," Lysander countered, the word 'brother' sounding more like an insult coming from his tongue. "But it happens so often, I shouldn't be surprised."

Rein's eyes bore into Lysander's, but the Warden of Shadows did not back down. Instead, he leaned forward and addressed the Warden of Echoes head-on.

"If you would stop accusing me of working against you, we could discuss a path forward like civilized adults."

Rein and Lysander were locked in a heated stand-off. Their Mythica-shrouded eyes housed their barely contained disdain.

"Fine," Rein conceded, leaning back into his chair, and I finally released the breath I had been holding. "Tell me everything."

And so Lysander did. From the Mark on the carriage to the attack in the Forsaken Quarters, he told Rein about the threats against me that had been piling up. I was shocked that he withheld any information about my nightmares and the incident in the fountain, but thankful for that nonetheless. Even though they were connected, my dreams and the attacks, it was a relief that Rein wasn't privy to how this sea creature was tormenting me.

I bit my lip as he described what he had found on the first attacker, the second Court Mark. The Forgotten Mark. It still stung that he had kept that from me as if I was too fragile to house a revelation so massive.

Lysander explained my ongoing training, the Mark sighting in The Court of Passion, and the ambush in Talisman that forced us to seek shelter in a cave. My cheeks heated at the memory, and I lowered my head, hoping Rein wouldn't notice the blush.

When Lysander described the vicious attack on the Prism Library, I tried not to wince. As the Mythica within me stirred, its explosive energy threatening to breach the surface, I felt the familiar surge of power coursing through my veins. The room around me seemed to slip away into darkness as my vision tunneled, and my instinct was to strike, to protect. I could sense the impending storm grow more vigorous and violent with each passing second as the memory of their masked faces crossed my mind.

A firm hand closed around my thigh, grounding me in the present moment. The touch was both reassuring and commanding, bringing me back from the brink of losing control. Lysander was so attuned to the subtle shifts in my demeanor and could visually see the rising cloud of power that he could easily recognize the signs of my spiral. The hand was gone a moment later, not to arouse any questions about our relationship, but the echo of his hand remained with me, grounding me.

When Lysander finished recounting our experiences to Rein, they settled back into their chairs, both seemingly lost in thought. I reached for my cup, hoping to calm the dull ache in my throat.

"I don't think I have to tell you that this is not a small matter any longer," Rein stated. "What have you made Miss Cromwell aware of as far as the origin of the Mark?" His eyes glanced over at me, and I felt hot under his assessing gaze.

"She knows that the Mark was once a symbol of a Court long forgotten," Lysander answered carefully. I watched Rein as he returned his gaze to my mate. There were a million threats and warnings raging in those eyes. Rein wanted Lysander to know that he was treading dangerously close to the line that the vow they had sworn would not let him cross.

"Warden," I interjected and immediately wished I could recall the word when his intense attention flicked to me. I swallowed the lump that formed in my throat and continued. "Perhaps you can tell me why a Court that doesn't exist is sending people who also shouldn't exist to harm me? The Warden of Shadows has been frustratingly tight-lipped." I could tell Lysander was impressed by my tactic. Throw the burden of proof to Rein and see him squirm as he navigated the delicate veil of the vow to respond.

"You'll know when I know," he promised. "For now, we'll need to get answers from your prisoners. That will be the first step."

My prisoners.

My breath hitched as the implications of that settled over me. Interrogation. Torture. Punishment.

"It's very impressive that you have chosen to train to prepare for more potential threats. That mindset is very worthy of a spot in my Court," he offered with an almost twisted grin. "I hope you plan to continue your training during your stay."

I nodded. "Yes, Lysander offered to assist me." Just as the words slid from my lips, I caught myself. Using such an informal address for a Warden of Verihda was a drastic slip of the tongue. I tensed, hoping Rein planned to ignore my mistake.

His head tilted slightly as his eyes danced between the two of us. "That won't be necessary," he said finally.

"I don't mind, brother. Your guards are too busy with their duties in your Prison to train an Uncourted," Lysander replied with a flippant hand toss.

"My guards and their duties are of no matter," Rein said, his red eyes fixing on me. "I will train you myself."

The room was so silent you could have heard a single drop of water splash against the cold floor. My palms burned with pain as my fingernails buried themselves into the flesh there. I knew exactly what he had planned for our training sessions and what he was expecting of me, and I also knew that I was intimately capable of doing precisely that.

He would craft me into a weapon of his own design, and with the fragile state of my Mythica, I wasn't sure I would be able to stop it from happening.

"You couldn't possibly have enough time for that," Lysander offered, trying to sound as nonchalant about the entire ordeal as he could, but I could sense the trepidation beneath the words. "You have an entire Court to run."

"Perhaps other Wardens were less hands-on in their approach to sway Lexa's loyalties," Rein offered a twinge of fury in his tone. "However, I will not make the same mistake." He stood from the table, and I was sure scorch marks were left on the surface where his hands had just rested. "Rest well, Miss Cromwell. Tomorrow morning, we begin your training."

As the heavy door swung shut behind the departing Warden, the thick silence that followed seemed to echo the weight of my impending fate. The chilling realization that tomorrow morning promised irrevocable change gnawed at the edges of my consciousness.

Lysander remained still beside me, a silent companion in the lonely hall, mirroring my powerlessness. The weight of shared dread hung heavy in the air between us. His eyes, usually ablaze with levity, reflected a somber acknowledgment of the inevitability I faced.

An unspoken understanding passed between us as we exchanged glances in the dim light of the Prison's confinement. He reached for my hand and held it tightly in the comfort of his own, but there was no comfort to be had.

The dawn would bring with it an inescapable fate, one not even the Warden of Shadows could prevent. Lysander and I stood together, facing the abyss of uncertainty with fear and the undeniable knowledge that, come morning, everything would change.

Twenty-Eight

Lilith was convinced that the best plan to collect the remaining Court Marks would be to remain at the Verihdian Institute while the Deans returned for the coming semester of study. While I was initially against such a passive approach, it was logical in practicality. There was no other place where every Court Mark would be present simultaneously. So now, it has become a waiting game. I detested waiting, but soon enough, it would all pay off.

Returning to the Veridian Institute with two Court Marks etched onto my skin brought a sense of triumph. The grandeur of its gothic halls seemed to bow in deference to the newfound symbol of power that decorated my skin. The Gothic architecture was once a testament to the institution's legacy, but now it felt like a backdrop to my ascendance. The towering spires and ivy-covered walls were no longer symbols of an unattainable goal but instead stepping stones on the path of my conquest.

My feet carried me through the darkened halls, past the unremarkable faces of the Uncourted students who called this place home. Their rather pedestrian lives seemed all the more feeble to me now that I had garnered more power than they could ever imagine.

Crossing the threshold into the ballroom was like a self-fulfilling prophecy. The last time I stood in this room, Lexa Cromwell had managed to make me feel… inadequate. She had somehow earned the attention and respect of all seven Wardens of Verihdia, but I knew that it was only a matter of time before it was me that she would be begging for attention from again.

I took confident steps across the decadent floor. The room was illuminated only by the candle in my hand, and its warm glow paved the way for me as I approached the platform.

The throne defied all notions of solidity and form. Emerald and black tendrils of thick and verdant smoke wove and danced, creating a mesmerizing display that challenged the very fabric of logic. The ethereal green smoke was suspended in defiance of gravity, packed together seamlessly to form the contours of a regal seat. And finally, I would claim it as my rightful place.

Climbing the stairs to the platform in the dim candlelight felt almost solemn. I was approaching the destiny I deserved. I hovered above the seat for a long moment, knowing that the moment I sank into the throne, I was crossing a previously unthinkable line.

Just as my knees bent and I descended toward the chair, the doors to the ballroom were thrown open. I startled back, taking a few careful steps away from the chair, and turned to face the intruder. Potential lies and explanations flooded my mind as the darkness-shrouded figure approached, but just as I planned to employ one, the figure stepped into the light.

"That's a tad premature, don't you think?" Lilith scowled, indicating toward the regal seat. I shrugged but descended the stairs to meet her on the ground floor anyway. I would claim my rightful space soon enough.

"Confident, I'd say," I replied as I reached her. She crossed her arms across her chest, and the corners of her mouth lifted in an amused grin. I leaned forward and pressed a chaste kiss to her cold lips.

"Guess who just arrived at the Institute?" She prompted.

"If it isn't one of the five remaining Deans, I would be severely disappointed that you interrupted me," I claimed. Her serpentine smile deepened.

"Which one?" I asked eagerly.

"Vitrola," Lilith answered. "She's just finished escorting Lexa and our Warden to the veil of Echoes, and she and her guard are resting here for the night before they travel back to Talisman in the morning."

I tried not to let the thought of Lexa dampen the good news, but I couldn't stop the envy that crept into the edges of my consciousness. By crossing the veil into The Court of Echoes, Lexa Cromwell has visited four of the seven Courts of Verihdia. The jealousy was so potent that I almost felt my skin shift into a verdant hue. She may be the first non-Warden to travel across every veil, but I would undoubtedly be the most powerful. That was going to have to be enough for me. For now.

"Let's not waste time then," I said as I brushed past Lilith and headed for the main doors of the ballroom. She quickly caught up to me, and together, we walked through the Institute's lively halls toward the Dean's wing. As we approached, the echo of voices down the hall caused our feet to slow. I shared a glance with Lilith, who urged me forward quietly. The murmured voices came into focus as we neared them.

"What do you mean they were attacked? How many?"

My eyes widened at the mention of an attack and the familiar voice that mentioned it. Instructor Thorne spoke in hushed tones, with an air of worry and concern.

"A dozen or so," Vitrola responded. "There were no casualties, but several injuries, including my Warden."

Lilith let out a small gasp, and I pressed my hand against her lips to silence her. I would not be found out and miss this opportunity because of her inability to keep quiet.

"And prisoners?" Oliver prompted.

"Eight. Delivered to The Court of Echoes this morning alongside The Warden of Shadows and Miss Cromwell," Vitrola continued. "Apparently, this isn't the first assault either, but my Warden didn't tell me much."

My mind flashed to the figure from the pub in The Court of Shadows. He had seemed so eager to assist me in eliminating my 'Lexa problem,' and I was so caught up in that promise that I hadn't bothered to imagine there were others who wanted her gone just as eagerly as I did. If Vitrola was to be believed, there were more assailants, and they were dead set on reaching Lexa Cromwell.

A familiar twinge of envy danced within my chest. Not that I particularly wanted to be chased down and attacked, but if I had anything to say about it, I would be powerful enough one day to warrant such blind determination.

"I trust you to be discreet with this information, of course," Vitrola said.

"Of course," Oliver offered quickly. One of them sauntered off, and I slowly dropped my hand from Lilith's mouth. She scowled at me, but again I shrugged.

"If it's Vitrola, I'll distract her while you go to her room and get the patch." She stood taller, brushing out some wrinkles in her tunic before moving around the corner to greet whoever remained behind.

"Ah," Lilith called out with feigned cheer. "Vitrola, I heard you were here tonight."

I smiled.

"Lilith, I didn't know you were at the Institute?" She sounded surprised. "I thought you were covering things at The Court of Shadows until your Warden's return?"

I rolled my eyes at the notion that Lilith could ever truly *run* my Court. She was a Vacant who was so easily manipulated that I had convinced her to do my bidding without so much as breaking a sweat. All it took was a few pretty words and passionate nights, and she forgot everything she'd ever promised Lysander.

As the two continued their monotonous conversation, I used the distraction to slip down the hall toward Vitrola's quarters. I only knew where it would be because I had spent a few nights here and there in Lilith's room down the hall during my time as a student.

To my pleasant surprise, the door was unlocked when I reached it. And it was deathly silent as I pushed it open and closed it behind me. The universe was giving me exactly what I needed. I couldn't help but smile as I rummaged through the packed bags that Vitrola had deposited here.

Clothes, rations, books. There wasn't much here, just enough for a few days away from home, so finding the rolled piece of enchanted parchment I had been searching for didn't take long. My fingers trembled as I closed my hand around it, lifting it from her bag. It was so close now. I could practically taste the newfound power.

I slid the rolled Mark into the waistband of my pants and slowly made my way to the door. Pressing my ear to the wooden frame, I listened for lingering footsteps outside the hall. When I was sure the coast was clear, I slipped out of the room and into the cold, empty hallway undetected. Pride bloomed in my chest as I took my first steps away from the room. The Mark felt warm against my skin beneath my tunic, and I couldn't wait to meet up with Lilith and finally add another Mark to my collection.

I was about to round a corner when I bumped into a tall frame. My hands came up to press the figure off of me, and I nearly scoffed at their uselessness when my eyes met his.

"Chandler?" Oliver asked, with shock on his face.

"Instructor Thorne," I replied, injecting as much nicety as I could muster.

"I had no idea you were back at the Institute," he offered. His voice had a hint of suspicion, but I ignored it.

"Just for the start of term," I responded. He nodded, but his eyes squinted with confusion. "I've been assisting the Dean of Shadows in her duties in our Warden's absence," I tacked on without bothering to hide my eager pride. His eyes widened.

"Is that so?" He asked incredulously.

"It is," I replied, with a hint of finality.

"What are you doing in the Dean's wing?" He couldn't hide the suspicion in his tone if he wanted to. It was painted so clearly on his face.

"Seeing Lilith, of course."

"Of course," he responded. Silence hung over us as we stood facing one another in the cold, dim hallway.

"Well, I better get going…" I offer, aiming to move past him.

"Wait," he called, placing a hand on my upper arm. I flicked my eyes at him. "How was Lexa's time in The Court of Shadows?"

I had to physically restrain myself from rolling my eyes. It was no secret that Oliver Thorne favored Lexa just as the Wardens were now. He treated her and her little clan like they walked on water. Save for me, of course. Even now that she wasn't attending this stupid school, he still asked about his prized student.

"She made a right fool of herself and only proved that she didn't deserve to be chosen for this honor," I stated, waiting for Oliver's shocked expression to return. He didn't react as I would have predicted. Instead, he sighed deeply and ran a hand through his hair.

"You always were so jealous of her," he whispered, but the words found their mark in my chest. Anger clouded my vision.

"You think I'm lying?" I scoffed.

"I think your Court Mark is showing," he seethed.

I tensed for a moment and almost instinctively went to press my hand against the newest addition to the tapestry of my skin, but it was in his eyes that I saw the comment for what it was—a slight against my nature.

"Good, I hope so. I plan to make The Court of Shadows very proud one day. You wouldn't know anything about making a Court proud."

I began to push past him, shaking his arm off of mine. I was several feet away from him when he called out once more.

"Be careful who you detest. People might just exploit that. Wouldn't want that, would we?" He said before slipping down the hallway in the opposite direction.

My feet remained planted to the ground as he walked away from me. His parting words echoed in my mind, and I allowed them the honor of rattling me for just a moment longer before shaking off the nagging feeling and moving through the Institute to find Lilith so that she could perform the ritual.

With this new Mark inked into my skin, I had only four left to collect. Then Oliver, the Wardens, and all of Verihdia would see that I was something Lexa Cromwell could never be.

Unstoppable.

Lexa

Twenty-Nine

As I ventured through the dark, winding halls of the Prison on my way to meet with Rein for our first training session, I felt a chill race down my spine with each echo of my steps on the stone floor. Somehow, this place was even more intimidating in the light of day - a feat I hadn't previously considered possible. I spent last night in Lysander's arms, hoping his embrace could stave off the nightmares. While the endless ocean and terrifying yet familiar creature hadn't appeared in my consciousness, the sounds of the Prison were nearly worse.

In the silence of the night, there was nothing to mask the screams that drifted through the halls like wicked omens. These screams were familiar and painful. I understood them. I had also been plagued by nightmares in the still of the night. However, thinking about the stark difference between me and them kept me awake long into the early morning hours. These prisoners didn't have a mate to hold them and protect them from the nightmares they were facing in their cages. No, they faced these horrors alone.

I tried not to think about the screams that would most likely be imprinted on my mind for the rest of my time in the Court and returned to the dining room where Rein had sent for me.

I was the first to arrive in the room and tried to look at it all through a fresh gaze. Perhaps Rein was worse than the cold, vile creature he showed in the darkness, too? Would the light reveal another side of him that was even more daunting?

The door swung open, and Rein sauntered in. He wore a similar red uniform to his guards, but he was decidedly more dignified, with medals and honorific insignias decorating the breast of the coat. His grey, cracked skin gave off the illusion that he may fall to ash at any moment, but I knew he was far sturdier than he seemed.

But it wasn't his uniform or even his burnt skin that made my heart skip a beat in fear. It was those eyes. And the fire behind them.

"Good morning, Miss Cromwell," he said as he came to stop before me. I bowed my head.

"Warden, good morning."

As I raised my head and met his gaze again, I felt them assessing me as if he was analyzing my skills, strengths, and weaknesses. He was watching me like a warrior who was preparing to counter any attack that came his way.

"I hope you found your quarters to your liking," he said, and I tried not to give anything away as I nodded. Did he know I hadn't spent the evening in my own bed but instead his brother's?

"Your home is lovely," I lied.

He pursed his lips and narrowed his eyes for a moment. "I recall telling you that I do not enjoy wasting time. Yours or mine," he started, and I felt my heart rate amp up. "So perhaps next time you speak to me, you will not waste your breath on a lie."

I inhaled sharply, and instead of responding, I nodded.

"Good," he turned on his heel with militant precision and headed back through the open doors. He didn't have to 'waste his time' and tell me I was expected to follow him.

The only noise that filled the hall was the sound of our hurried feet and my anxious breaths as we made our way toward the heart of the Prison. A few moments later, we arrived at a sizeable iron-barred door with an even darker hallway that lay beyond. Three guards had taken up posts at the door armed with sharpened swords and intimidating scowls. Rein barked a few orders to the three of them, and within moments, they opened the door and ushered us inside.

The iron gate closing behind me, nearly sent me into a spiral. The hallway suddenly felt like it was closing in on me. I don't know how anyone was expected to breathe down here in the chilled, thick, oppressive air. The prison floor stretched before me like a desolate expanse of despair, a labyrinth of iron bars and shadowed corners. Cages lined the corridor, and as I walked by, the faces that peered through the rusted bars told stories of lives marred by mistakes and regret. Eyes that I'm sure had once been filled with vitality now held a dim, haunted gaze. The prisoners within, deemed criminals by society's standards, seemed to carry the weight of the punishment they were being dealt in those broken stares.

They did not react to me or their Warden as we continued our trek. I'm not sure their feeble bodies had the energy to. In the dim light, I saw the weariness etched into their features, thick and deep lines of defeat. Slumped shoulders spoke to the heavy toll of their incarceration, the punishment they were being forced to endure. These were individuals who had likely committed unspeakable acts, criminals of Verihdia, the worst of our world, and yet, as I observed their collective surrender to the confines of the cages, a pang of unexpected sympathy stirred within me.

My Mythica raged against my chest, begging to reach into those cages and determine if their crimes warranted this sort of torture, but I willed it to calm. I would need as much control over my power as I could muster if Rein were leading me where I thought he was.

As we neared the end of one row and turned to face another wing of the Prison, I couldn't control the gasp that fell from my lips at the sight before me.

We had spilled from a hallway into the heart of the Sunken Province Prison Tower. I stood on the ground floor, and my head fell back as I followed my gaze up... and up… and up. The interior of the foreboding tower I had seen from outside was worse than I could have imagined. The space housed a dozen floors, each adorned with an intricate lattice of balconies and cages, creating a layered visual tapestry of incarceration. The tower's central core held a network of catwalks and staircases, crisscrossing in a complex dance of metal. The cages sat side by side and row upon row, climbing to impossible heights. As my eyes scanned the thousands of cells, I couldn't help but wonder if I had ever heard of someone being released from Sunken Province. Were they prisoners here for the rest of their lives, no matter the severity of their crimes? An uneasy feeling settled on me as Rein pushed forward.

I found myself wrestling with conflicting emotions - a recognition of their transgressions yet an unexpected sympathy for the frail remnants of humanity that resided like ghosts within the confines of the cages.

As we entered another hallway and left the tower of thousands behind, I couldn't help but feel relief despite still being led further into this Prison of nightmares. Rein came to a stop in front of a large iron gate, wider than the others, and as I peered inside, beyond the bars, I saw the faces of the masked figures who attacked me for the first time.

Once shrouded in the shadows of anonymity, their faces now stood exposed to my scrutiny. It was a peculiar feeling, seeing their faces uncovered for the first time when I already so intimately knew each of their worst fears and darkest deeds. As my eyes raked over their frames, my Mythica licked at my skin with the memory of their delicious terror. Their eyes widened as they saw me approach.

"Miss Cromwell, you are aware of who these individuals are, correct?" Rein spoke, drawing my concentration from the flashing memories that my Mythica was showing me.

I nodded.

"I think it's about time we discover what they are after, don't you?"

I did want to know. And I wanted more than the vague statements I got the last few times I used my Mythica on the attackers. However, I wasn't sure I was prepared for the methodology that the Warden of Echoes would choose to employ.

"You," Rein said in his deep, commanding tone. He was pointing toward one of the smaller-framed females. Her mousy brown hair was messy and matted, and her face was pale and gaunt. I instantly recalled the flash of fear I stole from her at the Prism Library.

Heights. Falling. Death.

My Mythica had latched onto that fear and forced her to feel it. To feel the sensation of spiraling through the air toward her inevitable death. She was crying on the floor at my feet by the time Lysander arrived to stop me. Her wariness of me was well-placed and deserved. I hated that I was something she was afraid of now. Would it be *my* face I saw if I stole her fears from her again?

The woman stepped slowly toward the bars, brushing off the hands of a few of her companions who tried to hold her back. She stopped a few feet away from the bars, a safe distance. Rein stared her down, watching her movements with his striking red eyes. I'm not sure how often the Warden dealt with prisoners personally, but I can imagine that when he was present for these 'sessions,' his eyes played a part in the creation of terror.

"What is your name?" Rein asked. I watched the girl as she decided if she would answer or not. It was a few moments, but she decided not, instead choosing to remain silent.

"That's the least intrusive question we have today. If you're already choosing to be difficult, I promise this will not be pleasant for you." Rein crossed his arms and watched the girl with his cold superiority.

"I won't answer your questions, so do whatever it is you plan to do and leave me be," she spat eventually, mustering more strength in her tone than I gave her credit for.

"Pity, I had hoped we could have made this easy." As Rein finished speaking, the girl's mask of bravado slipped ever-so-slightly before she regained composure. Then Rein moved with impossible speed. His hand darted through the enclosure's bars and toward the feeble prisoner.

By the time I registered the movement, his hand had already returned to his side, and the shimmering knife in his palm was dripping a deep crimson liquid onto the floor. My eyes flashed back to the prisoner, a tightness in my chest. Her eyes were wide, shocked, as blood poured from the wound across her neck down the pale column of her throat. Her shaking fingers attempted to press down onto the wound to staunch the bleeding, but it pooled ever faster. Her eyes met mine briefly, and I couldn't breathe. I couldn't move. She fell to her knees, then to the ground, and the dark pool of blood spread across the cell floor, slinking toward me like a serpent. I heard a scream. The other prisoners rushed forward, their arms cradling her head, and cursing Rein who simply pulled me back a few steps. It was over in a few moments, yet so much had changed. It wasn't until the dull ache in my throat registered that I realized it was me who had screamed.

My body shook as my eyes remained locked on her dead eyes. Life had drained from her and spread on the ground, staining my shoes. I suddenly felt sick. The room was spinning, and I needed my mate.

My Mythica registered the threat and was raging within me. It took everything I had to hold it back and keep it from attacking Rein. I would join the lifeless girl on the floor if he knew I could affect him.

I am in control.

I said the mantra repeatedly in my mind, trying to believe it as my heavy and shallow breaths slowed.

I think the other prisoners were verbally battling Rein, but the world was a muddled echo. I couldn't seem to focus on anything other than her eyes and the Mythica within me that begged to avenge her.

Lexa.

A voice was calling me through the blurred reality.

Lexa!

I couldn't place it. I couldn't look away from those eyes.

'Lexa!" Rein's demanding tone finally pulled my attention away. My breathing was erratic as I glared at him. He surveyed me as if he was disappointed in my reaction. "Perhaps you'd like to ask the next prisoner a question now?" I knew what he was prompting. He wanted me to find and exploit their fears, but I couldn't release the tight hold I held on my Mythica because if I did, there was no guarantee that it wouldn't turn its power toward him.

I couldn't find my voice to refuse, so I shook my head. He watched me, scanning my features for a spark of the monster he wanted me to be. It felt like minutes before he spoke.

"Very well," he said, finally. He walked past me, heading down the hall back the way we came.

"Lexa," a whispered voice called from the cell. My feet paused, but I didn't dare toss a glance over my shoulder at the dead woman on the ground or the other prisoners whose fates were undoubtedly similar. "We need to talk to you alone."

I shook my head, over and over, as if I was stuck in a loop, unable to break free as I shuffled down the hall following Rein, realizing that his path was immortalized on the pavement by crimson-stained footprints, and so were mine.

We reached the tower once again, and Rein turned to face me. I felt numb, the same sort of dread that coursed through me the first time I killed one of these Double Marked individuals.

"Consider that lesson number one," Rein began. My eyes flicked to him and saw nothing but determination in the fiery depths of his gaze. "We'll pick up here again tomorrow."

*

The days began to fall into a vicious cycle. I'd meet Rein, who would lead me through the suffocating halls of the Prison toward the cell where my attackers were held. I'd watch as he interrogated them, showing off his methods. I'd fight against my Mythica, which was becoming a more arduous task every day. Then I'd stalk back to my room, slide under the covers, and wait for Lysander to make it all disappear. But it never really did. No matter how hard my mate tried. No matter how many comforting kisses he placed against my skin. I couldn't close my eyes without seeing her lifeless stare looking back at me from behind my eyelids.

I knew Lysander was aware of the horrors I witnessed, but thankfully, he never asked me to recount them for him. He was the safest place in this Prison, and I desperately needed to feel safe.

Rein hadn't killed another prisoner since that first day, but that's not to say he wasn't violent. On the second day, he left the body of the feeble girl there as a 'motivator,' as he called it. On the third, he picked a new target and asked them about their name, goal, and Court Marks. For each hesitation, he took a finger.

By the end of the session, the prisoner had one left.

On the fourth and fifth days, he offered for me to take the lead, which I almost accepted just to stop the violence for a little while. When I couldn't follow through, he released a thick fog into the cell. I wasn't sure what it was, but when they started clawing at their red and raw skin, I had a pretty solid guess that it was a poison of some sort.

One week into my stay, I could tell that Rein was growing impatient with the prisoner's refusal to cooperate…and mine. He wanted to watch my Mythica work, and by the tenth day, I needed to release that energy so severely, but was too afraid of the consequences. We'd only learned that they were sent by someone else and sent for me, but nothing else. No matter what Rein threw at them, they would accept their punishment, accept their torture, and remain silent, save for the screams and cries of pain that nobody could stifle.

On the fifteenth day, the official halfway point of my sentence at The Court of Echoes, I finally understood why the Court was named as such. Because in the middle of the night, when the screams of the prisoners seemed to quiet, a new set of screams seemed to echo through my mind. Every cut, every assault, every second of the sessions that Rein had been conducting replayed in my mind all through the night, vicious echoes of the pain that he was inflicting on them each day.

Because of me.

Somehow, I managed to avoid using my Mythica despite Rein's insistence and its volatile nature. He thankfully hadn't pushed me too hard, but I had a feeling my *luck* would run out soon.

On the morning of my twenty-fourth day in The Court of Echoes, I woke up with the unfortunate realization that a weariness clung to me like a heavy shroud. This fatigue went beyond the physical and seeped into the very core of my being. It was not just the exhaustion of the body, it was the weariness of my spirit and the profound toll of witnessing humanity's darkest impulses.

The things I had witnessed here had left an indelible mark on my soul, and I knew, without a doubt, that I was changed because of my time here. I would never be the same. I just hoped I still recognized the person I was when I finally broke free from the shackles of Echoes.

I bathed and dressed with Lysander by my side as I did most mornings, and I could tell that he was growing worried for me because his eyes were filled with sorrow, and his touch was even more gentle. "I can't stand seeing you like this," he whispered as I finished dressing for the day. I had learned early on in my time here not to wear the clothes I cared about, seeing as they'd simply return to this room covered in flecks of blood and the memory of despair. So, instead, I fastened the buckle of the red shroud that Rein had offered me to wear.

"I'm sorry," was all I could say.

He rushed forward, pulling me into his embrace. "Don't apologize, little storm," he whispered into my ear as his hands drew idle lines down my back. I sunk into his hold, enjoying how his fiery scent reminded me of the comfort of our cave in Talisman, where we finally solidified our bond. I held onto that memory, allowing the warmth to flood through me and keep me alive in a place where all there was was death. I looked at him and saw his eyes dancing around the space above my head, watching my Mythica, which felt like a violent storm within me. I'd never kept it contained for this long before.

"What does it look like now?" I asked him.

"It's thrashing, angry. It's feeling trapped. I've never seen it look so… sentient. And I didn't think that could be possible," he whispered, almost afraid of the words as he said them.

"I've been holding it in, and it's getting harder," I admitted in the silence of my room.

"You can't deny your Mythica like that for much longer, Lexa," he said, looking back at the cloud of power above my head, visible to only him.

"It wants to attack him, Lysander. I can't use it on the prisoners like he wants me to because I know that the second I release my hold on it, it's going to go after him, and then he'll know." Tears began to stream down my cheek. His thumb wiped them away, and his emerald gaze searched mine, filled with so much empathy I thought I might burst.

"Come here. " He gripped my face and pulled my lips to his. I fell into his kiss, letting the passion and love between us silence the echoes for only a moment. His lips drank from mine eagerly, and his tongue swept into my mouth, searching for mine. I pulled him closer, pressing my breasts against his chest and searching for that relief. He was the reprieve I needed. He was the only thing keeping me alive here. "Give your pain to me, little storm. Let me battle the demons that haunt you."

Then, the overwhelming power began to dissipate. It was painful, but not as painful as it had been to carry around the volatile mass of rampant energy for the last several weeks. My eyes flew open, and I broke our kiss with a gasp as the feeling settled on me.

Vacant.

He had taken my Mythica again, and this time, I couldn't be happier for the moment of freedom from the confines of its torturous rage. The weight that had been pressing ever harder on my chest seemed to slip away, and I took the first full breath of air since I arrived in this Gods-forsaken Court. I felt light and airy. Free. I sighed, letting the emptiness that used to anger me, soothe the burns on my soul where the power had been clawing its way to the surface. For just a moment, I didn't have to fight.

When I opened my eyes and looked back at Lysander, his face was twisted in pain as my Mythica surged into him. Guilt surfaced again, and I pressed a palm to his cheek.

"Gods, Lexa," he winced. "You've been carrying this alone for too long." His forehead wrinkled in pain as he glanced down at me.

"You're in pain," I cried, pulling at his shoulders. "Give it back. I can't see you like this."

He shook his head and leaned down to press his forehead against mine. "I cannot make your pain disappear, Lexa, but I can hold onto it until you're ready to face it again."

I fell forward into his arms and sobbed.

"I love you," I confessed. It had been the truth for longer than I was willing to admit. His arms tightened around me.

"Your love is something I have never been worthy of, and the selfish part of me will never get enough of it," he kissed my forehead. "You know that I love you, too, right?"

I nodded, smiling through the sobs.

"Come with me," he said, stepping back and offering me a hand.

"Where are we going?" I asked, watching his microexpression for the obvious signs of my violent Mythica eating away at him. He was hiding it well, but I knew him better. I promised myself I wouldn't let him suffer it for long, but selfishly, I wanted to revel in its absence a little while longer.

"I'm accompanying you to 'training' today," he said as we made our way toward the door of my room.

"But Rein said you weren't allowed to come with us," I protested. Gods, I wished so many times he could have. But then again, I think I would have sought comfort in his arms amidst the horrors of the Prison, and then Rein would know exactly what we were to each other.

"I'd like to see him try and stop me."

Thirty

"I told you that you're not permitted in the Prison. How much clearer do I need to be?" My brother said with an air of authority that most people would bow down to. I was decidedly *not* most people.

"And I'm telling you that either I go with you today, or neither of us is setting foot past those gates." I folded my arms over my chest and tried to maintain composure despite the raging storm that was currently mine. The intensity was unbearable, a relentless torrent threatening to drown the essence of who I was. The Mythica, like a tempest of raw energy, clawed at the walls of my consciousness, seeking to reshape and redefine me. How Lexa survived this alone for weeks was beyond me.

My little storm is astonishing.

I could see the shadows forming in her eyes, and I watched as the cloud above her head became less and less docile with each passing day. I could only hold her and promise her we were almost done. I had half a mind to put a knife to my brother's throat for what he had been putting her through. He was the reason she felt this raw energy eating her alive. He should pay for it. He'd kept me from keeping my promise to her.

As the energy raged within me, I marveled at her resilience, the strength it must have taken to navigate the storm alone. My mate was more than merely 'powerful,' she was extraordinary in will, spirit, and heart. She was a woman undeserving of the pain she was experiencing. The pain I currently housed for her and would do again every day, if it meant she could breathe unhindered, even just for a moment.

Rein's eyes flicked toward Lexa, standing just off the side. She held her head higher than she had for weeks. There was even a ghost of a smile on her lips as she looked at me. The lightness she currently felt was worth every ounce of this burning, angry pain that now ravaged my body.

I'd managed to hold onto someone else's Mythica once for a full day, but that was an extreme case. I knew with the intensity of her Mythica, I would only be able to offer my little storm a few hours' reprieve, at most. I just hoped it would be enough.

"Lexa, would you mind giving me a moment alone with my brother," Rein asked, and I heard Lexa retreat from the dining room back into the hall. "What do you think you are doing, undermining me in my own Court? Need I remind you that I do not and will not take orders from an equal?" He seethed.

I rolled my eyes. "I'm not giving you orders, Rein. I'm setting boundaries."

He scoffed.

"Lexa Cromwell is disintegrating before our eyes, and don't act as if you couldn't tell." I tried to keep the rage I felt from coloring my tone. The Mythica underneath my skin swirled and tried to reach for Rein, desperate to make him submit to the power. I took a steadying breath and pushed the Mythica back. Now I could see why her eyes had been so hollow, and she seemed so lost and broken. It was taking everything I had to keep this energy at bay.

"She was fighting against her nature. Eventually, she wouldn't be able to fight it any longer, and she would finally submit," Rein offered casually. The Mythica within me forced me to take a step forward, begging me to unleash it against him. "Then we'd see what she was really capable of."

Clearing my throat, I try to mask the inner turmoil. "She's not an animal, and she's not a prisoner. You don't get to break her." I spoke with the most even tone I could muster despite the intense need to make him pay for what he's made my mate suffer. "Listen, I've seen her use her Mythica countless times." The said Mythica surged at the mention of its use. "It will not work if you go about it the way you have been." Not that I was privy to the specifics of what he'd forced her to witness, but I could infer based on the blood on her clothes and the hollow look in her gaze when she returned at night.

He looked like he would fight back for a few tortuous moments, but then he sighed, sliding a hand through his hair. "What do you suggest I do then? We have had these prisoners for nearly a month and have yet to discern any real information."

"Let her talk to them alone," I said. He began to protest, but I pushed again. "We can monitor from a distance, but you need to let her use her Mythica the way she always has. You can't force her to witness unspeakable acts of violence and expect her to proceed as normal."

"She's weak," he whispered under his breath, and I couldn't stop myself.

"If you believe that's true, you don't know a damn thing about Lexa Cromwell," I seethed. He held my gaze for a few tense seconds.

"Fine, let's try it your way. We will let her talk to the prisoners on her own." He clearly didn't like the idea but was running out of time and options. And I hated to admit it, but I needed the answers from those prisoners, too. How could I keep her safe if I didn't know what she was up against?

Rein left the room without another word and began the trek toward his precious Prison. Lexa fell in line beside me as we passed her in the hall, offering me a curious look.

"He's going to let you speak to them… alone," I whispered. She released a soft gasp. "I will be nearby. I'll control it for you. You just have to 'ask' the questions."

That seemed to calm her, and she nodded softly as we followed. The walk to the cell where the prisoners were being kept was not only cold and dreary but a tapestry of pain and suffering. No wonder my mate had begun to lose herself after walking this same path over and over again each day.

Rein came to a stop in front of a large cell, and I had to keep myself from reacting when my eyes settled on the sight before me. The prisoners were battered and beaten, their skin caked with blood. Their clothes were ripped and torn. Some it seemed on purpose to fashion slings for what looked to be broken bones, others just out of desperation and anger. There was notably one fewer prisoner than there was when we arrived, and I couldn't help but notice the stain of blood that sprawled across the cell floor. My heart ached that this was the nightmare Lexa had been forced to live during the day when I couldn't hold her to stave it off.

The prisoners who had Mythica, which I noticed back in Talisman, were now noticeably Vacant, thanks to my brother's Mythica-blocking bars and cells.

"Very well, Miss Cromwell," Rein said, facing us. "We will give you a few minutes to talk to them and get the answers you need."

"I'll remain close by to ensure her safety," I said, not leaving any room for him to protest. His tongue ran along the front side of his teeth as his anger bubbled, but eventually, he nodded and returned down the hallway. I could see him, but he was far enough that he wouldn't hear us unless we screamed.

"Go ahead, Lexa."

She nodded and took a few tentative steps forward to the bars.

"Don't get too close," I urged, but I hated how afraid I sounded.

"If you tell me what we need to know, he won't… he won't do what he's doing anymore," she whispered.

A male figure from within the cell came forward, his broad chest on full display, showcasing the Court Mark for Talisman, Forgotten, and the ugly, raw, and raised brand of Echoes. Three Marks. Dancing along those marks were long, thin cuts. Dozens of them. Deep enough to hurt. But not so deep as to cause accidental death. Rein was always skilled at causing maximum pain without wasting life. I shuddered at the memory that threatened to return. The Trial we both faced. The lengths we went to to win.

"We need to talk alone," the prisoner urged, looking over her shoulder at me. He looked young, mid-thirties perhaps, and handsome enough, but the time behind bars had not been kind to him, making him appear haggard and tired.

"Whatever you need to say to me, you can say to both of us," she replied, and my heart swelled with honor. She was the single most important thing to me, and she was claiming me as hers in small ways whenever she could.

The male didn't like that alternative, but I could sense that he felt relieved that their meeting today was not accompanied by torture.

"I don't want to use my Mythica. Please don't force me to," she said. The same words coming from someone like Rein would have been a threat, but from her, they were a plea.

"What's your name?" Lexa asked. I knew she was desperate to find answers, so maybe the 'training' my brother was forcing upon her would end.

The male looked over his shoulder at the others for a moment before responding. "Lachlan," he replied, finally.

"Lachlan," Lexa repeated softly. "Thank you for telling me that."

He nodded, eyes flicking to me again. Lexa's Mythica was chomping at the bit to be released, to get to the bottom of their attack, but I held it back with a tight mental grip.

"Why do you have two Marks?" She asked next. My breathing slowed as if I instinctively needed to ensure I could hear his response.

"So we can visit two Courts," he said as if it were a throwaway. A side-step away from revealing anything real, but that's not true. My eyebrows shot up as the words settled on me.

He's been to The Forgotten Court.

Lexa seemed to follow a similar line of thought.

"Have you been to both?" She asked, and the man instantly recognized his slip-up for what it was. He once again tossed his gaze to me to gauge my reaction. I gave him nothing.

"Yes," he said.

My heart rate sped to an almost uncomfortable degree as the implications dawned on me. That should have been impossible, and yet. The forest we erected, the measures we've taken. How did we let this happen?

"Where did you get the Forgotten Mark?" Lexa continued her line of questioning, as if the man hadn't just revealed something insurmountable.

"From my parents," he said pointedly. 'Parents' implied generations. Who knows how many more? My head was swimming.

"How many Double Marked are there?" She asked in a whisper.

Lachlan looked over his shoulder to have a silent conversation with his cellmates before turning back to us, and with his eyes locked on mine, he said, "Hundreds."

Lexa's Mythica jolted again, forcing me to stumble back a few feet. Lexa turned to look at me with worry in her eyes. I shook it off and tried to brush the intense feeling away, but I was unsuccessful. She turned back to look at Lachlan, and I took the opportunity to suck in cold mouthfuls of air.

"Why do you all keep coming for me? What do you want with me?" She asked. This time, an edge of anger slipped into her tone.

"We need you, Lexa," Lachlan answered, and Lexa groaned.

"That's not good enough anymore. What does that mean?" She begged, her voice rising. I could see Rein standing straighter in the corner of my eye as Lexa's call reached his ears.

"We can explain when we get there. Just help us get out of here," Lachlan said, pressing up against the cage bars.

"I'm not going to fall for your tricks! I've been attacked, chased, hurt. I'm done. Tell me why you want me!" She screamed, and I saw Rein move forward, taking quick steps to avoid missing the show.

The show that I was in charge of performing.

I took a calming breath before gripping onto the Mythica that swirled within me and ever so slightly let it drift outward. The cloudy tendrils of power danced along the air toward Lachlan, and just as it reached him, I let the silent question fall from my mind.

What do you want?

Lachlan leaned forward, pressing his forehead to the bars as the Mythica surged through him. It was violent and unrestrained, a product of the weeks of build-up, I'm sure. I couldn't hold it back if I wanted to. I silently hoped that Rein wouldn't get too close or I'd be the one being voted on at the next Wardens meeting.

I would never get used to the burning sensation that came from wielding this power. It was venomous and overwhelming.

Lachlan groaned against the power and tried to keep his secrets within his mind, but the Mythica had a hold on them, and it wasn't going to let them go.

"The… the trial…" he spit out through clenched teeth. "We want you to… complete the trial."

A shocked gasp fell from my lips before I pulled the Mythica back with a forceful grunt. Lachlan fell to his knees, and the others rushed forward to comfort him. Lexa was standing eerily still. I forced the Mythica back to its space within my chest and locked it up as best I could. It felt slightly less uncontrollable now that it had been let loose, even for the short time it had been.

I looked over to where Rein was advancing and felt the hair on the back of my neck stand on edge as I wondered what he had heard. There wasn't a doubt in my mind that he wouldn't hesitate to kill her if he'd heard the truth just now. I took a protective step toward Lexa, who was still frozen in her place.

"What did you find out?" Rein asked, his eyes darting between my shocked expression, the man on the ground, and the still Lexa.

"Let's head back, and we'll debrief," I offered, ushering Rein back down the hall. He eagerly headed forward, and I wrapped an arm around Lexa's shoulders to lead her as well.

"Come on, little storm," I whispered. "We need to go."

"Lexa..." Lachlan whispered from his place on his knees. "We need you, please."

I kept walking and helped lead Lexa away from the cell. Ignoring the way her Mythica seemingly wished to remain behind.

"What did he mean," Lexa whispered under her breath as we continued through the halls of the Prison. "What did he mean by that, Lysander?"

"We need to worry about what to tell Rein first, then we will deal with that," I whispered hurriedly. I was having difficulty forming full thoughts. There was too much swirling around in my mind, and the addition of Lexa's overactive Mythica only added to my frantic nature.

Rein didn't stop until we were back in the dining room, and finally, he turned to face us. "Tell me what happened," he asked me. Thankfully, he wasn't addressing Lexa, whom I was sure didn't know how to navigate this lie we were about to create.

"They got their Marks from their parents," I offered, knowing that was innocent enough information to share. "So somewhere along the line, a small group found the Mark and began using it on their children after they had already graduated and Pledged."

Rein narrowed his eyes and began pacing.

"How many are there?"

If I tell him the truth, he would want to act now, only putting Lexa in more danger than she's already in. He has a tendency to act first and think later, and I can't have Lexa caught in that crossfire.

"It's a small group, a dozen or so. We shouldn't worry too much about them," I said, hoping he didn't question me further.

"We can't let them grow," he said with a severe look in his blazing eyes.

I nodded, agreeing, as if he had just devised an incredible plan of action.

"I will take the liberty of following up on this threat as you and Miss Cromwell continue your journey. We can assume they haven't attacked again because of their small remaining numbers."

Again, I nodded.

"Thank you, brother. We'll both be glad you're looking into this issue." My brother wasn't run by his ego, but every Warden loved being told how important they were every now and then. I would know.

Rein then turned his attention to Lexa, and I hated how those eyes scanned her. "Miss Cromwell, you have impressed me. I'm glad you finally got over whatever was holding you back."

She didn't respond, and I couldn't because I was too busy holding the Mythica back from sinking its powerful claws into his subconscious.

"You are leaving my Court soon, and I want you to know that there will be a prominent position in my Court for you when you choose to return to me." It's a vicious prophecy, one I know he intends to fulfill.

Lexa bowed her head, a tear sliding down her cheek, and uttered the words, "Thank you for your guidance, Warden," before exiting the room. I watched her leave with sadness pooling in my heart while Rein watched her with a satisfied smirk plastered on his lips.

"I knew she would break eventually, and so beautifully too-" he began, but couldn't finish because my fist had made contact with his jaw, throwing him off balance and sending him stumbling back several feet.

"Have you lost your mind?" Rein sputtered through the blood that pooled in his mouth. He ran his thumb along his bottom lip and pulled it back to reveal the crimson liquid on his finger.

"No," I started, squaring off against him. "In fact, that was the most sane thing I've done since arriving in your Court."

He took a menacing step forward, his fist clenching at his side. "I never thought I'd see the day the Covetor would defend someone else's honor," he spat, and a mist of blood sprayed from his mouth. "A little girl, no less."

"Make no mistake, Lexa Cromwell does not need me to defend her," I begin, feeling her Mythic urge me on. "You've had enough time to corrupt her. We're leaving tonight." I began to walk toward the door, but he rushed forward and gripped my shoulder, pulling back with such force that I was tossed back a few feet and landed on my back on the stone floor. I exhaled in pain as the sharp jolt traveled up my spine from the impact.

"You're not going anywhere," he growled, stalking forward. "I've got six more days with her."

I pushed myself to my feet with the help of Lexa's Mythica, which almost felt like a physical hand pulling me up. "In the twenty-four days since Lexa has been in your care, she has been subjected to horrific things beyond comprehension. You've forced her to watch and participate in the torture of prisoners. You've disregarded her physical training. You've completely ignored the mental repercussions of your little 'sessions' and admitted to attempting to break her spirit so she would submit." I stared him down, unwilling to show him an ounce of weakness.

"We agreed to a schedule. The Wardens will see this as a slight, and you'll be punished," he yelled back, fury seeping through his pores and filling the room with a suffocating cloud of anger.

"Our siblings wouldn't think twice about siding with me after what you've done, and you know it. And something tells me they wouldn't be upset about you losing time to sway her loyalties away from them." The twitch in his jaw told me that he knew I was right.

"I deserve my time," he said in that stern tone that told me he was close to losing his cool. The red cloud of his Mythica was slinking down his arms and spreading toward me. It wouldn't work on me, but that didn't stop it from itching to try.

"You don't deserve another second of time with her. Not after the damage you've already done," I said, standing my ground. "I am taking Lexa out of this Court tonight. And you better pray to whichever God will still listen to you that you did enough to warrant her Pledge." I left him seething in the dining room. I would pay for this eventually, but Lexa was worth it. Her safety was worth it. We needed to hurry, though, before he could do something to stop us.

I rushed through the halls to catch up to my mate. I found her just outside our room, closed my arms around her waist, and pulled her into me. She gasped in shock but smiled and sunk into the embrace when she recognized it was me.

"What are you doing?" She asked, her eyes darting around the space to see if there were any prying eyes.

"We're leaving," I said, and the light that had been extinguished for far too long in her eyes sparked.

"Now?" She confirmed, and I nodded. She jumped up, throwing her arms around my neck and joyfully squealing. I chuckled softly and held her tighter for a moment longer before pulling myself back.

"We need to pack and go now."

She nodded eagerly and disappeared into her room to gather her things. I followed after her because I would sooner die than leave her unaccompanied in this Court again. She hadn't ever truly unpacked, a testament to how out of place she felt here, so there were only a few things left to gather.

"Does he know we're leaving?" She asked.

I nodded, wincing slightly as the pain in my back surged. It would heal, but that, coupled with the violent Mythica, was undoubtedly a heavy toll.

"He's not happy though, understandably. So we must leave before he thinks of some wild plan to keep you here."

She moved faster.

I watched her back as she scurried around the room, eager to leave and never return. I understood the sentiment. Her movements slowed, and I saw her back tense as a thought occurred to her.

"What about the prisoners?" She asked in a feeble voice. "I… I don't want them to suffer."

I sighed deeply because I, too, had felt similarly since seeing their state, but I also knew there was no way out of the Sunken Province Prison.

"We can't help them, Lexa," I whispered, the words getting caught in my throat as the thought settled.

"They don't deserve what Rein is doing to them," she replied, facing me. There was so much empathy behind the sheen of tears. I rushed forward and pulled her into my arms.

"I know," I answered. I'd always known my brother to be vicious. I was intimately aware of how far he was willing to go, in fact, but even those memories weren't enough to prepare me to see the aftermath of what he'd done to those Double Marked individuals. "You got him the answers he wanted. He won't be so… hands-on about their punishment any longer," I offered as a comfort, but I knew it wouldn't help much. "You helped them the only way you could. Hold onto that."

She nodded into my chest, holding me tightly around my midsection. "It's my fault they're here."

Her guilt slammed into me. Well, into her Mythica. It was potent and sorrowful. As the Mythica swirled in my veins - feeding on the guilt rolling off my mate - its power became overwhelming, threatening to slip through my grasp like sand slipping through desperate fingers. I felt the intensity coursing through me, a volatile surge that whispered of both untold strength and the looming risk of losing control.

Her guilt about the prisoners' fates was vibrant and painful, but the underlying guilt that I had first found that night of the Courting Ball was still present. I think it always would be. Her shame about withholding information from her brother. Twice now. It was an undercurrent of pain beneath the new, fresh wounds.

I took a long, languid breath, willing the Mythica within me to settle long enough for us to escape the confines of this Prison. As I composed myself, Lexa returned to her packing. I watched her intently, feeling her guilt pulse beneath her skin, her own Mythica seeking the chance to sink into the memory, to bring it forward. It pulled at my skin, threatening to burst out of me.

When we finished her room, we both moved to mine to do the same, and I did so with slow, methodical movements to avoid losing my hold on the power that was surging inside.

Finally, after a torturous few minutes, our bags were packed, and we were ready to take our leave. She reached out to grip my hand, and the Mythica saw the touch as an invitation to strike. It burst forward, and I groaned, pulling back on the magic with all my might. I withdrew my hand from her, closing my eyes and taking more settling breaths. When I finally felt like I had regained the delicate hold, I opened my eyes to find her standing before me. She searched my face, those crystal eyes seeing me so clearly, so intimately.

"Give it back," she whispered, gently brushing a hand against my cheek.

"I can keep it a while longer," I protested through clenched teeth, but she shook her head.

"I'm ready."

I searched her face for any sign of false bravado, but all I saw was love. I leaned forward and pressed a gentle kiss to her lips, willing her Mythica to carefully return to her. She moaned into my kiss as the power surged between us.

I kept my lips on hers long after the Mythica had disappeared from my veins, finally releasing me from its violent hold, but I couldn't get enough of her.

When I pulled back, I was greeted by the familiar sight of my mate surrounded by a thick black cloud of Mythica. It was calmer than it had been in weeks, but still, I hoped the burden wasn't too much for her to handle.

"How do you feel?" I asked, gently brushing a strand of hair behind her ear.

"Like I'm not alone," she said softly. "Thank you for saving me from myself."

I kissed her again, pouring every ounce of love and adoration into it before grabbing our bags. We made our way to the front gate without so much as seeing another living soul, but that didn't stop me from bracing for a fight around every corner.

The guard at the front of the Prison had not been informed of our departure, but didn't aim to stop us. A few minutes later, we were packed into a carriage and riding away from Rein, the Sunken Province Prison, and the secrets that were revealed.

There was a day looming on the horizon, but arriving far sooner than I wished, when I would have to reveal the truth - the harrowing reality of the Trial of Wardens and the potential horrors awaiting her should the Double Marked somehow succeed in their goal. I knew it was my duty to prepare her for the worst and protect her from ever needing to face it. However, in the present, I allowed myself the indulgence of selfishness, simply holding her until that inevitable day arrived.

Thirty-One

"What do you mean they're arriving early?" I heard Avalin exclaim from our shared living room. I threw off the cover that blanketed me and swung my legs over the edge of the bed.

"The message just came in. They crossed the veil an hour ago," Dean Salazar replied in an anxious voice.

I stretched my arms above my head, and a yawn stole my breath as I thought back to my crossing. As I crossed through the mystical veil into The Court of the Vanguard, a palpable shift in the atmosphere enveloped me, like a cloak of arcane energy settling upon my shoulders. The very act of passing through that ethereal boundary carried a weight, a subtle yet undeniable acknowledgment of the prideful price exacted for admission to this new existence of mine. For a moment, during the passage into the Court, I was forced to surrender to my sense of self-importance and welcome an embrace of unbridled confidence. I'd never felt such unrestrained conviction before, not like that. I felt like I could do anything I wanted, be anything I desired, and take what I had earned.

Of course, the veil's influence only lasted for a brief window of time before the familiar self-doubt settled back into my thoughts. I belonged in this Court not because of my unrestrained confidence but because I desperately needed to earn my spot. I was here because I put in time and work that I was proud of.

I stood from the bed, taking stock of my sore muscles from yesterday's training session. I sparred with two Gladiators and emerged victorious both times, but not without paying the price of that exertion this morning.

"How am I just now hearing about this?" Avalin cried. She was angry about whatever news it was that she had just received. I padded across the floor toward the door and pulled it open. Both sets of eyes turned to me immediately. Avalin looked beautiful, as always, but her eyes were wild and unrestrained. Salazar's gaze was just as heated but in a different manner. His eyes scanned my bare chest, and I suddenly felt very exposed.

"My Warden, is there a particular reason there's a half-naked Pledge in your personal chambers?" He asked, not removing his eyes from me.

"Yes, there is," Avalin said with a sense of finality.

Salazar rolled his eyes and looked back at her. "I came to you as soon as I heard. They'll be here later this afternoon," Salazar continued.

Avalin broke eye contact with me and sighed deeply, running a hand over her face. "Prepare the guest suite for them and tell the citizens that we will hold an honor fight tonight and that I expect the crowd to make me proud," Avalin ordered, and Salazar bowed his head.

"Of course," Salazar offered. He turned on his heel and headed for the stairs, but not before throwing me an accusatory glance. Salazar always saw my potential during my time in the Institute, but even he couldn't hide his pity that I was Vacant.

'You have potential, Axel. It's a shame that you have no Mythica.'

He wasn't saying anything I hadn't already said to myself a million times, but now here I was—a Vacant Pledge living in the personal quarters of the Warden of Vanguard.

Something to be proud of.

Once Salazar had retreated up the stairs, Avalin turned to look at me. There was a brief glimmer of heat in her gaze as her eyes raked across my chest and down my toned stomach. I ran my tongue across my bottom lip to avoid speaking and ruining how she surveyed me. She hadn't kissed me again since that night at my house, but she hadn't shied away from finding reasons to be in my personal space. She'd often pick the same couch as me, when we were sitting and discussing our plans for my sister's arrival, instead of the adjacent one. When she attended training sessions, she would come around behind me to help show me the proper way to hold weapons by placing her hand on mine and pressing her chest against my back. Joining me on my morning runs to my hilltop sanctuary. There was a sort of delicious and forbidden tension between the two of us, and I had no idea how I was supposed to navigate it.

Her eyes returned to mine and suddenly the stress returned to her features. "Axel, I need a fight tonight. A big one," she said, pacing across the floor.

"Ok, I can prepare the Gladiators," I replied tentatively, moving forward slightly. "What's going on?"

She stopped pacing and turned back to me. "Your sister arrived in The Court of the Vanguard early. She'll be here in a few hours."

A surge of excitement rippled through me, knowing that my sister, my companion from the earliest days of our lives, had crossed the veil into my home within this realm of pride. It felt like it had been an eternity since we last shared the same space, the most prolonged separation we'd endured since the day we were born, and the anticipation of our reunion danced beneath my skin, sending jolts of energy through my body.

Yet, beneath the excitement bubbled a subtle undercurrent of nervousness. Lexa had a way of capturing attention effortlessly, and she was the most coveted person in all of Verihdia. I couldn't help but feel a twinge of anxiety about potentially losing the attention of my Warden to my sister. Attention I'd become too accustomed to.

"We learned some…other information as well," she added and I raised an eyebrow in question. "Your sister has been the victim of several attempted attacks on her life since her tour of Verihdia began."

Fear sliced at my heart. "What? Is she ok? Is she harmed?"

Avalin shook her head quickly. "She's ok. But it was advised that we always be very diligent about her safety."

I nodded fiercely, processing the new information. "Who was it?"

Avalin's face contorted as she searched for the right words. "There are some theories, but nothing concrete."

I ignored the half-truth she fed me, chalking it up to need-to-know Warden business, but my heart was racing, and my palms were clammy.

"She's ok?" I confirmed again, and again, Avalin nodded.

"The Warden of Shadows has protected her well."

I thought about that momentarily, marveling at the image of the selfish Warden putting my sisters' safety above his own. It settled my anxious panic just slightly.

"She has understandably had a rough go of it, so we need something to offer that can take her mind off what she's endured," Avalin adds, her eyes searching mine for the residual panic.

"You need a spectacle to welcome her," I agreed. Swallowing the stress in my voice. "I will ensure the Gladiators are ready to put on a good show." I tried to mask the fear in my voice, hoping she didn't notice the shake in my hands.

"I'll meet you at the Coliseum in an hour," she said before sauntering up the steps. I ignored how her dismissal made me feel and quickly dressed to follow up behind her. Nearly fifty minutes later, the Verihdian Gladiators surrounded me on the sandy arena floor, stretching their muscles and preparing for a fight.

Raul and Klover were playfully pushing each other's shoulders. They had gotten close over the last few months, and I had to admit that the admiration between the two of them certainly made Raul a more tolerable person.

"Today's honor fight is a celebration and a welcome for a personal guest of our Warden," I said, watching as the Gladiators, who were spread across the area, turned to look at me. "Now, the rules."

They groaned.

"No excessive force and non-lethal hits only. Today is about beating your opponent without killing them or forcing them to choose between surrender and death." I leveled my stare at each of them. "Your Warden wants a good show, and I want all of my Gladiators to be alive for next week's tournament. Is that clear?"

The Gladiators grumbled under their breath, but each one finally nodded. They saw honor fights differently than I did. They still believed that the most honorable thing a Gladiator could do is prove themselves worthy in the crucible of the tournament by spilling as much blood as possible. In contrast, I believed the real honor is found in what they fight for. "Today, your battle isn't for blood and glory. Instead, you're showcasing everything that The Court of the Vanguard holds in high esteem." I saw a flash of red hair from the corner of my eye.

Avalin crept forward from the tunnel across from me and was watching me address my fighters.

"Today isn't about you. It's about your Court and your unwavering dedication to it. Your goal is to make your Warden proud and to bring pride to your Court. Does that seem like something you're capable of?"

The Gladiators rose to their feet and offered a guttural yell of agreement.

"Good." I smiled. I took a moment and paired off my fighters with people I knew they could show off against. I was putting together the show that Avalin wanted.

"Raul, we are one down after losing Fulcho last week." The memory stung. We lost our first Gladiator of the season during the last tournament. He refused to surrender.

Prideful fool.

Something I had tried to convey to him was that there was no pride in a useless death, but he saw only two options, either win the tournament or die trying. Unfortunately, he had landed on the latter. It landed on my shoulders harder than I thought it would. Gladiators die all the time. But this one was *mine.*

"Sit this one out today. Prepare for next week," I finished, but Raul growled his disapproval.

"I want to fight," he said with a fire in his eyes.

"Sit in the stands and watch. You might learn something," I teased. We had landed on relatively good terms after he realized I knew what I was talking about and could back it up, but he still had this almost juvenile eagerness that, sooner or later, would get him hurt.

"Go get suited up and prepare. The fight begins in a few hours," I announced, ignoring the glare that Raul was giving me.

They scattered in their pairs, discussing their tactics and plans to ensure an outstanding performance, and after offering a scoff, Raul followed. I released a sigh and ran my hands through my unkempt hair.

The internal conflict between the excitement of the coming reunion and the anxiety of competition tugged at my emotions. Lexa's presence would be a welcome beacon in the court, but the lingering fear of being overshadowed by her loomed large. It was a delicate dance between the joy of familial connection and the awareness of the hierarchical dynamics within The Court of the Vanguard. The next few weeks of my life would be one giant game, and the prize was Lexa's loyalty.

I loved my sister and wanted nothing more than to see her again. To embrace her and to spend time with her the way we always had. And yet, I had admitted silently that it felt nice to have something of my own here. Being a twin meant that so little of my life was mine alone. Being the Vacant mirror to Lexa's powerful image carried with it moments of shame. Not jealousy, necessarily, but disappointment that I wasn't reaching the potential that I think our parents expected of us when they gave us these names.

Did they expect me to be her equal?

I couldn't ask them because I still didn't know who they were. I understood it, mostly. The Wardens didn't want me to have to hide the truth from my sister, but I couldn't lie…it was painful. I did everything they told me to. I survived my illness, I trained, I made my Pledge, I found my new home, and still, I wasn't given their names. They could be around any corner, Icould pass them on any street, and I wouldn't even know it.

"Axel," Avalin's voice pulled my attention from its internal struggle. She had approached, stopping where the Gladiators had just vacated.

"Yes?"

"Why haven't you asked me to be a Gladiator?" She was observing me analytically, and I felt the air thicken around me, making it harder to breathe under her suffocating stare.

"I'm… I.. how," I stuttered, my inability to form a coherent thought frustrating and pathetic.

"Cassius may have mentioned something during our last run together," she added casually, her purple gaze tracking me as I stepped back toward the safety of my room.

"They had no right to speak for me. I am proud of the position you've appointed me to." I pressed my hands together in front of me, anxiously twirling my fingers.

"It's not just that, though," she said, tilting her head to get another good look at me. "It's the way you speak to them." She indicated after the Gladiators who had just retreated to the tunnels. "And to me," she added softly. "You speak so passionately like you believe in what is being done here in this Coliseum."

"I do believe in it. I always have," I answered truthfully.

She nodded."Is that something you want?" She asked.

"I love the opportunities you've already given me."

"It's a simple question, Axel. Do you want to be a Verihdian Gladiator? Do you wish I would have recruited you to fight instead of train?" Her voice was steady, devoid of any inflection, and her face remained a neutral mask, revealing no discernible emotion. I struggled to gauge her feelings in either direction.

I wanted to tell her that being a Gladiator has been my dream for as long as I can remember. I wanted to say to her that the thrill of being in the tunnels during the tournaments wasn't sufficient for me, and I yearned to hear those screams specifically for my sake. I wanted to tell her that I have trained my whole life to become the best fighter Verihdia has ever and will ever see, and I felt like I was wasting my potential training others to live my dream, while I remained simply a witness to their glory.

"You've done so much for me, I'm living a life I could have only dreamed of because of you," I offer, skirting the question yet again.

She pressed forward, closing the distance between us. "Axel," she said softly.

The sound of my name on her lips was so deliciously taunting that I tensed my jaw and closed my eyes to compose myself. Her footsteps continued, and I tried to steel myself against the onslaught of overwhelming emotion. Between what she was asking me and what her proximity was doing to me, I couldn't breathe.

"Do you want to be a Veridian Gladiator?"

"Yes," I exclaimed breathlessly, my eyes popping open to find my Warden just feet away. I could reach out and touch her if I chose to. "Yes, I do. It's been my dream for so long, Avalin. I've trained my whole life to become the best. I used to want it more than I've ever wanted anything." I found myself getting lost in that purple torrent behind her eyes; the air between us was fiery and tense. She was so close to me now, and I loved how the scent that invaded my nostrils had become so familiar.

She nodded, a small smile playing on her lips. "Then suit up and prepare. You'll fight Raul tonight."

The world seemed to decelerate as I absorbed the weight of her words. The opportunity I had relentlessly pursued was here, within my grasp, and a surge of euphoria and excitement coursed through me. I was on the brink of rushing forward, ready to pull her into an embrace and seal the moment with a kiss, but I maintained my distance.

"You're asking me to become a Gladiator?" I whisper the words, searching for confirmation of my wildest dreams come true.

She shook her head, and dread filled the place where joy had claimed. "You can't *become* a Gladiator, Axel," she said, stepping forward again until I could feel her breath on my lips.

I shook my head, willing the tears that were stinging my eyes not to fall. Her hand came to rest on my chest, and my skin felt like it may burst from the heat of her betrayal.

"Of course," I said. My voice was shaky and low as I avoided eye contact with the beautiful, dangerous woman before me. Of course, she would only be offering one fight. Not the whole season. I was naive to assume otherwise.

Her hand snaked up from my chest to just below my chin and pulled my head up so that I could meet her gaze. Her scarred skin was glowing in the midday sun, and I loved how her windswept hair gently danced around her face.

"You can't become a Gladiator because you already are one. You have been since the moment you first arrived here. Probably long before that, even. I see your fire, Axel, and I can't believe it took me as long as it did to do so." The tears fell entirely now as her words sunk in. "You are the truest definition of a Gladiator, Axel. You always have been."

The air crackled with a tension I couldn't deny. An impulsive urge took hold of me. The rational part of my mind argued it might not be right, but the pull was undeniable. Without thinking, I closed the gap between us and stole a kiss from the lips that had praised me. It was a kiss born from impulse, a daring act that held the promise of consequence. Yet, in that fleeting connection, the world momentarily melted away, leaving only the passion of an unplanned kiss lingering between us.

As I broke free from the overwhelming kiss, the taste of spontaneity lingered on our lips, and my heartbeat pounded relentlessly as an echo of the impulsive act. Her eyes were wide with surprise and held a hint of uncertainty, mirroring my inner conflict.

Time seemed to stand still for too long, and I found myself searching her amethyst gaze for a reaction. Was it a mistake to indulge in this connection again? The air buzzed with anticipation, and I braced myself for the aftermath of our kiss. Knowing that despite whatever consequences awaited me, it would have been worth it.

As the silence lingered, a subtle shift in her expression unfolded as the shock softened and the world around us resumed its normal rhythm. The memory of the impromptu kiss lingered in each breath and each beat of my heart.

"Apologies, my Warden," I said, stepping back from Avalin and the impossible draw I felt for her.

She scanned my features silently before a breathtaking smile claimed her lips. "You have nothing to apologize for," she replied. "I should go prepare for your sister," she began, and I once again felt the pang of disappointment. "I cannot wait to witness your first fight as a Gladiator of my Court. You've earned it." With a lingering look, she turned and exited the arena.

Her crimson hair seemed to flail wildly in the wind as she retreated. Once she was out of my eyeline, I finally felt my heart return to its resting pace, but the reprieve lasted only a moment before the reality of our conversation settled on me.

I am a Verihdian Gladiator.

The words felt too impossible to be true. And yet, they were. I had earned my spot, and despite my connection with my Warden - whatever that connection may be - there wasn't a shadow of doubt in my mind that I had earned this honor all on my own.

This outcome would have been mine regardless of who my sister was or what her loyalty meant to my Warden. This win was mine and mine alone, and I'd never felt more proud.

I rushed off the arena floor to find Raul and tell him about our upcoming rematch, something I was positive he had been itching for ever since I managed to beat him a few months ago.

With two anticipated events on the horizon, my heart swelled. The imminent arrival of my sister promised a desperately needed reunion, and it also heralded the opportunity to demonstrate that I was worthy of the title of Verihdian Gladiator and, perhaps more importantly, the title of my sister's brother.

Thirty-Two

The journey away from The Court of Echoes was tense with an undercurrent of dread. Until the moment we crossed the veil, we were constantly looking over our shoulders and expecting to see the red-eyed, monstrous Warden of the Court chasing after us, hoping to capture me in his malicious clutches once more. While I knew the mental scars of those weeks in the Sunken Province Prison would never leave me, the moment we passed through the vicious veil and I got my first lungful of uncorrupted air, I felt the weight of those days slip away. Save for the guilt that still rested on my soul and the unsettling truth that I was the cause for the Double Marked's suffering, which was logically a useless worry considering they were the cause of mine.

Lysander offered for us to stop at the Institute and stay there for the remainder of what should've been my time in The Court of Echoes, but I refused. Despite our strange encounter at the Festival, I missed Oliver, and I'd be lying if I said I didn't miss the ease of existence there, but I was in such a delicate and fragile place. I needed the one person who had always been there for me. My blood. My brother. Axel.

So, with my mate's hand clasped tightly in mine, we raced away from the horrors of the Prison and toward the only family I knew about. I couldn't ignore the fact that I was the only family Axel had, too, simply because of my selfishness. The regret stemming from my worst deed lingered persistently, a looming storm cloud that darkened and thickened with each passing day. It was a mistake that haunted me, a constant presence in my thoughts. The weight of this guilt became more evident as I endured the torments within the Prison. It took facing the brutal realities of that place for me to realize the gravity of my actions and what needed to be done.

I have to tell Axel the truth.

Lysander held a quick exchange with a guard just outside the Vanguard gate. As the carriage rolled through the shimmering amethyst veil to The Court of the Vanguard, I was transported once again to a world unlike any I'd ever experienced. How many lives had I lived since leaving the Institute? The crossover brought with it an almost excessive boost of self-assuredness. In fact, any lingering doubt or fear about revealing the truth to my brother drifted away with the Mythica within the veil.

"I want Axel to receive his envelope," I stated confidently.

My mate's eyes darted to me in question, searching my face for any sign of timidness in my choice. He wouldn't find it. He pulled the carriage off the side of the road, coming to a rest near the edge of a cliff that overlooked a stunning field below with a shimmering crystal blue creek that danced across the landscape. We were secluded here amidst the lush trees and gorgeous streaks of sun rays as they peaked through fluffy clouds.

"Are you sure about this? If we give it to him now, he may ask why he didn't get it after his Pledge," he said, turning to me, and I knew what he was implying.

"Yes, I'm sure." I nodded, smoothing the skirt of my dress. A soft breeze whispered through the surroundings, carrying the sweet fragrance of the long-stemmed purple flowers that adorned every hill and field on the horizon. The landscape unfolded before me like a picturesque panorama bathed in perpetual sunshine. The vibrant hues of the flowers contrasted with the lush greenery, creating a scene of unparalleled beauty. "I am going to tell him the truth. All of it."

Lysander's eyes softened, and a faint smile played on his lips, but it almost seemed wistful and melancholic. "How very… not selfish of you."

I saw the unspoken worry that was hidden behind his words. He saw a quality in me that didn't directly align with his Court. The silent question of my loyalty that lingered between us once again burned to life. He hadn't pressed me on it, although I knew he desired to. Without even using my Mythica, I could see just how badly he needed me to Pledge to him. It was something that I had toiled with over the last few months, but truthfully, the answer was clear. I just didn't let myself see it until this moment.

The vibrant sun cast a brilliant light across the landscape, and I felt its delicious effects warm my skin. The aroma of beautiful flowers threatened to overwhelm my senses, and yet the truth that I'd realized and admitted to myself was so clear and focused even through the haze of a new adventure.

I pressed my hand against his cheek and marveled at the way his dark canvas provided the perfect backdrop for my pale skin. The perfect contrast of light and dark. His uncertain eyes looked at me with a mixture of anticipation and hope. "If you still believe, for one moment, that after everything you've done for me and everything you *are* to me, that I wouldn't Pledge to spend my life at your side…then you don't know me at all."

As my declaration hung in the air, a palpable tension enveloped us. Then, with a surge of emotion, a radiant smile broke across his face. In that charged moment, the air seemed to crackle with the promise of loyalty. The bond I shared with him hummed, satisfied within the confines of my chest. His surprise and happiness mirrored my own, and before another word could be spoken, he closed the distance between us. The kiss that followed was an impulsive celebration of the new admission. It was a tender and passionate affirmation of the truth that had been laid bare. It was a moment suspended in time, where our hearts synchronized in a sweet harmony of surprise, happiness, and the promise of shared tomorrows.

He drew back, shoulders heaving as he composed himself. "You're mine?" He said, in question, wanting me to clarify my promise to him.

I pressed my chest into him, swinging my leg over his lap to straddle him. Once perched above him, I felt the familiar heat building in my core. He looked up at me as if I was the sun itself. Sacred, vibrant, beautiful. I would never get enough of the way he looked at me. I smiled at him softly before pressing a delicate kiss to the sensitive part of the skin at the base of his neck. His head fell to the side, and a moan slipped from behind his lips as I repeated the process on the other side. I peppered kisses against his skin, loving the way his body reacted to mine. His fingers dug into my hips, and his lengths hardened beneath me. I kissed a trail up his jaw.

"You may not yet be My Warden," I said, pressing one last kiss to his throat. The action earned me a low, sultry groan. "But you are *mine*, Warden."

He grew tired of my tortuous exploration of his skin and quickly dragged my skirt up past my waist so that I was deliciously exposed to him. Moments later, his length was free, and he was sheathing himself inside of me. We remained there, eyes locked and breathing ragged, as my body stretched to welcome his.

Wordless promises passed between us as I began to rise and lower myself onto him. His hips pressed up into mine, seeking his pleasure in the heat of my body. He kissed me again and again until our lips were bruised and swollen. His hands dug into my hips and directed me to slam down onto him with more force each time. Our moans melded together in a perfect symphony of pleasure and release. My core tightened around him as the bond that joined us thrummed and pulsed loudly.

"Make your Pledge," he growled, and the possessive fire in his eyes was enough to warm my skin.

"I, Lexa Cromwell," I breathlessly whispered between gasps and moans, as he so expertly orchestrated my pleasure. "Having completed my training at the -," I groaned as his hips slammed into mine. "At the Verihdian Institute," I panted. "Now humbly Pledge my allegiance," I whispered as tears of joy flooded my eyes. His hips slowed to a more leisurely and cherishing pace. "Loyalty," I said, placing a hand on his cheek, loving the way his eyes were glowing with both heat and love. "And life to you, Lysander Bladespell. I Pledge to you."

He groaned with satisfaction as my words fed his selfishness before resuming his wicked pace, playing my passion so perfectly. I was burning from the inside out—a phoenix in the presence of his love. Every thrust of his hips, into the deepest parts of me, was a claiming possessive motion that had my back arching, exposing my throat to him. He claimed the flesh there with his lips, his tongue, his teeth and still did not relent his punishing pace. I felt the muscles in my body clench as I neared the cliff of euphoria. Release tore through me, and I screamed out his name, feeling my core tighten around him as I rode the wave of pleasure.

He followed closely behind, slamming to the hilt as my name tumbled from his lips with a moan. Our labored breathing was the only sound that could be heard as we both descended from the heights we had traveled to together.

When I was sure my legs could function without wobbling embarrassingly, I slid off his lap and back onto the seat beside him. A delightfully light and freeing giggle bubbled from my lips, and Lysander smiled down at me, watching my face as I laughed. After a moment, he joined me, our voices mingling in a shared release.

In the aftermath of a month filled with the weight of unspeakable horrors, this was a surprising moment of lightness. It happened suddenly, unexpectedly, as if laughter had found its way back into the chambers of my heart after a prolonged absence. For a moment, it felt liberating - our shared laughter echoed through the air. It starkly contrasted the heavy silence and fear that had dominated the weeks before. It was a brief reprieve from the shadows that had clung to my every thought and action.

However, as the laughter subsided, the realization of the last month's harrowing events settled in. The weight I had momentarily cast aside crashed down on me with an overwhelming force. A profound sadness gripped my chest, and before I could comprehend the shift in emotions, tears welled up, streaming down my face.

Lysander, attuned to the depth of my emotions, abandoned the laughter and, with a gentle touch, began to comfort me. In that delicate moment, the juxtaposition of laughter and tears was a beautiful reminder of how much life I had lived - the good, the bad, and the painful.

"Thank you, I needed that," I admitted, wiping the tears from my cheeks and feeling my smile return as I met his emerald eyes. He held me close, running a gentle touch along my back.

"I will give you everything you need, Lexa, for the rest of my life," he vowed, and my heart leaped at the promise.

"I need you to give Axel his envelope," I said, still feeling the effects of the veil in my veins. While it wasn't quite as assured, the plan remained the same. I had to tell him the truth, and I needed to rectify the mistakes I made.

He nodded, pressing a kiss to my hair. "Avalin has it. I will get it from her when we arrive." And just like that, I knew that eventually, everything would be ok. Even if Axel were upset with me, giving him the information he deserved would be worth it. And he was my twin, my mirror, my equal, my best friend. He couldn't stay mad at me forever.

*

As we approached the Chaos Coliseum, the anticipation of my upcoming daunting task built. The intricate details etched into the towering stone walls seemed to tell tales of countless events witnessed within those walls, a testament to the rich history and tradition of The Court of the Vanguard. The atmosphere was charged with excitement as hundreds or thousands of voices echoed together from within the confines of the arena. Lysander stopped our carriage when we saw a familiar face. Salazar stepped forward to greet us and offered his hand for me as I descended the carriage. I smiled graciously at him and accepted his assistance.

"My Warden was delighted to hear about your early arrival. She has wasted no time preparing an evening of extraordinary festivities for you. Please follow me." He bowed his head slightly at Lysander in respect before turning on a heel and leading us into the arena. It was massive, much larger than the one in the Living Lands, and instead of sitting atop the land and climbing toward the stars, it was built into the ground, sloping toward the mysteries below the surface.

The energy was unbelievable as the patrons moved about, claiming their seats for the upcoming event. I had accompanied Axel to the tournament when it came to the Institute, but this was something entirely different. I could almost taste the ferocity of the spectators as they cheered and screamed as a prelude to the show.

Salazar led us to a guarded door just off the way, and soon, we descended stairs into the bowels of the arena. The echoes of screams muffled but did not disappear as we arrived in the tunnels that ran beneath the carved seats. Ahead of me, I saw a flash of red hair on the person whose back was turned to me, and I instantly wondered what The Warden of Vanguard would look like to me this time.

As we approached, Avalin turned, and I exhaled sharply at the sight before me. I was looking at an almost identical copy of Lysander, save for the red hair, purple eyes, and the ceremonial armor she wore. Another chuckle spilled from my mouth.

Lysander leaned down, pressing his lips to my ear. "In case you were wondering, you look beautiful with red hair."

I looked up at him, smiling at the adoration I saw there. He saw me the way I saw him. I resisted the urge to clasp his hand and bit my lip instead. He mirrored the action, and his eyes flicked to my lips as if to indicate precisely what he was thinking about.

"Miss Cromwell," Avalin exclaimed cheerfully, rushing forward to claim my hands in hers. I tried not to let the near-perfect mirror image mess with my mind as she greeted me. "I can't tell you how excited I am that you are here, and early no less. Lucky me!"

I smiled at her, releasing some internal tension as the realization that I was safe and this Warden was nothing like the last, settled the majority of my nerves. "Thank you for accommodating us earlier than scheduled," Lysander said, offering his hand for his sibling. She gripped his forearm in an embrace of respect.

"The honor is mine," she added, nodding to him before returning her gaze to me. The purple irises gleamed in the waning Vanguard sun. "We have prepared a fight in your honor tonight, a display of my best Gladiators and their strengths."

I smiled at her. I wasn't the biggest fan of the bloody brawls I witnessed back in the Living Lands, but something tells me that half the enjoyment of these fights is the atmosphere, and I was surprised to find myself excited about it.

"We have many incredible things planned for you to witness during your time with us," she continued. "However, I think I know what you are most looking forward to."

My smile deepened.

"Lexa, allow me to introduce you to my newest Verihdia Gladiator." She swept a hand toward the tunnel entrance to her left, and as my eyes danced that way, I saw him. There he was - my brother, a familiar face in a world that had grown increasingly unfamiliar. The sight of him triggered an overwhelming surge of joy and relief. At that moment, the months of separation and the burdens we had individually carried seemed to fade into the background.

Axel held his ground, tall and confident in a set of traditional Gladiator armor. A surge of pride and awe welled up within me. The transformation was striking. He stood there, a formidable figure, exuding strength and resilience. The traditional garb accentuated his every muscle, a testament to the rigorous training and trials he had undergone since we last crossed paths.

While his exterior seemed more rigid and composed, the beaming smile on his lips was all the invitation I needed to sprint across the expanse and toss my arms around his neck. As we embraced, our connection felt more profound than ever before. The weight of the shared experiences, the trials faced, and the challenges overcome surged through the simple act of holding each other. It was a reunion tinged with the bittersweet recognition of the hardships endured during our time apart and the hardships yet to come. But for this moment, there was only us.

He laughed eagerly, lifting me from my position and spinning us around. I laughed with him, my heart swelling with each echo of the melodic joy. My Mythica surged with recognition of the man in our arms as if it was just as happy to see my brother as I was. When my feet settled back on the ground, I pulled back from the embrace to get a look at my brother. His skin was tanned from the Vanguard sun, and he seemed older, more mature. He had lived an entire life since the last time we spoke.

"I see you two have already met," Avalin teased, a soft laugh in her tone. I glanced over my shoulder to see Lysander beaming at me. When my eyes returned to Axel, I again pressed my face against the rugged plated leather at his chest.

"We'll give you a few minutes. Avalin, if we may, I have something I'd like to discuss with you," Lysander spoke from behind me, and I ignored the tendril of fear that threatened to sneak its way into this reunion. I threw my arms around him again and hugged him until I couldn't feel my arms any longer.

"Well, if it isn't the most coveted woman in all of Verihdia," Axel taunted me, and I playfully smacked his shoulder. He laughed, stumbling back a step or two.

"That isn't important, not even in the slightest," I offer eagerly. "You're a Gladiator!" I stepped back and made a big show of admiring his armor. A proud smile danced on his lips.

"I am," he replied, pride beaming out of every pore. "As of today. This will be my first fight."

"I knew you could do it, Axel. I am so proud of you." I reached for his hand and squeezed, hoping he could feel the truth behind my words. A film of unshed tears pooled in my eyes. "You found where you belong."

His crystal eyes, a copy of my own, welled with tears, and he nodded. "I really did."

There was a surge of simultaneous pride and jealousy in my chest. Pride that my brother found his place and is thriving as he was born to, and jealousy that I, too, have found where I belong, yet I cannot disclose that information to him. Or anyone.

"Lexa," Lysander called, drawing my attention to him. He stood beside Avalin near a door. He held a familiar golden envelope in his hands. I looked to Avalin to try and gauge how she might have reacted to this development, but she wasn't looking at me. Her eyes instead were on my brother, a longing expression etched on her face. When I turned my attention to Axel, he watched her with a similar emotion. I silently filed that information away to discuss with him, but I had something much more important to discuss now.

"Axel, do you think we can go somewhere quiet and talk for a few minutes," I asked, drawing his eyes away from his Warden.

"Well…" he looked over my shoulder toward the arena.

"Go ahead," Avalin offered. "I'll get the show started. You're not needed until later. Enjoy your reunion." She smiled at him, and I couldn't help but find a familiarity in that gaze. "And Lexa, enjoy the show. I look forward to getting to know you after the event." She bowed her head to all of us and tried, and failed, not to toss another wistful look at my brother before heading down the tunnel toward the cheering crowd.

Lysander stepped forward, the envelope clutched tightly in his fingers.

"Yes, uh, follow me. There's another tunnel back here just for the trainers," he said, grabbing my hand and leading me down the sandy corridors to a more secluded area. Lysander followed closely behind.

When we arrived, I turned to face Lysander. "Do you mind giving us a few minutes?"

Fear flashed across his face as he hesitated. I stepped toward him, reaching for the envelope.

"I need to do this alone." I didn't pull the envelope from his grip. Instead, I just waited for him to release his hold on it. If he was worried that I'd peek at the information within and my loyalties would sway, he didn't trust me the way I trusted him. His hand slid from the envelope easily, without question, and my heart swelled. I looked down at the object in my hands.

The golden envelope in my hands was an embodiment of the answers I'd longed for. The identity of my parents was concealed within its elegant folds, and only a thin layer of parchment stood between me and my family.

As I traced the delicate contours of the envelope, the weight of its contents felt both tangible and elusive. The answers I had sought, the key to unlocking the mystery of my parentage, were now within my grasp. Yet, something had shifted within me.

For the first time, the need for that information to help me define my choices had dissipated. This envelope held the power to unveil the truth of my past, but the revelation no longer held the same urgency. Of course, I still wanted to know who my parents were, but I knew now that, without a doubt, whatever was on this piece of parchment, wouldn't change a thing. The choice had already been made. Made not by the ink on a document but by the journey I had undertaken and the person I had become as a result.

My choice was made because of the love I had fought against and the love I fought for. I was sure. Confident. Proud of my choice.

But there were other choices I wasn't so proud of that would soon be revealed. I tore my eyes from the envelope, noticing that the draw to open it myself had slipped away.

"It's not safe to be alone right now, Lexa," Lysander urged, glancing around the desolate tunnel.

"Warden," Axel exclaimed, walking forward toward Lysander. As he approached, I stepped to the side, and suddenly, two of the most important people in my life were face-to-face.

If Riley were here, it'd be perfect.

"It has come to my attention that my sister's life has been threatened," he said, a tense tick in his jaw. "More than once."

A tightness clawed at my chest, and I hated that he knew what I'd gone through. He shouldn't have to worry about me like that, not when he's found his happiness here.

"That's true," Lysander replied coolly, trying to hide his feelings for me behind a mask of indifference. "I assure you, I've done what I can to protect her."

Axel stood his ground momentarily before offering his hand for Lysander. After a brief look of surprise, Lysander accepted my brother's arm and allowed him to express his gratitude with a handshake. I tried not to let my giddiness show on my face.

"Thank you for taking care of her," Axel said, a slight choke of emotions claiming his words. Lysander nodded, a brief glimpse of his love for me showing on his face before he quickly slipped back into the persona of the Warden of Shadows.

"Of course." They dropped hands, and Lysander turned to face me. "If you know about the attacks, then you know why I shouldn't leave her unattended."

"She won't be unattended," Axel said, indicating to himself. "She'll be safe with me for a few moments."

Lysander looked back and forth between the two of us like he couldn't come to a decision. I offered him a single nod, and he sighed.

"Alright, but I won't be far," he said. "Keep her safe." He offered a lingering look to me before leaving. I watched him go, feeling the bond in my chest swell with love.

Once we were alone, Axel looked down at me with knowing eyes. "He seems to take his position very seriously," he said with the slightest undertone of jest. I willed the blush that threatened to dissipate and cleared my throat.

"Your Warden seemed unable to keep her eyes off of you earlier. Care to elaborate on that?" His face deepened with a pink tint, and he shook his head.

"I have no idea what you're referring to."

"Right," I taunted, bringing my hands to my hips. The motion drew my brother's eyes to the golden envelope in my hands.

"What is that?" he asked, but the haunted look in his eyes told me he knew intimately what could be housed in this envelope.

"You know what it is," I said, avoiding his searching eyes.

"Why do you have it?"

"Because it's yours," I said, swallowing the lump of guilt in my throat. "You deserve this." I held the envelope out for him, and his hands shakily reached for it. But before his fingers could grip it, he stopped. My Mythica rushed out toward him involuntarily, latching onto the desire for the knowledge within the confines of this envelope. I reined it in, barely.

"They're letting us open it?" His fingers hovered just inches away as if he was holding them above a blazing fire and testing how close he could get before he was burnt.

I shook my head. "Not us, just you."

His eyebrows knitted together as he scanned my hand and the object outstretched within it. "I don't understand. Why now? I was told I couldn't get this until you made your Pledge."

I felt the sting of tears in my eyes, and I bit my lips to keep it from trembling. There was no turning back now. It was time to tell him everything.

"I have something I need to tell you," I admitted softly. He didn't respond but instead observed my face. "I am the reason you didn't get this on the day of your Pledge." The admission was toxic on my tongue, like ash and flame.

"I know. They were afraid I'd tell you when you came to The Court of the Vanguard and influence your Pledge." He shook his head.

"No, they weren't," I whispered.

"What do you mean?" He asked, his tone even and cold.

"The Wardens gave me a choice. They said you could get your envelope without me, or they could withhold it until I got mine as well." Tears poured down my cheeks as the confession echoed through the tunnel.

"No," he said incredulously. "No, you … you wouldn't do that to me." He tried to convince himself, but something about the shock in his voice and the fear that my Mythica was tasting on him told me he wasn't so sure he believed that.

I bit back a sob and pushed forward. The sooner I said the words, the sooner I could start healing the damage I'd done. I steadied myself, knowing that what I was about to do might be the most painful thing I have ever endured. "It.. it wasn't the first time either," I whispered through the sobs.

"No," Axel said, taking a step back. I kept going. I had to.

"When you were sick…"

"Stop." He shook his head, tears spilling down his cheeks.

"When we weren't sure if you were going to make it," I sobbed. The words felt like glass raking against my throat. Painful and damaging.

"Please, don't-" Axel cried, but I pushed through.

"They were going to give this to you." I held up the offending envelope. "They were going to tell you so you could know in case you… in case you," I inhaled sharply, finding it more challenging to breathe with each passing second as my deepest regret was being laid bare before me. "They asked me if it was ok."

"Don't say it, Lexa," He warned, a mixture of disgust, pain, and sadness lacing his tone and features.

"I said no."

Axel turned his back to me, a sob wrenching from his chest. I cried, letting the tears flow fully and steadily. The words had been said. The truth was out. And I felt like the most despicable person in all of Verihdia.

"It is the one thing I regret most in my life, Axel. I acted selfishly. I was only thinking of myself, and I am so so sorry. I'm so sorry." I stepped toward him, placing a hand on his shoulder, but he quickly yanked it out of my grasp. A choked gasp was ripped from my lips.

"Don't touch me," he seethed.

"Axel, I know what I did was wrong." Despite my desire to reach for him again, I didn't move forward. "I will regret it for the rest of my life," I promised, sniffling. "I hate that I was ever the kind of person who would do that to you. But that's not me anymore, Axel. I'm trying to make it right." I held the envelope out toward him again, desperately attempting to close the distance between us.

My words found purchase, and he turned slowly to face me again, but it wasn't acceptance on his face. It was anger. Pure, unbridled anger. I tried to ignore the flash of vicious red eyes that slipped into my consciousness.

"Not that person anymore?" He asked, a hint of sarcasm in his tone. I took a step back, which he answered by taking one toward me. "You claim that you're not this selfish, *horrible* person anymore?" He spat the word, and I cringed at it. My Mythica roiled within my chest, begging to be let loose to protect myself. "So, tell me then, Lexa, why would my *sister* tell me this horrific thing that she did moments before the biggest fight of my life, huh?" Dread settled in the pit of my stomach as his words found me.

"I didn't…" I stammered.

"You didn't what?" He interrupted, taking another step forward until his chest touched the end of the envelope that acted as the only barrier between us. "Didn't think about it? Because all you could think about was absolving yourself of this guilt and not even considering how I would react."

I shook my head, unable to voice a response.

He was right.

I was the same selfish girl who told Oliver 'no' all those years ago. I haven't changed. I wasn't a better person. My Mythica raged against my chest, and I had to physically press my free hand to my chest to keep it contained as my brother stared at me with nothing but loathing in the crystal eyes that we shared. It was one thing to see my self-loathing in my own reflection but to see it in him was a special kind of torture.

"I'm sorry," I whispered, almost too quiet to hear.

He glared at me, my brother, the only family I have, with hate. And the worst part was…I deserved it. His eyes flicked down to the envelope in my hands briefly. He scoffed and turned to stalk off, leaving me and the envelope behind.

I stood there, alone with the haunting aftermath of my confession. The regret gnawed at my insides, and the sense of isolation deepened as the distance between us widened with each step he took away from me. My words lingered, a painful reminder of the irreversible damage wrought by my own hands. I was paralyzed to my spot by the weight of my mistakes.

As I replayed the scene in my mind, remembering the harshness of his gaze and the disdain in his voice, I had never felt so raw and exposed. It was a wound that cut deeper than any physical pain the Double Marked or the creature from beneath the waves had ever inflicted, a wound I had wreaked upon the one person who had always been my anchor.

In the silence that stretched before me, I couldn't help but feel like I had lost something irretrievable. The trust and love built from a lifetime of familial bonding were all sacrificed at the altar of my selfishness. I pulled the envelope to my chest, hating how cold it felt in my hands now, and slid into the front of my corset dress. I would hold onto it, unopened, until Axel was ready for it.

Consumed by the weight of regret, I failed to notice the subtle shift in the air. A sudden, jarring motion caught me off guard, and before I could comprehend what was happening, strong hands seized me from behind. The world blurred as someone forcibly turned me, and panic surged as I caught a glimpse of the familiar white mask. I tried to scream but whatever Mythica this figure had seemed to steal the very voice from my throat, silencing me. Then they began to drag me away.

The tunnel and the roar of the crowd became a fleeting backdrop as I struggled against the unyielding force pulling me. I tried to protest, to resist the hands that propelled me forward, reaching for the dagger at my thigh. I wrestled against the hold, and the density of my skirt but finally my fingers closed around the emerald-hilted dagger and I prayed for the spelled blade to protect me as it was designed to. As it has so many times before.

I attempted to slice at the figure, but their grip around my arms kept me pinned in place. I grunted in exertion as I tried to drive the dagger into the stomach of the figure, but my grunt and the attack were simultaneously silenced. A quick hit to my wrist caused the dagger to go spilling to the sand floor below.

I watched the dagger fall, and realization settled into place. I was going to have to fight my way out without it.

I squared my feet, drawing on the training I had received over my last few months. My leg shot up, making contact with the figure's gut. They folded over, and I tried to reach for the dagger, but another set of hands quickly pulled me back.

I was outnumbered, that was true, but what was also true was that I wouldn't go down without a fight.

Now, too far from the dagger to consider it an option, I charged the second masked figure and got my hands around their throat. Their knees buckled under the force of it, but again I was tossed back by the other set of hands. I fell onto my back in the dirt, and I felt a sharp shooting pain jolt up my back.

I sat up, watching the two figures stalk toward me. The dagger was too far, so I steeled myself and reached deep into my chest where that inky well of Mythica had always been. It was roaring, raging to sink its claws into these attackers. Just as I prepared to let the tendrils loose on these figures, something heavy and thick slammed against the back of my head, and darkness claimed me.

My last thought before my consciousness slipped away was that of my brother and Lysander.

Lexa

Thirty-Three

As consciousness slowly returned to me, I instantly became aware of a disorienting ache, a wicked roar, and the undeniable feeling of being restrained. The last memories I could recall came back in segmented pictures. Axel. The fight. The Double Marked attack. Blinking against the murkiness, I surveyed my surroundings and found myself tied up in the dim expanse of what appeared to be an old but oddly well-maintained repository.

Moonlight filtered through the high windows, casting eerie shadows across the worn metallic floor. The air carried the scent of dust and age. A sense of confinement settled in, intensified by the tight bonds securing me to an unforgiving surface.

A memory of the cages in the Sunken Province Prison flashed in my mind. This was decidedly different, and yet, a cage all the same.

As my eyes adjusted to the low light, the contours of the repository revealed themselves - stacks of forgotten crates and tomes of untold origin on dusty shelves.

With my senses fully returned, I could finally place the wicked roar that hummed in the background. The sound of distant crashing waves echoed through the space. It was both familiar and haunting, a vicious reminder of the nightmares that plagued me night after night and the creature who hunted me.

Had they finally kept their promise to find me?

As I strained against my restraints, to no avail, the gravity of the situation settled in. The moonlit windows above me offered no comfort amidst the solitude. Anxiety coiled within me, heightened by the unfamiliarity of my surroundings and the muffled echoes of the sea that seemed to mock my captive state.

The door at the far end of the space swung open, and a light from the hall spilled in, basking some approaching figures in a warm glow. I reached for my Mythica but found that it was absent. Not entirely gone, but the familiar storm within me was lying dormant. I felt the pulse of Mythica within my bindings and knew instantly that these shackles held the same properties as Rein's Prison cages. I was alone, tied up, and stripped of my Mythica. There was no escape.

Four masked individuals stopped before me, and I felt fear tighten around my throat like the coils of the creature's tentacles. I stared at them, refusing to show weakness despite my lack of options.

"Let me go," I growled. My throat was raw from the silenced screaming during the abduction.

"We can't," the closest figure replied smoothly. Her build told me that she was not one of the two who attacked me. Or I guess she may have been since I was knocked out from behind by an unseen adversary.

"Why am I here?" I spat at them, lacing all my rage into my tone.

The figure before me lowered onto one knee so she was on my level and slowly removed her mask. Olive skin with dark freckles dotted her face. She had soft brown hair that fell to just below her jawline. It was the brown eyes that sent a jolt of recognition through me. I gasped.

"Anika?" Her name burst from my lips. She smiled a soft, playful smile that reminded me of that brief tryst we indulged in before she Pledged to The Court of Passion two ceremonies ago. "What are you -"

"We have a lot to tell you," she offered in a sultry tone, but the mirthful delivery of her words made them no less terrifying.

"I don't.." I stammered, unable to form a coherent thought.

The second of the four individuals stepped forward. This one was obviously one of the two I had fought. He pulled his mask from his face. His features were pleasant enough for a kidnapper. His pale skin rivaled mine. His sandy blonde hair reminded me of the sand on the arena floor, and my heart constricted at the thought of Axel.

Did he even know I was missing?

Did he care?

"You have been very hard to get a hold of," the newly revealed figure spoke. "My name is Torin, and we aren't here to hurt you."

I scoffed. Tossing a betrayed look at Anika. We hadn't shared more than a brief moment, but I thought foolishly that earned me some loyalty.

"I'm tied to a chair."

"But you're not hurt," Torin pointed out.

"Cut it out, Torin," Anika sniped. "Lexa, please listen to what we have to say. It'll all make sense soon."

I shook my head. "I don't care what you have to say," I argued.

"You will when we tell you who your parents are," Torin said, and my blood ran cold. Suddenly, the room became unbearably small. Torin's eyes flicked down to my cleavage. No, not my cleavage, but the envelope tucked within.

I bucked against my bindings when he reached for the envelope that was tucked away in the top of my corset. These people had taken enough from me, and I wouldn't let them take this. I screamed and thrashed, my legs flailing in an attempt to push him back. I managed to make clear contact with his jaw, but not before he snatched the envelope, cursed and stepped back to cradle his face in his hand. He glared at me, holding the golden parchment in his hands.

"I'm trying to help you!" He yelled.

I sneered. "I don't want your *help*. I want you to let… me… go!" I screamed.

"Let her go," the masked figure at the back of the group said, finally contributing to the conversation. I diverted my eyes to him.

"You're kidding, right?" Torin exclaimed.

"Leave the shackle that binds her Mythica, but unbind her." The owner of the gruff voice seemed like he was attempting to speak lower than his natural voice could reach. Giving the impression that he was trying to appear more intimidating.

I didn't question it, though, because he offered me a chance to escape. I could get out of here without my Mythica. I'd have to.

"She needs to see what's in here," Torin argued, ripping open the envelope.

"Leave that alone!" I screamed, but he disregarded my pleas, pulling the cream parchment from the golden shell. Tears slid down my cheeks.

"Look at this," he said, stepping forward and turning the parchment toward me.

I shut my eyes tight, refusing to see what they were trying to show me. I wouldn't, not before Axel. I couldn't do that again. On purpose or not.

"Open your eyes, Lexa," Anika urged from behind me. I hadn't realized she had moved. But her deft fingers were unbinding me carefully.

"No," I yelled, preparing my arms to strike the second they were free.

The bindings on my wrists, save for the one keeping my Mythica at bay, fell to the ground, and I burst into motion. Tossing my hands out, I gripped the paper in Torin's hand and let my momentum carry me forward so that my head slammed into his. The pain was vicious, but he stumbled away, and I was finally free.

"Damnit!" he screamed as I rushed past him toward a large metallic door. My feet glided across the floor with purpose and strength. Each step toward freedom was another thing to fight for.

Axel.

Lysander.

Riley.

Oliver.

Myself.

The figures were closing in on me from behind, but I was quick, thanks to my training, and reached the door before they could stop me. Hope surged within me as I approached a door, the possibility of escape tantalizingly close. With a pounding heart, I grasped the handle and swung the door open, anticipating the sweet taste of freedom.

Before me was not the anticipated path to liberation. The expansive ocean sprawled in every direction as far as my eyes could see, encircling the island on which the enigmatic building stood. Waves crashed against the cliffs with unrestrained fury, creating a tumultuous barrier that seemed to mock my escape.

The illusion of freedom shattered, replaced by the disorienting reality of this isolated island surrounded by the raging sea. The realization hit me like a physical force, leaving me standing at the precipice of the doorway, staring at the tempestuous expanse beyond.

I was trapped.

"Lexa," a voice behind me whispered. A familiar voice. One that I had grown up with. Panic laced my veins.

"No," I whispered as the recognition settled on me. I closed my eyes, blinking away the tears that began to fall.

I felt the mist rolling off the ocean, pelting my face, stinging with the truth I didn't want to face. Opening my eyes, I let my eyes find the paper in my hands, knowing without a doubt what I would discover printed on its surface.

Breath alluded me as the words confirmed what I already knew. The paper slipped through my fingers, and I watched it dance away on the wind being carried out to sea, an escape I wouldn't be granted.

He stepped forward until I could feel his presence blanket me in that once comforting, familiar way.

"Everything will make sense soon," he whispered.

My mentor.

My friend.

My instructor.

My father.

Oliver Thorne.

"Welcome to The Court of Conscience."

ACKNOWLEDGMENTS

This story owes its existence to some very important people. To my husband, Zack, thank you for always being the first to read my work and keeping me motivated. Mom, you're my biggest cheerleader and fan - discussing these stories with you is a joy. Dad, thanks for teaching me grammar; I'm getting better with commas, I promise! Tricia and Mackenzie, my Beta readers, you've helped shape this world into the best it can be and words can't explain how thankful I am for your guidance and support.

Special thanks to Alison Turjancik, whose artistic talent brought my Court Marks to life. Melissa Nash, your stunning map of Verihdia is exactly what I always pictured, and Rachel McEwan, the spellbinding cover is thanks to you. Thank you all for bringing bits and pieces of this world to life with your art and talent.

Lastly, to you, the readers, thank you. Creating this world means so much more with you to share it with. Your support, kind words, and assistance have kept me motivated, pushing me to write the best story possible for all of you.

www.ingramcontent.com/pod-product-compliance
Lightning Source LLC
Chambersburg PA
CBHW030627310726
48979CB00003B/922
9781964036014